BECOMING THE CONQUEROR

BY JOSEPH T. PICKETT

BOOK I OF THE DEEDS OF THE NORMANS SERIES

THE AUTHOR'S OWN EDITION

2017

Joseph E. Pickett

N° 030/200

First published on Kindle in 2015.
First published in print in 2017.

Maps and genealogical trees created by the author.

All characters in this book are based on historical research and
the author's imagination. Any resemblance to real
contemporary individuals, whether living or dead, is entirely
coincidental and unintended.

Typeface of headings is Oronteus Finaeus Sm Caps.
Typeface of main text is Arial.
"Becoming The Conqueror" title lettering by Thierry Fétiveau
www.thierryfetiveau.fr

ISBN 978-1-9998700-9-6

www.JosephTPickettAuthor.com

TO MY GRANDFATHERS, DAVID AND GEORGE,
WHO LOVED SHARING GOOD STORIES, GOOD WINE,
AND MUCH LAUGHTER.

Dear Heather,
Thank you for all your support
on this wonderful writing journey.

In gratitude,

Joseph

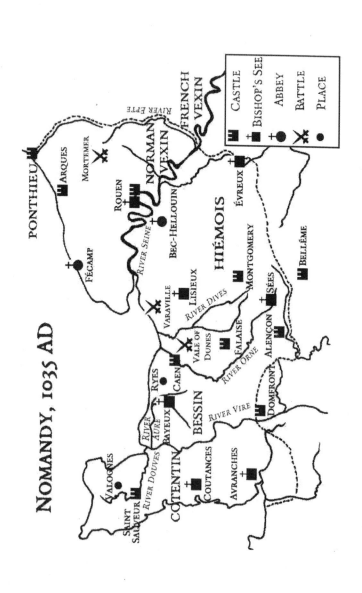

NOMANDY, 1035 AD

PONTHIEU

RIVER EPTE

NORMAN VEXIN

FRENCH VEXIN

ARQUES

MORTEMER

ROUEN

ÉVREUX

FÉCAMP

RIVER SEINE

BEC-HELLOUIN

HIÉMOIS

MONTGOMERY

BELLÊME

VARAVILLE

LISIEUX

RIVER DIVES

SÉES

ALENÇON

FALAISE

VALE OF DUNES

RIVER ORNE

DOMFRONT

RYES

CAEN

RIVER VIRE

RIVER AURE

BAYEUX

BESSIN

VALOGNES

COTENTIN

COUTANCES

AVRANCHES

RIVER DOUVES

SAINT SAUVEUR

CASTLE	▪
BISHOP'S SEE	✝
ABBEY	●✝
BATTLE	✗
PLACE	●

THE EMPIRE

BRUGES
GHENT
FLANDERS

RIVER SOMME

PARIS
RIVER SEINE
FRANCE

ARQUES
ROUEN

MERCIA
RIVER THAMES
LONDON
KENT
GELDEFORD
WESSEX
WINCHESTER
HASTINGS
ENGLAND

CAEN
NORMANDY
ALENÇON
BELLÊME
MAINE
LE MANS
RIVER LOIRE

BAYEUX
DOMFRONT
ANJOU

THE NARROW SEA

CYMRU
(WALES)

KERNOW
(CORNWALL)

DOL
NAONED

BREIZH
(BRITTANY)

RIVER LOIRE

THE HOUSE OF NORMANDY IN 1035

Richard I, †
Duke of Normandy
942-996

- Richard II, † *Duke of Normandy* *996-1026*
  - Richard III † *Duke of Normandy* *1026-1027*
  - Robert I, *Duke of Normandy* *1027-* ~ Herleva, A tanner's daughter
    - **William The Bastard**
  - Herleva = Herluin, Lord of Conteville
    - Odo
    - Robert
- Æthelred II Unraede, † *King of England* *978-1016* = 1 Emma of Normandy 2 = Cnut, *King of England 1016- King of Denmark 1018- King of Norway 1030-*
- Robert, Archbishop of Rouen
  - Mauger
  - William, Count of Talou
- William, Count of Eu

Eleanor = Baldwin IV, † Count of Flanders

Adeliza = Rainauld, Count of Burgundy
- Guy of Burgundy

Baldwin V, Count of Flanders = Adeliza, Daughter of King Robert II of France
- Matilda
- Baldwin

THE KINGS OF ENGLAND

Ælfgifu † of Northumbria = 1 Æthelred II Unraede, † *King of England* *978-1016* 2 = Emma of Normandy 2 = Cnut, *King of England 1016- King of Denmark 1018- King of Norway 1030-* 1 = Ælfgifu of Northampton

- Edmund Ironside † *King of England 1016*
  - Edward the Exile
- Alfred Ætheling
- Edward
- Harthacanute
- Harold Harefoot

Key

=	Marriage
~	Liaison
2 =	Second marriage
†	Deceased
King of England 978-1016	Years of reign

CHARACTERS

William 'the Bastard' - Only son of Duke Robert I of Normandy, whom he begot with Herleva, a tanner's daughter.

THE OLDER NORMANS

Robert I 'the Devil' - Duke of Normandy, William's father.

Osbern - Duke Robert's Steward. Lord of Crespon.

Archbishop Robert of Rouen - Uncle of Duke Robert. Prelate of the Church in Normandy.

Talou/Arques - William, Count of Talou and later of Arques. Brother of Duke Robert, thus uncle to William.

Mauger - Younger brother to Duke Robert and Arques.

Roger I Montgomery - Lord of Montgomery, Viscount of the Hiémois. Head of a powerful family. Close adviser to Duke Robert.

Hubert - Lord of Ryes. A humble vassal of Duke Robert.

Lanfranc of Pavia - A renowned Italian theologian in Normandy.

The Bellêmes - A powerful family with lands in Normandy, France and Maine.

THE YOUNG NORMANS

William FitzOsbern - Son of Osbern the Steward. A childhood friend of William's.

Osbern the Monk - William FitzOsbern's brother.

William & Roger Montgomery - Sons of Roger I Montgomery.

Guy of Burgundy - William's cousin. A son of Count Rainauld of Burgundy & of William's aunt. Of legitimate birth, unlike William.

Nigel - Viscount of the Cotentin. A vassal baron of Lower Normandy.

Ranulf - Viscount of the Bessin. A vassal baron of Lower Normandy.

Hamon the Long-toothed - A vassal baron of Lower Normandy.

Eudo - Eldest son of Hubert of Ryes.

De Warenne, Bigod, Picot - Vassal Norman barons.

THE NEIGHBOURS OF NORMANDY

Henry I - King of France. William's overlord.

Geoffrey Martel - Count of Anjou. A rival of Normandy. To Normandy's south-west.

Baldwin V - Count of Flanders. To Normandy's north east.

Matilda - Baldwin's daughter.

Herbert - Count of Maine. Control disputed between Normandy and Anjou.

Enguerrand - Count of Ponthieu, whose lands lie off the Norman border with Flanders.

Guy of Ponthieu - Enguerrand's younger brother.

THE ENGLISH AND THE DANES

Alfred Ætheling & Edward - Exiled sons of the deposed Æthelred Unraede, King of England, and his wife Emma of Normandy, Duke Robert's aunt.

Cnut - King of Denmark, England and Norway.

Harold Harefoot & Harthacanute - Cnut's sons.

Godwin - Earl of Wessex. The most powerful man in England.

Swegen, Harold and Tostig - Godwin's eldest sons.

.I.

I Sing of Arms and of a Boy

Chapter 1

Falaise, Lower Normandy. 1035 A.D.

It was an autumn day when the news reached Normandy. The trees had already turned to fire and now the land howled. Normandy breathed in and the orchard swayed with much creaking of branches. Normandy breathed out and beasts roared on pennants. Through this angered land, William ran.

He ran as fast as his legs would carry him. His heart thumped against his chest. He chanced another look behind. As he turned back to where he was heading, he realised his danger all too late as his enemy leaped down from the nearest apple tree.

William drew his sword. Everything was at stake.

"Come on then, if you're man enough," came the taunt.

"I'll soon wipe that smile off your face."

The crows circled above as the two warriors sized each other up. William felt his heart pace faster. He held his breath a moment, offered up a silent prayer. Then he attacked.

"Normandy!" he cried, and with a crash brought down his sword, only to have it checked by the other's shield. In a flash he saw a blade flicker towards him, his own shield barely meeting it in time. As his enemy pushed all his weight behind his shield, William took a step back, wrong-footing him. He stuck out his leather shoe and tripped the fool up.

"Do you give up?" he asked, pointing the tip of his sword at the knight's chest.

The answer came in the form of a foot hooking around his ankle, bringing him down to earth with a dull thud. His adversary leapt to his feet and put the tip of his sword to William's throat.

"Yield!"

William reluctantly admitted defeat – on this occasion.

"Well done, my boy!" Osbern the Steward beamed with pride at the two seven-year-olds playing with their little wooden swords. He had just returned from one of his many trips to sort out a quarrel amongst two barons. William looked grudgingly up at FitzOsbern. Since William's own father had set off on his pilgrimage to the Holy Land and entrusted him into his Steward's care, Osbern had treated William as if he were as much his own son as FitzOsbern.

Osbern strode up to the two young boys. His smile seemed to hide some worry. There were heavy bags under his eyes. The dirt on his tunic showed he had come straight to this orchard below the keep of Falaise without bothering to change out of his riding clothes. The Steward patted FitzOsbern on the back, before sending him to let his wife know he had returned.

"Come here, William," he said wearily.

His deep voice sounded so gentle for one who commanded respect throughout the land. William obeyed, bowing dutifully and brushing the dirt off his backside. Somewhere nearby, a bell started to toll. Osbern winced at the sound.

"I have news from the East, William."

An ominous lump caught in William's throat. He coughed.

"You have heard from my father, my lord?"

"William, your father is dead."

3

The words struck as a thunderbolt. In the distance, another bell began to echo the first.

"Dead?"

Osbern nodded. "In Nicea, on his return journey."

"But how?"

"He fell ill," the Steward said, though William thought he saw Osbern's eyes flicker away for a split second. "And now you must be brave and strong for your mother – and for Normandy. You are our Duke, now."

"No! No, that's not true" William shouted, then turned and ran away as fast as he could through the apple trees.

Tears streamed down his face, blurred his vision. He caught himself as he tripped on an unseen root in the undergrowth. All he wanted was to escape – to escape to some safe haven, to some hole in the ground where he could just curl up and forget everything he had heard. He gulped the cold morning air; it was like choking down frozen water.

Reaching the last tree of the orchard, he could run no further. He collapsed onto the sodden soil and leaned his back against the coarse bark of the trunk. Wrapping his arms around his legs, he buried his face in his knees and sobbed, shaking uncontrollably.

A crow called from somewhere nearby. Peeping out of his cocoon, he saw it perched atop the huge rocks on which he and his friend William FitzOsbern had only earlier that day been playing under the shadow of Falaise keep. Now all was gone and Normandy growled in anger as thunder rumbled in the distance – an approaching storm.

A heavy hand gripped his shoulder, making him jump.

"William," Lord Osbern's gruff voice said.

He looked up at his father's steward, towering over him.

"William," the steward repeated, "stand up."

He didn't want to, but daren't disobey the fierce warlord.

"Your father *is* dead, William."

"No, he can't be. They're wrong. They're wrong!" he said, shaking his head.

"He's dead, boy," Osbern said sternly. "Your uncle, the Count of Talou, saw him fall. He buried him with his own hands and brought the news here from the Holy Land."

William shook his head again and tried to turn away. The steward grabbed him with both hands.

"Look, boy," he said. "Look at the crows. They are looking at you. And at me. They watch us all, all the time, waiting for us to fall. We live with death near us every day. Remember that. Your father is gone and nothing you nor I can do will bring him back."

William turned to Osbern again. The steward's countenance softened as he took in the seven-year-old's quivering lip and scared chestnut eyes peeping out from under his fiery red hair.

"Come here," he said, holding out his arms.

William gladly accepted the hug and burst once more into tears. The steward's chainmail hauberk felt cold against his face.

"It hurts," Osbern said. "I know it well. I was fortunate to have my father a few years longer than you, but it scarce made it easier to lose him. You cry now. Cry and let it all out."

William clung on to him, weeping until he was drained of tears and could cry no more. Eventually, he stepped back as the steward loosened his hold.

5

"There," Osbern said, ruffling William's fiery hair. "Now, no more tears. Your father was duke of Normandy, don't ever forget it. He would let no man see his moments of weakness and nor must you."

William nodded, wiping his eyes and snuffling.

"Your father left strict instructions. Bastard or not, you are his only son. He made us all swear to follow you, before he set out on his pilgrimage. That makes you our new duke."

William frowned. He was only a boy. He was no duke. His father was the duke of Normandy, not him. Even with his father gone, he could never truly be duke. The steward seemed determined, though, and got down on one knee, placing his palms together.

"You must put your hands around mine, William."

He did as he was told.

"William, Duke of Normandy, I humbly pledge my sword, service and life to you. Will you accept my homage? Will you let me serve you as steward, as I served your father?"

William nodded. Osbern raised his eyebrows, waiting. William cleared his throat.

"I accept your homage, Steward Osbern," he said, his little voice trembling.

Osbern beamed at him from behind his silver-grey beard, his steely blue eyes twinkling.

"Now," he said, standing up. "Go and find my son. I must convene a council; there are many affairs to set in order. I am glad you and he get on so well, as you will be seeing a lot more of each other, now that you will be in my household for good."

William's eyes widened.

6

"Can I not go and live with my mother?"

"No, William, I'm afraid not. Your father betrothed your mother to Herluin of Conteville, one of his knights, remember. Her place is by his side and your place is at court. You are Duke William of Normandy."

William looked at his feet.

"Do not worry, young master," Osbern added, seeing his disappointment. "I shall send for your mother. She will want to kiss your hand. You are her duke also."

He smiled fondly and strode off in the direction of the great stone keep of Falaise, his left hand resting on his sword hilt.

William kicked a clod of earth. He remembered laughing as he had once tried to stomp around in his father's big shoes. How could anyone expect him to wear them so soon?

"Normandy is a land forged in fire and blood, my son; fire and blood." So Duke Robert had told William before leaving for the Holy Land. "Our forefather, Rollo the Viking, cut this rich swathe of rolling hills and fertile meadows out of France. He won these sweet orchards, these cool streams, these menacing forests in which we hunt, for his people and his heirs to preserve. He won it with this."

Duke Robert drew his sword and gave it to William, who struggled to lift it in his little arms. It was a plain sword, by all accounts; a cold straight blade, a simple guard with only the slightest curve away from the dark leather grip and a heavy pommel. No embellishments, no fancy patterns; just a brutal weapon, the tool of a conquering Northman.

"He plunged it deep into France, my lad, into the heart of Paris until the French king himself begged him for peace. Rollo was merciful and left Paris. He kept his conquered lands, which the French king had no choice but to gift him. And so Rollo settled here with our people in this land of the Northman; Normandy."

William looked at the sword, wide-eyed. He longed to be a hero like Rollo, fighting through whole armies to win land and glory. He frowned as he noticed an inscription on the blade, near the hilt.

"What does this say, sir?"

"It says 'Diex aie', my boy, *God helps*. When at last Rollo had settled in peace, he cast aside the pagan gods of old and found the one true God. He knew that He had helped bring peace and justice to the land. Yet we must continue to fight for that same peace and justice. Our enemies are ever restless. Whether jealous neighbours or our own unruly people, we must keep them in check, and so this sword can never rest easy in its scabbard. You are my only son and heir, William. One day it will fall to you to wield this sword and rule over Normandy."

As the Duke said these words, William felt the sword growing heavier in his hands. He went to put it down, but he couldn't let go of the grip, try as he would. The ground under him grew uneven, turning into marshland.

"Father," he called out. "Father, help me!"

Duke Robert seemed not to hear and turned away.

"Father, please!" William struggled, but still the sword was firmly stuck to his hand and weighed him down, as his legs sank further and further into the marsh.

"HELP ME! FATHER!"

As his head disappeared under the Norman soil, the last sight he had was of Duke Robert striding away, without a single backward glance.

William awoke with a start, drenched in cold sweat. Had it all been a dream? As his eyes grew accustomed to the darkness, he found himself curled up on his bed in a small room on the topmost floor of Falaise castle.

Just a dream, he sighed. He crept over to the window and pulled aside the curtain. The hound which had been sleeping at the foot of his bed gave a small growl of discontent as the full moon flooded the room with its eerie light. William breathed in the cool air. As he stood there, he became aware of raised voices coming from the main hall just below. He crawled softly along the floor and lifted up a corner of one of the sheepskin rugs. Through a crack between two floorboards, he could make out several figures in the hall.

"Duke Robert was quite clear," boomed the gruff voice of the Archbishop of Rouen; "Steward Osbern and I are to look after his son and his duchy."

"Those instructions were for his time on pilgrimage," William's uncle Talou barked. "Now that my brother is dead, we must decide who will take his place."

William felt his breath catch in his throat as the nightmare of reality returned.

"His son takes his place, of course," Osbern said.

"He's just a boy!" Talou said.

"You swore an oath, along with the rest of us." Osbern's calm voice was suddenly full of menace. "Or have you so soon forgotten your fealty?"

"We all swore homage; that is true," another voice put in, "but this land requires a man to lead the duchy. Until he is of age, William will be Duke in name only. Normandy needs a strong leader."

Though he could not make out the face of this other man through his small peephole, William needed no clues; the voice was one which had long dominated his father's court.

"Talou is right," continued Count Roger of Montgomery: "we must decide who is to rule in the Duke's stead."

"I see no reason to dismiss my nephew's instructions," the archbishop said. "Whether dead or abroad, the Duke is not here. He appointed Osbern and me to be custodians and we will continue to follow his orders until his son is ready to take on the burden of a duke. You will, of course, be consulted on the great matters of Normandy."

"Duke Robert trusted me to run many of his affairs, as well you know, and –"

"But he did not appoint you custodian," the cleric interrupted Montgomery.

"He could not have foreseen his death," Talou objected.

"He did, though, else why have us all swear allegiance to his son so early? He knew how dangerous his journey would be."

"The people know what Duke Robert's wishes were," Osbern said. "They were read out in every church in the land."

"I wonder who organised that," Talou grunted. Montgomery scoffed.

"The Duke's wishes are beyond question," Archbishop Robert said, ignoring the *pique*. "Now let that be an end to it."

With that, William heard the hall door swing open and two men leave. He could not tell what it was that his uncle Talou muttered to Montgomery, as the already faint words were lost in the sound of heavy footsteps coming up the winding stairs towards him. William scrambled to his feet, rushed to pull the curtain shut and leaped back onto his bed, just before the door to his own chamber opened.

"They will cause us trouble," Osbern said to the archbishop as they came in.

"I know. We must remain vigilant. These are dark days indeed."

He opened the curtain and the two men turned to look at William, who was making a poor attempt at pretending to sleep.

"How much did you hear?" Osbern asked him. The honesty on his face disarmed William, who looked down at the floor.

"Only that my uncle and the lord Montgomery don't want me as duke."

"Montgomery and Talou will have to do as they are told," the archbishop said. "As will any other who tries to defy the authority of the rightful duke."

"You needn't worry about that yet, though," Osbern said, sitting on the edge of William's bed and putting a hand on his shoulder. "You have enough friends to protect you until you are ready to rule. All the same, you must remember that cunning men such as Montgomery will always be looking for ways to take advantage."

"What should I do?" William asked Osbern.

11

"Focus on your Latin," the archbishop said, "for an educated and sharp mind is the only thing which can outsmart cruel cunning."

He ruffled William's auburn hair.

"Why don't you take some rest, Archbishop? I will stay with William and see that no harm comes to him."

The Norman prelate nodded his thanks. He winked at William and set off back into the darkness.

CHAPTER 2

ROUEN, UPPER NORMANDY. 1036 A.D.

The blow struck Alfred hard on the shoulder. William winced at the sight of it, but the English prince stood unshaken. Ever since William could remember, Alfred had been in Normandy. He had a brother there also, Edward, though he was not very talkative and always seemed distant, lost in thought. Alfred was friendly and often played with William when he had the time. Exiled princes have plenty of time. He had a kind face, with wrinkles around the eyes from much smiling. His hair was fair and his eyes blue; so typical of his Saxon origins. Rather than the short-cut Norman style, he wore his hair long and sported a thick beard. Everyone at court knew and respected Alfred; none more so than William, who now sat watching him in awe as he took on one of Normandy's best warriors in a game of wrestling. The punch to his bare shoulder showed what regard his opponent paid to the rules.

"Steady on," Osbern said to his over-zealous champion.

Alfred waved away the Steward's concern as he stood grinning. If there was one thing he relished, it was a good dirty fight. The two wrestlers had stripped down to their breeches to fight in this lush green orchard. The shade of the apple trees offered some small respite from the heat of the summer sun which leaned life to the land of Normandy, ripening its crops and feeding its people. Alfred's long hair hung damp against his cheeks, his muscular arms bulging as sweat ran down his chest. William watched him as he sized up his opponent, trying to calculate his next move. Mistaking his cunning for distraction,

13

the Norman lunged, thinking to land a kick in Alfred's ribs. The English prince was too quick and side-stepped the blow. Grabbing hold of the Norman's foot, he kicked the other from under him and the knight fell hard on his back. Alfred leaped on top of him and pinned him down.

"Yield?" His grin spoke of victory.

"Yielded," the Norman conceded.

Alfred got up and, laughing, took his beaten adversary's hand and pulled him up.

"Your men fight well, Duke William, though they could perhaps do with a touch more training."

He winked at Osbern.

"Congratulations, Prince Alfred. If you carry on beating our warriors so easily, you won't need to return to England; you'll already have conquered Normandy."

William ran up to Alfred, his little eyes sparkling.

"Why don't you stay and fight for me?" he asked eagerly. "The Count of Anjou would never dare fight against you."

"Count Geoffrey is a formidable enemy. Few men could conquer so much before their fortieth year," Alfred said. "Besides, my people need me. It is time the House of Wessex was restored."

"Come, William," Archbishop Robert said. He had just joined the small group of spectators. "Leave Prince Alfred to rest. You and I have work to do."

"But I want to learn to fight!"

"There will be time enough for that when you are older. The Steward will teach you that when he sees fit. For now, you must

14

learn to read and write. You must learn the lives of the saints and the Lord's message."

"But why? I will command armies. I won't be reading books in Church!" He folded his arms.

"A duke must first learn what he is fighting for. Then, to command, he must be educated," the Archbishop said sternly.

"Archbishop Robert is right, young Duke William," Alfred said. "Unless you have God on your side, there is no point in fighting. Learn the Lord God's message. Learn to read and write; your men will respect you for it. Only when your men respect you can you make your enemies fear you."

"You fight, though, Alfred!"

"*Prince* Alfred," the prelate corrected him.

"I fight when I must," Alfred agreed, "but the greatest fights do not take place on a battlefield; they take place at court and in church. And for now I must wash, for no one will have a king who is covered in muck."

"Go with the Archbishop, William," Osbern said. "Prince Alfred and I have business to see to when he is ready."

William reluctantly followed his great-uncle the Archbishop to the small chapel where they had started William's schooling. It was more convenient and discreet than the great cold cathedral of Rouen where the Norman prelate's see was.

"Now," the Archbishop said, "let's go back to the story of King Solomon the Wise," he said pointedly.

William was not listening.

"King Solomon?..." the Archbishop prompted him again.

"Why is Prince Alfred not King of England? And why does he talk of leaving now?"

The Archbishop raised an eyebrow, but decided he might as well teach William something of use, even if it wasn't from the Good Book.

"As you know, young William, Prince Alfred and Edward's father was King Æthelred of England. He was a fair king, so I understand, but the Danes are ever greedy for land and wealth. When they came to ravage the coast of England as so often they have done before, Æthelred listened to poor council. He let them take much of his land and acted too little too late and had to flee here. His eldest son Edmund fought valiantly. He fought so well his enemies and friends alike called him Ironside. Edmund Ironside held the Danes at London, forcing the Danish King Cnut to share power in England."

"And what happened next?" William said, eyes wide open and fixed on the Archbishop.

"Edmund died. So did his father Æthereld in the same year." The Archbishop shrugged. "The Lord moves in mysterious ways. He took brave Edmund before his time and Cnut took over all of England. Æthelred's widow is Emma, my own sister, and so she naturally sent Alfred and Edward here for safety. When Æthelred died, Cnut took Emma as his wife. Now Cnut himself is dead and his son Harold Harefoot, from his previous wife, has claimed the English throne. Prince Alfred, however, plans to take back the throne and rejoin his mother in England. And so you, young William, will be a relative of the King of England."

"Is Prince Alfred going to war?" William had visions of knights crashing over open countryside to cut down the evil Danes.

16

"Perhaps," his great-uncle answered vaguely. "Now, King Solomon the Wise…"

"Oh, please, Archbishop! Tell me! I can keep a secret. I promise!"

"I should hope so too; no duke of worth ever opens his mouth unless he has to."

"Please…"

The archbishop put down the bible once more. It was a wonderful leather-bound parchment with majestic capital letters of gold and red and blue and green. These kept a close watch over the black ink of the text which stood to attention in straight bold lines. Yet William gave it not the least thought. He watched the prelate very closely for any hint of Alfred's plans. The archbishop sighed in resignation.

"What I am about to tell you, you must keep to yourself. Tell no one, do you understand?"

William nodded, hardly able to contain his excitement at being in on such a big secret.

"There is a man in England, a Lord Godwin, whom they call Earl Godwin of Wessex. Wessex is the richest part of England. This man was Cnut's biggest supporter after the Danish conquest. But he will not support Cnut's son. Instead, he has sent word to Prince Alfred. If the Prince joins him in England, Godwin says he can raise a whole army to overthrow the Danes. It can only work if Alfred is there, though, as many of the English think he will not come and wouldn't dare risk their lives unless they have seen him."

"Will Alfred win?"

"Only God knows that. I have asked the Steward Osbern to give Alfred men so that the prince can join Godwin safely. All we can do is pray. And so, let us read about the life of King Solomon the Wise."

"I'm coming with you," William said sternly.

"Indeed?" Alfred said with a fond smile. "And why would you want do a thing like that?"

"The Archbishop says that it is right that Normandy supports the true king's return to England. As I am Duke, it is normal I should join you."

Alfred chuckled at the bravado. Whenever he laughed, small lines appeared at the corners of his eyes. William had grown to like this amiable Saxon, whose thick beard and long wavy fair hair made him look like he belonged to another age, not just another land. Whenever he heard the tale of Rollo and his Viking warriors arriving in Northern France in their long boats, he pictured men just like Alfred with his wild hair. The English prince clapped William on the shoulder, the friendly blow throwing him bodily forwards.

"Archbishop Robert is right, of course; Normandy does well to stand up for justice. We will soon throw the Dane out of England forever. But you must stay here," he waved his finger at William. "The Steward needs you here."

"But I want to fight with you!" William protested.

"I would be glad of the help, but our duty must always come first. You made an oath to serve in Lord Osbern's household until you are old enough to learn the skills of arms. In this world, good and bad men are sorted according to how true they stay to their oaths."

William looked sullenly at the ground. It wasn't fair.

"Besides," Alfred said, "Edward isn't coming and he's my own brother. Perhaps when things are more settled and he comes to join me, he will ask the Steward if you can come too. It is only fair that a duke should be thanked by those whom his duchy helped to free. There will be many feasts to celebrate victory over the Danish invader."

William chirped up a bit at the prospect of a victory feast.

"You promise I'll see England?"

"If your lord lets you, yes. For now, I must be on my way, or there will be no victory at all. Now that Cnut is dead, I must strike before his son Harold Harefoot gets a hold over England. Earl Godwin will be expecting me in two days' time. He's not a man to be kept waiting."

"Ah," boomed Osbern. "There you are, William. Were you trying to steal my best warrior from me, Prince Alfred?"

"I must admit I did try," Alfred said, winking at William. "But the Duke here was adamant that he should stay by his oath-lord's side."

"And well he does to remember it. I know what you Saxons are like!"

The two men laughed. William laughed along with them, a big grin on his little face, though quite what the Saxons were supposed to be like, he did not know.

"Alfred says he'll send for me to celebrate his victory. Can I go?" William pleaded.

"*Prince* Alfred," Osbern corrected him.

19

"Prince Alfred," William dutifully repeated. "Can I go, Lord Osbern? Please!"

"Perhaps, if it's safe enough." Osbern glanced over William's head. "Here comes trouble."

Alfred and William both turned to see the Count of Talou, William's uncle, striding towards them with Alfred's brother.

"Edward!" said Alfred. "Come to be the first to pay your new king homage?"

"You know you needn't ask for it," Edward bowed. "Take care, won't you brother? Harefoot may sound like a simple brute, but it's said he has his father's ruthless cunning."

"All the cunning under the sun is no match for righteousness. Besides, now Godwin is behind me, the other nobles will be more confident about joining me."

William saw that this did not seem to reassure Edward one bit. Alfred saw it too.

"I will be careful, Edward," he said. "Heaven knows you fret enough for both of us, though."

Talou cleared his throat. "Everything is ready, Prince Alfred. You must go now, if you are to make the tide."

"Thank you, Lord Talou. And thank you William, for lending me your troops." Alfred smiled at him again.

William was pleased to have such an important role, even if the decision had actually been taken by the Council, it was still done in his name, he told himself.

"I trust you will remember – and remind Godwin – that it was Normandy which gave England back its King," Talou said.

"I shall be sure to tell the Earl. Upon my coronation at Winchester, I will ensure that Normandy gets the reward it rightly deserves."

William could tell that his uncle was pleased with that answer, though Osbern almost imperceptibly smirked as Talou wished the Saxon a safe journey.

"God speed you home, brother," Edward said. "Give my love to our mother, though she has done little to deserve it. It should have been she who sent for us, not Godwin"

"Thank you Edward; we will be together again before long. This time we will enter London as victorious rulers, not running away in the middle of the night."

"I pray for it," Edward said.

With that, Alfred spurred his horse down towards the ships that waited to carry him across a ruthless sea towards his home and the promise of a throne. He stopped a moment to wave back to William.

As the sails were dropped and the stone anchors lifted, the first chill of autumn could be felt in the air. William watched as a dead leaf fell from an old oak tree. The wind carried it off to sea.

CHAPTER 3

"Go on," said Talou to the haggard looking man who stood before him. "Why should this neighbour of yours think he could suddenly move the boundary stones between your lands?"

"Well my lord, it's like this; the land was given to my father by the Lord of Plessis. Now that both my father and the good lord are dead, he thought he'd get away with it."

"That's a lie, my lord!" said the defendant, an ill-favoured peasant with a flat nose which told a tale of many a drunken brawl. "He's taking you for a fool. The markers were always there."

"Silence," Talou commanded. "I will not suffer impertinence in this court."

William, who was sat by a window at one side of the hall, looked up from his carved wooden knights which Osbern had made for him by the light of an evening fire, to see what all the raised voices were about. His uncle was sat on a chair raised upon a small wooden dais. To his right, in the place of honour, was Edward. The English prince leant over and said something so softly that only Talou could hear it.

"Prince Edward, here," Talou said, "has helpfully pointed out that there should be a written grant of land from the lord in question. Do you know anything of such a document?"

"No, my lord. I can't read," the first man said pitifully.

"Well of course you can't, but the priests from your village can. We shall send for them to see if any such document was entrusted to them. In the meantime, you will both…"

Whatever Talou wanted of them was lost as his voice trailed away, for at that moment they were interrupted by the door swinging open and Osbern striding in. He bowed to William before turning to Talou and Edward.

"My lords, I have news from England," he said in a grave voice.

Talou dismissed the crowd of petitioners with a wave of the hand. As they shuffled out of the hall, William moved closer to his uncle, eager to hear news of Alfred.

"My lord Edward," Osbern said in a faltering voice, "I am sorry to have to inform you that your brother Alfred Ætheling is dead."

Edward gripped the arms of his chair, in too much shock to say a word.

"How did this happen?" Talou asked for him.

"This man will tell you better than I." Osbern beckoned to a Norman soldier who had been standing nervously near the door.

William saw that the man's clothes were all muddy and frayed. His face was pale and gaunt, as if he hadn't eaten properly in days. Bruises on his face showed he had been recently beaten.

"Who are you?" Edward asked. "How can you be sure my brother is dead?"

"They call me Gilles, my lord. I was in the Ætheling's party which landed in England."

"Tell me all you know," Edward commanded.

"My lord, we landed at Pevensey Bay. Earl Godwin met us there, as planned, with a company of armed men. He said they were his hearth warriors and, though some of them seemed of Scandinavian stock, we thought little of it. So many Vikings have

23

settled in England over the years... The Ætheling led us West towards Winchester. He insisted on being crowned there before marching on London. He said it was only right for a king of the House of Wessex to start his reign in the town of Alfred the Great." The soldier coughed, his voice grating in his throat.

"Get him some water," Osbern barked.

"Carry on," Edward insisted, impatient to hear the whole dreadful tale.

"The Earl talked him into making a detour to the hills overlooking London. He said that more men would join them there, so Alfred would be safer." The man gulped the water he had just been handed by a servant. "We reached a place the English call Geldeford and made camp there for the night. I woke up to the sound of muffled screaming. As I turned to get up, I was hit over the head. When I came to, my hands were bound."

He stopped, looking down at his feet. William could tell he was finding it hard to relive the memory.

"Go on," Edward insisted again.

"There were too many of us to keep us all prisoner. They killed some three hundred of our number on those hills overlooking London before leading the dozen or so survivors, along with Alfred, into marshlands to the north east of there, on the other side of the great river. There they blinded the Ætheling with a dagger. They did the job all too crudely; the knife went in so deep that the Prince collapsed on the soggy ground. After a few moments, he lay still..."

Edward closed his eyes, as if to block out the gruesome image. William felt all the warmth leave his body on hearing how the English prince had died.

24

"How is it that you were able to escape?" Talou asked with just a note of suspicion.

"In the mist and confusion, I managed to give my guards the slip. I hid in the marshes for three days, to be sure that they wouldn't still be looking for me. Eventually I made my way down to the river and convinced a trading boat from Flanders to take me as far as the French coast. I made my way down from there."

"Did Godwin show any remorse that my brother died so?" Edward said.

The soldier thought about it for a while.

"He seemed put out, though more due to inconvenience than any remorse."

"Inconvenience?" Edward spat in disgust.

"Yes, my lord. They wanted to force the Ætheling to renounce his claim to the throne."

"And stop Prince Edward from also claiming the throne," Talou finished the thought.

Edward banged his fist against his chair.

"Such treason! Such villainy! Cold blooded treason from one who wanted our support to be the greatest earl of England. He is not so. His guile is nought but godlessness. Godwin the Godless; let him be known as such throughout the land."

Edward's bloodlust and fury seemed to sear just below the surface, turning his usually pale complexion bright vermillion.

"What will you do now, my lord?" Osbern asked, though he clearly regretted the words as soon as they were spoken.

"I will sail straight up the Thames and not rest until I have buried Godwin in unhallowed ground."

25

"My lord Edward, if I may," said Talou. "You are in shock, and rightly so. What caring brother would not want revenge for so grievous a deed? But I must advise caution at this stage. The Ætheling's fate has shown us that the Dane Harold Harefoot's hold over the English nobles is stronger than we had thought. To attack again so soon, no matter how just the cause, would merely play into his hands and risk your own death. Who then would lead your people?"

The look Edward gave William's uncle then was one of murderous defiance.

"Understand, Prince Edward; to have committed such an act of savagery towards my good friend Alfred of England, Godwin has earned the eternal enmity of Normandy. We will see that you have your revenge, but we must have the courage to wait until the right time to strike. A sailor who sets off in a storm is foolhardy, not brave; you are no fool."

Edward reluctantly nodded.

"So, young William," said Talou, turning to the eight-year-old who had been following the conversation attentively, "you will have the honour of Edward Ætheling's wisdom a while longer. Are you not lucky?"

William dutifully bowed, as Edward seemed taken aback at being addressed for the first time by his brother's title.

"Montgomery, a word if you please," said Archbishop Robert. William had been following his great-uncle towards the cathedral of Rouen when Montgomery had come out of a nearby tavern with his usual entourage of surly knights.

"Yes, my lord Archbishop?" The perfunctory greeting barely hid the scorn.

"I have heard disturbing reports of your men intruding on the lands of your neighbours and dealing out justice as they saw fit – or rather injustice, I believe."

"I can assure you, my lord, my men obey only my orders." Montgomery gave him a sly smile.

"Really? I thought they obeyed the orders of the Council, as should you."

"You forget, my lord, that I am on the Council," Montgomery answered through pursed lips.

"Being on the Council and being the Council are two very different things, my lord. All matters of justice must be passed by me, and the other members."

"But you were far away here in Rouen. There was no time to send word to you. And besides, we can hardly be expected to summon a full Council just to deal with a few vagabonds."

William could sense the tension between the two men. The archbishop put a reassuring hand on his shoulder.

"These were no mere vagabonds. They were your neighbours whom your men" the cleric jutted his chin disparagingly at the knights who stood protectively around their lord "took upon themselves to rob of their possessions and show every kind of insult."

"These reports must be false, my lord Archbishop," Montgomery said coolly. "If my men had undertaken such actions, they would indeed have been punished."

"My reports are never wrong – and well should you know that."

27

William saw the prelate's knowing look. Montgomery's features seemed to harden under the scrutiny, as one who has just realised that his actions have not been as secret as he might have hoped.

"Very well; I will make sure that they stay within my borders in future."

"Just make sure your borders don't move then. Come William." William felt his great-uncle's hand firmly guiding him away. "Good day, my lord Montgomery. I shall be most vexed if I hear any more of these reports."

"You will not, my lord Archbishop," Montgomery bowed. "Good day."

"Upstart," the Archbishop said as soon as they were out of earshot. "You must watch out for men like him, William. They plot and scheme and if you turn your back for one moment, you will find a dagger in it thrust right up to the hilt."

"But why does he disobey your orders so?"

"Because he thinks he can get away with it. He is right; Normandy is a long stretch of land, with much distance between us and him. He can do as he wills and we can do little but watch from Rouen."

"What can we do, then?"

"I will send word to the Steward. Lord Osbern's estate of Crespon is in Lower-Normandy, and thus much closer to Montgomery's lands. If there is further trouble we will strike out from there."

"But why is Lord Montgomery allowed on the Council if he is doing such evils things?"

"He is there, young William, because he has much support. Your father, God rest him, made Montgomery a powerful man. No doubt he needed a strong man to watch over that part of Normandy. But now that he is dead, Montgomery has cast off what loyalty he felt towards the ducal household. Perhaps he never truly had any loyalty and your father simply let him get away with it as a necessary evil. Who knows? All I do know is that he will continue to cause us trouble."

He stopped and turned to face William. Kneeling down, he looked him in the eyes. William looked back into those steely hard eyes framed with greying eyebrows and deep creases. They spoke of years pouring over manuscripts by candle light or else keeping a watch over the ever troubled lands of the North men.

"Remember, William, that you and you alone are Duke. There can only be one true master of Normandy. One day I will die. I am an old man. By rights, I should have disappeared long before your father, yet for now I am still here."

William thought painfully back to the day Osbern had told him of his father's death.

"When I do at last die," the Archbishop continued, "men such as Montgomery – or even closer to home – will seek to take advantage. They will do what they can to diminish your authority in your own lands. They will go back to the dark days of reckless warlords snatching food from each other's table. You must not let that happen. When I die, you must rise up as your father did, and his father before him. You must summon the strength of Rollo. It flows in your blood as it does in mine. You must be a lion of Normandy. Remember that."

William nodded, more out of duty than out of belief.

"You aren't going to leave me, are you?"

His great uncle smiled and ruffled William's red hair.

"No, William. I am old, but I flatter myself in thinking that I have some years of strength left in me. Death must wait until you are ready to take up your role of Duke."

CHAPTER 4

A bell started to toll dully somewhere in the town. Just as William went to stick his little head out of the window to look for the cause of this new and unexpected sound, the door to the hall was flung open so hard it nearly came off its hinges.

Osbern the Steward instinctively leapt to his feet and started drawing his sword. As he saw that it was William's uncle Talou, he let the blade slide back into its scabbard – though he kept his hand on the pommel.

William saw the look on his uncle's face. It was a mixture of worry and anger. His hands and rich green tunic were covered in blood.

"My lord, what has happened?" Osbern asked in alarm.

Talou, seeing William, ignored the question and rushed over to his nephew. He embraced him tightly. It took William aback. His uncle wasn't usually one for such shows of affection; he had always been so stern. The blood on him stained William's shirt.

"Oh, my dear nephew! Dear child!"

"My lord, what on earth has happened?" Osbern repeated, putting a hand on William's shoulder to reassure him.

"My uncle Robert is dead," Talou said in a trembling voice, so uncharacteristic of his usual strong self.

"The Archbishop is dead? How?"

"Murdered. Sliced open from gullet to gut. In his own cathedral, no less!"

"Dear God," Osbern crossed himself. "Has the perpetrator of this foul deed been caught?"

"He has not. I just found my uncle myself, lying in a pool of his own blood before the altar." Talou drew back. "You must take young William here to a safe place. Until we find whoever did this, he will be in danger."

"Of course, my lord, but do you not wish to come with us? You may be at risk yourself."

"Thank you, but no. Someone must stay here and restore order in the town. When word of the archbishop's death gets out, all havoc may break loose."

"Then let me take charge of the city. My men are the finest soldiers in all Normandy. We shall see peace and order maintained, you may be assured of that."

"I do not doubt that, good Steward, but your place is at our duke's side and I will not leave the city. It would look as though I were running away. My uncle Robert was the symbol of authority and continuity, while William here is still young. With him gone, the people will need reassuring that another member of the ducal family is there to guide them. I will bear the burden of that responsibility... Until William comes of age, of course. We cannot let the House of Rollo fall."

"As you wish, my lord," Osbern said, with clear reluctance. "Where shall I take the boy?"

"To Herluin of Conteville's castle. He will be safe enough there for the time being. If anyone should question it, we can easily defend it as a perfectly natural visit to his mother's. I'm glad my brother had the sense to marry her off to a solid man."

"To Conteville it is then," Osbern said to William. He knelt down and put both his hands on William's shoulders. William could feel the strength in the steward's arms. "Listen here, young master. You must be brave once more. Your great uncle Robert is dead. We must go to your mother's now. She will be pleased to see you."

William felt strangely numb. He had known little of the Archbishop, yet it was all so hauntingly familiar, as if he were reliving the moment when he had been told of his father's death. He bit his lip and nodded. The Steward nodded back. The shadow of an approving smile appeared in the corner of his lips.

"Do you think my lord of Talou will manage to restore peace?" Conteville said.

They were sat in his modest hall, within the safety of its timber palisade atop a motte – one of the defensive mounds which had been springing up increasingly quickly throughout Normandy these past years. Herluin of Conteville was a kind enough man, William thought, as he sat on his mother's lap, wrapped in a fur-trimmed cloak. The soft fur against his cheeks was as comforting as it was warm. Herleva, his mother, passed her fingers through his soft red hair.

"If any man can keep order in Normandy, it is the Count of Talou. He has but to look at the mightiest warrior to turn him into an obedient pup," Osbern said.

"How was Rouen when you left the town?" Herleva asked in her gentle voice.

Osbern thought about it for a while.

"Quiet, my lady. Eerily quiet. One might have thought the place deserted."

"The people were scared, no doubt," Conteville said.

"Yes," said Osbern, "and yet it seemed more than simple fear of violence. Archbishop Robert was so much a pillar of Normandy that his sudden passing has left a hole. The people know not to whom they can turn for justice."

"It's as if my dear Duke Robert had died again," William's mother said, before looking apologetically for mentioning her former lover's name. Herluin hardly minded. The late Duke had been a generous man who had clearly loved Herleva.

"Indeed it is," Osbern said. "We must now pray that Talou and his brother Mauger don't meet too much resistance. There are always those who seek to take advantage of such dire events."

"Do you think they will catch the assassin?" Herluin asked.

Osbern shook his head.

"Not unless someone chooses to claim responsibility for it. Too many people stood to profit from the prelate's death. Archbishop Robert was fair but firm, and always knew how he wanted things done. A man of such character will always have plenty of enemies."

Conteville grunted his agreement.

"What about my boy?" Herleva said, kissing William on the forehead. "Is he to live in fear for the rest of his life?"

"Alas, my lady, every duke and prince is born with a sword hanging above his head," Osbern said, though when he saw the lady's pained expressed, he was moved to add "but rest assured; I am here to ensure the sword stays securely in the air." He smiled, hoping to allay her anxiety some little bit.

"So what next?" Conteville asked in his throaty voice.

"We do our duty. The young duke, here, must be given the best possible chance of a peaceful reign. To that end, Talou and

Mauger will govern the land until such a time as he is ready to take the reins. I will keep the peace with my men. And you, young sir…" he turned to William, who peered nervously over the fur trimming of the cloak "You must learn how to fight and how to be the duke your father always knew you could be. Are you ready for that?"

"Yes, my lord," William said in a small voice.

"Right, then let's get started."

"So soon," Herleva said. "You've only just arrived. Can I not have a few moments more with my son? He is safe enough with me, my good Steward Osbern."

"It cannot wait, my lady," Osbern said, causing a tear to appear in Herleva's eye. "It is precisely so that you can have more time with your son that we must start now. Do you have a spear and shield for young William, my lord Conteville?"

"Certainly. I will have my squire cut the spear down to length for him."

"No," Osbern said. "Let him have a full sized spear and the heaviest shield you have. That is what will be used against him, so he had best get used to it. Besides, he needs building up. Come, William."

He held out his hand for William to take. Herleva held William close, not wanting to ever let go of her baby child. William pursed his lips, threw off the cloak and, after giving his mother a kiss, walked over to the steward.

"Now, dear wife," Conteville said, putting his hands on her shoulders. "Let the boy become a man."

Herleva sniffed back the tears and put her hand on her husband's.

"You're right, of course," she said with the faintest hint of a tremor. "William, my boy, you listen to the good Steward. Your father put his faith in him, and so must you."

"Yes mother."

She smiled at her brave little warrior.

"I'll look after him, my lady. Don't you worry about that."

William saw his mother nod as Osbern pulled him out into the yard.

William was soon kitted out with a spear and shield. He wore a heavy leather jerkin and a short sword hung in a scabbard at his side. From a nearby forge, a smith could be heard working on a coat of chainmail to fit William. The sound of his hammer hitting rivets into the rings to hold them in place echoed about their ears. *Tap, tap. Tap, tap. Tap, tap.* The measured and repeated rhythm was that of a man well versed in his trade, who had spent many a long winter forging armour.

"Now remember: you need a firm arm to hold your shield. Your life depends on it. Think of a tortoise. Your shield is your shell. Your arms, legs and head should never stick out past the shield unless absolutely necessary."

"Yes, lord," William said, doing his best to keep his left arm steady under the weight of the heavy wooden shield. His hand tightly gripped the handle of two crossed leather straps, while another pair of straps, running side by side, held the shield firmly against his forearm. Osbern was stood opposite him, wielding a long training spear. The iron tip had been replaced by a ball of cloth filled with straw.

"Ready?" he asked William, who nodded and gritted his teeth.

36

Osbern lunged forward, striking the centre of the shield. William staggered backwards, only just staying on his feet.

"Your arm wasn't bad," Osbern said, "but watch your footing. Turn to your right."

William turned so that he was now sideways.

"Now put your right arm back. Turn your left foot forward, put your right leg back a bit and look at me."

William did as he was told, feeling much more stable.

"Good. When I move to attack, I want you to take a step forward with your left foot. Lean into your shield, but keep your right foot firmly in place. Ready?"

Osbern thrust the spear forwards a second time. As he did, William took a firm step towards him and leant hard against his shield. The force of the blow sent a shock all the way up his arm into his shoulder. Yet he held firm. When he looked up above the metal rim of his shield, he saw the steward beaming with pride.

"Alright?" Osbern said. "I dare say you have the makings of a fine knight."

They practised this for a full hour. Time and again the spear was thrust hard at young William and time and again he went one step forwards to meet it. Eventually, his left arm was so numb from the repeated shocks that they were forced to stop for a break. Osbern patted William on the shoulder with approval. William flinched as the Steward had chosen to tap the very shoulder which had been taking the brunt of the attacks. They sat down on the side of a nearby drinking trough as one of the servants brought them water. William gratefully gulped down the water, glad to be relieved of the shield's weight, which had seemed to increase more and more as the afternoon went by. He sensed Osbern looking at him and turned to meet the man's gaze.

"Tell me, William: why do we fight?"

William was taken aback. "Because we are knights, my lord," he said confidently. The Steward chuckled.

"You're not a knight yet, young sir. But that is not the answer, anyway. Think about it. Why do we fight? What is the aim? What is the purpose?"

William frowned as he thought hard.

"To kill our enemies?"

"Any man who fights to kill his enemies cannot rightly call himself noble or knightly," Osbern said in a stern voice.

"Why do we fight, then?"

"We fight to defeat our enemies, to bring them under our control and force them to accept our rightful authority."

"Why not just kill them? That way they can't fight us again."

"You can kill one man," Osbern agreed. "But then another of ambition will take his place and rally his supporters. If you show mercy, though, then your enemy must show gratitude and submit. When a leader submits to your Justice, his men must follow suit."

William thought about what the steward said.

"Then why did the archbishop get killed? Should his enemies not have made him surrender instead?"

Osbern smiled.

"That is a very good question, young William." He scratched the nape of his neck and sighed. "I'm afraid that not all men are knightly. Not all men are as clever as you or me. Men who have not intelligence, nor faith, nor a loyal heart, will lower themselves to the most underhanded villainous tricks."

"So how can we beat them?"

"It is our duty to seek them out. Such men have a habit of making mistakes. And when they do, you must bring them before God's good Justice, where all can see them be tried. Only when they are fairly found guilty can you use the most severe of punishments. Be mindful, though, to show mercy where you may. Only God can give life, so you must be sparing in taking it away."

William looked thoughtfully at Osbern, who smiled back.

"Come, now, William. That's quite enough resting. Pick up your shield. We have much work to do."

CHAPTER 5

FALAISE, LOWER NORMANDY. 1041 A.D.

"My lord Edward, are you certain that you want to do this?" Osbern said, voicing the concerns of many of the assembled lords. "It could easily be a trap."

"It could," Edward agreed in his softly accented French.

"Since your brother's death, you are the only ætheling left – the only Saxon worthy of the throne."

"Which is precisely why I must go. If Harthacanute is sincere in wanting a brotherly reconciliation, then this may be the only chance my country ever has of regaining its freedom from the Danish yoke."

"Or it could be the time when the last English ætheling is killed."

"You forget Edmond Ironside. His son is also in exile and could just as easily return to take the throne, if I were to die."

"Ironside's son has vanished. No one has heard of him for years. Besides, you are the only one who could sway the people."

"Exactly, so either way I must return to England. I believe Harthacanute to be sincere. In any case, I have no intention of merely counting on his word."

Osbern raised his eyebrows quizzically. William looked up, keen to hear what Edward meant. He had warmed to the Saxon prince. He knew he would never be as close to him as he had been to Alfred, but what Edward lacked in charisma and friendliness, he made up for with his calm temperament which spoke of efficiency – as well as a certain ruthlessness which

40

William, now fourteen, guessed might be hidden beneath the surface.

"Surely you did not think that I had remained idle while the Danes strutted around my kingdom? Nor that I would venture blindly into the lion's den after what they did to Alfred. There are many earls and thegns back home who have suffered under Cnut's line – many who had received little help from Godwin, the scheming Earl of Wessex. I have been in regular contact with those loyal Englishmen. If there is the slightest hint of danger, the Danish lords in England will wake up to find their throats being slit and whole armies springing up throughout the land." Edward clearly relished the look of surprise which now showed on the faces of his Norman friends. "Forgive me for not confiding in you, but I had to be sure that the Danes would not find out before I got to England. It has already been arranged. The Earl Godwin will be sent to keep an eye on the Welsh, who have conveniently agreed to cause trouble – though that agreement was hardly necessary, as I cannot remember a time when the Welsh were not causing trouble. My best man at court will stay close to Harthacanute. Any problems and Harthacanute dies."

"Why not simply kill him right away and be done with it?"

"Let us give him a chance first. England needs a peaceful transition, for once. Besides, I do believe he will soon be dead anyway."

"My congratulations,' said Talou. "It seems we have all underestimated you, my lord."

Edward nodded graciously.

"Let us hope that Godwin and his Danes have done me the same favour."

William sat with his uncle Talou to his left and Osbern to his right. They were in the great hall at Falaise, the walls of which were lined with men. On the right stood the greater lords of Normandy, dressed in their finest clothes – their scabbards hung limp at their sides, for Osbern had made it a rule that none save the duke's guards may bear arms within the ducal residences. The lords had come from all across the duchy to witness this event. It was a moment many of them had long prayed for. For others, it marked the end of a lucrative alliance and its perks of dubious legality. Either way, not one man present was indifferent or ignorant of the importance of the moment. Such a radical shift in the balance of power had not been seen since the death of Duke Robert four years earlier. Even the Archbishop's murder had not caused so much upheaval.

Across the hall stood William's uncle Mauger, now archbishop in William's great-uncle's stead. Around him were all the bishops of Normandy, to remind those present that this judgement was from God, not just the ducal Council, for treason is contrary to God's own laws.

"Bring forth the traitor!"

Osbern was armed with all the trappings of his office. As Steward and head of the ducal Council, he was fully armed in his mail hauberk with a vicious-looking mace in his hand. It was a mace which had forged justice throughout the land even in the days of the old duke, a mace of such presence that it appeared on its own to command the room. At his neck hung a heavy chain with a large circle of silver on which was the duke's emblem, crowned with a cross and framed by the words "Iuste Et Fideliter"

– justly and loyally. Glancing sideways at Osbern, William saw the man who had kept the querulous barons of Normandy in check. Osbern the Steward was a warlord in all his glory. Now he would flex his muscles and deal out punishment to the one who deserved it so. In he came.

Even as he entered the room with his hands in chains, he looked as one who knew himself to be superior to all his betters. Though all present had known who to expect, the sight of him sent a shudder through the crowd, as though it had all been mere small talk and wishful thinking without the substantiation of the body. His eldest son came with him, to witness his fate. One of the guards pushed him, so that he would kneel. He elbowed the man away and spat towards Osbern's feet.

"You, Roger, sometime Count of Montgomery, will kneel before your Duke." Osbern's imperious voice would have made lesser men quake in their boots.

"Kneel? Before that little turd? That imp? That brat? Never."

Osbern nodded to the nearest guard, who brought the butt of his spear crashing into Montgomery's back. The latter flinched, but stayed upright until the guard kicked his leather shoe into the back of his knee, sending him to the ground with a thud. Montgomery looked daggers at Osbern.

"You think yourself so righteous, do you not, Osbern?"

The Steward gave no answer.

"Well let me tell you this: you leave Normandy in grave danger. This duchy has ever been ruled by powerful men. A lack of strong leadership is what cost the French kings this land. Now you would have us lose it in turn by placing this weak bastard on the Norman throne. So which of us is the real traitor?"

43

The last remark seemed directed not at Osbern but at Talou. William looked at his uncle. Talou's expression was impassive. Whatever alliance or sympathy had existed between him and Montgomery had clearly died the moment one of them found himself in chains.

"I see," Montgomery said, "so it's like that. Well, Talou, I hope that your new-found faith in the boy is worth it. Personally, I think you're a damned fool."

"There is nothing new-found about my faith in our duke. I only ever stayed close to you so that I could keep an eye on your devious ways, as the good Steward here knows well. It seems I was right to, given the present state of affairs."

"Yet you spoke as I did about the boy and —"

"Whatever I said was to lure you into trusting me. If you believed it, then more fool you."

William saw Osbern give his uncle a furtive glance before turning his attention back to Montgomery.

"I won't waste any more of these good lords' time. Roger Montgomery, this Council has found you guilty of withholding the taxes due to your duke, of taking lands and monies which were not yours by right, of disobeying direct orders from the Council and your duke, and of plotting treason against your duke, whom God appointed to rule over us all. In the presence of the lords of Normandy, spiritual and temporal, I hereby sentence you to banishment from the duchy... for life."

The assembled lords murmured.

"Your lands are forfeit to the duke," Osbern continued. "Should you return, it will be the duty of every man bearing arms to put you to death."

"My lord, please!"

It was William Montgomery who spoke.

"I beg you, show mercy. My father served Duke Robert loyally. Anything he has done since was done out of love for Normandy and out of the need to preserve discipline and enforce the laws of the Council."

Osbern was unmoved.

"Your father here has sown the seeds of rebellion. Far from upholding this Council's decisions, he has trampled over our authority and, by extension, over his duke's authority."

"That whelp has no authority," the older Montgomery said. "You may cast me out, but I swear that it will but postpone the inevitable. He will never be duke."

"You see, young Montgomery, your father is utterly unrepentant. Consider yourself lucky; Lord Talou had asked for his head to be struck from his shoulders. Be gone."

As the guards pulled them away, the young Montgomery gave Osbern a look of pure loathing.

William stirred in his bed when he heard something – a scuffling sound – followed by a stifled cry which chilled his very soul. As he bolted upright, he was pushed back down by a forceful arm. He looked up and saw a burly man running out into the hall, his head masked by a hood.

William turned back towards the foot of his bed. As he looked down, he froze in terror. His eyes had fallen on a shadowy figure on the ground; it gave a spasm, and jerked again, a gargling sound coming from its mouth. He crawled across to turn the figure over and cried out in horror. Brave Osbern looked up at him. His throat was slit.

William lifted the Steward's head. As Osbern looked him in the eyes, he was suddenly aware of how old the loyal man looked. He had always seemed so solid, immortal even. Now his grey beard turned to crimson and a tear appeared in his eye. The last expression on his face was one which would stay with William until his own dying day. Some men die in fear, others in anger. Not Osbern. The last expression on Osbern's face was one of apology.

The old man closed his eyes for the last time, leaving William feeling alone in the world.

Winter was upon him. As Osbern's blood warmed his cold hands, the immortal land died.

CHAPTER 6

William of Talou was built like so many of the Norman castles in his custody, stern and sturdy. His solid legs and boots served him as well as any motte to support his heavy frame. His broad shoulders and portly stomach were as solid as any keep. To this he added his resilience to withstand as great a siege as any fort might. Yet, as most defences in the land were made of wood, he knew that it was sometimes worth giving in a very little – for when the timbers bend some small amount, it saves them from breaking altogether.

In short, he was just the kind of lord a young duke should have for guidance – though perhaps not one a young lord would *want* for guidance.

"How did he get in?" Mauger asked. They were gathered in the archbishop's chambers in Rouen. Osbern's body, carefully wrapped up, had been taken to the nearby chapel.

"One of the guards was killed by the main gate," Talou said. "I came up as soon as I saw his body. It had been quickly hidden behind some barrels."

"And the other guards?" Mauger said. Talou merely shrugged.

"No sign of them. Whoever did this must have paid them off."

"They can't have got far," said Herluin. "We have men all over the town and barring every route out. We're bound to catch them."

William stood silently in a corner of the room, looking around at the assembled lords. Any one of them might have been behind the murder. It was no secret that all were jealous of

47

Osbern's privileged position at court. He had been free to deal out justice in whatever way he saw fit to keep the relative peace and he had never been one to shy away from using that authority.

William's look settled on Osbern's son, who stood in the far corner. FitzOsbern's eyes were fixed on William with a look of anger. He stared, unblinking. William shook his head in denial. There was little he could have done to save his friend's father.

"So what's to be done with William?" Mauger said, drawing William's attention back to the conversation.

"I could take him back to Conteville," Herluin offered. "He will be safe there and I know his mother will want to keep him close until we are sure that the danger has passed."

"No," said Talou. "He must stay here and show himself to his people."

"He might still be at risk of assassination!" Herluin protested. Talou raised an eyebrow.

"He is a duke. He will always be in danger. Someone will always be trying to kill him," Talou said, now looking William in the eye. "To be a duke is to have the sword of Damocles ever hanging over your head." Osbern had told William's mother that very same thing. Now he lay dead in the chapel - all to protect William.

"Damocles was a king," Herluin pointed out.

"Being a duke of the Normans is worth more than being king of any other land," William said, summoning his courage. Talou gave him a look he had never before seen on his uncle's face; a look of approval.

"William must stay here. It is where he belongs, not hidden behind his mother's skirts," Talou said. "Besides, he will be far safer here than at Conteville, I dare say."

"And yet your high walls did not save the Steward!" Herluin flushed vermillion. "This town stinks of corruption."

"It was not corruption which killed my father!" FitzOsbern's trembling voice piped up. "It was cowardice." He looked daggers at William. Talou looked from FitzOsbern to William and back again.

"William knows well the pain of losing a father, FitzOsbern," Talou tried to calm him.

"Yet he didn't lift a finger to try to save mine! And this is our duke?" FitzOsbern clenched his fists, his whole body shaking.

"I was asleep!" William said. "There was nothing I could have done."

"You could have fought!"

"Enough," Talou said. "Enough. Understand that our enemies will ever seek to disunite us, to have us fight each other rather than them. The only way to defeat them is to show them that nothing is so powerful as to break us apart."

Talou's words were lost on FitzOsbern; though he did keep silent, his countenance lost none of its resentment.

"And what is to be done about Osbern's killer?" Herluin asked. "If we don't catch the guards, how will we ever find him out?"

"Can you remember anything, William?" Talou asked. "Anything at all about the man?"

William shook his head. "It was too dark. He was medium height and hidden under a cloak."

FitzOsbern scoffed.

49

"Until we catch the guards, there is little we can do, then," Talou said.

"There's no knowing how far ahead they are. A couple of men could easily slip away in the night, especially if they had horses waiting. This hardly looks like a spontaneous murder, so they must have planned a getaway," Mauger said.

"The killer could still be here, of course, hiding in the open," Talou pointed out. "If he is, then he is bound to slip up sooner or later."

"So all you plan to do is wait?" FitzOsbern spat.

"Your father was a remarkable man," said Talou. "He was strong, of course, but what made him truly wise was his ability to decide when to charge in and when to keep his sword sheathed. If fighting blindly can harm your interests, then it is better to wait until the picture is clearer. They could have tried to kill Osbern when he was alone. Instead, they did it where he should have been safe. If they took such a risk, it could only have been for one reason."

He let his words hang in the air until it finally dawned on William.

"They wanted to kill me."

Talou nodded.

"Perhaps they did not even expect Osbern to be there. We may never know. What is clear is that things did not go to plan. William should have died. No doubt the intruder took fright when William woke up. If he had stayed a moment longer after you shouted out, William, he would have run into me and would soon have met his Maker. Osbern's presence saved your life."

The thought sent a chill down William's spine. It was not the first time he had been in danger, of course, but it was the first time death had come so close. Were it not for a coincidence – or perhaps some instinct on Osbern's part – it would have been William's body now resting in the chapel. He looked over at FitzOsbern. His friend's face was pale, as anger gave way to grief. It occurred to William that his friend, through his veil of tears, had not seen until then that William should have died instead. Perhaps he wished it had been so; William could not begrudge him the thought. Some wounds run deep and only time can help. There would always be a scar.

William knew that FitzOsbern craved that which he himself had craved at his own father's death. He wanted revenge.

Talou was right, of course; they could do little until someone talked. To act now could cause more harm than good. In the shadows of that candle-lit room, on that winter's night, William made himself and his friend a promise. He vowed that, no matter how long it took, he would find Osbern's killer and give his friend the revenge he so bitterly needed.

Nothing can beat the thrill of the hunt. No excitement is greater than the rush of blood as predator pursues quarry. From a very young age, William had taken to the sport in all its forms. One of the few memories he had of his father was being taken out into the forests around Valognes in the Cotentin to show him how to hunt deer with bow and arrow. William had been but six at the time, but the stern Duke Robert believed his only son and heir ought to be taught the harsh facts of life at the earliest opportunities.

Stags, he had told William in his gravelly voice, were proud creatures which were worthy of the same respect a man should show his noblest enemies. They lived in structured communities with a hierarchy, just as men did. They were not malicious creatures, the duke had said. True, they destroyed parts of the surrounding woods, and yes, they needed to be killed so as to provide food for the household, but they were nonetheless to be respected and admired for their ability to outwit many hunters.

After two hours of searching for broken branches, disturbed ground and other tell-tale signs of a deer passing through an area, they had finally found their quarry – a large stag with impressive antlers which told of long years spent commanding the area and watching of the heard.

"It is all part of the natural order of things," the duke had told William. "We must eat and keep a healthy stock of animals for future meals. To do this, we remove the oldest member of the herd, that way the younger males will take his place and protect the females. When they are old and large enough to provide us with food, they in turn will be killed; so the cycle goes on."

William had nodded, though thinking back on it, he realised that he had perhaps not realised the full meaning of his father's words.

"Are you going to shoot it now?" he had asked in a timid voice.

"Not now," had come the gruff reply. "Not yet. We're upwind of the beast. If we move in closer, it will catch our scent. We have to find a better position. When we have it where we can be confident that it will go down on the first shot, then I will strike. You must understand, William, that sometimes you only get one chance. If you cannot be sure of success, best wait and stalk your prey. Soon enough it will make a mistake." Robert nodded at the beast calmly drinking from a stream. "Look at it. It does not even know that it is hunted. Why should we rush? Until it senses its danger, we are free to take what time we need."

They stayed there, crouched behind the bushes, looking down into the lush green valley.

"Come," said the duke through his thick brown beard with its flecks of silver. "Let's see if we can't find a better spot."

They moved around the valley in a wide half circle, taking care to keep behind the cover of the densely growing oak trees and nettle bushes. The stag, still seemingly calm, set off in search of food, or perhaps simply to look for another member of its herd. William and his father followed the beast from their new downwind position. William was eager to go in for the kill, but the duke held him back, insisting on waiting until the conditions were at their best.

Finally, after many hours of stalking the animal, they came to the outskirts of a clearing in which the late afternoon light reflected off the surface of a small lake. The stag had stopped to drink again. It had stayed near enough to the edge of the clearing to make a shot strike home with sufficient strength to kill. At that distance, Duke Robert could hardly miss. The foliage around their hiding place gave plenty of cover.

"Stay here and don't make a sound," he told William.

The duke crept forwards, drawing an arrow from the quiver slung over his back. William watched wide-eyed, hardly daring to draw breath. His father gently rested the arrow upon his left hand, which held the bow. He clipped the horn nock of the arrow on the string. Adjusting his footing to get a strong and stable position, he paused for a moment. The stag's ears pricked. The animal lifted its head. Had it heard the duke? Robert waited with baited breath, staying as still as a statue. The stag looked across the water, away from him. After a short while which felt to William like an eternity, a small hare came hopping out of a patch of undergrowth. It stopped, sniffed around and hopped off back into the safer depths of the forest.

The stag seemed to relax at having found the cause of the disturbance and resumed its drinking. Duke Robert began to draw back the string. He did it slowly; William could see the concentration on his father's face from his hiding place just to the right. The duke's dark eyes never left his target. As the string went back past his thick brown beard, the beast lifted its head again. It made as if to turn – too late. With a flash of crimson the arrow struck home, finding its way into the creature's neck. A bleat of agony and it darted towards the safety of the woods, in spite of the deep wound to its neck. Robert swore. He leapt out of his hiding place to pursue the animal, which struggled to keep its footing as blood gushed forth from its wound. It collapsed just before reaching the tree line. The duke dropped his bow and drew his sword. William plucked up his courage and ran to join his father. The animal, in its ultimate desperation, thrashed wildly about with its hooves, churning the earth of the damp clearing. The duke looked down at it. To William, it seemed the animal looked back at his father, its eyes full of an implicit plea for mercy. The duke sighed, lifted his blade and put the magnificent beast out of its misery and this world.

Robert walked over to the lake and washed the blood off his sword. Having wiped it dry on a corner of his tunic, he sheathed it and drew his large hunting knife. He turned to William, who stood gazing open mouthed at the animal.

"Come here," he said, offering his son the knife. "Show me how well you can deal with a stag."

Following his father's instructions closely, William started by slitting the beast's hide in a single clean line from the gullet downwards. Aware of his father watching his every move, he rolled up his sleeves and forced himself not to wince as he reached into the carcass. The animal's warm blood covered his hands. He pulled out the bladder, taking care not to burst it lest it should spoil the meat. He leant forwards and plunged his arm deeper still into the animal and grabbed hold of its innards. Tugging hard, he pulled out the stomach and intestines. The duke knelt down and checked both for any sign of disease. When he was satisfied, he made William remove the heart and lungs, telling him that this was called the red offal, in contrast to the white offal of the intestines and stomach. Again, the duke inspected these closely and determined that no healthier stag had ever died. It would make a fine feast.

He tied the offal into two neat bundles which he put into a bag William held out for him. Here he took the knife back from William. Looking for the joins between the upper and lower parts of the limbs, he cut deeply. With a single slice at each part, he severed the lower limbs and discarded them – an offering to Nature in return for what he had taken. What carrion inhabited the woods would soon be scavenging the treat. He put hooks through the carcass to pin it all together.

"Wait there while I fetch the horse", he instructed William.

As he stood guard, William found his gaze drift from the large patch of blood on the ground to the beast's eyes, still open and pointed towards the late afternoon sun. He was struck with how quickly the lordly animal had gone from master of these woods to an empty shell. He felt ashamed almost of the part he had played, but forced himself to remember what his father had said about the natural cycle.

There would be a great feast in Valognes that night.

CHAPTER 7

VALOGNES, LOWER NORMANDY. SPRING, 1042 A.D.

"You are certain it was him?" William said.

"Positive," FitzOsbern insisted. "One of the stable boys overheard him. Montgomery's eldest son William organised the whole thing."

"We must be sure," Talou said. "These are precarious times we live in. The Montgomeries have many supporters; we cannot simply execute one of their number without proof."

"Perhaps that is precisely why we do need to do away with him," Mauger said. For a bishop, he could hardly be accused of faintheartedness. "Roger Montgomery was allowed to gather such power as to challenge the ducal house and all because he had been close to our brother Robert. He trampled all over this Council's decisions. Are we to let his son do the same?"

"He has not defied us openly," said Talou. "How are we to justify an execution?"

"He does not need to defy us openly. There are others who would seek to usurp William's position. We cannot afford to let any part of Normandy become hesitant in obeying us."

"You seem to forget, uncle Talou, that this man went so far as to enter my chamber and kill the Steward as I slept. He might as easily have killed me if I had not awoken. Who's to say he wouldn't try again, given the chance?"

"If we kill him, you could risk an open war," Talou said. "Would you tear your duchy asunder?"

"Would you let my father's murderer go unpunished?" FitzOsbern said. "What coward shies away from delivering justice?"

"Calm down, FitzOsbern," Mauger said. "Talou is merely pointing out the dangers of starting a family feud."

"Starting a feud?" spat FitzOsbern. "This all started long before today and not by my hand. My hand will finish it though."

Talou scoffed.

"You are still very young, FitzOsbern," he said. "I do not expect a boy of merely fifteen years to understand the fine balance which we must temper ourselves to achieve. Not all problems can be solved by the sword."

"What of my authority?" William asked. "I have yet to mark my fifteenth birthday, but my authority – with this Council's guidance – cannot be weakened. I will soon be of age, after all, to rule alone."

Talou raised an eyebrow. William would have to tackle that particular obstacle in due course.

"He has a point," Mauger said. "William Montgomery is guilty not only of murder. Osbern was the duke's appointed officer. That makes it a treasonous offense. We can try him for that."

William watched his uncle Talou scratch his beard. His dark eyes glimmered by the light of the fire which crackled in the great hearth.

"Fine," Talou said at last. "Let him be killed. He won't be found guilty of treason, though. The only witness we have is one of Montgomery's own men. He would never testify against his lord. He might not even live long enough to testify, given Montgomery's past record."

"What do you suggest then?" Mauger asked.

"We must find some way around the matter. If it looks like murder, we risk a feud. We must be seen to act lawfully."

William looked into the fire. An idea started to form in his mind.

"Montgomery does not yet know that he has been found out, I take it," he said to FitzOsbern.

"No. He does not. The stable boy kept his mouth shut and came straight to me."

"If he did find out, how would he react?"

"Make a run for it, I suppose," said Mauger. "Try to join his father at Henry's court. The only other way of going about it would be to risk an open war."

"Which he isn't prepared for yet," William said.

"Neither are we," Talou said. "It would take months to assemble an army large enough to take his fortresses, not to mention the supplies necessary for a prolonged siege."

"Then he must find out when he is at his most vulnerable," William said. "When he makes a run for it, we can make as if to arrest him. It will, of course, be a pity that he will die when trying to escape from our men."

FitzOsbern grinned.

"Clever,' Talou said. "Very clever. We will make a duke of you yet."

"I am a duke," William said.

Talou smiled.

"Which is why it will be your men who do the deed."

"Indeed, I trust you, as a leading member of my Council, to exercise my authority in this matter," William said. "Let

FitzOsbern join you, though. We owe him that much for not having been able to keep his father safe."

Talou looked at FitzOsbern, clearly weighing up the odds.

"Very well, FitzOsbern; you may go," Talou said. "Be sure to obey my orders though. This is a ducal mission, not a bloody revenge."

"I will show Montgomery the respect he deserves, don't you worry," FitzOsbern said.

The answer hardly seemed to reassure Talou.

"Are you ready, my lord?" William Montgomery called.

"I am indeed. We can set to it at once."

"Are you sure you do not wish to take some men with you?"

"Positive. We have your men to protect us, and I have nothing to fear from you, do I?"

"You do not, my lord, of course."

"In any case, I have had to send Talou and FitzOsbern away on business."

"Business, my lord?" Montgomery seemed surprised.

"Oh, just some locals squabbling. The usual nonsense, but I don't expect them back before sundown. So you and I shall have plenty of time for the hunt."

The news seemed to please the man, who was more than ten years William's senior. Talou had a great presence and tended to overawe even more experienced men. To have the Duke to oneself on a hunt through thick forests was a rare privilege – and opportunity, if any dared take it.

"Then let us go. Ride on!"

With that they set off across the fields around Valognes. William felt alive with the wind running through his hair. He enjoyed few things in life as much as a hunt. This hunt would prove particularly satisfying, he thought, as he rode next to his quarry.

They passed into an apple orchard which William knew gave good cider and soon found themselves entering the dense forest which surrounded Valognes, making it such a favourite hunting ground of his. In the darkness, where only thin rays of light penetrated the thick green cover of leaves, they searched for some animal to pursue. William tried to guide the party where he wanted, but Montgomery's huntsman was adamant that he had seen a stag in some other part of the forest and took them on a merry dance in quite the opposite direction, further and further west. William was beginning to think the whole day might end up being a waste of time when finally they saw not the stag in question, but a wolf. Curiously, it appeared to err alone. Just as they saw it, so did it too become aware of their presence and dashed off, not west, but east, right past their very noses. William thought it most unnatural, yet who was he to turn his nose up at such a chance?

"After it! Quick," he shouted, touching his spurs to his horse's flank and darting off in pursuit of the animal, with Montgomery and his men hot on his tail. East and east some more, they went, swiftly covering the ground they had ridden through that whole morning. William gave chase to the creature, though never risking getting too close. He needn't have worried, for the fear which drove the wolf lent it more speed than any horse might have covered through the tangle of the woods. Eventually they came to a spot which William recognised. As a crossing of two paths appeared ahead, he saw the wolf dash down the left fork. He glanced behind. None of Montgomery's men would have been close enough to see past him. He could not have planned it any better himself.

"Make haste, my good Montgomery! It went this way," William cried back to his host, pointing to the right. "Normandy! Normandy!"

If such a war cry was out of place in a hunt, Montgomery showed no surprise. Men oft got caught up in the thrill of the chase. It was good practice for battle.

"Normandy!" They all took up the cry, unaware of what William shouted it for, but eager to please their duke.

As they hastened round the bend in the right fork, William was the only one to see the tell-tale glint in the trees up on the slope to their right.

"Normandy," he shouted one last time for good measure.

The last knight appeared behind him. Then it happened. It happened very swiftly indeed. Flashes through the air preceded cries of agony and whinnying of horses as men and steeds were thrown to the ground. Some few, perhaps three or four, men were still on horseback. They recovered quickly, as befits trained knights, and turned their mounts about. It proved a fatal error. Had they kept their momentum, they might just have ridden straight through those few archers into the safety of the deeper woods. The pause gave Talou the time he needed to charge down from his concealed position of the rise and block their escape route with his own troop of some twenty good and loyal knights.

William flashed a grin of teeth at Montgomery, who alone seemed to have kept his cool and thus far avoided harm. Seeing William's smile and recognising Talou, he realised that this was no group of brigands.

"My lord Duke," he said, trying to remain calm. "I do not understand. You let your uncle kill my men and say nothing? They are all true Norman knights and as loyal as I to you."

"As loyal as you are to me?" William scoffed. "And just how loyal *are* you to me? Can you think of no reason why I should act so?"

"Indeed, my lord Duke, I cannot. Since my father's banishment – before that, even – I have been loyal."

"You Montgomeries ever think yourselves clever, so superior to the rest of us. It seems that your education will not save you now, though. You see," he gently edged his horse closer to Montgomery's, "I know your sin. It was confessed by one of your own men. A stable boy told me so, having heard it himself."

"Sin? What sin?" Montgomery said, failing to hide the doubt which appeared in his eyes.

"I knew it all along, in truth, yet I could not quite be certain of it. It was dark that night. I had slept too soundly, but now I see it all as though it had been mid-day. It was you. You were the one who pushed me back even as old Osbern lay dying, choking on his own blood."

"I protest, my lord, you are mistaken," he stumbled on his words, looking around for help. "My lord Talou, you must see the madness in this."

"There is madness indeed, but that madness lies with you. Did you really think that you could do such a deed and never be punished?"

"You have done such things yourself," Montgomery spat. "You were in league with my father!"

"I was, it is true. Yet I was only feigning to be his friend that I may prevent such a crime. It was to my great sadness that I did not continue to keep a closer watch on you, else the Steward might still be alive."

Montgomery looked from William to Talou and back again. Then he laughed. It was the callous laugh only a traitor might muster at such a time.

"You may have banished my father, but my house is still strong. I will join him, if you so wish. There we will rebuild our forces and Normandy will pay the price. The shaky word of one stable boy will not see me hang."

"You will die sooner than you might make one move towards the edge of this forest!"

It was FitzOsbern who shouted this. He came down the slope, emerging from the trees in all his anger. He wore full mail and carried a spear. At his waist hung that same vicious mace which his father had borne when banishing Roger Montgomery.

"Why if it isn't little FitzOsbern. What a happy coincidence," said Montgomery. "I see now why you drew me into the woods rather than fight me in the open. Quite the little coward. I wonder whether your father would -".

Whatever Montgomery wondered of old Osbern would remain a mystery as FitzOsbern's spear flew straight into his horse's chest. The beast threw its rider to the ground. With a

64

blood-curdling cry, FitzOsbern charged down the slope towards his enemy. Leaping from the saddle without so much as stopping his mount, he drew his mace. As a stunned Montgomery tried to get up, FitzOsbern swung his weapon with all his might, bringing it crashing down onto the older man's helmet. The sound echoed through the woods. Even through the metal, bone could be heard breaking. Montgomery dropped to the dirt once more – this time for good. FitzOsbern crouched down beside him and bashed his mace again and again in dull thuds on Montgomery's body.

"Enough, FitzOsbern!" Talou shouted. "He's dead."

Sweating, the youth stood up. He spat on Montgomery's corpse, before throwing his mace down one last time for good measure.

"Now he's dead."

The knights from both sides who had been watching the fight stood with jaws hung open. William Montgomery, favourite son of one of the most powerful families in Normandy, had been a man in his prime of some twenty-five years. Yet the ferocity with which this fifteen-year-old youth had beaten his corpse to a pulp in cold blood was something which they would not likely forget.

"Good," said William, with a nod of approval to his friend. "Now that's done, perhaps we might return to the castle. I'm starving. A good hunt always works up an appetite."

Talou raised an eyebrow.

"What do you want us to do with the rest of them?"

"Will they talk, do you think?" William said.

"They might – if they are foolish enough."

"Then I leave them in your good care, uncle, to do as you think best." He turned to FitzOsbern. "Come on, let's get you cleaned up."

His friend was covered in Montgomery's blood.

"Messy things, animals."

They rode off, back down the path. As they headed out of the forest and into the orchard, William thought he heard screaming from behind, though the trees muffled the sound.

And as the first blossom appeared in the orchard, the immortal land was born again.

Chapter 8

William leant over a small trestle he had had brought to his chambers in this castle of Rouen to break his fast. His hounds lay dozily by the small fire which chased away the chill of the morning. He had planned to go on a hunt that day, but found he had little appetite for his food either. He sat there playing with it absent-mindedly. He whistled and one of the slumbering dogs pricked its ears. It stretched its paws before padding over to droopily rest its head on William's lap. Its nose sniffed tentatively at the table, the spread of which was just out of its sight. William smiled faintly. At least someone was hungry. He broke off a piece of bread and held it out. After the briefest of sniffs, the hound's curiosity was satisfied and it snapped up the bread. William stroked its head, feeling the soft fur on its ear.

FitzOsbern was stood by the window, looking out of the open arch at the activity in the fields below. William was sorry to deprive his friend of the thrill of the hunt, though he sensed the drizzle outside meant that he was just as content as William to laze around indoors for the time being.

"What are you going to do?" FitzOsbern interrupted William's reverie.

William shrugged.

"I'm not sure, yet, to be honest. I can't be everywhere, but whenever we're away in Rouen, the barons of Lower Normandy seem to be a law unto themselves. Not a day goes by when news doesn't come in of some fresh dispute. One might almost think there were two Normandies."

"What the Hell is he doing here?" FitzOsbern said, looking out into the yard. The corners of his lips curled down in disgust.

William rose from his chair, to his hound's disappointment, and rushed over to see with his own eyes whom the unexpected visitor was. As a young man approached the keep, William sensed his friend shaking with anger beside him. William sighed. This would likely be a pleasant encounter for none of the parties present.

A tap at the chamber door signalled the arrival of Talou. He nodded his head in the curtest of bows. William was growing into a man – a man who would soon be duke in his own right. It was courteous for Talou to show him the respect William hoped to command.

"Roger Montgomery's second son, Roger, is here, my lord. He requests an audience with you."

"Did he say what he wanted?" William asked.

"The devil take him and his father! And all Montgomeries that walk this earth!" FitzOsbern shouted, punching the table so hard it nearly flew off its trestles. "Whatever he wants, you can be sure he's up to no good. Just send him packing to join his father!"

Talou coughed.

"Yes, uncle?" said William.

FitzOsbern glared at the older man.

"If I may, it would be unwise to banish him. His father was banished for he had committed treason and we had the proof. Without some form of evidence or a widely accepted crime, we can do nothing lest it set an example to others that they can settle their scores out of hand. Your father, FitzOsbern, knew that well. He only banished him once we had the proof and it was common knowledge."

"He's a Montgomery! That's proof enough."

"The Montgomeries still have influence. Even from afar, Roger the elder is able to send bribes and threats which we can do very little about. He is sheltered by King Henry, on account of that same influence. We can't touch him."

"I could touch him and so could my sword," FitzOsbern said.

"And all the time," Talou continued, ignoring the interruption, "the barons of Lower Normandy squabble. The Montgomery lands south of Caen are ideal for keeping the lesser barons in check. William, the Duke of Normandy cannot be in both Rouen and Falaise at the same time. You need a balance in Lower Normandy. Montgomery was that balance."

FitzOsbern threw his hands out.

"Are you saying my father was wrong to banish him?" FitzOsbern was fuming.

"Not in the least. But we must now have an answer to this problem. I gather that Roger the younger is much more ready to listen to reason. He is well educated – much more so than his rough brother William was. It would be far better to have a Montgomery whom we can control. If you gift him his father's lands, he will be indebted to you. In return, you will have a lord to keep Lower Normandy in check."

FitzOsbern scoffed, turning back to look out into the yard. The dog joined him, as if sensing FitzOsbern's sadness. It was rewarded with a rough pat on the head and a scratch behind the ear.

"William," Talou said softly, leaning over William's chair, "you must see that this cannot go on forever. Where we can solve these problems, your dukedom will be more secure. You will wield more power and be able to accomplish greater things. Tend your land, let your crop ripen. Only with a stable and prosperous Normandy will you be able to see off threats from outside. We have been fortunate thus far. What happens if Anjou, ever restless and hungry for land, attacks us whilst our barons squabble?"

"Anjou?" FitzOsbern said. "Better risk a difficult war with Anjou than trust a Montgomery."

"If you cannot guarantee the safety of Lower Normandy, its barons will turn to one strong enough to offer the sort of protection the House of Montgomery gave."

"Protection," FitzOsbern repeated in disgust.

William turned to his friend. They were both but eighteen years of age, yet how much had they already lived through? Their fathers were gone; FitzOsbern's murdered and William's dead in suspicious circumstances. William's tutor the Archbishop of Rouen had lasted little longer. The English Ætheling Alfred had been killed through deceit. Death and treason were their childhood memories. Now William's duchy hung in the balance. And the key to its security? Trusting the son of the man who murdered his only true friend's father. He could feel FitzOsbern's suffering. Such wounds run deep.

But Normandy was suffering. Its streams ran red with the blood of its own people, for there was disorder. Without order – without structure – there could be no peace. The land which should be ripening in preparation for the summer was left uncared for as man dropped his tools and reached for his spear, fearful of what his neighbour might do next. Normandy was truly the land of the Northman and those North men reverted to tribal ways of old, answering only to strength – or to the absence of it.

"William," Talou said, "you must make a decision."

The decision might be taken by the Council, for William had not yet been given his arms and thus was not yet a full duke, though the time approached. His uncle was preparing him. It was time he knew the full burden of his office. He felt like the boy of seven years' age who had been told his father was no longer there to protect him. That cloak of boyhood which had shielded him from much of the politics was gone.

"Send him in, my lord of Talou."

His uncle nodded and left.

"William!" FitzOsbern said in a voice full of pain. "Please."

"I must hear him out, at least, FitzOsbern. I loved your father like my own. This pains me more than anything else. I would that there were some other way, truly. I hope you can forgive me."

"I will always follow you; you know you have my faith. But I beg you; reconsider. To return the house of treason to power; that is madness."

As the door clicked open again, the hound's ears pricked. It looked round excited to see whom this might be to pay him some attention.

Talou entered the small room and bowed pointedly.

"My lord Duke; Roger son of Roger, the former Count of Montgomery."

The man who followed him knelt before William, his head bowed.

"My lord Duke," he said in an accent which spoke of much education.

"Stand up, Sir Roger." William gave him no title of lordship for he had none. His father had forfeited it with his treason.

As he rose, William took time to study his guest. He was slightly older than William – perhaps twenty-three or twenty-four. His build was slender, albeit fairly tall. His dark hair was neatly trimmed and his chin cleanly shaven. The cloth of his tunic was a deep red, which must have cost a small fortune; such richness of colour requires dying many times. The silver chain about his neck held a finely crafted cross and on his right hand he bore a ring, also of silver. William noted with some amusement the faintest hint of ink which Montgomery's careful scrubbing had failed to clean out from under his nails. What sort of knight fights with a quill?

"Speak."

"My lord Duke, I have come to pledge my service to you."

"It is not yours to pledge. It is your Duke's already," FitzOsbern said. William saw the nervous glance Montgomery gave FitzOsbern. He could hardly blame him, given the story which had somehow got out about the brutal manner in which the young FitzOsbern had caved in William Montgomery's head.

"I do not deny it. I have always been Duke William's servant. My circumstances are not exactly usual, though. Since my father's exile and my brother's… I can understand that my own loyalty may be called into question and I have never had the chance to swear it." He turned back to William. "My lord Duke, I am not my father. I am not my brother. I warned William not to meddle as he did."

"So you admit that you knew of his plans to kill my father and did nothing," FitzOsbern said with relish.

"No, that is not true, I swear. I heard him talking and thought it nonsense. My brother always was reckless, but on my honour, I never dreamt he might do something so villainous. His soul became so black that I no longer knew him for my brother."

"And your father," William said, "what of him?"

"My father and I have never seen eye to eye, even when I was a little boy. William was always his favourite. He sent me off to the Church, but when he was exiled, my mother sent word that I should return to Montgomery castle. Since my brother's death, I am the eldest male of my family still in Normandy. The Church is no longer an option."

William could not help but see honesty in Montgomery's eyes. Looking at him again, he resembled his father not one bit. If he was not skilled in battle, perhaps he would be less of a risk than his father. In the present situation, William could think of no better solution.

"If we entrusted you with your father's former lands, how would you deal with the present unrest?"

Montgomery seemed taken aback at the question. He looked to Talou as if expecting the older man to laugh at such a joke, but Talou's face was as serious as ever.

"Well, my lord Duke…"

Montgomery thought about it a short while. FitzOsbern crossed his arms like a stern abbot sure to be disappointed by his neophyte's answer. Montgomery cleared his throat.

"I suppose I would give the most troublesome barons a share of my stock of grain during the Winter months in exchange for

73

their laying down their arms. If they refused, I would take a conroi of knights and torch their own grain stores. I believe that after doing this two or three times, the remaining barons would see sense and comply with your orders, my lord Duke."

William had to stop himself from smiling. The man was clever. Fear and bribery was a classic approach, but one that was proven to work. By tying loyalty to the winter's supply of grain, Montgomery would ensure relative peace all the way through to the following spring.

"Very well. My lord Talou, take note; we hereby name Roger our Count of Montgomery, for such is our good pleasure."

"My lord, thank you," Montgomery said, visibly astounded at such good fortune. "You will not regret it, I –"

William put up his hand to silence him. He walked over to Montgomery and kissed his cheeks. He lingered to whisper in his ear.

"If you betray me, your brother's death will seem like a pleasant way to go compared to that which I shall make you suffer. Understand?"

Montgomery nodded silently.

"Good." William stepped back. He caught sight of FitzOsbern's venomous look, but was proud of his friend for not questioning his decision in front of Montgomery. "My lord Talou, would you show the good Count out?"

Talou led the new lord out, before returning to join them.

"This is a big mistake, William," FitzOsbern said. "I hope you know that."

"He will behave; I am sure of it – especially with my steward keeping a close eye on him."

"Your steward?" FitzOsbern lifted his eyebrows, for William had no such man yet.

"Yes. I think, uncle Talou, that it is time FitzOsbern here took up the office his father honoured so well. Wouldn't you agree?"

"Indeed, my lord Duke," Talou said. William felt sure his uncle would have happily taken the office himself, having in a way exercised it during his minority. But Talou was a man of the World and would have known the inevitability of that moment. "I am sure that young FitzOsbern will serve you well. His loyalty is beyond any doubt; that is the most valuable of all virtues."

FitzOsbern knelt before William.

"Thank you, my lord Duke." William felt odd to be addressed so formally by his childhood friend in private. "I will serve you to my dying day."

"Get up, you soppy fool," William said, and threw his arm round his friend. "Come on, let's have a drink."

Normandy tossed and turned. The storm had started in the night, coming in from the north to batter the orchards and strain at the churches' rafters. William sat in his hall at Rouen, deep in thought. On such a rotten day, there was little to do. He could not hunt and there is a limit to how many times a man can sharpen his sword. For now, the well-honed blade of his father's sword rested against the table. It calmed William to always have it within reach. The uncertain years of his youth had given him the unconscious habit of glancing towards the door every few moments. Too many of the people he loved or respected had met their ends within the confines of their own homes. William was not going to let that happen to him. He always felt less at ease when FitzOsbern was away, as he was that day – gone to manage the estates his father had left him.

"Whenever you are ready, my lord," Roger Montgomery said.

"Are you so keen to lose?"

Montgomery smiled. He had won the previous four games, yet William would not lose face. Roger had been fortunate enough to have an uninterrupted education. His own had been less than constant on account of his tutors having the discourtesy of dying.

William made up his mind at last and moved his tower. The glint in Roger's eye told him instantly of his mistake. Roger moved his bishop with a confident gesture.

"Check mate, my lord."

William looked at the board, at his error and at Roger, who was smiling even more. With a swift backwards swipe of his arm, he sent the chess pieces flying across the room. Losing was not a feeling he was ever going to get used to.

"Hasn't anyone ever told you, Roger, that it is good politics to let your liege-lord win from time to time?"

Roger bowed his head.

"I could indeed let you win, my lord, and no doubt your bad vassals do. Yet I would be doing you a disservice. Far better you should lose to me here and learn how to beat the rest of the world."

"I could beat you any day."

"With a sword, perhaps," Montgomery conceded. "But who's to say it will always be a sword which you are fighting with?"

He stooped down and picked up the piece of chess he had just beaten William with and put it on the table between them.

"Beware of bishops, William. They fear not the sword and still wield the power to destroy and no castle you own will hold them back."

There was a knock at the door and Talou appeared, soaking wet and dishevelled by the storm. He paused to catch his breath.

"My lord," he bowed. "A message for you."

He handed William a folded parchment. William noted the opened seal.

"You know what it says."

"Yes, my lord. I'll warn you now, you won't like it."

"How sensitive is it?"

"The whole world will know soon enough."

William handed the parchment to Roger, who seemed surprised.

"This is King Edward's seal," he said.

"That is correct," William said. "Read it, please, and tell me what I should know."

"King Edward has the pleasure to inform you of his marriage to Edith, daughter of Earl Godwin of Wessex."

"Godwin's daughter? I sincerely doubt there was any pleasure in that. What on earth possessed him?"

"Godwin's is a wealthy family. It is a sensible match," Talou said.

"No, there must be more than that," Roger said. "The enmity between them is no secret. King Edward could have married any woman in England – or from any of the royal families of the west. Something must have changed. Perhaps he no longer has the support of Leofric. The Mercian Earl is almost as powerful as

Godwin. If Leofric caused trouble for the King, with Welsh problems ever present on England's borders and the northern thegns constantly bickering, Edward would have needed help closer to home. Perhaps Edith was the price for keeping his crown. This way he pacifies Godwin, who will expect to have a grandson who is king of England."

Talou raised an eyebrow, clearly impressed at how well informed Roger was. William wondered how Roger had gained such knowledge of the politics across the narrow sea.

.II.

A HARVEST OF DEATH

CHAPTER 9

VALOGNES, LOWER NORMANDY. MAY, 1047 A.D.

William woke up sweating. He shivered in spite of the warmth. He got up and went to the bowl kept on the table by the door and splashed the cold water from it over his face. It had been months since he'd last had that dream of Osbern's death.

He went out of the hall, still unnerved by his dream, in the hope that the fresh air would wash over him and bring him back to reality. Normandy slept still.

He sighed. Montgomery's plan had bought him some time with the barons of Lower Normandy. Now the stirrings of rebellion, so often seen before, were emerging once more to threaten the fragile peace of the land. By the Grace of God and the watchfulness of his guardians, he had lived long enough to attain his majority. But being of age to be a duke and actually wielding the powers of a duke were two very different things. Even now he was suffering from the circumstances of his birth.

Bastardy was nothing new. Many a lord bereft of legitimate heirs had sired and appointed a son begot outside wedlock. But when powerful rivals of ducal stock and pure noble parentage were to be found, there would always be those who would use William's bastardy against him. William had clung to power, to an illusion of power, for what it was worth. Now he had to deal with two turbulent viscounts who had defied their rightful lord.

Nigel of the Cotentin and Ranulf of the Bessin held lands in much of Lower-Normandy and they had set that region ablaze by quarrelling amongst themselves. Taking up arms against each other, despite Roger Montgomery's best efforts.

Their daggers may be pointed at each other's throat, but their blades were waving perilously close to the single thread of hair which held the Damocles sword above William's own head.

These two petty lords of Lower-Normandy needed to be brought to heel – or bought out so that they would quit the field of their own volition – before others of more malicious and devious motives could exploit the situation.

It had to end. The dissent, the lawlessness, the bitter feuds between neighbouring lords – it all had to end. Yet William's coffers were sorely barren. The years of his minority had seen lords using the fractured power of his house to withhold monies he was rightly owed. Even now he had few truly loyal men upon whom he could count.

Feeling the cold soil beneath his bare feet, William dropped to his knees and prayed.

He crossed himself and rose to his feet, aware of a presence nearby. He turned and saw Taillefer, a jester from Bayeux who had regaled William and his host the previous evening with his juggling and his song of Rollo, William's ancestor from Scandinavia – the north man who had created Normandy with fire and sword. It had filled William with pride, as well as the ever-present fear that he would be the last of his line to reign over the region. Yet Taillefer was a jovial young man, of about William's own age, perhaps slightly younger, who had a genial and contagious smile. He had been heading back to his sleeping place after answering a call of nature when he had caught sight of his duke praying. Seeing that the young lord was downcast, he smiled amiably at William and bowed to him, the bow quickly turning into a handstand, which had the desired effect of making

81

William chuckle under his breath in spite of his forlorn mood. He returned the compliment offering Taillefer a round of silent applause.

He wandered back into the hall, wondering which of them was the real fool of his court. Taillefer, having answered the need which had awoken him at such an early hour, returned to the patch of hay in the stables which served as his bed for the night. He had just started to doze off when he heard someone outside. The duke had no doubt abandoned his poor prospects of sleep in favour of a stroll in the fresh air – the hall in which the occupants of the manor and their attendants slept could get rather musty during the night, hence Taillefer's own preference for the stables. At least the horses didn't snore quite so much. The sound of clinking mail, however, brought him fully back to his senses. There was no way that his lordship could have armed himself so quickly.

The jester lay motionless, listening, straining to catch any indication of who the armed man might be and why he had chosen to come at such a time. Perhaps this was simply a visitor or messenger who had chosen to ride through the night rather than stop for rest. Yet somehow Taillefer doubted it. As he listened, he heard that there was more than just one man. Three dismounted. This was all wrong; they had chosen to leave their horses behind the stables, rather than ride into the yard and leave their mounts with the other horses. They were clearly walking in all too stealthy a manner and were talking in hushed voices.

"Remember now; hard and fast. No hesitating and no parlay," came an authoritative voice. "And for God's sake Hamon, keep the noise down!" This last was angrily hissed at a man whose horse had got restless, no doubt sensing the tension in the air.

"Don't you worry about me, Nigel; I'll have the bastard's throat cut open before he's even woken up."

"Well that's a pity", grimly muttered a third, younger man, "I would have liked to see his face when he realised who had come to end his days."

A sword audibly scrapped out of its scabbard.

"Just kill him", said the first voice, "and kill him properly. We can't afford him escaping. You know the penalty for treason, and even a wounded dog can still bite. Besides, you know our orders. It's not even worth keeping him alive for the ransom, what little of it there'd be."

Taillefer had heard more than enough. He crept out of the front of the stable, taking care not to disturb the manor horses, and rushed over to the hall, before these unwanted visitors made their way into the yard.

"My lord!" he cried, hammering on William's door and hoping that he would hear him before the noise alerted the intruders. "My lord, make haste! Lord Nigel has come with armed men and means to slit your throat!"

Within his chamber, William stood shocked. A moment later, having crossed himself, he opened the door.

"Where?"

"Behind the stables, my lord. I heard men plotting your murder. Lord Nigel gave the orders."

"Brave Taillefer," said William, before bolting out the back door as he heard footsteps in the yard. He ran behind the hall, the earth cold under his feet, as he'd not had time to pull on his shoes, let alone don his mail hauberk and sword. He paused in the shadows of the night as he reached the side of the hall and, peering round towards the front of the building, saw his would-be assassins rushing, swords at the ready, towards the main door. In the gloom he struggled to make out who they were and only knew of Nigel's presence amongst them thanks to Taillefer. Making the most of their turned backs, he ran towards the stables. Being bereft of chain mail and shoes, he was able to move unheard and reached the back of the stables unnoticed.

Not having time to saddle his own steed, he leaped into the saddle of one of the aggressors' horses and quickly fumbled his feet into the stirrups. The horse reared, startled by this sudden and unexpected approach. Holding the reins tightly in his left hand, he slapped the beast's haunch with the palm of his right hand and it bolted off into the night, with William holding on for dear life.

As he set off on his bid for safety, he heard his assailants shouting from the courtyard, as they realised that their quarry had just slipped through their fingers. They would already be rushing to their mounts, though one of them would have to wait until he could get one of the stable horses saddled, giving William a slight edge. But despite that narrow head start, he was far from safe. Never having dreamt that Nigel would dare try to ambush him, William had ventured out alone in the heart of Nigel's own viscounty of Cotentin. He swore as he remembered his sword still rested by his bed. He needed to get out of the Cotentin, and fast. As he rode south, he soon found the river Merderet. He knew that if he followed its flow south, he would soon reach the estuaries that marked the end of the Cotentin peninsula. With any luck, once he'd entered Ranulf's viscounty of Bessin, Nigel would be hampered by Ranulf's troops, as they continued to quarrel.

As he hastened to cover the ten leagues or so that separated him from his only hope of safety, barefoot and unarmed, on the back of a stranger's horse, William's mind reeled with the thoughts of what had just taken place – and what he would do if he made it out alive. Only the previous evening, he had been a young duke making merry with his vassals, entertained by a court jester, before riding out to assert his authority over two petulant viscounts. Now, one of those viscounts had tried to murder him and, far from riding out to stamp his authority, William was a fugitive, fleeing half-dressed on a stolen horse, fearful for his very life. So much for having left behind him the fear of his childhood.

As the land awoke, William left the mouth of the river Merderet behind him and came to the wider river Vire. He had glimpsed no sign of his pursuers, but knew that they could not be far behind. What's more, they would be able to take the roads which he had been fearful to use, not wishing to be seen by anyone. After all, these were Nigel's lands. Who knew what an ambitious young sergeant might do if he came upon an unarmed duke to whom his lord was hostile?

By luck, he had arrived at the estuary of the Vire just as the tide turned to the flow. He quickly sought out a ford in the growing light and crossed it, reminded as he did so of how God had saved Moses and his followers by holding back the sea. It seemed the Almighty had heard William's prayer after all. The

85

swift tides which were notorious in this part of Normandy would soon make the river impassable to his hunters.

Once across, he allowed himself to ride along at a slower pace for a while. Through a lightly wooded area, he came to a small church standing alone. William lead his stolen horse to water in a nearby stream, then tied its reins to the branches of a tree and went into the Church. As the nerves of the chase abated somewhat, he became acutely aware of just how tired and hungry he actually was. He could not afford to stop long enough to attend to those particular needs. The church was empty, the light echo of the steps of his uncovered feet making the only sounds within. Kneeling before the Cross, he offered up a silent prayer of thanks to his Saviour for having granted him protection thus far and implored his guidance to finish his journey back to his birthplace of Falaise and the safety it promised. Only once he was back with his friend FitzOsbern and his uncle William of Talou would he be able to rally his strength and reassert his position as the rightful duke of Normandy.

For the time being, having rested a short while on his knees before God, he summoned more of his reserves of will power to regain the saddle and set off on the next leg of his journey. The long trudge through the county of Vexin would present almost as many risks as his flight from the Cotentin. Ranulf may be Nigel's sworn enemy in their disputes over the bordering land of their two territories, but he had no love lost for William either. Since his father's death, the lords of Lower Normandy had been a law unto themselves, caring little of what the Duke's household over in Rouen thought. He would hardly welcome his overlord with open arms. William was still an unarmed nobleman riding alone on an exhausted horse through a land in a state of open war. The memory of his father was unlikely to be sufficient protection against any rogue elements he might meet on his way home. The only blessing was that whilst Nigel and Ranulf were warring with each other, it kept them from effectively rising against William.

From the church, he managed to quickly find the river Aure, which ran parallel to the coast, around the outskirts of Bayeux, before splitting into the branches which went south and around either side of the town of Bayeux. William followed the northern bank of the river, ever mindful of avoiding the paths which others might take and constantly on edge, out of fear of being caught by his pursuers, who would surely be able to make a good guess of where he was headed and how he would try to get there, or of being taken captive by one of Ranulf's patrols.

As he reached the turn in the second branch of the river, he decided his best option was to leave the river behind him and ride with his face to the sun. As it was morning, this would at least take him in a roughly eastbound direction. Another hour's ride saw him safely beyond Bayeux. He should at least be less likely to meet Ranulf's troops, as they would be concentrated around the border in Nigel's county of Vexin, he must have slipped through their lines unnoticed. But if he had managed to do so easily in the early hours, his hunters would no doubt have had the same ease. His stop at the church, though necessary, and his lack of spurs to encourage his horse more determinedly would have given them the time they needed to make up somewhat for having to ford the Vire further upstream. But as the weariness began to set in again, William knew that he would have to stop soon to find a fresh horse and some food and clothing. And a sword would at least make him feel a bit more at peace.

It was mid morning when he came across a beaten track. He followed it through the trees and the dense branches soon gave way to a clearing in which stood a wooden hall with stables on one side. William slowed the pace of his horse, wondering just what welcome he would get; a chance to regain his castle at Falaise or the greeting of drawn steel and a promise of soon rejoining his assassins or their rivals?

Hearing a horse's steps approaching outside, a man appeared from inside the hall. He was a stout fellow, with dark hair showing the occasional strand of silvery-grey. His solid build and stern face, his confident stride and his sword belted at the ready by his side even in his own home, all spoke one clear message to William; this was a man who was used to fighting his way through the challenges of life and not one to be crossed. William swore gently under his breath. He remembered the man from a few years earlier. The last time he had seen him he was being reprimanded at a session of the ducal court by William's uncle, William of Talou. The man had been accused by a nearby church of having encroached upon its land. Where the Church was concerned, William and his uncle thought as one mind; they both wanted to ardently protect the Lord's servants from the ambitions of the worldly lords of Normandy, for the barons of the north of France were ever trying to increase their wealth and the Church was sadly often a victim, being the soft target that it was.

Why steal from your armed neighbour when the Church did not wield a sword? This man opposite him now had been forced to relinquish the disputed lands and had hardly taken kindly to the loss or to the stain on his honour. But the Church must be protected. William still remembered the glowering look he had shown his uncle of Talou. And now here they were; William on a blown horse exhausted and unarmed, in front of one to whom his closest adviser had shown scorn. He was hardly likely to be sympathetic to William and had stayed well clear of the ducal court since that day.

Would the man even recognise William? He had, after all, been only a boy then. And now he was a young man sat of another's horse, only half-dressed and bereft of the few trappings of a duke which he normally wore. He looked more like a fugitive felon than a duke of France. He was half-tempted to pass himself off as a man of lesser birth to claim asylum. But how could he later regain the loyalty of his people if now he shrank from the duties given to him by his father and by God?

William swallowed, his throat dry from the dust of the long road.

"I am William, your duke." He said, his voice braver than he felt. The dice were rolled. He waited to learn his own fate, as the man in front of him now had waited for his all those years before.

The man fell to his knees and William offered up yet another silent prayer.

"My lord duke; what brings you to Ryes in such circumstances?" Hubert asked, rising slowly to his feet.

"It seems that there are those who do not wish me to be their duke… not alive, at least. And you, Hubert; where do you stand?"

"Why my lord, I stand before you." William smiled in thanks and soon told him the story of his rude awakening and how Nigel and three others unknown had tried to kill him and were without a doubt still hunting him now.

"Eudo! My good lad," shouted Hubert to a young man who had just emerged from the hall. "Go arm yourself, and tell your brothers to do the same! And have Alain saddle my best horse and your own. Make haste now, boy!"

The youth looked from his father to the stranger, unaware of whom William was. He didn't ask any questions of his father, compelled by the urgency in his voice. He rushed back into the hall to do as he had been told.

"You cannot linger here, my lord; it isn't safe. Let us find you some food and clothes. Then take my horse. My sons will escort you out of these parts. To Falaise?"

"To Falaise," William acquiesced. "Your kind and loyal service will not be forgotten. Are you not tempted to hand me over to these rebels? They would reward you richly, probably even more richly than I could afford."

"But I would not be rewarded by God, for He made you my duke."

William nodded in recognition of the faithful words.

"And besides," continued Hubert, "I've always thought Nigel was a bit of a tight git. Almost as much so as my lord Ranulf."

William laughed out-right at that, grateful to have happened across the company of one of the few so loyal.

"By God's will, Nigel will rue the day he ever thought to cross me."

Though still tired, William felt replenished from having hurriedly eaten some bread with honey and an apple. He was now sitting astride Hubert's fine war horse, the man's three sons were also mounted and armed. The weight of his chainmail hauberk felt reassuring, the links on it glistening in the mid-day sun, as they prepared to set off. It felt good just to be alive and ready to defend himself. Let them come now, he thought, though prudence warned him against any rash actions. Falaise first. Then rest. And then he would be able to sort out this sorry mess and have Nigel locked up in chains.

"Go now, my good lord Duke. If they come this way, I will do what I can to hide your tracks." He turned to his sons, his face filled with pride and concern. "Do your duty to your duke. I swore an oath to his father that I would follow his rule. All the barons of Normandy swore that oath, though it seems some have forgotten it again. You are men of Ryes, and true Normans. I know you will not let me down. Take care to stay well away from the main roads on your way to Falaise. God speed you safe."

He bowed to William, who returned the favour with a gentle nod of his head and they were off, spurring away through the trees towards the south and safety.

Hubert set about hiding the horse William had arrived on. He tied it to a tree some distance behind the house, where any passers-by would be unlikely to see it and went back into the courtyard in front. He saddled his second-best steed and went along the narrow track which led the way from which the young lord had come. He casually led his steed up and down the path, with all the laid-back demeanour of a lord surveying his estate. Barely an hour had passed when he heard the sound of hoofs grow near. He sat up straight in his saddle. From round the tree line came Nigel, viscount of Cotentin; this was the rogue who had tried to kill his duke. His fellow conspirators soon appeared behind him. Hubert stopped his pacing. This was not possible. How could such a pact have come to pass? The man who came to Nigel's side was all too well known to Hubert, for he had visited his home on many an occasion. Regaining his composure, he went forward to greet his guest.

"My lord Ranulf. What brings you to these parts?"

Ranulf, Nigel's sworn enemy, had clearly joined his rival in this grave act of dishonour. It was almost beyond belief; two of the most powerful barons of Lower Normandy had risen up against their duke and tried to kill him in the dead of night.

"We are after a fugitive, a lone rider," said Ranulf gravely. "He caused great offence to lord Nigel. We are reconciled in not letting common villains escape the rule of law, whatever the circumstances between us."

Hubert flickered a glance at Nigel and saw that he was smirking at the open lie.

"Come man!" insisted Ranulf. "Have you seen him or not?" The viscount of Bessin was on edge, eager to know if he would be the one to overthrow the duke or if he would soon be facing the consequences of rash and impetuous treason.

"My wife did see someone, as it so happens," Hubert lied placidly in his own turn. "She could not see his face, for he had a cloak drawn up tight and was in great haste. He was headed east, no doubt towards Caen. With your leave, my lords, I will show you the way."

"Lead on, then!" shouted Ranulf.

Hubert led them east, in a plausible direction for William to have taken. He was in fact happily fleeing south with the loyal man's sons. And so Hubert took Nigel and Ranulf on a merry dance across the rolling hills near the coast, riding hard until they eventually accepted the inevitable.

"It's no use!" fumed Ranulf. "The little turd has got away."

"He must have turned off on a different road or perhaps took shelter en route. Either way, it's certain that we'll not find him now, my lord."

"Then the hard work is about to begin," said Nigel, "and God help any poor sod who ends up on the wrong side."

"My lord?" asked Hubert, feigning a quizzical look.

"Go back to your wife," said Ranulf through gritted teeth. "We have business elsewhere."

"Come! We must make haste!" shouted Ranulf to his companions.

He then left Hubert truly puzzled, as they set off not back west towards their own lands, but off into the east. Hubert did not have time to see what further mischief they were about. Duke William needed to be told of Nigel's new alliance with Ranulf. He turned his horse and made for Falaise with all speed.

CHAPTER 10

"Crush them! Let's ride straight over there and crush them both now!" William FitzOsbern insisted, as the Duke William watched him continue to pace up and down the hall.

Hubert had brought in the news that Ranulf had joined forces with Nigel and had even been one of the four men who had tried to kill William. Now a fiery FitzOsbern was stoked all the more for having heard William's tale of what had woken him before the incident at Valognes; the dream of FitzOsbern's own father's murder.

"They're only a couple of petulant barons and their cronies; we'll give them a hiding they'll not soon forget," he said, jabbing the table with a straight index finger, as William often saw him do when he wanted to make a point.

"You underestimate them at your own peril, FitzOsbern," came the grave voice of William of Talou. Thus far he had stood calmly by his nephew, arms folded, patiently letting the young FitzOsbern reel off his diatribe.

"Consider this, my lord," he said, moving closer to William's chair, "but a few weeks ago, they were merely irresponsible fools, bickering amongst themselves, just asking for you to chastise them. Now they've put aside their differences and hold their castles against you, not against each other. And they've already tried to kill you once."

"Any fool can carry a knife!" FitzOsbern objected.

"Yes, and that knife will still be sharp, fool or no fool. Let us bring them to heel, yes, but not by charging in there blindly like a boar onto a hunting spear."

William saw FitzOsbern make to retort, before thinking better of it and resuming his pacing.

"So what do you suggest, my lord of Talou?" William asked his uncle, whilst taking a goblet of wine from the table in front of him in the hope that it would help him to think more clearly.

"Go to King Henry of France. He will see the sense in helping to put down a rebellion on his Northern border. I will send a good man to parlay with the rebels."

"Parlay?" FitzOsbern shouted in disgust.

"Parlay," Talou flatly replied. "For whilst they are talking, they are not fighting. It will take us time to assemble an army large enough to defeat them and for the King's men to join us. Weeks, maybe months even. Do you expect Nigel and Ranulf to sit around on their backsides and patiently wait? I say we parlay."

"William, any time we give them will be time for them to rally more men to their banners! Crush them now!" FitzOsbern said.

William knew that something had to be done and it had to be done quickly. He was the Duke of Normandy. The duty of ensuring peace within his lands was his and his alone. He had to make a decision and he knew he would only have one chance to make the right one. Move in too slowly and the rebels would have a chance to strike the first blow and fight on the ground of their choosing. Move in too soon and he would risk defeat through lack of sufficient men. Timing was everything.

He took a deep breath, his nostrils filling with the smell of stale wine; the rushes on the floor had not yet been changed from the previous night's drinking.

"We will act now," he said, raising a hand to stop Talou from interrupting. "I won't keep running away. My whole life has been running away and it stops now. My people look to me to make safe these lands and I don't intend to let them down. So help me God."

"But William, there is no way we can raise a large enough force to stop them. We can't even trust half your vassals until we know how deep the plot runs. And we've precious few funds to hire mercenaries," Talou said. "You must rely on your own milites alone."

"My men are all fine knights. And as to the rebels' followers, when they see their rightful duke of the battlefield, they will rally to me."

"And what of Guy of Burgundy? Will you be calling on him to fight?"

"You mean do I trust him?" William replied.

"Quite. He may be your cousin, but don't be fooled. He's ambitious and popular in parts of your lands. If his father the count of Burgundy decided to support him..."

"He wouldn't dare!" said FitzOsbern.

"He might," said Talou "We've all heard Guy's grumbling."

"Oh I've heard the grumbling well!" William said through gritted teeth. "He thinks that just because I'm the son of a tanner's daughter I'm unfit to be duke. He thinks that his noble birth should give him the right to be duke in my stead, but just watch him try! I'd tan *his* hide well and truly!" William shouted, banging his fist against the table.

"But will you have him fight for you?" Talou repeated, "for you have need of his men."

"I gave him Brionne, didn't I? And Vernon! Those are two of the most solid castles in the land. That was the price of his fealty. Even he wouldn't be so stupid as to bite the hand that feeds him."

"He saw them as his by right, though, just as he does your whole dukedom."

"I've kept his ambition on a leash so far, haven't I?"

"But this rebellion might unleash it."

"I will keep him close by me. If there's the slightest sign of treachery from him I'll kill him myself."

"You would do well to call on the King of France, nephew. If Guy did turn on you, you would certainly be outnumbered. Call on the King, nephew."

"My decision is made, my lord of Talou," William said markedly. He resented how his uncle could still patronise him as if he were talking to a young child. "We will strike them now!" William roared "And Nigel, and Ranulf, and any other who dares side with them will soon know who the rightful duke of Normandy is!"

He saw his uncle's face take the resigned expression of one who knows further argument is futile.

A smiling FitzOsbern stepped forward, his eyes alight with relish at the thought of a good battle.

"I shall send word for the barons to muster their men, my lord," he said.

Talou reluctantly joined them in planning the coming campaign. William could tell that he was still uneasy about going to war without the King of France, but the decision was made.

William would not be bullied by his barons any longer and his retribution would be swift. As they stood in their council of war, studying the best approaches to their enemies' forts, the door to the hall suddenly burst open. In strode Eudo, Hubert's eldest son. He bowed to William; as he straightened up, the look of apprehension he bore was obvious.

"Well? What news from the Bessin?" William asked.

Eudo hesitated to speak.

"I take it you bring word from your father," William said.

Eudo nodded, clearly dreading having to deliver whatever tidings he bore.

"Speak man!" William shouted at him impatiently.

"My lord Duke, Guy of Burgundy has raised the ducal standard above the ramparts of Brionne. He has joined the rebellion and claims to be the true duke of Normandy."

"What?" William spat across. Eudo flinched, as if expecting William to strike him. The two men were of a similar age, but the duke's strong military frame was already impressive.

William turned and walked over to the window. He needed time to take in the full implications of the dire news. As he looked out over the eastern slope which lead down from the keep to the bailey in which the labourers lived, his eyes were drawn to ravens perched on the jagged rocks. Their cries filled the silence within the hall. William thought back to the carefree days when his father was still around. He would have been down playing on those rocks with FitzOsbern; two children playing at mock battles. How times had changed. The reality of it was quite different. This time, the very survival of the duchy was in

William's hands, and it seemed he had lost the battle before it had even begun. The folly of youth, William cursed himself.

He felt someone approach and the steady voice of his uncle Talou spoke the only words that could be expected.

"You now have no choice; you must go to the King, or else lose all you have."

William entered the small room nervously. It was dark already, with only a modest fire in the hearth offering warmth. He gently closed the door behind himself. His mother, the lady Herleva, sat in a high backed chair with a sheepskin thrown over her knees for added protection against the night's chill. It was summer already, but she felt the cold, as older women often do. She turned to look at William, her face full of affection.

He felt shame.

"Ah, my William," she said. "My dear sweet boy. Come closer, that this ancient woman might see you."

He duly obliged and went to kiss his mother on both cheeks. He felt her dark eyes roving across his face, taking in his every flaw.

"I have failed, mother," he said with a sigh. The pang of guilt seemed as a lance plunging deep into his heart. "Father entrusted his land of Normandy to me and I have not protected it as I should have. Rebels are beating down the gates and I must beg France for protection."

Herleva smiled tenderly at him, her kind eyes unaffected by the passing years which each left another line on her face. She reached out for his hand. He frowned at how rough her hands still were all this time since she had left her father's tannery to join his father the duke and later her husband Herluin.

"No, my dear son; you have not failed Normandy. Normandy has failed you. Your dukedom should have been given to you intact, yet this land is ablaze with the folly of lesser men. Your time has now come. King Henry of France may have given you your spurs, but Normandy can only be ruled by Norman steel. Your father knew it only too well. And so it is with Norman steel that you must take back your dukedom from these rebels. With Norman steel shall you take your rightful place."

She reached behind her chair and produced a long object carefully wrapped up in a plain piece of dark green cloth.

Even before she had unwrapped it, he knew what it was, though he could not quite bring himself to believe it.

"I thought it had been lost in Nicea."

She shook her head.

"It came back to me, swathed in your father's travelling cloak."

"Why did you not tell me?" He had longed through those fear filled nights and hollow days for his father's presence, and there it was; Duke Robert's sword.

"We thought it best."

"We?"

"Steward Osbern and I," she said, with some surprise at his needing to ask. "He loved you deeply, you know, as did your father. Men never say such things, and rightly so. They must appear strong. Their armour cannot have weak links. Yet they cared greatly for you. We thought you had burden enough to carry, without adding the weight of your father's sword to the load. You were not ready."

101

"I was not worthy," William said, looking at his feet.

"It was not your time to prove yourself. Your time has come now and you will rise up to meet the challenge, as did your forebears."

She held out the sword. As he pulled the hilt, the steel blade glinted in the fire light. In the groove, those two words spoke out between the two crosses.

"Diex aie," he read aloud.

"God helps," his mother said. "Remember that. You are the rightful duke of Normandy and therefore have God on your side. He will not abandon you if you stand up for your rights. So go forth and meet with the King. But know that it is your sword which will rule, not his."

William looked up at the King of France. Henry was a man of about forty. His face was that of a calm and welcoming host, but his real nature was belied by the quick and calculating dark eyes which William felt digging away at his very soul, trying to uncover what secrets lay therein.

William met the gaze defiantly.

"So you have got yourself in trouble with your barons and you want me to sort it out for you," Henry coolly summarised the discussion so far in a typically perfunctory way.

"No more trouble than you had yourself when my father had to come to your aid," William said. The corner of Henry's lip curled up at the remark.

"True, your father the duke helped me out. But as I recall, he was one of many to come with men. You are asking me, in effect, to do your job for you."

"If I must fight them alone, I will, my lord King."

"And win?"

"I certainly don't intend to fight and lose."

"But you do not have enough men to win alone, or else you would not be here."

The words lingered in the air. William watched Henry get up and go over to a table in the corner of the tent. He poured out two goblets of wine; the servants had been dismissed to give the two lords complete privacy.

"The first role of a French duke is to ensure peace throughout his lands," the King said.

"As is the role of a *Norman* duke," William answered.

"Remember just whom your king is, Duke William! You talk as if you are the next Rollo, leading a brave army of northern warriors, and yet here you are come to beg me for help!"

"I have no intention of begging."

"Well you should! Because without my support, yours will be just another name added to a long list of counts and dukes whose barons have grown weary and over-thrown them. If you are lucky, you might just make it out of Normandy alive, but where would you go? Anjou hates you. Brittany resents you. Flanders would happily extend its land into the rich fields of Normandy. The only safe way out would be for you to join the King of England. You sheltered Edward during his exile, yes, but I can hardly see him giving you men to fight your way back to Normandy; especially when his own position is so precarious. No king would be so foolish as to risk his own throne for a duke who has already been supplanted."

103

William marked the words carefully. Henry's message was clear; lose this fight and I'll let somebody else take your place.

"So your choice is simple, William; exile in England or death in Normandy. That is what you face without my support. You might wish to reconsider your previous stance on begging."

"It will have to be death in Normandy, then, if you are refusing to help me. But if the promise you made my father Duke Robert to uphold my birth right isn't enough, if the sin of perjury doesn't scare you, then perhaps a more worldly consideration will persuade you."

"Perjury?" the king balked. "Perjury!"

"Just so, my lord King."

William watched the King regain his calm. His scornful eyes met William's again.

"And what is this worldly consideration, then?"

"Of your own lands' security. Think about it, my lord King; as you said, when my people first came to these shores, they came as raiders. Warlords rampaged throughout northern France and threatened Paris itself. The only thing which halted their advance was the firm leadership of my forefather Rollo. His discipline brought peace to your realm. And now you would throw all of that away by letting the rightful Duke of Normandy be overthrown by a hot-headed fool? Guy will not command the loyalty of Normandy. All you will get is a divided land of lawless warriors eager to increase their wealth. Rest assured, my lord king; they will be heading here first."

"I know how to defend my borders; rest assured of that."

"For a time, perhaps. But others will be sure to make the most of my downfall. The Duke of Anjou hates me; you said so

104

yourself. When Geoffrey sees the chance, he will naturally do all he can to bring Normandy within his power. And if he does manage to combine the strength of Anjou with that of Normandy, he will be more powerful even than you. Besides which, I hear that he has been in talks with the Holy Roman Emperor."

"Geoffrey of Anjou, unlike yourself, is already wise in the ways of the world. He knows that a crown is to be respected."

William kept his cool despite the barb.

"I do respect your crown, my lord King. That is why I want you to keep it on your head. All I ask is that you help me to keep the coronet which rightly sits on my own head. In so doing, you will strengthen your own rule."

"My crown's security owes nothing to you."

"For now, my lord. But the winds of change rarely give much notice, as I have found at my own expense. Assist me in weathering this storm and I will remember it. Leave my ship to sink and I'll not forget it."

William saw the King's eyebrow rise.

"You are brave, young William, but you have much to learn in the craft of diplomacy. Idle threats seldom go down well. If you must threaten someone, be sure to do it from a position of strength."

William pursed his lips. After years of guardians and older barons trying to moralise, he had grown sick and tired of it. Talking to the King was like listening to his uncle Talou's patronising manner. He forced himself to bow insincere thanks for the lesson.

"I apologise, my lord King, if I have caused offence."

Henry gently nodded acknowledgement for the concession.

"So will your Majesty help me?"

"I will think on it further. Good day to you."

William bowed himself out of the tent. An anxious FitzOsbern was waiting for him.

"Well? What did he say? Will he be sending his troops?"

"I think," William answered, "we had best look to our own swords."

CHAPTER 11

A FIELD SOUTH OF CAEN, LOWER NORMANDY. AUGUST, 1047 A.D.

William leaned forward over the pommel of his saddle to pat his steed's neck firmly. It had been a hard ride from Falaise. He had sent Talou ahead to organise the muster of the loyal barons and their men. FitzOsbern came galloping up the column; William had entrusted his childhood friend with the ducal banner, a position of some honour. As he spurred his horse to catch up, William saw the beaming smile on his face. At least someone was getting some enjoyment from the present situation.

"What a sight!" FitzOsbern shouted to William. "Makes your blood run warm, doesn't it?"

"It certainly does!" William answered. "I only hope that more are on their way. We'd be hard pressed to beat Guy, Nigel and Ranulf with just this few. Come; let's go find out who else is awaited."

He trotted over to the nearest sentry.

"You there! Where is the count of Talou?"

"Over there, my lord Duke," the man answered, pointing towards a large oak tree in the middle of the field, where William could just make out a group of men standing around a table.

William turned to FitzOsbern.

"Have the men find food. Then join me."

William spurred his horse down the slope and past the rows of tents. Men bowed to him as they recognised him riding past. He dismounted further down the slope and entrusted his horse to a good man to look after.

As he made his way through the camp, he hid the doubt which gnawed away at him. This 'blood-warming sight', as FitzOsbern put it, could hardly call itself an army. William had scarcely managed to get any hired swords; men who sought profit through battle were not exactly keen to join a forlorn cause.

Henry had sent no word of his own army. William remembered the King's words. His father had had to come to Henry's aid, because too few men had rallied around him to save his crown. Even fewer men would be willing to risk their lives to help the duke of a land which they had long been wary of.

The fact of the matter was that the King wasn't coming. Henry was merely going through the motions of an overlord who wanted to appear to be doing his duty of protecting his vassal. William knew that he would not actually go so far as to risk his own position. He would simply accept as his vassal whichever lord survived the coming battle. William, Guy, Talou; it all mattered little to the King of France. A Norman duke was a Norman duke; just as long as he made obeisance and kept within his own borders, the King would let him rule his lands as he saw fit.

As he approached the group, William overheard his usually stoic uncle Talou swearing at the top of his voice.

"How could this happen? I thought we'd got between them."

"It seems Guy slipped his troops through the net during the night. We have too few men to cover the whole of the area," another answered. "By the time our scouts spotted him, it was too late for us to ride out and intercept him."

"If only William hadn't been so hot-headed with the King we might actually have stood a chance of beating them. For all his bravery, his pride may be our downfall."

"Our pride is what makes us Normans, my lord of Talou."

William's firm voice startled the men who hadn't seen him coming. "I would sooner lose my life than forsake my pride, for without it I would not be a worthy duke of Normandy. Whichever way the coming battle goes, we shall show the King of France what a true Norman is made of."

"Forgive me, my lord Duke," said Talou, "but what does pride matter when we have so few troops? This man has just told me that Guy of Burgundy has linked up with Nigel and Ranulf's forces. I had hoped to keep the two apart, but we simply do not have enough men."

"If we had wanted to keep them apart and fight them piecemeal, then we should have attacked them immediately, not wasted time dithering and going to the King of France! If Henry really felt duty bound to come, he would have come without expecting the duke of Normandy to beg. From now on Normandy looks to Normandy."

Talou frowned at that remark.

"Now, what is our strength? Who else is coming?" William said.

"My lord, no one else is coming. You have what you can see around you; six-score knights and about three hundred men of the commons. That is all."

William kept his expression calm. He would be sorely pushed to defeat Guy's men with only one hundred and twenty knights and three hundred peasants on foot .

"Well what of Ralph Tesson? I don't see him here."

"Hubert has sent word that Ralph has joined the rebels."

"You're not seriously trying to tell me that all my barons have turned against me?"

"No, my lord, not all. Some knights from Caen are here. The Episcopal towns Evreux and Lisieux have also rallied to your banner."

"At least the bishops know whose side God is on, then," William grunted.

"Many of the barons are too scared to pick a side. They have sent excuses instead of troops. Some say they are too old to fight, others that they don't have enough men to spare from their own defences. They may be loyal to you, but the duke's seat is far away in Rouen. Ranulf and Nigel are much closer and to incur their wrath by siding with you would mean a much greater punishment."

"What of Montgomery?"

"The rebels are close to his own lands and he pleads to be allowed to stay there to protect his people."

"So what strength do the rebels have?"

"Ten-score horse, my lord," Talou replied flatly, "and twice our foot."

"Ten-score?" William replied incredulously.

"They heard of your meeting with King Henry. They knew they wouldn't be able to beat us if we joined forces with the King, but they can't go back now. So they're throwing everything they have into this fight. Everything. They've practically emptied their castles of the garrisons in order to have more men to fight. They've drawn support from Anjou and Le Mans in exchange for the promise of territorial concessions. Every single knight, squire and man at arms they could bring will be on the field."

A wry smile spread across William's face. He saw that his uncle Talou was puzzled by his reaction.

"So if we beat them here, then we will finish the lot of them."

"But my lord, you are missing my point; we cannot defeat them. There are just too many of them."

"Never mind the odds; this will see an end to it, one way or the other. I would stand our six-score brave and loyal knights against any thousands of deceitful and heinous traitors."

"Surely we would do better to fall back to Falaise and defend ourselves from there. We could send out envoys and try to negotiate or buy more time to win over the King of France. They say King Henry *is* coming."

"Perhaps he is," William said, "but only to accept homage from the victor. No. I have waited long enough. Now it's time to pick a fight. They may be many, and we may be few, but more than that is needed to win a battle. We all share a common and noble cause, which God wills us to defend. They are each out for their own personal gains. We are all valiant Norman knights. They are counting on the support of strangers from Anjou and Le Mans, who will not risk much for victory. I will not abandon one more inch of Norman earth to these rebels. The time has come to play the final game."

Talou pursed his lips, but finally nodded.

"Now," William said, "where have the rebels set up camp?"

"South of Caen, my lord Duke, about five leagues west of here."

111

"Excellent. If we can entice them to fight us here, they will not be able to run far. They'll have Caen and the sea to their left, the Orne to their backs and I dare say they'll not risk going too far south, for it would take them too close to Falaise. They'll want to fight us soon, too, while they still have such good odds. They know that their allies from Anjou and Le Mans won't want to stay in Normandy long; especially if they think the King is on his way. I just need to get them to attack before they realise that the King is not actually bringing an army."

"Favourable ground; that's what will bring them on," said Talou, now more enthusiastic, as any true Norman is for a fight. "We can head over to a place I know of near here; the Vale of Dunes, the locals call it. A wide open field, good for cavalry, and far enough away from Caen that Guy and his men won't feel as if they are exposing their backs. That will bring them onto our swords."

"That and an insult to Guy's pride; he's a rash fool. I know just the person to goad Guy," William said. "Ah! And here he comes now!"

Talou turned to see FitzOsbern striding towards them.

"So," said FitzOsbern, "what have I missed?"

William took in his friend's confident, boisterous manner and smiled at Talou.

"FitzOsbern, my dear friend, it just so happens I have a small task for you."

The young man looked quizzically around the table.

CHAPTER 12

FitzOsbern had done his job brilliantly. William hadn't even needed to ask him what had happened at the rebel camp; his friend's gleeful face said it all. He could just picture a fuming Guy of Burgundy, swearing at this upstart cousin who had dared, undaunted, ride up to his very tent and before all his supporters toss at his feet a dead hare and a flask of wine. William had bidden FitzOsbern proclaim to Guy that William, being his loving cousin and generous liege-lord, did not want him to fight on an empty belly and that this *feast* was all Guy's due share of Normandy. To tell him that by the morrow's last light, he would be kneeling at William's feet; whether it would be to renew his homage or as a captive bound in chains was his choice alone.

Guy was sure to have appreciated that. His pride spurned and the fire lit in his belly, he was bound to rush headstrong into battle and heedless of the risks; just what William wanted. To have all his foes charge recklessly onto one field would be the only way of putting a definitive end to the struggle. Could a war be fought and won in one day? William certainly hoped so. To vanquish all or to lose everything; that was all he asked. An end to the prolonged quarrelling, to the bittersweet taste of a dukedom without power; that was all he had craved these last years. True, Normans had ever lived by the sword. And yes, his guardians had managed to limit the mayhem that could easily have ensued, though several of them had paid for it with their lives. But between his over-bearing guardians and his recalcitrant barons, he knew the great power of Norman dukes,

113

ever needed to keep a warrior race in check, risked being lost forever through successive weakening.

But how to bring about this victory? He trusted those lords who had rallied around him, but they were few. He had but a hundred and twenty knights, and three hundred men of the commons, who were merely peasants armed with little more than clubs and the occasional spear. He could count on them to keep their heads down, and little more. His milites were his one chance of victory. They were his household knights, his oathmen. They were all sworn to fight and die for him. Today, he would repay that trust by taking them to the jaws of Hell. Let Talou command the peasants. William would lead his milites across that field to take on the foe.

Guy had managed to assemble near enough a thousand men, of which almost two hundred would be knights. Those were poor odds by any reckoning. Still, William had some hope. He had chosen his spot carefully. At this, the great cross roads by the ford of Berengier, he could deny his enemies the opportunity to get around behind him. On his right flank was an area of marshes which only a fool would even consider trying to cross, which meant that Guy's numbers would count for little on that side. His left flank was more exposed, so he would put his sterner fighters there.

William signalled to his men that they should stay where they were, before pressing his spurs to his horse's flanks and riding out into the field.

William could see why they called it the Vale of Dunes; the place was all hills covered in wheat. In the sun, the pale crops made the slopes look like the sand dunes merchants and travellers spoke of in far away hot lands. In front of his lines was a gentle sloping hill; the fields of wheat had been abandoned by the local farmers on seeing soldiers drawing near. By this day of early August, the wheat had already been harvested towards the lower part of the hill and in the valley, but further up they had not yet been able to bring in the crops. William had not wanted to risk his horses stumbling in hidden holes and his men to struggle to run through the tall stems, which is why he had stayed in the valley. But as the slope was so mild, it would hardly make much difference. The valley was a rider's dream; there were no hedges to go round, no large rocks to break a horse's stride, no woods in which treacherous men could hide. All men's deeds this day would be done in the open, in full view of all others and of God himself. As he bowed his head, he appealed once more to the Lord for his protection. God made mortal men dukes and only He could judge the worthiness of their cause.

He looked back at his army and sighed. This was little more than a glorified hunting party, and Guy would use his far greater force to turn them into the quarry. What more could he do to defeat the rebels, other than pray? Their leaders; that was the key. Capture or kill those disloyal barons who had brought about this uprising and their fickle followers would soon scatter. Guy of Burgundy, Nigel of Cotentin and Ranulf of Bessin, those treasonous would-be murderers with their thug, Hamon the Long-toothed; all would pay. William swore in the middle of that field, before God Almighty, that these traitors would pay the ultimate price.

He was brought out of his deep thought by the urgent sound of a horse galloping towards him at full speed. As the rider drew away from the ducal lines and hastened nearer, he realised that it was his uncle Talou who was waving frantically to attract his attention. God help us, William thought, what more dreadful news could possibly be flying his way? He hurried to meet his uncle.

"William!" his uncle cried, struggling to catch his breath.

"What is it? What news? Do you bring word of the rebel army?"

The older man shook his head, still panting from the ride.

"Well what then?" William pressed him.

"My lord… the King is here!"

William's jaw dropped. For a moment he just sat there on his horse, lost for words.

"Henry? Here?" He saw his uncle nod fervently. "He surely means to wait nearer, so that he can sooner accept homage from whoever wins the field."

"Not with a thousand men on foot and twelve-score knights, he doesn't."

"One thousand?" William repeated incredulously. "Where are they?"

"Just coming up from the south, my lord. They made camp in a ruined Roman village not two leagues from here after marching through much of the night. Their horses were blown and their men too tired to reach us before now."

William offered up a prayer of thanks, for the coming of these thousand men was surely as much the work of God as that of King Henry of France. Warmth flooded back into his heart as he contemplated the full scale of what this meant. Guy and his pack would be eagerly crowding the field, expecting to look down from the hill onto a ragged bunch of men huddled around their master. Instead, they would find themselves confronted not only by the ducal household, but by the full force of the French royal army. The King's power may have diminished somewhat since the fall of Charlemagne's empire, but it was still one of the most powerful armies in Western Europe.

William rode with his uncle back to the Norman lines. As he did so, the king's herald arrived with a small vanguard of knights, all finely armed and kitted out, their swords and chainmail glimmering in the early morning sun. Talou introduced William to the herald.

"Fairly met, Duke William of Normandy. Our lord King bids me send you his most heartfelt wishes. He embraces you as a father does his loving son and would have me proclaim to all present that the King of France remembers his loyal vassals and is come to enforce his appointment of you as his Duke of the Normans."

"Please give your King my thanks, good herald. But for your proclamation, no words are needed. The King's presence here will speak louder than any."

The herald nodded, reluctantly taking the hint. William had no desire for the King of France to claim the victory as his own before the battle was even under way. If the victory was seen as French rather than Norman, then the relative independence which the descendants of Rollo had enjoyed would risk being utterly shattered. He may have learned that he now had a solid means of stopping Guy from gaining power in Normandy, but that wasn't just so that he could hand it over to Henry of France. There was only one answer to this particular problem; he would have to be sure to take the rebel leaders himself, before the King's men had the chance.

"The King would know where he can bring up his men," the herald prompted William.

"Bid your King come up on the south. If he is ready to hold the left flank, then I shall duly hold the right."

If Henry lost his nerve and fled, William would still have the marshes protecting one of his flanks, rather than standing alone and exposed.

As the royal troops duly took up their position, Henry himself rode up to William, who dutifully inclined his head. He had to at least be civil to one who had brought so many men.

"Greetings, my lord King! I thank you for joining me on this good Norman field!"

"Good morning, Duke William. I am come to enforce the laws of France; in defying my vassal, these rebels have also defied their sovereign king. Let us redress this injustice together."

"Indeed, my lord, I…"

Their conversation was cut short by the arrival at the top of the hill of a group of horsemen. William could sense the men around him brace themselves to meet the full force of the rebellion. The tension caused by these knights was palpable, even the horses seemed to feel it. As he looked across the field at the rebels, he realised that they had already finished filing into position. This was no army, merely a group of some fifty riders and their servants.

"Who are these men?" Henry asked him.

As he strained to make out faces in the far off crowd, William caught sight of a stocky bearded knight who sat under a pennant bearing the shape of a wild boar. How often he had thought with amusement how ironic that symbol was, for the man in question bore little resemblance to the creature in spirit, even if he did have the heavy build of the beast. Where a boar charges in a determined rage, this man was of such an over-cautious nature, so racked with doubt, that his fellows always wondered if he would ever charge at all. And now he sat in the enemy vanguard opposite William. How fate played with men.

"That is Ralph Tesson, my lord. I know him well, for he used to ride with my father duke Robert," he said, turning to the king who acknowledged the news with a grunt.

"So whose side is he on?"

"I believe," William began to say, studying the man who now appeared to be having a heated discussion with his advisers, "that he is on our side."

As Henry gave William a quizzical sideways glance, Ralph suddenly shot out from his ranks and charged down the slope, straight towards the two men. Bellowing a war cry, he threw his spear down on the ground and lifted a leather-gloved fist in the air. As he darted towards the combined army, Henry made his horse take a few smart steps to the side, leaving William alone. The latter held up his hand to forbid any of his men from coming between him and his assailant. Instead, he sat calmly in his saddle and waited for the knight to come nearer in his most uncharacteristic and alarming frenzied charge. At the very last moment, William realised the man was not going to draw his sword, so he dropped his own lance and let the fist come down to strike him jovially on the shoulder. His chainmail took the impact and Ralph simply stopped his horse and smiled at his

119

duke. The men around them sat in bewilderment. William coolly returned the smile, a wave of relief washing over him.

"My lord Tesson, what is this?"

"My lord Duke, I have been true to my word; I promised my liege-lord Ranulf that I would be the first to strike you and I have done just that."

"You do not wish to fight for him then?" William asked amused.

Ralph blushed under his mail hood.

"My lord, I had to show my fealty to him for he had threatened my family. But I could never have brought upon myself the perjury of taking up arms against my duke," he said defensively.

Where are the traitors now?" William asked; he saw the relief in Ralph's eyes at not having been counted among the traitors, though William had yet to make up his mind as to the man's fate, in truth.

"Coming up, my lord Duke; they must be, for they were not far behind me."

It would have made sense for Guy to choose Tesson to lead his vanguard, as he would want to keep a close eye on deceitful Ranulf and Nigel, and keep a close rein on hot tempered Hamon Long-teeth; but he should have better calculated Ralph's lack of nerve. It was a liability that had cost him before the battle had even begun. Now he had lost an ally, along with some fifty knights.

"Tell me," William began.

"Yes, my lord?" Ralph said, eager to find a way to regain his duke's favour.

"Do Guy and Ranulf suspect you may betray them?"

"No, my lord! They last heard me speaking with all intent on advancing their cause!" He bit his lip, quickly realising how foolishly enthusiastic such a statement was. William let it pass.

"Very well. If you love me as a true vavasour loves his overlord, you will do exactly as I say. Let Guy think you still stand with him. Hold your forces off on the side of the hill. He will expect it, as you are admired for your caution." Ralph blushed at that, realising the insincere flattery was really poorly disguised criticism. "He will think you are acting as his reserves, when in fact you will be acting as mine."

The King of France, who had been following the conversation closely, lifted an eyebrow to that.

"You are fortunate indeed to have so forgiving a duke; it is well within his right to have you put to death for your treason."

"My sovereign King, I was ever faithful in my heart."

Henry's only reaction to that was a sly glance between the two men.

"I do forgive you, Tesson, as God is my witness. Now do your duty and show me the same loyalty as you showed my father," William said.

"I will, my lord. My thanks to you, good Duke."

Tesson nodded to the two lords and rode off to take his place up the side of the hill.

"You show him too much leniency, lord William." said the King. "How can you be sure that he will remain loyal?"

"He knows we will win. Why side with a man who has nothing to offer save a share of his shame and a place next to him in his gaol cell?"

"We haven't won yet and you've now put him on our flank."

121

"I have put him on your flank, my good King," William said with the hint of a smile. "To strike a duke is one thing, but Ralph would never dare ride against God's anointed King of France."

Henry glared at William, but kept his temper.

"Then I hope that the duke whom God's anointed King chose will be equally blessed."

"God protect you also, my lord King."

Henry nodded to William and set off to join his knights on the left flank. As he did so, he passed to lord of Talou.

"Have a care, my lord; your duke is keen to make a great name for himself and it may yet be his downfall," Henry said. The two men had known each other some time and a mutual respect had grown between them.

"I shall do my best, my King." Talou said thoughtfully. "He may seem impetuous, but in him flows the blood of Rollo. We expect much of him, though he is still young."

William looked out across the field that would soon be filled with the sights and sounds of war; horses charging, spears and arrows flying through the air, blood flowing, men screaming and enemies ever coming to fill the gaps left by their fallen comrades. He had never been in a battle before, let alone commanded an army in one.

To his right was the marsh. To his left stood King Henry with his men. Beyond him, on the side of the hill, Ralph Tesson waited with his group of horsemen. William's own horse scraped one of its hooves through the soil of the freshly harvested wheat. William stroked its neck. Suddenly he saw its ears prick as it listened intently. He gazed at the top of the hill where there was now movement in the next field. Through the swaying heads of wheat which had yet to be gathered there, men came over the crest. Just a dozen at first, then another score, until a full thousand troops, some two hundred of them mounted, covered the crest of the hill and it seemed as if every head of wheat in the field had been turned into an armed man to confront William.

He carefully scoured the hill in search of the different pennants. In the centre was Guy of Burgundy's banner. To Guy's left, nearest the marshes, William saw Ranulf of the Bessin's arms.

Further up the hill, opposite the King, he could just make out Nigel of the Contentin's pennant next to that of Hamon Long-Teeth.

If the top of the slope appeared covered with men to subdue William's followers, it was nothing next to the shock that the newly arrived rebels must have felt. To see the golden lilies of the French King's blue banner flying next to the Norman duke's pennant with its two lions would have been devastating to Guy and his fellow conspirators. All the same, William was aware that many of his men were daunted by the sight of so many mail-clad warriors come to cut them down, like a second harvest of the field. He turned to steady his troops.

"You see, my lords and good and faithful men, these wretches, who think to intimidate you into cowardly submission with the mere show of their spears! For their own vile reasons, they skulked through the night and meant to kill me, their rightful duke, appointed by God to deliver justice in this land of Normandy. Well let us deliver that justice now! You may see them and feel fear, but look at you yourselves; they came here thinking to fight a mere five hundred of you, yet now find you to be nigh on two thousand! Woe unto them who thought to overthrow God's law and the natural order of this land! We shall be the Lord's retribution, as He guides my sword."

"William, look!" FitzOsbern hissed quietly, nodding towards the enemy. William turned to see a small group of riders coming to parley, as custom dictated.

"What terms should we offer?" Talou asked.

"The same terms they offered me that night at Valognes," William said curtly. He turned back to his men. "You see? They are already coming to weasel their way out of this desperate situation they have got themselves into. Will you let them simply walk away, when they would have shown you little mercy and put your families to the sword? Because I won't! So will you follow me now to hand out God's punishment? Will you fight?"

"Yes!" came the men's thunderous roar, filling his heart with pride.

"God helps!" he shouted the Norman war cry!

"God helps!" echoed across the field, as the men raised their spears in the air. William turned his steed to face the foe and swung his own spear round to order the charge. The horns sounded and the duke's whole body of cavalry surged forwards.

At that moment, the emissaries riding out to negotiate stopped in alarm. Far from a civilised conversation, they found themselves facing some six-score furious knights charging towards them, followed like a tidal wave by many hundreds of foot soldiers. This was not how things were done. William saw them hastily bring their horses about and rush back to the safety of their own lines.

CHAPTER 13

On the other side of the field, King Henry swore. What did the foolish youth think he was doing? He had not even met the envoys to try to find a compromise and had instead bolted towards the enemy lines, without so much as softening them up a bit with his archers or bothering to consult his King. True, the leaders of the rebellion must know what fate awaited them if they meekly gave themselves in, but the presence of a royal army was a potent argument in finding a solution. Instead, the young duke was impetuously throwing himself into an unsupported cavalry charge. Damn these ambitious youths who had brought about this sorry state of affairs. He would have to talk to Talou when all this was over. If the man's idiot nephew hadn't got himself killed first, that was.

William spurred his horse up the slope, exhilarated at finally having the chance to show them once and for all just whom the duke of Normandy was. After these long years of being nothing more than a puppet for his guardians and barons to play with, he was now unleashing his full fury upon those who had thought to depose him. He roared his defiance at them. Glancing over his shoulder, he saw that his knights had been almost as taken aback as the rebels by the sudden order to charge and were only just managing to keep pace with him. FitzOsbern was just behind him on his left, with Talou to his right. William turned back to focus on Ranulf's men; they had just started down the slope to counter his attack, using the hill to quickly pick up speed. He caught sight of a confident rider who snarled in his direction. On this summer morning, the rebels faced a further difficulty; they face full east, so they had the sun in their eyes as they rode down the gentle slope towards William's men. William smiled. As the knight rode out, spurring his horse towards him, he didn't even see the spear fly from William's hand. It caught him hard in the shoulder. The strength of the impact threw the man clean out of his stirrups and tumbling to the ground a few paces in front. William drew his sword and moved on past, leaving FitzOsbern behind him to finish the job with a swift lunge of his own spear.

The man who next headed towards William knew his business. As he drew near, he sharply pulled on the reins, taking his horse just beyond the reach of William's sword and breaking his spear on William's shield. The force of the charge should have embedded the spear's point in the wood, but William had been fortunate that it had instead stuck on the steel boss. All along the line, similar engagements were taking place, and William was soon over-taken by his knights. Knowing his back was covered, he turned back to meet the man again. Both had lost the impetus of their charge, and so they cautiously brought their horses close together each having a care to cover his mount's head with the lower part of his long shield, guarding it from just the sort of attack that William himself had carried out on the first man.

Their bodies now level, they clashed the bosses of their shields together, each using his weight to try to force the other back. The rebel spat, straining against William. As they leaned into each other, William saw the man's features distinctly. Under the rim of his helmet, a long scar ran down across his eye; a token of some previous quarrel, no doubt. He cursed at William, calling him every name under the sun. Sweat ran down his brow. Clad in iron and leather, every man baked in the searing heat of summer.

Suddenly the rebel leaned back in his saddle, hoping William would fall forward and expose his back. It was a classic move which William had trained for and been expecting. He let himself fall forwards, covering himself with his raised shield and putting all his weight behind his sword which he thrust out. The blade scraped along the metal ring which lined the rebel's shield, only to stab thin air. He heard the man chuckle above him, having made his horse side step just in time to avoid William's sword. William gritted his teeth and swept his blade up in a reverse swing. The chuckle became a yelp as steel connected with jaw bone. It was William's turn to grin. As the knight was blinded by pain, he stabbed sharply, sending his sword through the man's good eye and deep into his skull. He pulled back his sword and turned to find his next opponent, vaguely aware of a spray of blood next to him.

All the while, King Henry sat and watched. And Normandy burned.

CHAPTER 14

Normandy burned and King Henry just sat and watched. He watched the folly of youth, which is ever a wondrous spectacle of heroic heedlessness and incalculable lack of calculation. The young duke, for all his love of God, seemed intent on throwing himself into the very jaws of Hell, putting enemies to the sword whilst being blissfully unaware of the perils he himself escaped through luck as much as any actual fighting ability. Granted, Henry had to accept that his initial throw of the spear to despatch the first rebel had been beautifully executed; but the second foe should by rights have pieced him from belly to backbone. Those first actions had just been visible to Henry, for the field was not that wide and his position slightly up the slope gave him a good vantage point, particularly as William had left most of his knights in his wake, so the king had seen it all. But now little could be made out in the press of the battle. The field was shaken by a whirlwind of men and horses, of swords, spears and shields, of bellowed battle cries and the shrill shrieks of the wounded. And all the while, King Henry sat and watched.

He just sat on his horse and watched, for there was little point in rushing in. Were he to launch himself to William's aid, he would soon find Nigel and Guy crashing into his own exposed flank. They did not go to their ally's help, for they feared just the same of the King. And so Henry just sat and watched. As he did, he saw a messenger leave Guy's battle line to ride over to speak to Ralph Tesson further along the hill. Curse the young Norman duke for having left that fool on his flank. William may trust him, yet Henry knew that he would simply wait to see what the

128

outcome would be before intervening on the side of the soon-to-be victor. He turned back to try to make out which way the battle was going and was appalled to see that the ducal forces were beginning to buckle under the strain of the rebels' determined resistance. Appalled, but not entirely surprised. Desperate men with much to lose and little hope of clemency in surrendering will ever fight with more brutality and dogged determination than a cornered boar. And so Henry had to make a choice; risk his own men's lives in saving a petulant youth or simply accept the homage of another petulant youth. It was hardly a difficult decision to make. After all, why should the king of France defend one who barely recognised his authority? Had the duke not dug his own grave, his pride being his spade? In fact, he could even secure Guy's loyalty by taking William's forces in the rear. A simple choice indeed. And so King Henry of France charged.

William was fighting between two rebel knights, struggling to keep the one on his left at bay with his shield, whilst meeting the other with vigorous blows of his sword. FitzOsbern had been pushed back by the increasing press of Ranulf and Guy's men. He had not seen his uncle for some time now. He began to grow anxious. Talou's tedious sermons may tire him, but he had been there to watch over William since before his father, Talou's brother, Duke Robert had left for his ill-fated pilgrimage to the Holy Land. He dearly hoped Talou was alive. The din of battle, the deafening thunder of hooves, of iron hitting iron, of wood splintering rang in William's ears, reverberating through his helmet and he continued to struggle against his two assailants. His left arm was straining under the repeated blows to his shield. He turned to look at the man to his right. He was snarling at

William, perhaps the man hadn't even recognised him. William raised his sword to deflect yet another blow, the force of it jarring his arm. He pushed the man's weapon safely wide and brought his own around in an arc, making use of the momentum to plough the blade towards his neck, but the man managed to dodge the worst of it, tipping his head so that the sword simply glanced off the curve of his helmet. It was then William's turn to move swiftly back, narrowly avoiding his left eye being gouged out by the tip of his foe's sword.

Just then the noise of the battle changed. It was not a great change, merely a different pitch of cries, as if somewhere on the field men who had been hard in the fighting were suddenly startled by a new danger. William and those he fought all instinctively turned their heads, pausing as if by mutual consent to find the cause of this uproar. The beating on his shield ceased for a moment. And that moment was enough. William pounced and the knight to his right could do nothing to stop him, for he had thrown his full weight in his saddle behind his sword and caught the man square in the chest. The sheer brute force of it drove the point clean through the chainmail, prising the links apart. William felt the blade grind against his enemy's ribs and push into a lung. The man gasped, wide-eyed, unable to believe what had just happened. His horse, startled by the awful sound, carried its dying master off into the chaos of the field, leaving William to hurriedly yank his weapon out from the man's chest. The knight to his left, who had been trying to break his shield apart before the lull, saw the fate of his comrade and renewed his attack with twice the vigour; so much so that William's shield was pushed hard against his helmet and it was all he could do to stay in his saddle. The hammering stopped for a moment. He knew it was now or never. He brought his sword round swiftly from behind his shield and, as it neared the man, lowered his shield to take aim. But the man managed to parry the blow, knocking his weapon wide and exposing William to the killing blow. But the blow never came. For the man on his left was now none other than FitzOsbern.

"I hope you don't mind me barging in like this, William, but I couldn't let you have all the fun." He said.

"All the fun? I was beginning to think that you'd quit the field altogether," William chided him. He glanced down and saw his former opponent lying on the ground with a spear embedded where an eye used to be. His horse must have freed itself of the rider's weight. "Speaking of hiding away, where's Talou?"

"Not seen him," FitzOsbern answered, aware of the concern William had tried to hide in his voice. William looked across to see what had caused the alarm on his left flank. It was growing nearer.

"What's going on over there?" he asked FitzOsbern.

"The King's finally decided to shift his royal arse and do his share of the fighting."

William saw that his friend was right. The King, whose contingent was larger than any other on the field, had sent a detachment of knights crashing into Ranulf's flank. The rebels on that side of the field thus found themselves confronted by men both to their front and their right. It was carnage and chaos. Men and horses shied away from the dreadful killing ground, all training melting away in the panic. Confusion reigned as those in the second ranks found their paths blocked by the fleeing men seeking to get clear of the charge on their flank. William seized the initiative; he'd not forgotten his vow to deal with the rebel leaders personally.

"Come," he told FitzOsbern. "With me, you brave and noble Normans!" he bellowed, spurring his horse into the disordered enemy ranks, hacking about him with God's own fury.

"Guy," he roared. "Where are you, you traitorous dog? Why do you hide behind braver men than yourself? Are you so scared to face the results of your own evil act? Come and fight me!"

He knocked a shield aside with a powerful sweep of his sword against its edge, bringing back his hilt to smash into the knight's jaw, before he had time to recover. William smiled grimly as a satisfying crunch told him of broken teeth.

"Guy," he shouted again. "You coward!"

He slashed at another rider, who swerved his steed out of William's path, desperate to stay well away from the young man's furious onslaught. William was about to go after him, but through the gap left by the fleeing rebel, he saw his quarry.

CHAPTER 15

King Henry smiled. The power of the French crown had much diminished since the days of Charlemagne. The reach of the King's arm curtailed so much that many of his vassal dukes paid him homage merely as lip service, effectively treating him as nought more than another lord. And understandably so, Henry thought ruefully, as the lands over which he could exercise his power were now reduced to little more than a duchy around Paris. But this day, all that was changing. This was the day that the King of France had set out to impose his will and the will of God over the lands of the lords of Northern France. Today the crown of France was brought out of the dusty chest and polished anew. For the King had made his choice. He would save the callous youth and in so doing reaffirm the once ubiquitous power of the sovereign of France. And so he had sent three conrois of knights to smash into Ranulf's flank, causing much alarm in that quarter. The nearest rebels could not move out of the way, for their own allies were blocking their escape. The King's men were free to seize the advantage, hurling their spears into the chaos and slaying many a foe. The dead could not fall to the ground for the shear press of horses and men. Any poor soul who stood on foot among the horses was in great danger of being crushed between the beasts. The rebels further down the slope could not have moved away to give their comrades room, even if they had been aware of what was going on, for the marshy ground William had carefully chosen to have on his right flank made any movement on horse in that area impossible.

Seeing the impact his knights were having against Ranulf and Guy's men, Henry left the young duke to seize the initiative – Heaven knows he had needed the help! – and turned to lead the greater part of his troops against the rebels of the Cotentin and Guy of Burgundy's men. As King, he naturally rode with a bodyguard of France's best knights in the second line. He would not emulate William's rashness in charging in first. That was not the role of a true leader. As he ordered the attack, his heart warmed to hear the French war cry. "Mountjoy!" echoed the call across the field. "Mountjoy! St Denis!"

As one man, the royal knights started towards the rebels' right battle on the higher part of the hill. This was no reckless charge. They went at a slight canter at first, keeping the line straight, then gradually picking up speed until they all came to smash into the enemy at the same time, each man's steed almost touching the next horse's flank. Nigel and Guy had kept their men back, wary of the Royal knights opposite, and had thus witnessed from across the field how the King's first conrois had punished Ranulf for leaving his flank unprotected. Though, of course, their absence contributed somewhat to that lack of protection. Even so, Nigel still seemed quite cautious; perhaps assaulting an anointed King of France was not what they had expected when they joined to take on their duke. Perhaps it was simply the awesome sight of the battle which checked them. Either way, their counter-charge bore little impetus, so that the King's men smashed into their lines, their conrois driving in deep like wedges to prize apart an already split log.

A rebel knight, bolder than the rest, had caught sight of the King and now threw himself at him. His furious assault was so sudden that the royal guards scarce had time to see him. The rebel thrust his spear full into the King's chest. Henry was thrown clear out of his saddle. The rebel cried in triumph at his great feat of arms. Such an act would be sung of for generations. He would himself savour the victory little, though; alone among the King's vengeful guards, he was overpowered and put to death.

The nearest guards dismounted, anxious to see if their monarch yet breathed. They had little chance to make a thorough examination, for Henry sat up and swore, cursing every man under the sun. His usual calm and considered complexion had been chased away by the shame of being unseated. He scarce noticed the broken links in his mail hauberk. Ever cautious, he had doubled it with a thick leather jerkin covered in scales of iron which the rebel's spear point had failed to pierce.

Henry saw the relief in his men's faces.

"Well don't just stand there!" he shouted, fuming. "Get me up on a horse! Would you let them go unpunished?"

"My lord, the man is dead," one of them said, helping the King to his feet.

"He should have died before getting anywhere near me. What were you all playing at?"

He snatched his horse's rein from the man's hands and swung up into his saddle.

Looking over the huddle, he saw that the rest of his men had formed a protective screen around him. This meant though that the rest of his army had not seen him since the moment he was thrown to the ground. Henry had to show them he was alive, lest they should falter against the rebel scum.

"Must I do everything myself?" He grabbed a spear from his steward. "This time stay close to me. You might even learn something."

With that he pushed through the front rank of his knights. A cheer went up as the French saw their King ride out unhurt from a blow which would have killed any other man. Even the rebels paused as this Achilles emerged to deal out retribution. Under the blood red morning sun, the King of France, protected by God, commanded the field on this feast of Saint Lawrence.

"Men of Normandy!" he shouted to the rebels "See now your anointed King whom you sought to supplant by overthrowing the Duke we gave you. Surrender now or pay the price of all traitors."

His fury was undoubted by any who could see him. He turned to his vassal lords, raised his spear and shouted.

"With me now. Montjoy!"

"Montjoy! Saint Denis!"

As one, the lords of France charged anew into the rebel lines. Taken aback by the abrupt and sudden élan of the King's conrois, Nigel's front rank buckled as men sought to avoid the furious sovereign and his fierce knights.

"Montjoy! Saint Denis!" The battle cry of France echoed across the field.

From his position further up the slope, it must have seemed to Ralph Tesson that the day's work was turning into a very one-sided affair. The French cavalry pressed its advantage, leaving their infantry to finish the job by swiftly despatching the wounded enemy with short stabs of daggers.

After the battle, William would come to hear how at that moment Ralph finally made up his mind and charged. Tesson later claimed to have deliberately waited until the right moment to strike. William knew the truth – knew that Ralph had in fact waited until he saw a clear victor emerging before choosing where his allegiance lay.

Seeing the centre of Guy's line collapse opposite Duke William and the King pressing Nigel hard, Ralph Tesson must have realised that the time had come to make a move if he was to claim any of the credit at all. There could only be one victorious side and it was clear which it would be. As Nigel's standard was waved in a call for reinforcements just below him, he answered by charging into the rebels' exposed flank.

His reasons mattered little, for either way the effect of his late charge was devastating. Nigel, who had been little surprised at Tesson's reluctance to commit to battle, was caught completely off guard when Tesson sent his knights crashing into his right flank. The infantry which had been left there were entirely unprepared to be assaulted by cavalry. As spears flew into them, they panicked. There was nowhere for them to go. They were utterly annihilated by the treacherous attack.

Nigel found his senses quickly enough. He knew he could not risk the panic spreading to his knights.

"Saint Saviour!" he shouted his rallying cry. "Saint Saviour, to me!"

His disciplined milites expertly closed up their line and turned to face the new threat. Though the King kept pressing their front and Tesson was now on their flank, the knights of the Cotentin were not going to give in just yet. They stood by their colours and their Count.

Looking down into the valley, Henry could see why. For all his skill with a sword and youthful bravado, the young duke was failing to overcome Ranulf of the Vexin and Guy of Burgundy.

CHAPTER 16

William pushed his way through his men to ram his horse between two rebel knights. He hacked away with his sword, caring little if he was actually inflicting any damage. All he wanted was to cut himself a path through to Guy. The smell of spilt blood and crushed wheat filled his nostrils. The sounds of metal hitting metal, of wood splintering, of horses whinnying and men crying filled his ears. Swords and spears flew past his eyes, yet he was only dimly aware of them. The only thing which was of any consequence was reaching his traitorous cousin.

"Guy, you dog! Fight me!" He shouted over the din of battle. "Fight me!" He was shaking with rage.

Guy turned and saw him. His cousin's face was one he no longer recognised. All the warmth had drained from it, giving way to cold-blooded ambition and malice. He smiled at William. It was the smile of a wolf greeting a sheep.

A rider stepped between the two men. William punched his sword hilt into the horse's mouth, causing it to throw the man to the ground. William had not bothered to check whether it was a foe or a friend. The fool should not have got in the way of vengeance.

William pointed his sword at Guy, who took up the challenge. Men sensed a change in the flow of battle and parted to let them through. His cousin smirked at him. William could feel the sweat trickle down his face from the heat of the summer sun which made the day's labour all the more tiring.

"*Duke* William," Guy said, the words sounding somehow ridiculous from his mouth. "A hot day for it."

"Not as hot as where I'm sending you, Guy. You traitor." William said, bringing his horse level so that their shields touched.

"You think I'm the one going to Hell? For wanting to free our people from a weak and illegitimate duke?"

"For trying to kill your rightful duke, chosen by God and to whom you swore homage. Homage is given for life. It is a bond nothing can break, as well you know."

Guy laughed.

"Chosen by God?" Guy spat in disgust. "Would Zadok have anointed Solomon if he'd been a bastard? 'A bastard shall not enter into the congregation of the Lord.'"

William felt his blood boil at the insult. Who did this retch think he was, to dishonour his mother so?

"Cur. What small hope you had of mercy is over."

"Only the victor can give mercy. Look around you. The King is not come for you. Your men are already beaten. He will make peace with the victor."

"We are not beaten yet," William said.

With that, he roared in defiance and thrust his sword at Guy's face. Unprepared for it, Guy had no time to bring up his shield and clumsily fell back in his saddle. The tip of the sword gave Guy a nasty cut across the eyebrow, though he was lucky not to suffer worse. William brought the blade back down, but Guy was already leaning forwards again. Taken aback by the swift recovery, William only just avoided the tip of Guy's sword which came perilously close to his throat. Had his horse not chosen that very moment to take a side step, almost as if sensing the danger William was in, the blade would have cut clean through his windpipe. As the sword went past his neck, he saw the chance and took it; dropping his own weapon, he grabbed Guy's arm and pulled with all his weight. William saw a flicker of astonishment in his cousin's face before head-butting him in the jaw with his steel helmet. A satisfying crunching sound was followed by a yelp of pain.

William kicked his spurs. The horse obediently lurched forwards, pulling Guy clear out of his stirrups. Weighed down by his mail, Guy fell to the ground with a dull thud, his face covered in blood.

"Seize him!" William shouted to his nearest sergeants. "And be sure to keep him alive... for now!"

Two men grabbed the traitor and pulled him to the back of their ranks. FitzOsbern spat in Guy's direction as he caught up with William.

"You got the turd, then?" he said with relish.

"One of them," William said. "But there are more still out there."

They looked out across the field. Further up the slope, to their left, they saw that the King's charge had lost its impetus. Against all odds, Nigel's Cotentin contingent was managing to hold its own. A pity such a good leader should be on the wrong side, William thought.

Henry's men were still fighting hard, probing for weaknesses. William desperately needed to deal with those rebels still stood opposite him, who were on the verge of breaking his knights. Seeing their leader captured had caused Guy's men to relent somewhat. If only he could deal with Ranulf, he might come out on top in this lower part of the field.

"They're a stubborn lot, aren't they?" FitzOsbern said. "What's to be done?"

"Finish them, of course."

"Good; I'm starving. We broke our fast hours ago."

William laughed. Only FitzOsbern could think of eating amidst the terror and slaughter of a battlefield.

"Come, let's find you something to eat, my friend." He said with a sly smile. "Find me Ranulf!" he shouted to his men.

William's men pressed on, testing their enemy, searching for gaps in the line – just enough to start opening it up.

The rebels would not give in. They knew that they had already crossed the Rubicon. There could be no turning back now. Any man who tried to overthrow his lord knew that he had either to kill him or be killed himself. The only alternative was perpetual banishment – to live the worthless life of the outlaw. A liege-lord is a giver of land, and of the rich rents that land provides. To forsake one's lord was to forsake one's home.

Thus the rebels fought on with the tenacity of a cornered boar whose very tusks were given the added strength of despair. William needed to convince them to give in or to break them altogether.

That was when he saw his uncle. He had lost sight of him for some time and now he saw why. Talou was among the rebels. Had he planned it or was it a spur of the moment decision? William cared little; for all that mattered was the sight of his uncle William, Count of Talou, among the rebels.

What a glorious sight it was. Talou had led the lightly armed men of the commons on the long slow walk through the marshes which protected William's right flank. The knights of both camps,

142

so busy with their fighting, had scarce noticed the peasants making their way through the water-logged ground, half hidden by long grass which grew there. Now the infantry had emerged to hit the rebel left flank. It was complete chaos. Rebel knights were pulled unceremoniously from their saddles and had daggers brutally thrust into the unprotected parts of their bodies or else had their steed hamstrung so that the beasts would fall to the ground among much flailing of hooves.

Henry smiled wryly as William's vassal belatedly entered the fray with all the swagger of another Hercules. Nonetheless, the effect was devastating as Nigel's flank collapsed. The King's men, joined by William's left flank, soon surrounded the rebels of the hill.

Unrelenting, Henry's men pushed again and again, hacking, stabbing, throwing and thrusting at the rebels on the hill, determined to break them. Those knights of the Cotentin were exhausted. Most, as Nigel, fought on foot, having had their horses killed from under them. Yet their leader would not yield. Henry could not help but admire the man's dogged determination to soldier on against the odds, no matter how futile it seemed. Nigel, Viscount of the Cotentin, was proving to be a formidable warrior. Even as his standard bearer fell, the butt of a spear protruding from his belly, Nigel dropped the splintered remains of his shield and grabbed the flag. A French knight tried to take it from him and was rewarded with a sword in the face. The blood splattered across the tattered banner.

"Saint Saviour! Saint Saviour!" Nigel's rallying cry echoed through the noise of battle.

143

The French relented, pulling back in order to regroup and charge anew.

"Wait," Henry said. He pushed his horse to the front, men doing their best to make way for him in the press of steeds. Resplendent in his polished armour trimmed with blue cloth beneath, a gold circle on his helmet serving as a crown, Henry looked every bit the warrior-king. As he came before the rebels, Nigel lowered his sword and bowed. He handed his flag to the man next to him.

"You have fought valiantly, Lord Nigel, Viscount of Cotentin. I have not seen such a display of bravery in many a year." He took off his left glove and pulled a silver ring from his finger. He tossed it to Nigel, who caught it with no little dexterity. "Take that ring as a mark of my respect."

"Thank you, my lord King."

"Yet sorry I am to see you join in so dishonourable a rebellion against the Duke whom I appointed with God's grace to watch over you. What have you to say for yourself?"

"My good King, I do not sin against God's law. There are many wrongs in the land of Normandy. Many men give this weak Duke ill advice and it risks tearing our land to pieces. I only acted so for the good of my people."

"Your *weak* Duke has very nearly won the day. See how the boy whom many thought to supplant is now a leader of men. Your people would be best served to follow his word and live in peace." Henry looked down at Nigel, thinking he saw a flicker of doubt beyond the resolution. "Yet I am prepared to offer you a way out. Leave Duke William's side and come to my court. I have need of good men and I do not think your soul is all black."

144

Nigel frowned.

"My lord King, I am a Norman. I cannot abandon my land so readily."

"Your Duke will likely have you executed. Publicly, I must support this. Come to my court, though and you will be richly rewarded."

Henry was growing impatient. He would sooner have Nigel's sword on his side, for the Dukes and Counts of Northern France were ever a cause for concern. There was no knowing whether he might not one day be back here fighting against William rather than for him.

"My sovereign, you offer me money to complete my rebellion through desertion. But my cause is just. Were I to take riches, I would corrupt my soul, and that I will not do. I must surrender to the Duke of Normandy, my liege-lord – not the King of France."

Henry scowled, but kept his temper under control.

"So be it."

William felt a lull in the pressure against his shield. He chanced a glance over its rim and realised it was all but over. Ranulf, seeing his allies surrounded by the King's men up on the hill, turned tail and galloped away. His followers, so inspired by this act of bravery, followed. The whole army of the Bessin melted away. William grinned at FitzOsbern.

"Shall we?"

"Why not," his friend said with a smile. "A brisk ride would do me good."

William took off his helmet and lifted it high.

"I am your Duke," he shouted to his men, "and we have victory! Now let's get the rewards. Finish them!"

The gleeful cry of the saved rang out and his men launched themselves in pursuit of Ranulf's men. As the rebels ran into the top field of wheat which swayed in protest at being so disturbed, William led his men to the harvest.

Those on foot were cut down where they stood. The slowest horsemen were taken for ransom, if they were lucky. Most were thrown from their saddles to water the crops with their blood. With that sudden rush of salvation comes the hunger for revenge, and so William's men showed no mercy. Bodies were trampled under their horses' hooves.

Those who managed to get away from the battlefield fared no better. William had chosen his spot well and his gamble was now paid off. As Ranulf's men neared the River Vire, their one chance of safety, they found themselves atop a steep bank. Those in front had no time to stop their steeds and tumbled down the steep bank. Trees and bones snapped under the weight of falling horses. More riders followed and men found their deaths at the bottom of the bank.

Some further back saw the danger in time and made it unharmed down to the water, finding less steep paths. It saved them not. The river was deep and their chainmail heavy. Beyond the river were lush green fields and beyond those were woodlands which might hide them long enough to allow them to escape. They would not set foot there. Where one man might have swam his horse across, a whole army sought to ford the river Orne. It was barely twelve feet wide, but it was deep enough and pulled men to their deaths. The tide was on the ebb as Normandy angrily swept the men downstream, that no blood should sully the green fields beyond. This Rubicon they had been so eager to cross that morning was now the Styx and spelt the Hellish end of the rebel knights of the Bessin. Their bodies were carried away to block up the watermills used to grind the wheat for the small town of Caen, turning the water there red.

William watched the spectacle in awe. This divine retribution of the land was as beautiful as it was cruel. Ranulf himself would not risk the crossing and, out of options, was promptly captured by the ducal vanguard.

Justice would be done. William returned to the battlefield, pausing as he neared the hill.

"What day is it?" he asked FitzOsbern.

"The feast of Saint Lawrence, I believe."

"Then we shall build a church here in thanks to him. On this day, he has once more saved a grail from the hands of iniquity."

And the bloody land of Normandy rested at last.

.III.

A MOST TREACHEROUS HOUSE

Chapter 17

"It was a wonderful victory, William," FitzOsbern said.

"Indeed," Talou said, "at the end, it *was* a wonderful victory, my lord."

"I thank you; you and all my loyal lords and men," William said.

After much gloating at saving Normandy in spite of William's character, King Henry had given William leave to deal out punishment as he saw fit, though he had cautioned him not to let the Viscount of the Cotentin live. Nigel, he had said, was of a deceitful bent and would cause Normandy much suffering. William had dutifully thanked his liege, much though it galled him.

He now took in the sight of his assembled lords, wearing all the fineries of their high positions. The walls of the hall in Caen were lined with soldiers. These lords were those loyal to William, but time and death had taught him to trust little and take many precautions.

"Loyalty must be rewarded as earnestly as treason is punished. That is one lesson for which I may thank my late uncle the Archbishop and your own father the Steward, FitzOsbern – God rest their souls."

"Amen," said Talou.

"And so reward you, I shall – such as you deserve. Uncle Talou, you warned me against fighting. You told me that victory could not be achieved and counselled me to offer the rebels terms. You doubted my abilities as a commander, judging me too young. In short, with your advice, we would not be here today."

Talou bowed low in obeisance, knowing better than to speak.

"Yet," William continued, "without your skill on the field and your good direction in seeking the King's help, we would not be here today either. For that, we thank you dearly."

Though he could not make out his face, William could sense his uncle smiling. He sensed also FitzOsbern's irritation.

"Throughout our minority, you stood by us, bearing much of the burden of office. We therefore gift you the castle and lands of Arques, which of late were still bestowed on our cousin Guy of Burgundy. Arise, Count William of Talou and of Arques."

The newly-appointed Count of Arques gave a deprecating smile of recognition, though William suspected he thought it no more than he deserved. Arques must surely have known then that nothing could be the same again. William may have needed his uncle's help, but the Vale of Dunes, when word spread, would show all of France that the land of Normandy well and truly had a Duke once more.

"Nigel fought bravely, surrendering when he knew it was over. I will need men like that to control the duchy. He is to live in exile for five years. After that, he may return to his lands, of which I deem only a third forfeit to me."

"Five years and a pardon?" FitzOsbern spat.

"A generous act of mercy, my lord," Arques said. "And of Ranulf?"

"Ranulf," William sighed. "An unrepentant traitor. And not just a traitor, but a coward. Nigel at least had the strength of his convictions. Ranulf saw an easy prey and took the chance. He thought nothing of his vassals nor of Normandy. There can be no mercy for such a man." He summoned a nearby knight, who came to kneel before him. "Ranulf, former Viscount of Bessin, is held under guard. Tell his gaoler that we find him guilty of treason and he is to be executed behind closed doors. Have him buried outside sanctified ground and with no marker for his grave. Go!"

The man went slightly white at having to deliver such an order, but he obeyed nonetheless.

"Make sure Guy hears of this, Uncle Arques. It should elevate his thinking."

"I've no doubt of it. There will be other Guys, though. Others who will try to take your place."

"You're quite right." William said, with a sideways glance at his uncle. "There will always be those who think themselves greater than their duke."

"That is why you must sire an heir as soon as possible," said FitzOsbern. "An heir of good breeding, who will strengthen your position."

"I have already thought of that. It is all in hand."

Both his friend and his uncle looked at him in surprise.

"Well," Talou said, "who has taken your fancy?"

"Matilda, the daughter of Count Baldwin of Flanders, is of marrying age and is said to be rather attractive."

"Matilda of Flanders?" Talou said. "Are you sure?"

"Quite," William said. "Why does that surprise you?"

"She's said to be very rash and strong minded. It's said she's already known a man's touch. Some English thegn, as I understand."

"Brithric, I think," FitzOsbern said.

"That's the one. Edward made him his ambassador at Baldwin's court and the damned fool went and seduced the count's daughter. So much for diplomacy," scoffed Talou. "And she, even more the fool, throws herself at his feet, against her father's wishes, only to be cast aside in favour of an English girl."

"So they say," FitzOsbern said.

"Nothing matters more than what they say," Talou said. "Would you take her for your wife?"

"I would have her as my duchess," William said. "Think about it; all the recent dukes of Normandy saw it fit only to have lovers. I would give our land a great dynasty in which Norman courage is strengthened further with the noble stock of Flanders and France."

"How can you call a girl of that behaviour noble?" Talou asked, throwing his hands in the air.

"She is the grand-daughter of King Robert the Pious of France; that means the blood of Charlemagne runs through her veins! She is also of the line of King Alfred the Great of England! What nobler wife could you find?"

"And if she runs amok?" FitzOsbern asked.

"She won't, not with me as her husband. She is young, but she will learn to do as her duke commands," William said, growing angry with their objections. Why were they so intent on stopping him from having the one woman he knew he ought to have?

"I see that you will not be swayed in this," Talou said.

"I will not," William agreed with an impatient sigh.

"Very well then, I will make the necessary enquiries, my lord."

"They are already being made," William said. He could not tell who was most taken aback, his uncle or FitzOsbern.

"Being made? By whom?" Talou said.

"I have sent Roger Montgomery to the court of Flanders. If Baldwin agrees, we shall be married as soon as possible."

"Why did you send Montgomery so soon? Why didn't you consult me?" Talou said, growing red in the face.

"You are being consulted," William said, trying to keep his own temper.

"After the horse has bolted! You should have waited for advice, William; I know what is best for you."

"I have other advisers, uncle, and I am duke in my own right, in case you hadn't noticed."

"Your advisers are hardly any more experienced than yourself! What use is that?"

"They are all loyal to me, though, unlike many of my father's generation. I need good and loyal men."

"I would hardly describe Montgomery as loyal," FitzOsbern said. "His father is a traitor, his brother as well…"

"In case you didn't notice, he did not join the rebels. Why stay loyal when this would have been his ideal chance?" William said.

"He wasn't loyal enough to stand by your side," FitzOsbern said, looking somewhat hurt.

"I thank you for your loyalty, FitzOsbern, I truly do, but it is time you let your quarrel with Roger go. His father is banished and his brother William is dead. We avenged your father, though

I'm sorry it took so long. Going after Roger won't bring Osbern back," William felt his friend's pain. "I must have unity at my court if Normandy is to survive."

"Well, Montgomery?" William asked, as Roger returned at last. "What news from Flanders?"

"I have made the appropriate enquiries of Count Baldwin. He is quite as well disposed as you are, my lord, to forge a union between our two lands. He has trouble enough with his northern and eastern neighbours and welcomes the prospect of an alliance which could ensure peace to his south – especially with such a promising young lord as you."

"Excellent," William said, beaming. "Then we can proceed."

"But what of the dowry, Montgomery?" Arques interjected. "Did you get from Baldwin any indication of what he had in mind for William to take his daughter off his hands?"

William looked from his uncle to Roger. It was true that he was ever in need of funds, in spite of the recent lands he had been able to confiscate from the rebels. Much of those new possessions would have to go towards strengthening the loyalties of those who had supported him. He could not risk a fresh rebellion.

"So?" Arques pressed. "What has Baldwin to offer Normandy?"

"You must remember that Flanders is not the richest province. There will be some contribution, of course, but we ought not to expect great riches."

Arques scoffed.

"In other words, you have failed to secure a decent dowry."

155

"I have secured a greater reward than that. This union will bring to the house of Normandy royal blood, as well as a strategic ally. Had Baldwin offered no dowry at all, we would still come out of it much strengthened." Montgomery gave William a knowing glance. "The lady Matilda's reputation for beauty is well deserved, by the way. She is not the tallest lady, but she is a beauty."

"Good," William said. "So where do we take it from here?"

"I have left Hubert of Ryes in Flanders to conclude the arrangements. We should hear back from him in a few days' time."

The days dragged by as William waited. He filled them with hunting and practising at the quintain. William wished he could have gone to Flanders himself to meet Matilda in the flesh, but he dared not leave Normandy so soon after the rebellion. After two weeks of tense waiting, Hubert finally arrived to give William the news.

"Is everything settled?" William said. Too anxious even to sit, he paced up and down the room.

"Count Baldwin will be only too happy to proceed with the marriage. There remains only the formality of sending word to Rome for a formal Papal blessing."

"Is that quite necessary?"

"Count Baldwin feels we ought to do this properly."

"Very well, make the arrangements for it."

"Yes, my lord. But…" Hubert's words trailed away.

"What is it?"

"The lady Matilda does not look favourably on the marriage."

William chuckled.

"Well what has it to do with her? If her father agrees, why should she object? Especially given the rumours about the Saxon, she should be glad to have a husband at last."

"Alas! She has a strong will – uncommonly so for a young lady of her rank. She is adamant that she will not marry you, my lord. I left her father trying to convince her, but if he cannot prevail upon her better judgement, it could make things... complicated at the altar."

"Does she give a reason for rejecting me?" William asked through gritted teeth.

"She says – and please forgive me for being the messenger of such insolence – that it is unheard of that a daughter of Charlemagne's line should marry the bastard son of a Viking brigand's line... and of a tanner's daughter."

William froze mid-pace.

"She said what?"

"I would rather not repeat it, my lord... A silly girl's tantrum..."

"By God, I'll not put up with any such talk when she is my wife!"

"Well that's just it. I'm not sure that she will be your wife. Baldwin seemed to be rather downcast when I left. I don't know that he has the heart to put his daughter through a forced marriage. He may not succeed in getting her down the aisle."

"Right," William said. "Well if he doesn't have the backbone to make his daughter do as she's told, I had best go there myself and sort her out."

"My lord, please..."

157

"No one insults my mother. She will have to learn respect, Hubert." He pulled open the door. "Boy, fetch my horse! I travel alone, Hubert."

With that, he stormed out.

"Well, Hubert," said FitzOsbern with a smile. "You've done it now."

CHAPTER 18

THE COURT OF COUNT BALDWIN, FLANDERS.

William spurred his horse through the gate, left wide open as the land was at peace and so that traders could come and go freely. He stopped just long enough to ask one of the nearby guards where he might find Baldwin's daughter. Seeing an important-looking lord on a costly warhorse, the guard answered.

"She is at prayer in the chapel, my lord. If you will wait here, I will let the Count know you have come to see his daughter. May I ask who you are, my lord?"

If the guard had kept his wits, he would not have told William the lady's whereabouts before Baldwin had been informed. William's answer was to kick his spurs, sending his steed flying up towards the chapel which he could just see at the top of the hill. As he neared, the bells started to sound and the doors swung open. The nuns stepped aside to let a party of courtly ladies out. Leading them was a small yet elegant young lady with chestnut hair. She wore a pure white dress lined with fur against the chill. She seemed perfectly relaxed, in complete control of the party. The proud expression on her face left William in little doubt of who this was.

He stepped his horse forward until he looked down at them.

"Lady Matilda, I take it?"

"I don't know how things are done wherever you come from, my lord," she said coolly, "but in Flanders, it is customary to dismount and introduce oneself before demanding it of others."

He was taken aback at being rebuked thus, especially from a woman. Nonetheless, he swung out of his saddle. He saw her disdainful glance at his dirty travel-worn clothes.

"I am William, Duke of Normandy," he said. It was the journey which made his breath catch in his throat as he spoke, not her dark beautiful eyes which met his defiantly. She made a good job of keeping her serene air, though William could tell she was shocked to meet him in person at her father's own court, unannounced, as she came from prayer.

"Ah," she said, as if his identity was sufficient explanation for his lack of courtly manners, "so this is William of Normandy; the bastard who thinks himself worthy of marrying a daughter of Charlemagne." She turned to her ladies who took the hint and giggled.

The mockery was more than he could take. He lunged forward and grabbed Matilda by the hair. This daughter of Charlemagne had clearly not expected anything of the like and let out a small cry of alarm. He pulled her towards him. Her hair felt silky in his rough palm. She looked up at him, startled.

"You call me a bastard? I am duke! By what right do you defy me when your father thinks me worthy of you?"

"You are the grandson of a tanner and your behaviour this morning is proof enough of that!"

He slapped her, the strike reddening her pale cheek. She pleaded with her eyes, but kept defiant with her words.

"What nobleman hits a lady thus?"

"I am the son of a great duke. The blood of Rollo, who cowed the Kings of France, flows through my veins."

"And like Rollo, the petty Viking brigand, you take by force that which is not yours by right!" She spat venom at him. He slapped her again. Her feet caught on the hem of her dress and she fell back onto the muddy ground, her pure white cloth dirtied by the earth. William stood over her as she lay there, staring into his eyes looking every bit like a lamb which has been cornered. He watched her chest rising and falling. Montgomery had not lied about her beauty. A shout from the other side of the courtyard alerted him. As a group of guards ran towards him with spears ready to strike, he leaped back into his saddle. He could not help but look upon her one last time, before kicking his horse into action. As he spurred out of the gates, the guard there was thrown back against the wall. William did not stop until he had passed the river Somme .

"Such an arrogant girl! Baldwin was clearly far too soft in bringing her up," William fumed. He was pacing up and down the hall of his uncle's new castle at Arques. "That such a girl should think herself greater than the duke of the Normans. She got what she deserved."

"Perhaps," Arques said, "but now we must brace ourselves for the consequences of your actions, nephew."

"What were my actions, but to demand that to which her father had already agreed?"

"William, you rode into the court of the Count of Flanders, without his permission, and struck his daughter as she was leaving the church. Put it whichever way you want, it doesn't look good. Even if he had sympathy with your anger, Baldwin won't let it stand. If he did, he would look weak. You can be sure he is making his plans for war as we speak, and so we must decide how to meet this threat."

"To Hell with Baldwin! If he can't even bring his own daughter under his authority, what chance would he have against us?"

"Flanders is not the country of idle peasants that it used to be. Baldwin has worked hard to bring in much trade and boosted his textile industry. That new money will buy him what men he needs to wage war, no matter what his own skill on the battlefield. Would you have Normandy flooded with mercenaries?"

"He can do what he likes; we will not be beaten." William had gone too far and he knew it. He was beginning to seriously regret slapping Matilda, but he was loath to admit as much to Arques.

"Remember the Vale of Dunes? We were nearly finished there. And don't think Henry will be so willing to help a second time, especially given the provocation. He does as much trade with Flanders as with us and he won't risk losing that revenue."

"You fret like an old woman, uncle."

"For God's sake, William! Have you learned nothing from me? Your uncle Mauger and I have been working hard to keep this duchy together. Now you would throw the fruits of our labour out the window for the sake of your pride?"

"Nothing is being thrown out. As duke of Normandy, I had an agreement with Flanders. Flanders broke that agreement. Would you have had me show weakness? Anjou is ever looking for some sign that we could be beaten. The Vale of Dunes showed we still have mettle. If Flanders chooses war, so be it. Even if Henry won't help, we have friends in England who distrust Flanders. Edward will stand by me, if it comes to it, but it won't come to it."

162

"At least make some conciliatory gesture," Arques suggested.

"To have it thrown back in our face? No. If Baldwin wishes war, he will have war. Either way, I will have Matilda at the end of it."

He was burning with desire for her. He couldn't understand it. He had only seen her for a fleeting moment, yet he longed for her more than he had for any other woman before. Of course, the choice was purely political and her lineage no doubt added to the beauty. Yet there was something in those doe eyes, that confidence, that heaving chest which stirred something in him. He could not get her out of his mind.

Arques could tell that it was pointless arguing further. William watched as he walked over to Roger Montgomery.

"Surely, Montgomery, you do not wish war."

"Not with Flanders, no. But William is right; we cannot now appear weak. What is done is done. We must ride this storm out."

"And ride it out, we will," FitzOsbern said, slouched in a chair. He wore his chainmail, for he had been out training his men, rather than have to make small talk with Arques and Montgomery.

They all stood in silence, the only noise being one of William's hounds snoring softly by the fire. William looked at the beast sleeping without a care in the world. How peaceful it must be, he thought. The silence was broken by heavy footsteps, as a sergeant came in with a grave look on his face.

"My lord, a messenger has arrived from Flanders."

William waved an absent-minded hand that he should come in.

"Try not to be too impetuous, William. There may still be a way out," Arques said, to his great annoyance. When would his uncle learn that he was no longer a child?

The Flemish herald strode in. He was a tall man, who stood as straight as a spear. His broad shoulders spoke of years practising with sword and shield. The quality of his chainmail and the fine cloth of his tunic beneath it told William that this was a man of some standing in Baldwin's court, no mere errand boy. As he came to the centre of the room, he looked around at the assembled lords, his disdain plain enough.

"I am Baldwin, son of Count Baldwin of Flanders." He spoke with the same peremptory tone as his sister Matilda, William thought. "I take it you are William."

He was looking at FitzOsbern as he said this. William followed his gaze. What did he see? He saw a warlord, armed for battle, the only person in the room to be seated. Of course he should assume FitzOsbern was the duke. William smiled and winked at FitzOsbern. The opportunity was too good to resist.

"He is indeed William," William said, before the others had a chance to contradict him. FitzOsbern nodded.

"Greetings, Baldwin, son of Baldwin. What message have you from Flanders?"

"My message is one of anger. You recently came to my father's court, my lord, without invitation and struck my sister, the lady Matilda. You will pay dearly for the offence."

"Will I now?" FitzOsbern said. "And how will I pay?"

"You will pay with the tears of the women of this province and the unanswered cries of babies whose fathers have fallen to the swords of Flanders. You will pay with the destruction of your crops and the burning of your villages. You will pay with your flesh that shall feed the crows."

"Brave words, young Baldwin," William said to the Flemish heir who could not have been more than three years his junior. "But next time you insult a Duke, best make sure you insult him to his face. I am William, Duke of the Normans, son of Robert the Magnificent, victor of the Battle of the Vale of Dunes. Such presumption does you no credit."

Baldwin stood bewildered, growing red in the face.

"You told me he was William," he protested.

"So I did, and so he is," William smiled. "He is William FitzOsbern, my steward. And this is William, Count of Talou and of Arques."

"And is he William as well?" Baldwin asked facetiously, pointing to Montgomery.

"He is Roger, Count of Montgomery."

Baldwin bowed to Roger, who bowed back; the Montgomery name was respected throughout France, in spite of Roger's father's betrayal.

"Now that that is sorted, would you do me the honour of threatening me again properly?" William said, as he walked up to Baldwin and looked down at him. Baldwin was no weakling, yet William towered over most men. The effect of this was to give Baldwin a momentary pause for thought. He had just opened his mouth to speak again when the door to the hall swung open and a chamberlain stepped in.

"What is it?" William barked, not breaking his stare with Baldwin.

"My lord," the man said, "another messenger from Flanders."

They all turn in surprised. William looked quizzically at Baldwin but saw that he was just as taken aback as the rest of them. The new arrival entered the room. He bore a striking resemblance to the first envoy.

"Robert?" Baldwin said. "What are you doing here?"

Robert raised his eyebrows at the scene before him. He had clearly not expected to see his brother standing nose to nose with the Norman duke. Nonetheless, he lost no sense of etiquette. He bowed to William and the gathered lords in turn.

"Duke William, I bring a message from our father, Count Baldwin of Flanders. He bids you forget what words might have passed between you and my brother on his behalf." Robert looked at his brother with concern, visibly hoping nothing too damaging had yet been said. "He prays you will see this as no more than the excessive words which members of one family can sometimes exchange in the heat of the moment."

"Members of one family?" Arques asked.

"Yes, my lord, for he bids you accept our sister Matilda's hand in marriage."

The room fell into stunned silence. No one had expected this. Baldwin was the first to recover.

"What is this, brother? Is he sure of this?"

"He is quite sure," Robert said flatly. "What say you, Duke William? Shall we be brothers?"

"That all depends," William said. "What does the lady Matilda say? She was quite adamant that she would not marry me under any circumstance."

"That may be so, my lord, but I do not foresee any further problems."

166

"She accepts the Count's decision?"

"No, my lord; the Count had desired to break it off. The lady Matilda said otherwise. She insisted that she could marry no other man than you."

"What?"

"Indeed, she said that for you to chastise her in her own father's court showed that you were made of far greater stuff than she had thought. So I would offer you my hand to shake."

"And I take it gladly," William said smiling, "brother".

CHAPTER 19

William's footsteps echoed through the silence. This place was not far from Rouen, the heart of Normandy, where merchants came and went in a constant bustle of activity. Yet in this valley he could have thought himself entirely cut off from the world. The only other noise to be heard was the gentle flow of the beck which gave the abbey of Bec Hellouin its name. The second half of the name was for its founder and abbot, Hellouin. It was not that great man whom William had come to see, though. Another was making a name for himself here.

William pushed open the door he had been directed to. Inside was a simple room. The only furniture was a small uncomfortable-looking bed, a stool and a plain lectern at which a lone cleric was writing by the light of a candle. He wore the black habit of his Benedictine order with no embellishments. His back was straight and he was so intently focused on his work that he scarce seemed to notice his visitor. His tanned skin hinted at his Italian homeland which he had left at Hellouin's request specifically to set up a school within the abbey; such was his reputation throughout Europe as a theologian.

At length, he put down his quill and, without taking his eyes off the parchment, spoke.

"I wondered when I would have the pleasure of your visit, Duke William."

"You are fortunate to be under the protection of the Church, Prior Lanfranc, else I would have had you brought to me in chains."

The Italian smiled. He met William's gaze with piercing blue eyes which seemed to look straight at William's soul.

"I am indeed pleased that God's servants are not subservient to temporal lords in these parts – whatever else may be wrong with the Church in Normandy."

"That may be so, but your office does not exist to challenge the Duke's authority."

"It exists to spread the Pope's authority, as the Lord's representative on Earth. And that is all I did."

"It was not the Pope's decision to ban my marriage to the Lady Matilda of Flanders."

"The letter I received bore His Holiness' seal. It was explicit in its instructions."

"Yet why should the Pope decree such a thing? This act threatens the very peace of our land. By supporting it, you have let the doors wide open for our enemies. Were you bought?" William felt a rage burning within him.

Lanfranc frowned.

"Unlike many of your priests and bishops, I cannot be corrupted. My judgement is only ever based on spiritual considerations. The Pope is clearly aware of some proximity between yourself and the lady Matilda. In case you did not know this aspect of cannon law, any two persons connected by blood cannot marry. It is clearly stated in Leviticus."

"There is no close connection between Matilda and me."

"It need not be close; within seven degrees, that is all. His Holiness has applied God's law and rightly so."

"Yet the same rule does not apply to others, it seems. How many lords of France have married their cousins? Why do you suppose the Pope has singled me out?"

"If others have not followed cannon law, then their souls will pay the price. You do not make their sins less by committing the same sin yourself, my lord."

William threw his hands in the air. He could see his future slipping irrevocably out of his control and Matilda leaving Normandy never to return. He drew a deep breath and tried to calm his temper. The prior was clearly not a man to be intimidated, and threatening a renowned clergyman would hardly convince the Pope to reverse his decision.

"Please, prior, sit down."

Lanfranc perched himself on the edge of his bed as William pulled up the stool.

"I understand your position, truly I do. Your reputation as a man of learning is clearly deserved. That much is plain. Now let me speak honestly."

"I think that would be a good idea."

"What you say is true; the lady Matilda and I are indeed related, however distantly. I was not even aware of the connection myself until recently, so remote it is. Most people are related within seven degrees if they search hard enough. Were it common place for this rule to be applied so rigidly, I would of course renounce the lady Matilda."

"It is not for you to decide, my lord. That prerogative is the Pope's."

"And what if the Pope was advised on ill council?"

"The Pope is infallible, Duke William," Lanfranc said in his heavy Italian accent. He leaned towards him and raised an index finger. "You are treading a dangerous path."

"I would not dare to question the Pope's judgement. I am merely pointing out that there are those who would be glad to see my marriage to the lady Matilda – and the ensuing alliance between Normandy and Flanders – blocked for reasons other than spiritual. Would you have the Pope used as a tool in worldly politics?"

"Of whom do you speak? If anyone has sought to dupe the papal council, then I will report it at once."

"I do not know who is behind it, though I have my suspicions. I only know that whoever did this was not acting in the Church's interests. Far from it, in fact."

"Even if that is true, it does not change anything with regards to your planned marriage. That marriage remains contrary to God's law."

"What if the Church in Normandy needs the lady Matilda?"

"What do you mean?"

"You have said yourself that the Church in these parts is corrupt. Alone, I am not strong enough to reform it and bring it back to its true purpose. But with Matilda at my side, with all her learning and love of God, as well as the backing of her father's county, I can set to work in cleansing the Church of its evils."

"Even if that meant dealing with your own family?" Lanfranc stared fixedly into his eyes.

"Even if that were the case. I cannot do this alone, nor without a man of God to direct the required changes. You would be that man. If you can convince the Pope of the virtues of making my

171

marriage an exception, I will ask him to give you his blessing to organise the Church in these parts. He has great respect for you, I understand. He will not refuse."

William sat back and let the Italian think about it for a while. He had long been preaching that the Church needed pruning of its evils and its wayward priests. William was now giving him the chance to go beyond mere words and carry out what changes he saw fit, with a Papal blessing, no less.

"If I were to agree to petition the Pope for you," he said, "His Holiness would want some form of penitence from you and the lady Matilda."

In the shadows of the room, William smiled to himself. Lanfranc would do it. They were down to the last details of the deal.

"I agree, prior. If the Pope accedes to my request, the lady Matilda and I shall each have an abbey built as thanks to God. You shall choose its priests and nuns, if you please. Then together, prior Lanfranc, we shall rebuild the Norman Church for the good of all."

Lanfranc took one last moment to think, and then stretched out his hand. William took it.

"Praise be to God," Lanfranc said.

"Amen," William said.

Chapter 20

William pushed open the door to the solar. Matilda was sat on a small stool, in front of which a wide piece of plain cloth was stretched over a wooden frame. From the doorway, William could just make out some pattern drawn on it. His bride-to-be did not notice him arrive, so deep was she in concentration over a piece of embroidery in her lap. He watched her carefully push the needle through the fabric, pulling it down and then back up again to the upper side.

He took in the sight of her long flowing chestnut hair, of her bosom rising and falling. An arrowslit in the wall let a ray of light creep in behind her, hinting through the white linen of her dress at the pert forms of her young body. William clenched his fist in frustration and longing.

"You may leave us. I wish to speak to the lady Matilda alone," he said to the two ladies who had been working with her. They exchanged a knowing glance, before dutifully curtseying to him as they left.

"My lord duke," Matilda said, blushing. "I did not hear you arrive. I thought the hunt would last some time longer."

"Indeed," William smiled.

He pulled the bolt of the door shut. Matilda glanced nervously around the empty room.

"My lord, I-", she started, before he silenced her with a finger to his lips.

"You need not fear me, my lady. We are to be husband and wife, after all. Is it not proper that I should have some moments to speak to my bride alone?"

173

He strolled over and looked over her shoulder at the work she had been so engrossed in. It was a battle scene in which a valiant king led a charge against fierce enemies with pointed helmets. Matilda followed his gaze.

"It is the story of Charlemagne, my ancestor, fighting off the heretics. We are making a frieze to present to the cathedral in Rouen - with your permission, my lord," she added hastily.

"Of course," he said, putting his hands on her shoulders. "It is only right and proper that you should honour your ancestor - especially as he will be my ancestor also, through our union."

She looked up and smiled at him, relieved at his approval. It was a smile of such candour that he immediately dismissed any shadow of the rumours regarding Matilda and the Englishman Brihtric who had been at her father's court. She was pure, without a doubt. An unspoilt cloth on which his own tale would be embroidered.

He crouched down behind her, his legs either side of hers. His hands slid down her arms. He sensed her breathing grow faster as his body pressed against hers.

"My darling Matilda," he whispered in her ear.

"My lord, please," she said softly. "We are not yet married."

He breathed in. A sweet smell of rose water teased his senses. How he wanted her. Yet he knew that it was not possible. He would not have his first-born tainted with the same bastardy which others had tried to hold against him.

He cleared his throat.

"I am keeping you from your embroidery, my lady," he said, fighting to regain some composure. "Forgive me."

She seemed to relax at the words, grateful that the moment had passed. William kissed her cheek and stood up, though his hand may have brushed over her breast as he did so.

"I bid you a good afternoon, my lady."

She stood up and curtseyed, with the look of a doe who had just escaped the hunter's arrow.

He threw back the bolt of the door and left. He thundered down the stairs to find FitzOsbern joking with the guards over a cup of wine.

"Don't you have duties to attend to?" William snapped at the guards, who promptly leapt to their feet and rushed about trying to look busy. "Come on, FitzOsbern; we must rejoin the others."

"William, are you alright?"

"I'm fine," he retorted. "God help me, but I could murder His damned Holiness the Pope right now," he said through gritted teeth, tightening his grip on the pommel of his sword. They returned to their horses and to the one hunt which William could pursue that day.

Chapter 21

William was proudly telling his lady about Normandy's growing renown for rearing fine warhorses, when he heard a shout from the bailey.

"William, come quickly!" It was FitzOsbern whose call interrupted William and Matilda's *tête à tête*. The air of panic, so uncharacteristic of his confident friend, brought him down to earth with a thud. Pausing only to look longingly into Matilda's eyes one last time, he rushed out of the stables into the bailey.

"What the devil's going on?" he asked, as people rushed around the place gathering weapons.

"Geoffrey of Anjou has invaded."

"Invaded? Where?"

"The Bellême lands."

"You mean they crossed Maine just like that? Didn't Count Herbert try to stop them?"

"God knows what happened; all I do know is that Angevin troops have been spotted near both Alençon and Domfront."

"Christ," William sighed. "Assemble my council."

"I've already sent for them and ordered the muster."

The news took a moment to sink in. William had known he would have to face Anjou sooner or later, but he had thought he would have time still. What a fool he had been to let himself get distracted, even by one as beautiful as Matilda. Now it seemed Geoffrey had already got a foothold in Normandy without anyone so much as trying to stop him.

"What is happening, my love?" Matilda said, emerging from the solar. FitzOsbern bowed and grinned at William, guessing more than had really happened - for William had kept his promise to Matilda - before rushing off to organise the muster.

"I am going to war and you are going to your father's; that is what is happening."

"I shall do no such thing," she answered defiantly.

"I love your determination, my dear, but now is really not the time. I need you to be safe; go to your father's."

"Do you think any of them would dare lay a hand on me? This war is on Normandy, not Flanders. I will stay. Besides, until our wedding receives the Papal blessing, I daren't leave Normandy for fear that my father's advisers might try to talk him out of it."

"Do you think they would?"

"Every court has those who are favourable to another power."

How true, William thought. He sometimes wondered whose side even his uncles were on.

"Very well, stay if you must. I could not bear to lose you. But please, stay here at Falaise and don't go out from the walls of the keep."

By the time he reached the hall, Arques and FitzOsbern were already having one of their usual shouting competitions. Lanfranc stood silently by the hearth watching them. The few lords who lived near by, Montgomery among them, were leaning over a crude map of Normandy. They all fell silent as William entered – all save Arques.

177

"We must try and negotiate a peaceful outcome," he said. "Perhaps Geoffrey can be bought off. If we gave him the county of Maine, it might appease him."

William raised a hand to silence his uncle.

"Tomorrow, we march on Alençon. I will not risk giving them the time to strike up from there. That would risk dividing the land in two."

"We need time to gather provisions," Montgomery said. "There's no telling how long we will be out there."

"The provisions will have to follow us. De Warenne," he turned to a stout young lord with an eager expression, "I'm putting you in charge of sorting out our supplies. Send messengers across the duchy. Every village is to contribute grain and salted meat. Have extra stores built here at Falaise. We will use them as a central storage area and send out rationed provisions from here to our outposts."

"Yes, my lord," De Warenne answered.

"Surely, William, you mean to negotiate?" Arques said.

"I have already ordered the muster. Montgomery, you wait here until the rest of the army is assembled; send half the men to Alençon, then join me with the rest at Domfront. I will head there as soon as I have established the situation at Alençon. If we get there soon enough, we might just be able to stop Geoffrey taking the town."

"It will be done, my lord."

"My lord Duke," Arques said.

"FitzOsbern," William said, ignoring his uncle, "you ride ahead tonight and see what the situation is like at Alençon."

"As you wish."

"For God's sake, William, will you listen?" Arques banged his fist on the table. All eyes turned to him.

"I am listening, Arques. What is it you have to say?"

"Geoffrey is eager to extend his lands. He clearly means to use Domfront and Alençon to prevent you from stopping him from taking Maine. What care we for that county? Let him have it and we may have peace."

"Peace? Peace? To have Geoffrey of Anjou breathing down my neck all the time from the safety of Domfront's high walls is hardly my idea of peace. I did not defeat a rebellion merely to let my neighbour take castles on a whim. Besides, King Henry came to our aid at the Vale of Dunes. He did it because it was his duty as our overlord. Now it is my duty as his vassal to see order restored in Maine. And let's not forget the Bellêmes are vassals of the King also. It is our duty to protect them."

"Maine cares not for duty. It is vassal to Normandy, yet its counts do as they please. If the King asks for help, that is another matter. He is quite capable of protecting the Bellêmes if he so chooses."

"My decision is made, Arques. An invader threatens two castles which are keys into Normandy. I will throw him out. There is nothing more to discuss."

"Really, William, you must see the sense…"

"Have you not questioned your duke's authority enough for one day?" FitzOsbern spat at him.

"Our lord the Duke has indeed been quite clear," Lanfranc said. "We all respect your experience, my lord of Arques, but I think any further discussion would be irrelevant."

"Thank you, Prior. Now about your business, everyone. We have much to do before the morning."

The lords filed out of the hall.

"Oh, Prior Lanfranc," William said. "Could I have a word?"

Lanfranc nodded, as Arques shot him a look of pure loathing. William waited until all the others had left and closed the door.

"Lanfranc, I want you to press ahead with our plans. Make your way to Rome as soon as possible."

"You do not feel it best to wait until the present matter is resolved?"

"On the contrary; it is more urgent than ever that I should be married and produce an heir. If I were to die and leave the duchy without an heir, I fear Normandy would descend into chaos and would be easy prey for the Angevins."

"As you wish, my lord."

"There is something else. I am growing uneasy. Something doesn't seem right. I want you to see if you can pick up anything in Rome. Someone doesn't want me to marry Matilda and I need to know who, in case they try anything more desperate."

"I will endeavour to do my best, my lord, though I must warn you that I am no politician. I would not even know how to dirty my hands with such affairs."

William smiled.

"Don't underestimate yourself, Lanfranc. I believe you may have some hidden talent there."

CHAPTER 22

Alençon was only forty-five miles from Falaise, but it was a difficult road between the two towns, little more than a dirt track winding through deep woods. William had waited until third hour before setting off with his small force of knights. There were only a hundred or so of them. Still, there should be enough of them to discourage any attack on Alençon. He had already sent out orders to assemble more men. The lands confiscated from the rebels at the Vale of Dunes would go some way to pay for hired swords. The promise of further land should attract plenty of eager knights to his banner. Once the reinforcements from Falaise arrived, he would be able to hit out at Geoffrey's other forces in Domfront from this position of strength. He took with him only mounted troops, for Alençon needed help before it was too late. These were his own milites, his oath-men, loyal household knights who had been with him at the Vale of Dunes. With them went adolescents from noble Norman families who had pleaded with their fathers, and with William, to be allowed to join his household. Youths are ever drawn to lords who offer success and have proven themselves in battle. William had chosen the most promising of them and intended to put them through the same rigorous training he had received from old Osborn and his other tutors.

It was beginning to get dark and William was about to admit that they would have to set up camp for the night when a lone rider came galloping out of the trees at full pace. William's guards made to intercept him, but William recognised the man just in time.

"Stand down," he ordered them.

The knight waved them frantically out of the way. William touched his own spurs to his horse's flanks and went to meet him. FitzOsbern panted heavily from his ride, trying to catch his breath.

"William, Alençon!" he managed at length to say.

William's heart sank. They were too late.

"They have locked the gates. The harvest is all brought in and the land around is bare of cattle."

"You are sure it has fallen?"

FitzOsbern shook his head.

"It hasn't fallen," he said. "Not to the sword, anyhow. The Bellême flag and that of Anjou fly side by side."

William cursed. The Bellêmes – he had always known they were their own men, but even so, he had not expected them to side so openly with his enemies.

"Any other sign of Geoffrey's army?"

"Nothing," FitzOsbern said. "Not a soul outside the walls and I saw no evidence of a large force passing through there."

"They must have struck a deal beforehand, then, to hand over their town so soon."

"Traitorous scum!"

"The King will be none too pleased, either. You can be sure they will have closed the gates at all their castles," William said. "How far are we from Alençon, anyway?"

"Barely eight miles. The land falls down to a low valley around the town. You can clearly see it from the tree line."

"Good, I'll have word sent back to Montgomery. Tell everyone to get some sleep. I want them all up before dawn."

William turned his horse and headed back up the road along which his knights had been travelling. Far from being the short sharp attack he had hoped for, it looked unavoidable that this would be a series of long drawn-out sieges. That meant he had only one thing on his mind: food. Of course, he needed men, horses and weapons. Above all, though, he needed food. An assembled army could strip a land bare in the blink of an eye. It would have been bad enough moving through enemy territory, where such acts would be legitimate, but this was Normandy. He had to provide for his whole army; not just soldiers, but all those who went with them. Armourers, smiths, fletchers, bowyers, priests, squires, farriers – not to mention the inevitable straggle of wives and children – would all be mouths to feed. He only hoped that De Warenne had got on with his task. Heaven forbid the consequences otherwise. What kind of duke would he be if he brought a plague upon his own lands?

Dawn rose. William had spent much of the night despatching riders to the four corners of Normandy to hasten the reinforcements he had ordered and ensuring that the barons would cooperate with De Warenne in gathering provisions. He had at length returned to awaken his men before leading them forwards to the southern ridge of the woodlands which the locals call the Forest of Escouves. Conscious that the trees could hide many dangers, he had ordered scouting parties to scatter themselves at regular intervals around his lines. Anyone trying to get a message in or out of Alençon would have to make their way across the low plains around the town and would soon be spotted. Behind, though, the woods could offer safe passage to a whole army moving between Domfront, to the West, and Sées to the East; both were under the stewardship of the Bellême family. Sées should not cause too much trouble; it was a poorly protected place and, though its garrison could threaten his supply line, William guessed that they would want to keep a low profile in the hope that he would choose to concentrate his efforts on Alençon and Domfront. He was quite happy to oblige them.

Domfront, however, was a different kettle of fish. The indomitable giant stood towering over the dwellings below. With broad stone battlements and a solid keep, it was perched high on a mighty rock whence it would be looking for the approach of its prey. Yes, Domfront would be quite another thing altogether. At present, though, he had Alençon to deal with.

"Come," he said to his captains, "let's take a closer look."

They led their horses cautiously off the ridge of the forest, eyes searching the surrounding land for any hint of danger. None came. As they reached the low flat land, William had his troops fan out around the town. There was little chance of a surprise attack by the enemy, as they could see for miles. The only danger could come from within the town or from the woods behind them. Those woods had filled up during the night with reinforcements. Until he found a way of taking the town, with its wooden palisade on a high mound, his task was to prevent anyone from entering or leaving the town. There was no telling how long this affair would last; a short assault might break the place or the town could hold out in a long siege, forcing William to wage a war of attrition. Sieges are ever won by whoever has enough food to last longest. He set about isolating the town.

Fear and doubt is a great weapon. William would cut off the town's lines of communication so that the only news from the outside world would be that spread by his own messengers. He had his men set to digging trenches and cutting wood from the nearby forest to reinforce the earthworks with makeshift walls. Their defence would have to face both the town and the rear of their lines, for there was no knowing when Geoffrey of Anjou might come with a relieving army to try to lift the siege and resupply the town.

As they worked, William and FitzOsbern went as close to town as was safe. The soldiers and town folks had gathered atop the walls to see what their enemy was up to. It was too far to make out any faces, but the wind was low, as if the land held its breath.

"You poor men of Alençon!", William shouted to the townsfolk. "Your leaders have betrayed you. Anjou is no friend of Normandy. Whatever promises Geoffrey has made, be sure he shall honour none. Were he to win, he would do nought but rule you with a rod of iron. You would all fall under the Hammer of Anjou. Will you be guilty of refusing your rightful lord? And how will you answer the King? I am not an unjust man. As your duke, I make you this offer: open your gates, hand over your leaders and I shall spare your lives. You shall keep two thirds of your lands and your children will grow up in good health and honour. What say you?"

William waited.

"Do you really think the Bellêmes will let themselves be handed over?" FitzOsbern said. William shrugged.

185

"It can't hurt to put some doubt and dissent in their ranks. Even if they don't give in now, it's bound to fester when the hunger starts setting in. And you never know, we may just get lucky. Let's see what they have to say."

A single arrow flew down from the ramparts and struck the ground just in front of them. FitzOsbern's horse reared in alarm and he swore while trying to calm it. William chuckled.

"I take it that means no," he grinned at his friend. He drew his sword from his scabbard and held it high for the townsfolk and soldiers to see. "So be it. Behold the will of Normandy! Behold your retribution! The next to enter the gates of Alençon will be death."

They turned their steeds and re-joined their troops who were getting muddier by the minute digging the earthworks.

"Bigod, come here," William said to one of his barons who was organising the defence.

"My lord?"

"I will presently march on Domfront. Montgomery should be en route there as we speak. Can you manage with half the men here?"

"I should think so, my lord. They don't appear ready for a sortie against us and our scouts have reported no sign of Anjou's army."

"Good. If anything does happen, send word at once. I just need you to hold them. Do nothing unless you hear from me personally."

"As you wish, my lord."

"Get the men together, FitzOsbern."

CHAPTER 23

The larger part of the army trailed a long way down the road through the trees. William was eager to get to grips with the castle at Domfront, but at this rate they'd be lucky to be there in two days more.

"For God's sake, Arques, tell them to get a move on. This isn't a Sunday stroll through the countryside."

"It's not the easiest road to manoeuvre along. It was a mistake to march on Domfront so soon. The men are still tired from the road to Alençon. Why not let Montgomery deal with Domfront?"

"Because it is one of the greatest forts in all Normandy. I must take it myself."

"I'm not sure that there is much that you will be able to do at all. It has never fallen to an attacking army and the Bellêmes are no fools. They will have made provisions enough to last a year or more; of that I have no doubt. This was planned a long time ago."

"Well, we have little choice. We must break them one way or another."

"You will watch your army waste away, consumed with hunger and illness. And when you are at your weakest, Geoffrey will come with his army, fresh and at full strength, and they will ride your men into the dirt."

"You would still have me negotiate with the Bellêmes, but that I shall never do. As for Geoffrey, he has much territory to cover and many quarrels with his neighbours in the south. He may yet find himself overstretched."

His uncle raised an eyebrow.

"You would not listen to me when I advised caution during the great rebellion. Will you not listen to sense now?"

"I always listen to your advice, Arques, but a duke must make difficult decisions. What price would the Bellêmes ask? As for Geoffrey, he is not called the Hammer for his willingness to meekly negotiate. I have no doubt he would settle for an agreement. I am just as sure, though, that even if we were to give him Maine, it would not appease him. He would simply strengthen his hold there and lie low until such a time as he could strike us again with even more resources. So no; I will not negotiate with Anjou or Bellême. That is final."

Arques looked utterly disgusted, but knew William well enough to keep his peace. Just then, FitzOsbern caught up with them.

"It's no use," he said. "We'll not make it there for another two days at least."

"Are you getting nervous?" William teased.

"Just keen to teach the traitors a lesson."

"Aren't we all? Come on; let's see what the ground ahead is like. I leave you in charge of this rabble, Arques."

FitzOsbern waved to William's bodyguard who headed up the main road to escort them.

"No," William said. "I'm sick of this road. Let's see where this leads."

He headed for a track up the bank to the right of the road and into the forest. The knights followed, having to squeeze through one at a time. Further up the slope, the ground evened out and they started picking their way through the trees. William felt the cool breeze across his face. It was liberating not to have to wait

189

for stragglers or to have to supervise pushing carts out of ditches. He was a young knight with his companions, quite carefree, roving deep into the forest where time itself seemed not to exist. He felt as if this were a hunting party on the lookout for some quarry to pursue. Then he saw it; a lone stag stood atop a rock. William held his hand up and his party came to a standstill. He could not help but admire the beauty of the beast, proudly raising its head to the failing evening sun.

All of a sudden, the creature turned its head away. Its ears pricked. Then it was gone. William looked around, trying to make out what predator had startled it. There it was. A glimmer. Just a glimmer. William could not be sure. Had he imagined it? No, there it was again; the tell-tale sign of light glancing off a spear tip.

A dozen questions raced through his mind at once. Who were they? Why were they here at this secluded spot? Was this some lone knight or were there more of them? The obvious explanation was that these were scouts from Domfront or from Montgomery's force which he went to meet. It seemed strange that Montgomery's men should be hiding when they were supposed to be meeting up with William. Had they let a group of scouts from Domfront slip past them? It was unlikely. Everyone would doubtless be hidden behind Domfront's high walls by now.

He put his fingers to his lips so his men would keep quiet. He indicated that they should wait there and slid out of his saddle. FitzOsbern followed suit and the two of them crept through the dense woods, wincing every time they stepped on a twig. The noise seemed to amplify in these woods that were strangely quiet. Even the birds and beasts seemed to sense something out of place and had hidden themselves without a sound. Stealthily moving down the slope towards where he had spotted the light, they drew near the edge of the trees.

There, in a clearing, was a group of armed men, all mounted – not just half a dozen, but hundreds. They bore no banner, but their intent was quite obvious, as they were watching the road, just beyond the next line of trees at the bottom of the slope, ready to attack.

"Christ," FitzOsbern said under his breath. "How many do you make that?"

"One hundred? Maybe one-hundred and fifty? How many have we?"

"Thirty."

"They must have known we were coming today."

"Did one of their scouts spot our army?"

"I doubt it," William said. "Come on; let's go."

They carefully returned to their escort.

"So what do you want to do?" FitzOsbern said. William scratched his chin.

"They're expecting an army," William said, "so I say we give them one."

FitzOsbern grinned.

William had his small group of milites spread out. These were his closest and most loyal knights. They had fought by his side on the bloody fields of the Vale of Dunes. They had put their faith in him and been rewarded with victory and a share of the spoils. They knew the elation of seeing an enemy flee and wanted to feel it again. Not one of them questioned him when he told them what they were about to do. They made their group fan around the clearing in an arc. William gave the order.

"Charge!"

Spurs touched horses' flanks and the knights bellowed their war cry as they went crashing through the trees towards the large enemy force.

It was pure folly. Arques would be telling William just that, had he been with them. Why attack when he could simply return to his main army? The army was a long way behind, though, and William knew that the enemy would fall back if they did not see them before night closed in. He needed to see off the threat now while he knew where they were, or they would merely hide elsewhere on the morrow.

So with thirty men, he charged at one hundred.

They raged and rampaged, that small band of knights, eager to deal out death. The enemy, alarmed at such a chaotic noise, turned to see what awful foe had fallen upon them. And what did they see? Knights charging out from the woods around them. The very army which they had planned to ambush had turned the tables and were about to trap them as they would surely push them back onto the waiting spears on the road below, just out of sight. Faced with such a fate, the enemy made the only rational choice. They turned and fled, hoping to lose their pursuers in the depths of the forest. It was total mayhem as three hundred warriors made a bid for safety.

William knew that he could not risk putting too much pressure on the enemy; if he did not let enough of them escape, they would be forced to try and make some kind of stand. If that happened, they would soon realise how few men he actually had.

William was surprised at the speed at which they were able to get through the trees. Heading west in pursuit, he saw why; a second clearing lay just beyond the first. In that open ground they had more room to manoeuvre once they had passed the first line of trees.

"Prisoners!" William shouted to his men. "Get me prisoners!"

There were now only a few dozen rebels left on the nearer side of the tree line. William's men were out of immediate danger. He doubted that they would turn on them now, as they must have been counting their lucky stars for their escape.

"Leave them," he ordered two of his men who seemed eager to make their way through the trees. "Just get me prisoners."

The last rebels were almost out of reach when FitzOsbern thundered past William, roaring like a daemon, and hurled his spear hard into the hind of one man's horse. A shrill cry came from the beast before it threw its rider to the ground.

"Good man, FitzOsbern," William said, putting himself between the downed rebel and the only way to safety. He looked round to assess the results. Some two dozen rebels lay dead or wounded in the clearing – most were those who had been closest to them and had little time to react.

"Any dead?" he asked.

"Not among our lot," FitzOsbern said. "We've been damn lucky."

"You believe in luck?" William spat on the ground towards the fallen rebel. "These men died because they were too careless to post sentries behind them."

"They've cleared off, the rest of them," FitzOsbern said looking past William. "Just think," he said to the man on the ground, "if you'd all had your wits about you, you might have captured the duke of Normandy himself."

The rebel stared wide-eyed at William.

"But surely that was what you'd planned, wasn't it?" William leaned down from his saddle to meet the man's gaze. "You knew I was going to be on this road today, didn't you?"

The rebel kept silent.

"Very well; have it your way. I know one or two men who will take great pleasure in loosening your tongue."

William led his horse to the tree line. The second clearing had a lake on its far side. It was large enough for his army and made an ideal place to regroup. He would send messengers out to bid Montgomery join him there with the rest of the levies.

"Head back along the road and tell Arques we'll make camp here. I'll make sure the rest of them don't come back."

William turned to the young soldier who claimed to have grown up in one of the villages near Domfront. He needed someone with good local knowledge.

"What is this place?" he asked. They were looking at a small ruined building which stood at the edge of the lake. It was little more than a hovel, lost amid the overgrown nettle shrubs.

"It's a hermit's lodge, m'lord, built in the old days, when these woods were still young. It's said…" The soldier's voice trailed away.

"Yes? Go on," William said.

"Just rumours, my lord." He shook his head. "I won't trouble you with them."

"Go on," William repeated firmly.

"Well, it's said that only one man ever lived there; a troubled soul who'd committed an unspeakable sin. He came here to seek solitude and God's forgiveness."

"And did he find it?" FitzOsbern asked.

"He went mad, m'lord, in the end. One day, he just disappeared."

"Just like that?"

"So they say m'lord. But he still haunts the place," the boy said, before seeing the look on William's face. "Well, so they say, m'lord. D'you see?"

"I do indeed see," William said. He looked past the boy at his army setting up camp in the clearing. "Now you see this; I don't want a word of this superstition talked of in the camp. We have enough real enemies to deal with, without putting a ghost in Anjou's ranks. Is that clear?"

The boy's face flooded with colour as he mumbled an excuse.

"Right, now be off with you."

The soldier needed no more prompting, bowing his head before running off to find his friends.

"Are you afraid of the ghost?" FitzOsbern asked with a grin.

William raised a sceptical eyebrow.

"Come on; let's have a drink while they get the tents up."

The shrill scream filled the night air.

"There's no point being brave. It will only end in your death."
William looked the prisoner in the eyes as the red hot iron was

195

pulled away from a bare thigh. The smell of burnt flesh filled his nostrils. "You can still walk away with your life. I'll even let you join my ranks and make you a wealthy man. I can be very generous, you know." He let the man catch his breath as the pain subsided. "All I need is a name."

"I'll not stain my honour with betrayal," came the defiant reply.

"You already have. You have betrayed your duke, as I take it you are Norman."

"My allegiance is to my lord and to God."

"But your liege-lord is my vassal. He holds his lands from me. By extension, all that is yours comes from me."

"I'll say nothing."

William shook his head at such foolish stubbornness, before having the man branded a second time.

"Just tell me who told you I was coming," he said, when the cry had died away. "Then we can forgive the part you played in it."

William thought he saw a flicker of doubt in the man's eyes.

"Just kill him, William," Montgomery said. "He knows nothing and it will do the men's morale good to see an enemy swinging from a gibbet."

"Oh, he knows," William said. "And he'll soon speak if he has any sense."

He knelt beside the man and held out his flask of wine.

"Why protect someone who has left you for dead?" he asked the prisoner. "No rescue party has come. Three hundred men fled and not one tried to save you."

The rebel licked his dry lips, weighing his options. Footsteps approached and William turned to see Arques.

196

"So, who is the traitor?" his uncle asked.

"He hasn't told us yet."

"Best not trust anyone then," Arques said so softly that only William could hear.

William saw his uncle's glance at Montgomery, but pretended to ignore it.

"Think hard," he said to the prisoner. "You only ever have one second chance."

With that, he headed off to eat.

A hand clasped William's shoulder. He instinctively reached for his sword, in its usual place on the side of his straw mattress, only to have it knocked out of his hand.

"It's me, William!"

He sat up and stared through the darkness of his tent to see FitzOsbern looking down at him.

"What the Hell is it, FitzOsbern?"

"You'd better come and see this."

William followed his friend out into the early morning mist to the place where they had left the prisoner the previous night. He took a flaming torch from one of the guards and held it towards the rebel's face. Blood trickled from his slit throat to form a small pool around him. Beside him, one of William's guards also lay dead.

CHAPTER 24

William walked through the crowded streets of Rheims. The new Pope, Leo IX, had called a great ecclesiastical council in the city to make his mark upon the clergy. He was known for his views on simony, that pervasive practice of selling religious offices to the highest bidder, and his distaste for those priests who chose to take wives. This council would be his opportunity to stamp out those practices, once and for all.

King Henry was having none of it. He saw the council as nothing more than papal interference. For him, Leo was yet another meddling pope who sought to dictate his will to kings and princes, to set himself above all other men.

William had received the same message as all Henry's other vassal lords; they were strictly prohibited from allowing their clergy to attend the council.

The French king might as well have ordered a bird not to fly or a wolf not to hunt sheep. The lords of France may have cared little for the finer point of canonical practice, but this was an opportunity not to be missed for the world. They knew that such an assembly would draw lords from all Christendom to Rheims. In one week, they would be able to carry out more diplomacy than in years of slow negotiations which required envoys to travel for weeks just to bear one message.

The merchants knew it too. They had been drawn to the city like bees to honey, sensing profit on an unparalleled scale. They rubbed their hands thinking of all those lords; some rich, some eager to present themselves as rich, some in need of hard cash and ready to sell for the lowest price.

And so William now walked through the streets of Rheims in what resembled not so much an ecclesiastical gathering as the largest market he had ever seen.

His men were back at Alençon and Domfront, entrusted to the command of his uncle Talou, in what was turning out to be a long, slow game of siege, which would be decided by who gave up first. It was no easy thing to keep two besieging armies fed. They were already being tightly rationed, for the sieges might last years.

And here William was, surrounded by the finest produce silver could buy. There was wine from Burgundy and Champagne, cider from Brittany and Normandy, mead from England and beer from Bavaria. Trestles heaved under the weight of foods of all kinds laid out to feed the many travellers who were arriving in droves.

Stalls were covered with woven cloth from Flanders and fine silks from the East. Spices William had never even heard of were being sold by eager merchants from Africa, that arid land William was told was nothing but an endless world of mountains made of sand. There were jewels of the most intricate detail he had ever seen, set with precious stones of all the colours imaginable.

William made a note to buy some for his future wife later on; it was only right that Normandy's first proper duchess should have jewels befitting her status. He would leave no man who saw her in any doubt that she was *his* wife, with all the noble blood she would bring his future offspring.

He looked up. Towering above the town was the great cathedral of Rheims. It was where Henry himself had been crowned - a further insult to this king who could not even control his own lands effectively.

William's uncle Robert, the Archbishop of Rouen and prelate of the Norman Church, had travelled to the city a day early and was no doubt inside the cathedral, taking part in debating the matters of the church. Let them talk, William thought, just so long as Lanfranc found time to sway the Holy Father to his will.

William's own reasons for coming were to ensure that his new alliance with Flanders did not waver before the marriage could take place. Baldwin was used to lengthy negotiations, of course. Still, William was not going to risk losing Matilda now.

He turned down a side street and found the house he had been looking for.

"Tell your master that Duke William of Normandy wishes to see him," he told one of the guards at the door. The man looked at William's escort of half a dozen knights, led by FitzOsbern.

"Wait here," William told them, before following the guard in without invitation.

As he stepped into the main hall, he found Baldwin deep in conversation with another man. He was of medium height and solid build, about William's own age. He was well-dressed, with a rich emerald tunic. His crimson cloak was bordered with an elaborate pattern and clasped with a broach of solid gold. He wore his light chestnut hair loose and had a thick moustache. William guessed that he must be from Denmark or somewhere thereabouts.

"Ah, my good Duke William," Baldwin said, hastily rising from his seat and striding across the room. He seemed somewhat flustered and William could not help but notice that his guest's face showed surprise at hearing his name.

William bowed to the Flemish count.

"Count Baldwin, it is a pleasure to see you again so soon."

He looked over at the guest.

"Oh, forgive me," Baldwin said, "allow me to introduce Tostig Godwinson, just arrived from England."

It was William's turn to be surprised. So this was one of Godwin's sons - the very Godwin who had betrayed the Ætheling Alfred to his death all those years ago. William could still remember the day Edward's brother had set sail on his ill-fated attempt to take back his rightful throne from the Danish usurper.

"I am honoured," William said, forcing himself to bow to the Englishman.

"The honour is mine, I assure you. Now," Tostig said, turning to Baldwin, "if you will excuse me, I have business to attend to elsewhere. I am sure I will see you at this evening's feast, my lord. We shall talk again then, if it pleases you, on this happy union."

"We shall indeed," Baldwin said.

Tostig bowed again to both men, before making to leave.

"Oh, my lord Tostig," William said, as the Englishman was heading for the door; "a word of caution. Some years ago, a friend of mine found, at his expense, that the journey back to England can be a dangerous one - even for a man of more noble blood than yours. So take care, my lord. I should hate it for England to lose another lord that way."

Tostig stiffened at William's reference to the Ætheling Alfred - and the implied accusation. He forced himself to put on his best courtly smile under his bushy moustache.

"I thank you, Duke William, for your advice. I trust we shall meet again one day."

"I am sure we shall. Give your father my best regards."

Baldwin pretended not to notice the barb in their voices, as he motioned for William to take the place Tostig had just given up.

"So, my lord, what brings you to my humble lodgings?"

"Does one need a reason to visit one's future father-in-law, my lord?"

"Of course not, my lord Duke."

"I am sure that it will not be long before your daughter and I receive the Pope's blessing," he said. "Unless..."

"Unless?" Baldwin repeated, confused. He followed William's glance to the doorway through which Tostig had just left. "Oh, I see! No, my lord, rest assured; it is a misunderstanding. Lord Tostig had come to ask for the hand of my sister, the lady Judith."

"Indeed? A most happy occasion," William said, meaning quite the reverse. So Baldwin was planning an alliance with the house of Godwin. No wonder he seemed uncomfortable, associating himself with William's natural enemy.

"I am fortunate to have found good husbands for both my sister and my daughter," Baldwin said, hoping to smooth things over with a compliment.

"Who was the pretty boy with the nose hair?" FitzOsbern asked, as William left the house some time later.

"That was Tostig Godwinson," William said through gritted teeth.

"What? I wish I'd known. I would have parted his head from his shoulders."

"Perhaps you'll get another opportunity one day, though I would much rather deal with his father directly."

"Come on," FitzOsbern said, patting him on the shoulder, "let's get a drink."

CHAPTER 25

CONTEVILLE, LOWER NORMANDY. WINTER, 1050 A.D.

William sat by the fire in the corner of the small hall. A warm sheepskin was draped over him and the smell of the animal filled his nostrils as the warmth of the fire dried the damp out of it. Rain continued to fall outside. He thought of his men, camped around the rebel-held towns which he had yet to break. He was failing them and, in so doing, making the threat of a victory for Anjou all the more real. As if that wasn't enough, he had yet to uncover who the traitor was. The man was still at large, somewhere, hiding behind the face of a loyal subject and no doubt plotting William's downfall.

It mattered little, though. Not now. Not here. Here he was safe, for this was the hall of old Herluin de Conteville, in which his mother lived in peace and modest comfort. Herluin was not the richest of men, nor the most powerful, but he was the best a tanner's daughter might aspire to - more than that, even. To marry a landed knight was quite an achievement. William's father had done well in making the match between them. Herluin had got new lands and Herleva had a home and a protector.

The flames crackled in the hearth as William lay back, mesmerised by his mother's work. Herleva was sat on a stool, with a distaff tucked under one arm, and busy spinning a spindle with the other. He watched as she put a new piece of wool on the forked end of the wooden distaff. Taking the loose end of the thread which was wound about the spindle, a short stick with a round stone at the end acting as a weight, she carefully pulled at some fibres in the new piece of wool and gently twisted them into the thread. The lightest of tugs showed that the thread was holding onto the woollen clump. With a confident flick of the wrist, she dropped the spindle, making it spin and thus tightening the sinews of wool. She recovered the spindle and pulled again at the bundle of wool, linking more fibres in and starting over again.

William smiled at her concentration and dedication to the task.

"Why don't you get a servant to do that for you, mother?"

She looked up and smiled back with motherly love.

"I've been doing this since I was a little girl," she said in the gentlest of voices. "More than one cloak which you have worn started its life in this way. Would you have us go cold?"

"You are mother to a duke now. I sometimes think you forget that small fact. You need never want for anything any more."

"My dear boy, how could I ever forget that? I see so much of your father in you."

William was touched. He had heard the compliment before, but from the person who had known his father the best, it truly meant something.

"Thank you, mother. So why work so hard?"

"I enjoy it; it keeps me occupied." She looked into the fire, eyes glazing over as if lost in thought. "It keeps my mind occupied, chases away the daemons."

William frowned. "What daemons?"

"It is no easy thing being mother to a duke, especially one of Normandy. I sometimes think that our people are cursed; cursed never to be at peace in a land of our own. We came here from beyond the seas, driven by a promise of peace in a fertile land.

We saw off the threat from the French, yet for how long have we fought amongst ourselves?"

"We fight against Anjou now," William pointed out. She merely smiled. It unsettled him, somehow, as if he was once again a little boy who did not understand the wide world.

"As you say, William. But when I'm spinning this spindle, it helps to banish the dark thoughts. You have your father's strength of mind. Strong men never lack bitter enemies, even amongst their own friends or kin."

William opened his mouth to speak when the heavy door swung open. A great furry shape stomped in growling.

"Argh!" It said. "Bloody freezing out there. When will it ever stop?"

"When you stop bloody swearing, Odo, no doubt," said another soaking wet form following it in before kicking the door shut behind it. "So we might as well start building an ark now."

"Now then, boys, is that any way to talk in the presence of a duke?" Herleva said.

"William!" Robert greeted his half-brother. "What on earth are you doing here? Shouldn't you be out fighting Count Geoffrey, the rogue?"

"Him and those traitors the Bellêmes," Odo put in. "I knew they were only ever out for their own interests."

"I think we all knew it was only a matter of time. No lord can faithfully serve three masters at one time; especially when one of those masters comes from the House of Anjou.."

"Still, you'll give them a thrashing, eh?"

"Oh I'll give them a thrashing. You needn't worry about that. For now, I've got them bottled up in Alençon and Domfront. I've left Montgomery to keep an eye on them."

"So why didn't they rise up in Sées also? They control that town too. Why let your men come and go so freely?" Robert wondered.

"Money and religion," Odo said. "Sées is on a vital trade route. If the Bellêmes are to survive, they can't afford to cut off such a rich source of revenues; road tolls, market taxes, and I would happily wager that the Bishop of Sées is not above selling religious pardons. All the while, they know William cannot attack a bishop's see without risking the Pope's displeasure; which is hardly something he wants to do when trying to get His Holiness to approve his marriage."

William looked approvingly at Odo. Such border politics were complex affairs when so many parties were involved, yet his brother clearly had a good grasp of the matter. Such cunning would serve him well.

"Come," William said to them both; "take some wine with us."

Odo and Robert were William's half brothers, in truth, as old Herluin was their father. Yet the two of them were as dear to him as any brothers could be. Herleva had made sure they did not spend too much time at court during their youth – William knew she feared for their safety. William was four years Odo's senior, with Robert a couple of years younger still. William could still picture Odo as a little boy trying to lift William's sword as he himself took a break from the quintain at which all squires are taught to practice daily. Now though Odo was of an age at which he could be expected to take on some real responsibilities. That was good, as William had decided to throw him straight into deep water.

The brothers filled their cups and pulled up stools, having dutifully kissed their mother who rewarded them with affectionate smiles.

"So tell us, William; what are you doing here?" Robert asked.

"You are not pleased to see me?"

"Of course I am, but you are in the middle of two sieges, preparing to face an army from Anjou at any day and trying to get married."

"The latter is the most dangerous, I might add," Odo offered.

"You can't really expect us to believe that you've come all this way just to share a flagon of wine with us."

"Not with the wine you drink, Robert," William teased. "You are quite right. I do have another matter to deal with."

"Which is?" Robert said.

"I have come to make Odo here –" he slapped Odo on the shoulder "Bishop of Bayeux."

Robert almost choked on his bitter wine. Their mother gasped. Odo himself just sat there, mouth wide open. William grinned with satisfaction at having caused such a reaction.

"Odo!" Robert said "Bishop of Bayeux?"

"Well why not?" William said. "I believe the office is within my gift."

"But he doesn't know the first thing about religious matters. He's hardly ever listened to priests, let alone trained to be one."

"That hardly matters, Robert. The previous man to hold that noble office was about as Godless as a man can be. He tried to unseat his lawful duke, my father and his own cousin, on more than one occasion."

"That's certainly true," Herleva tutted. "Hugo was faithless and far too interested in his worldly gains to be of any value to the Church."

"That's as may be," Robert said, "but is that reason enough to make poor appointments a custom?"

"I hardly think Odo would show the same disregard for the Church if he became one of its leading men," William said. "Besides, our bishops are as much landowners and barons as they are men of the cloth. They speak on my council and hold wealth and influence throughout the land. As such, I need men whom I can trust."

"Surely your scholar Lanfranc would be better suited to the task."

"Lanfranc is on business for me in Rome. I do not wish the see of Bayeux to lie vacant at such a critical time. Besides, I have other plans for Lanfranc."

"Plans? What plans?"

"Never you mind, Robert," William said. "Why are you so against Odo's appointment, anyway? Don't you want to see our brother elevated?"

Odo glared accusatorially at his younger brother. Herleva looked quizzically at him. Robert folded his arms, denial on his face.

"Of course I want Odo to succeed. But we have no lands and little experience in the great matters you deal with."

"Everyone has to start one day. I should not have been duke so soon, yet I am." He frowned. "Perhaps you are jealous."

"Certainly not!" Robert protested.

"There's no shame in admitting that you are eager to prove yourself too. That is the mark of any man who may rise later."

Robert's gaze drifted away into the fire.

"So, Odo; what do *you* say? Will you take up this great challenge? Will you serve your duke and your God as Bishop of Bayeux? Or do you also think that you are not suited to the task?"

"I will be honoured, brother… my lord duke."

Herleva went over to kiss Odo on the forehead, beaming with pride.

"Kiss your brother's hand, my son. You are to be one of his faithful men."

Odo knelt in front of William, who offered him his right hand, and kissed the ducal ring.

"Now drink some wine and cast away your sword. A man of God may not draw blood. Your formal ceremony will have to wait until you have been accepted into the orders."

"My brave boys." Herleva smiled. "My worthy Norman men."

Robert still looked morosely into the flames.

"Oh come, Robert; cheer up!" William said, with a sparkle in his eye. "Don't be so glum. I have not forgotten you."

Robert looked up as curiosity got the better of stubbornness.

"It may not have crossed your mind, yet, but the Bellêmes are not alone in rebelling. Other fellow Normans also chose to put their faith in Anjou. They made a very poor choice and will pay the price. Who then shall reap the rewards?"

"You?" Odo said mischievously.

"Perhaps." William conceded. "But I need good men to manage the lands. The Count of Mortain must have a good firm hand and be an honest man. The present holder of Mortain is a disloyal and dithering idiot. He will find that when all this is over, as it soon will be, my council has declared the forfeiture of his lands. And you, Robert, will take his place."

"Me? Count of Mortain?" he repeated incredulously.

"I would trust no one more than my own brothers. Don't let me down."

CHAPTER 26

WILLIAM'S CAMP AT DOMFRONT, NORMAN BORDER WITH MAINE. MARCH, 1051 A.D.

Drip. Drip. Drip. The sound of water running off the tent seemed interminable. William reluctantly accepted that he was not going to get any more sleep. He reached for his woollen tunic and pulled it over his shirt. He swung his legs over the side of the camp bed and checked them just before they hit the ground. Pulling on his leather shoes and tightening their straps, he grimaced. As he stood up, his feet went straight through the straw and sunk into the mud.

Mud. Every bloody day for the past month. Was this rain of biblical proportions a sign from God that he was transgressing? True, Domfront was technically in Maine, but as the Bellême family were custodians of both Domfront and Alençon, he could hardly have dealt with one and not the other. He cast the thought aside.

He called for a man to help him lift his heavy chainmail hauberk over his head and onto his shoulders. Though there was no sign of an imminent fight, the dangers of his adolescence had taught him caution. The bedraggled form of a sentry showed itself at the flap of his tent.

"Good morning, my lord."

"Only if you're a frog is this morning 'good' by any means," William grunted. The sleepless nights and poor meals had made him irritable.

He studied the man more closely as his eyes adjusted to the early morning light. His face was growing gaunt. Heavy bags under his eyes told of a night spent trying to stay alert on guard duty – any man caught asleep would be whipped. William was determined to maintain discipline. In such conditions, men needed an order to their day, or his army would wither. To look at this man, it was withering already. They had yet to see anything more than the occasional skirmish, yet his men were already turning into ghosts. The months that rolled by were intended to starve the castle of Domfront into submission. Perhaps the garrison was on the verge of breaking; William had no way of telling. What he did know was that his own soldiers were growing hungrier by the day.

Despite his ever-increasing efforts, the supply of food had become unreliable at best. Not four days ago, a convoy of grain coming down had been set upon and disappeared. He expected FitzOsbern back that noon at the latest to report on when the supply of grain due from Vire would be arriving.

"My lord?"

The sentry fidgeted. William realised he had been staring at the man for some time.

"Help me with my mail."

The hauberk donned, he strapped on his sword belt and set off to inspect the defences. As he left, he turned to the sentry.

"Find a fire to dry off your clothes and get some rest. I have need of good and loyal men. We may soon be in battle."

"My lord," the man nodded.

Why had William felt the need to tell the man they would soon be fighting? There was no sign of a coming battle. Indeed, the latest report from Anjou told him Geoffrey was still tied up in a war down on his southern borders, not here in Maine. He would not be coming to lift the siege any time soon.

He waded through the mud which had been turned into small trenches through the repeated trudging of men at arms going to and fro. He had chosen to stay in the bastion he had had built to the north of the town. This way he was the most visible to the people in the fortress-town above. He looked up at the beast astride its high rock. What he would not have given to storm it rather than wade in so much mud. To attempt it would be nothing short of madness. Still, the rain brought sickness, worsened by the lack of food, as though the land of Maine sensed an intruder and fought against him.

Yet what of the people locked up in that castle? How must they be suffering? It was weeks since anyone had last tried to smuggle in food. Their granaries must be running low. Yet they held out still. Was there something which he failed to see? He shrugged. Brooding served no purpose. He walked over to the wooden wall where a group of soldiers had clustered around the flames of a small brazier which crackled and steamed as they tried to get the damp wood to take. They greeted him.

"Any sign of FitzOsbern?" he asked.

"No, my lord. The Steward is not yet returned."

"SOLDIERS APPROACHING!"

The cry came from a sentry atop the parapet.

"Where away?" William called back, hurrying up to the walkway.

"East, my lord."

From out of the nearby forest came warriors of a bygone age. A full three dozen men with thick beards and flowing blond hair.

The early morning sun glinted off the heads of their great war axes. Many bore the great round shields which had fallen out of fashion in France. Among their number was a man with tonsured hair and garbed in fine cloth. Next to him was a younger man in a plain black robe. Even at this distance, William recognised the pair. He saw FitzOsbern had met them along the way and chosen to escort them to the camp.

"Open the gates!"

He rushed down the embankment, sliding in a less than dignified manner on his posterior in his haste. He ran across the yard to meet them.

"My lord bishop!" He greeted Robert of Jumièges warmly. The Norman had gone over to serve in King Edward's court in England. Edward always did trust a Norman over an Englishman, for which William could hardly blame him after Earl Godwin's actions. "Welcome back to France."

"Thank you, my son. It is indeed a great pleasure to see this land once more, though I see it is under the sword again."

"But a passing inconvenience. You have nothing to fear." He turned to the young priest, a man in his twenties. "Brother Osbern FitzOsbern! Welcome home!"

Osbern bowed. He did not look much like his father. He had chosen to leave soldiering to his brother and go into the Church. Perhaps his father's untimely death had pushed him towards the scriptures, yet he had never seemed quite suited to war, William thought. William FitzOsbern had inherited their father's solid frame and strong jaw, though Osbern had the same steely blue eyes with their unwavering resolve. That resolve was set on doing the bishop's work.

"Why don't we all go somewhere warmer?" FitzOsbern said. "Then you may care to hear the news from England. My men will look after *our other guest* while we talk." William noticed the gleam in his friend's eye, but could tell FitzOsbern wanted the news to come from the bishop, so he pressed him no further on that subject.

"Indeed, please Bishop, come to my quarters. They should have a fire on the go. And you also, Osbern. We have little food, but what we can spare is yours." He waved them in the direction of his tent and lingered a while to stay a few paces behind with FitzOsbern.

"What news of the grain," he asked in a hushed voice.

FitzOsbern pursed his lips.

"A bad business, William. A bad business. We found the convoy two nights ago – what was left of it, anyway. The guards and drivers were dead. Cut down by cavalry, to judge from the wounds to their faces and necks. Whoever did it knew they were coming and chose their place well. They did it by a shallow stream."

William grunted. Clever. After the ambush, they might have made off upstream or downstream. Either way, they would leave no tracks behind for William's men to follow.

"Who the Hell is doing all this? Anjou must have an inside man. I am sure of it now."

"Yet you still trust Montgomery?"

"Don't start that again, FitzOsbern. You have as good a cause to hate that family as any, but Roger is not his father, nor his brother."

"A Montgomery is a Montgomery. Treason is in their blood."

216

"He has done me good service."

"As his father did Duke Robert good service."

Their conversation was brought to an end as they joined the others in the tent. His uncle Arques had hurried to join them upon hearing of the Bishop's arrival. He looked as if he had got about as much sleep as William. The flap had been rolled up so that they might feel the warmth of a fire which a servant was tending to just outside. William had another bring them wine and food. He bade his guests sit down.

"So, what brings you to France?"

"We travel to Rome, Duke William."

"Rome?"

"For this purpose." The Bishop produced a piece of parchment with the seal of King Edward at the bottom and, at William's request, read it aloud. As he did so, William's eyes widened. He patiently waited for the Bishop to finish.

"Archbishop? You, a Norman, are to be Archbishop of Canterbury?"

"And prelate of the Church in England, that is correct."

"See how fortune turns," FitzOsbern said.

"But how is it possible? Surely Earl Godwin objected. He would have wanted one of his own favourites to take up the position."

"He did indeed," the Bishop said, "yet here I am, on my way to receive my pallium from the Pope himself."

"How did Edward manage it? He couldn't even choose his own queen, having instead to take Godwin's daughter."

"Listen to this next part," FitzOsbern put in, unable to help himself.

217

"Earl Godwin has far greater things to worry about than who is the new archbishop. He is banished from England, and his sons with him."

William looked at Arques to see his uncle was just as astonished as he was.

"How did that come about?" said Arques. "No man in England had a stronger position than he."

"That is quite true, yet the lords of England are far from united. The Earl Leofric of Mercia has many supporters. When Edward wanted to be rid of Godwin, he struck a deal with Leofric and the other earls that they should benefit from the downfall of Wessex. His only condition was that he should choose his advisers and the next archbishop. In exchange, Leofric sees the back of his old enemy Godwin, with the King's blessing, no less, and has a free hand to rule in central England."

"And the Queen? What of her?"

"The Queen, it seems, was much of the problem. Godwin hoped she would give the King a son, that a grandson of Wessex might rule the country. King Edward, as you well know, is of a feeble constitution. England's Kings are too often short-lived and many fear Edward will be no exception. If he dies while his son is not yet of age, Godwin will be *de facto* King. The son Godwin wished for has not come, though."

"So what has become of the Queen?" William said.

"Edward has given up on her. He never truly wanted her – it is said he has no appetite for her, preferring to seek comfort from God. Now he has decided his wife should do the same and has packed her off to a convent. If she takes vows – as she must – he will be free to take another wife and produce an heir. Of

218

course, he could never have taken such a course with Godwin still around."

"And you think he will take another wife?"

"Who knows. He seems quite disheartened. I wonder if he even has the appetite for any woman now. Which brings me to the reason for my making this detour." He waved to FitzOsbern, who promptly left the tent. "With your permission, my lord."

"Of course," said William, slightly puzzled.

After a moment's wait, FitzOsbern returned, with a firm hand on the shoulder of a young boy. The child could not have been more than five years of age. He looked around him with curious eyes at this assembly of powerful men. William saw the boy shiver.

"Duke William," said the Bishop, "this is Hakon Swegenson."

"Swegenson?" William said. "Do you mean...?"

"Yes, my lord. This is the child of Godwin's eldest son, Swegen. The same Swegen, you will recall, was sent away in disgrace by the King and his own father, for his actions with a certain abbess. Yet Godwin kept his grandson near him. It seems he and Harold, his second eldest, are fond of the boy, in spite of his father's sins."

"Come closer, boy."

FitzOsbern pushed the reluctant child towards William.

"You are supposed to kneel to a Duke," William said sternly in Latin, so the boy might hopefully understand.

The boy's lower lip began to quiver, but he obeyed.

"Now, look at me, that I may see your face. So... You are Godwin's grandson, are you? Firstborn of the next generation of traitors. I wonder if it would not be kinder to kill you now and save us much future trouble."

With this William drew his sword. The boy eyes opened wide in fear of the long steel blade. William stood up and placed it on Hakon's shoulder before drawing it back to strike. The Bishop looked appalled.

"But no," William said, gently lowering his blade. "An innocent boy cannot be made to suffer for his grandfather's villainy. When you sin for yourself, boy, then I will punish you. For now, you will be in the care of my priests. They will teach you to obey God's law."

"Indeed, Duke William," the Bishop said with no small relief, "King Edward bade me place the child in your care, while his father's family is abroad."

"I shall be sure to keep a close eye on him. I only hope for his sake that Godwin behaves himself." He turned back to the boy. "You realise why you are here? You are here so that we may be sure that your grandfather does not try to harm the King. If he does, then I shall have to kill you, whether I want to or not."

The boy shifted uneasily. Just a lost boy in a foreign land, as Edward himself had once been when the Dane took power in England. Youth ever pays for the reckless choices of the old. Such is the way of the world.

CHAPTER 27

The rain which William had begun to think would never cease had finally stopped. Now Normandy was shrouded in a sullen mist which lingered in the air to chill the very bones. William hardly noticed it though, as he stood in the churchyard. He felt numb all over. His brother Robert, whom he had already allowed to have himself called Count of Mortain, stood beside him. Opposite them, their brother Odo was solemnly reading Latin from a large leather-bound Bible which an old monk held before him. In spite of the fineries which Odo wore as symbols of his high office, William did not see a Bishop of Bayeux; he saw only a grieving brother.

He looked down at the form which lay in a linen cloth in a small hole in the sodden ground. He pinched himself, hoping to wake from this living nightmare. His mouth felt dry. For all the deaths he had known in his childhood and on the battlefield, he still felt the raw pain of loss.

No one can replace a mother. Yet there Herleva lay in the earth. It was all so unfair. William was not ready to say goodbye. His mother deserved better than this. After all that she had given to Normandy, she should have had the grandest of ceremonies to mark her passing. Where were the crowds of tearful people? Where were the two-hundred knights with black feathers on their horses' heads? Where was the grand procession of monks from each and every religious house in the land?

Instead of the grand ceremony befitting a duchess of Normandy, Herleva had the burial of a mistress married off to a poor knight. Old Herluin of Conteville himself already had his place in the small churchyard, having died suddenly in the Autumn. Now the last chill of the Winter had brought his wife a fever from which her ageing heart had not recovered. So she went to join her husband, in this small forgotten corner of Normandy. Her assembly of clerics was her bishop son and one monk. Her grand procession of mourning knights were her two warrior sons. As the Latin faded, William knelt by his mother's grave and wept. He wept inconsolably – glad for a time of the lack of people to see their duke's weakness – feeling even more powerless than the child of seven who had lost his father. He ran his hands through the soaking earth piled up ready to cover the grave, driven by some compulsion to feel the blanket under which his mother would sleep from now on.

He felt Robert put a hand on his shoulder and grip tightly. William could tell it was as much a comfort to Robert as to himself. He at last forced himself to relent from sobbing, feeling totally dried of tears. A dull thump was the only sound to break the silence as Odo closed the heavy Bible. He walked away, followed by Robert. Only William remained there, unable to leave his mother's side. How long he stayed there, he could not tell. Time hardly seemed to matter any more. Eventually, he heard soft footsteps approaching.

"Come, William." Matilda spoke in the gentlest of voices. William turned to look at her.

"Are you still ashamed of who my mother was?"

"I was never ashamed. She did such wonderful work in producing such a son as you. She will be proud of you."

William looked upon his mother's body one last time, before the spades started to cover it up forever.

"Come," Matilda repeated, holding out her hand.

"I'm covered in dirt," William said apologetically.

"You are covered in your mother's Normandy, which is as noble a shroud as any," she said. "Come."

William stood up and the two lovers walked off, hand in hand.

CHAPTER 28

A HILL NEAR ALENÇON, LOWER NORMANDY. APRIL, 1051 A.D.

William lay in the dark watching the town, searching for any sign that the enemy knew of his coming. All seemed quiet. Save for the closed gate, anyone nearing Alençon might think it a town at peace. Normandy wore a veil of mist, making this an ideal night to attack. The news Roger Montgomery had brought William had been welcome indeed; a spy, having slipped out of the town, had told Roger of a weakness in Alençon's east ramparts. FitzOsbern had been sceptical, cautioning William against trusting Montgomery, but William needed to break the Bellême strongholds soon. A disturbing number of reports had reached him that Geoffrey of Anjou had put an end to his problems in the south of his lands and was now turning his attention back to Normandy. William could not risk a relief force arriving while his army was still divided between besieging Alençon and Domfront.

Keeping an army assembled for such a long period of time was having a devastating impact on his finances. The men needed paying. Food provisions were scarcer than ever. The nearby villages and towns were all growing mutinous at having troops draining their resources and pillaging for profit or entertainment. Only the other day William had had to hang three men for taking liberties with a farmer's daughter. He had promised his knights and sergeants glorious victory against Anjou. Instead they got months on end in tents that would never

224

dry, trudging on empty stomachs through mud that pulled men in to die of sickness.

William turned to look at the men he had brought with him. They looked half starved, yet there was fire in their eyes. Even the long march through the rain had not put out that flame. They were thirsty for their enemies' blood, eager to pay them back for what they had endured these many months past. They wanted blood and they would have it. There would be nothing subtle about this attack. No men could be spared from the besieging forces to make a diversionary assault on the far side. Instead, William had to place his hopes on the fog and the secrecy of his preparations. He would throw his forces at the eastern wall and batter it until it collapsed. The spy had told Montgomery where the weakest spot was and that was where they would concentrate their forces.

What if the wall didn't give way? William pushed the thought out of his mind. No matter how well or poorly prepared the garrison of Alençon was, he would smash his way into the town before noon. However many men it took, he would hurl them at Alençon's walls with more devastation than Joshua's trumpets. Far better to lose men to the sword than to morale-fraying disease. Beyond his men, all lying on the reverse slope of that hill near the town, William thought he could just make out the faintest glimmer. Dawn.

"Time to go," he whispered to FitzOsbern and Montgomery.

They nodded and sent word back down the lines.

William drew his sword; the blade rasping against the rim of the scabbard seemed the only sound in the night. A very quiet night, William thought. He kissed the blade near its guard where

225

the letters were etched into the metal. *Diex aie.* With God's help he would see victory.

As one man, the Normans rose to a crouching position. They slowly made their way over the crest of the hill. No one was foolish enough to talk, for arrows have a way of punishing indiscretion. Yet William was painfully aware of the noise they made as they went. Chainmail jangled, hooks rattled, spears knocked against shields as men clumsily searched for a footing in the dark. William felt terribly exposed. He was a skilled horseman, but horses serve little use against high walls. He had nonetheless kept a small cavalry group in reserve, hidden in the woods to the north with strict instructions to cover his retreat if things should turn ill.

What was that? William stopped dead in his tracks. He held up a hand and those behind him came to a halt. He thought he had heard something – some noise from the ramparts like a high-pitched whistle. As he looked up, he could see no one on the ramparts. That was odd. Something seemed wrong. He was not going to call off the attack now. He crossed himself and started forward again. He reached the ditch. In front of him was a small gate used to bring in the crops and for travelling traders. This was where the spy had told them to attack. A wooden bridge which had once spanned that part of the ditch had been destroyed. At the bottom, the defenders had sunk logs which they had carved into wicked spikes.

"Now," he hissed.

Men rushed up to the ditch and hurled in bundles of kindling and thatch stolen from the deserted houses on the outskirts off the town. The pile soon reached the top of the ditch, forming a small causeway for his men to cross.

"With me," he said, before leaping onto the makeshift bridge.

He caught himself just in time, as one of the bundles fell off to the side. His men followed close behind, keen to get into the town and away from that exposed ground in front of the walls.

"Bring up the ram!"

Six particularly burly knights hurried up to the wall with a battering ram. Before the heavy metal-capped log could be swung, a shout came from the ramparts above them, followed by a flaming torch arcing high over their heads, bright in the night sky. A dozen more were thrown down, lighting up William's assault party even on that misty night. The top of the wall soon filled with men – not partly-armed men caught by surprise, but a host of warriors clad in chainmail, with helmets securely fastened, belts strapped at their sides and carrying many spears and bows.

"Shields up," William shouted. "Shields up!"

Lifting his own shield above his head, he felt another connect with his.

"The scum knew we were coming," FitzOsbern said, bringing his shield closer to protect William. "I told you this was a trap. Never trust a Montgomery."

"A trap it may be indeed, but not one of Montgomery's making. I am sure of it," William said, glancing over to where Montgomery was trying to get ladders pushed against the walls, only to have the defenders push them back down.

"What do we do now?" FitzOsbern asked, grunting as an arrow's point drove itself through the wood of his shield.

227

"What we came here to do. Come on," he said, hurrying over to the ram. He held his shield over it, his men following suit, to give the bearers protection while they swung their charge. "Heave!" The ram crashed into the timbers.

"Heave!" Another thud. The wood, far from being rotten, had recently been replaced. The ram had little effect, bouncing off the timber. A spear thrown with considerable strength from the ramparts found a gap in the shields, hitting one of the men wielding the ram full in the chest. He was thrown back by the force of the impact, falling against William whose mail was splattered in blood. William swore, pushed the dying man out of his way and grabbed hold of the ram.

"Heave!" He rushed at the gate with all his strength, the other bearers doing the same, none wanting to be the man who let his duke down. A satisfying crunch told William they had at last done some damage. Again and again they hit the wall, but the gate stood strong. How could the bar of the gate not break with so much battering?

All the while, arrows, spears and stones came down around them, picking off anyone unlucky enough to be exposed.

Then came the jeering. It was indistinct at first, as men's words were lost in the wind and the noise of battle. Then William was just able to make out four words, repeated over and over.

"Hides for the tanner! Hides for the tanner!"

He let go of the ram, causing the other five men carrying it to buckle under its weight. Stepping back from the gate, he looked up at the surround from under the rim of his helmet. The defenders and townsfolk had brought up animal skins which they waved in his direction.

"Hides for the tanner!"

He felt cold rush through him. Standing in silence, he was unaware of the arrow which flew right past his face. FitzOsbern hurried over to cover him with his shield again.

"William, for Christ's sake; watch out!"

William nodded towards the ramparts. FitzOsbern, recovering his breath turned to see what had made his friend stop in the middle of a battle.

"Oh Jesus, William," he sighed. "I'm sorry."

"Sorry? Sorry for what? It is not of your doing."

"No but – "

"But nothing. My mother lies in the sodden earth and this scum think to insult her." He swallowed, fighting a lump caught in his throat. "Well if they take me for a tanner, then I will tan their hides alright."

The cold had turned to fire and with fire he would break them. He rushed over to the ditch and grabbed one of the bundles of thatch.

"Get out of the way," he shouted to the men nearest the gate, before hurling the thatch against it.

Seeing his plan, FitzOsbern called some men over to help lift bundles out of the ditch and pile them against the wall. One unfortunate knight was struck with an arrow as he leant over the ditch. The blow, though not piercing his mail, pushed him off balance. The poor soul fell into the ditch, impaling himself on one of the spikes. The ditch being robbed of its makeshift bridge, they would now have no way of falling back. They would have victory or death.

FitzOsbern picked up two of the torches which had been thrown down from the ramparts and joined William at the gate.

"Shall we?"

They thrust the torches into the thatch. The thatch was damp and smoked so much that they had to step back. The rain of arrows relented, though, as the archers on the walls could not see for the smoke. William smiled to himself as flames gradually sprang to life. Growing bolder and bolder, they reached up, dancing against the gate. Above them, someone shouted for water. It would be too little too late. The fire burned hotter and soon the timber of the gate itself caught fire. A fetid smell lingered; the fur on the hides was smouldering and shrivelling from the heat.

"Burn it all to the ground, FitzOsbern. Burn the town to ashes."

The Norman knights and men-at-arms, full of blood-lust, were now hurling torches and flaming bundles of thatch over the low ramparts. Screams echoed within the town, piercing the night air. Plumes of smoke rising from within told of houses catching fire.

"Send word to our cavalry," William said to FitzOsbern. "They're to ride over to the western gates and stop anyone escaping. Send a good man. If he's quick, he should be able to climb out of the ditch under the cover of this smoke."

Montgomery came to join them. William noted the sour look FitzOsbern gave him as he went off to send out the order. Did FitzOsbern have a point? Could Montgomery have deliberately led them into a trap? If so, why would he have come himself to die?

"My lord," Montgomery said, "we can't stay here long. The smoke will soon clear. Why not try sending a force against the western gate or the fort above? They would not expect that and we can be confident they will have neglected that side of their defences."

"You would lead them?"

"I would, my lord, if you so order."

There it was, William thought. He had found his traitor, the one behind the disruptions to the grain supplies. It all made sense. FitzOsbern had warned him, but he had been wilfully blind. Roger was clearly doing his father's bidding. What better way to break William than inciting a rebellion and leading him into a death trap where no one could accuse him of murder? Men die in battles. That is the way of things. William still could not bring himself to believe it.

"My lord?" Montgomery had a puzzled expression on his face.

William patted him on the shoulder.

"I was just thinking on what you said. Thank you, but no; we shall not risk dividing our forces. We shall soon be within the walls. Once we are, the town will fall. You will stay close to me."

"Honoured, my lord."

William would deal with him later.

"It's done," FitzOsbern said, rejoining them.

"Excellent. Now, let's teach these fools a lesson. Form up! Shields on me!"

His men did not need telling twice. These were the veterans of the Vale of Dunes and had seen him snatch victory from the jaws of defeat. They trusted him to deliver again. Shields locked into place around him.

"Ready? Charge!"

He ran at the gate and reaching it, threw his whole weight behind his shield. The men pressing behind him and the impetus of their charge ripped the gate open, its doors falling right off the charred timbers to which they had been secured. William stumbled over something. Whether it was a defender's corpse or a piece of debris, he neither knew nor cared. He struggled to stay upright and continued to advance. Soon he was checked by a hard strike against his shield. He thrust his sword out instinctively and felt it grind into the links of a mail hauberk. A sudden release of pressure told him it had broken through to skin. He pulled the sword back and continued to press on, knocking his enemy to the ground. A small cry told him the man behind him had finished the job with a sharp stab.

"Normandy," he shouted. "Normandy!"

His knights echoed the war cry, smelling victory.

A heavy weight knocked into his shield, forcing him to bend his knees under the strain. A blade swung overhead, knocking his helmet askew. He swore and pushed hard against his assailant. Next to him, FitzOsbern stabbed out at the man, who parried his blow.

Seizing the moment, William crouched down, lifted his shield and leapt up, putting all his strength behind his blade. The sword buried itself deep into the rebel's unprotected groin. Warm blood covered William's hand as he struggled to free the weapon from the enemy, who fell to the ground and lay writhing in spasms of agony until FitzOsbern dealt the mercy blow.

Seemingly out of nowhere, a knight charged on horseback towards William's small group. FitzOsbern was aware of it too late, as the knight knocked him to the ground. William stepped forward to protect his friend, only to be kicked hard in the shoulder by a flailing hoof. Clutching his shoulder in agony, there was little he could do but watch the knight wheel round to kill FitzOsbern. The spear was poised to strike him full in the chest when William saw something fly overhead. It was a sword which would have cut the man's arm off, had it not first struck into his shield. Turning to see who had thrown it, William saw Montgomery running unarmed towards the knight who was struggling to free his shield of the weight of the sword which had embedded itself in it. The man turned his attention back just in time to see Montgomery. He tried to bring his sword up, but Roger was already beyond its point. He grabbed the knight's leg and pushed hard, throwing him out of the saddle. Having slapped the horse's hind so that it bolted away, he picked up the spear which had fallen and mercilessly drove it into the man's throat so hard that it pinned him to the ground. After a gargling sound and a few violent spasms, the knight lay dead. Montgomery recovered his own weapon and pulled FitzOsbern to his feet. William, recovering, could hardly tell which of them seemed most uncomfortable. FitzOsbern nodded his thanks, astonishment on his face.

William gritted his teeth against the pain and pulled himself up to find his next opponent. There were none there to fight. He turned to see the rampart nearest the gate deserted and more of his men flooding onto the surround from the ladders which were at last staying up.

He walked over to the fallen knight and pulled the man's helmet off.

"William Bellême," he muttered. "Well, well. Now you see the value of Geoffrey Martel's friendship. Go look for help from Anjou now."

"No mercy," he said to his men. "Take want you want. This town will be no more."

Thus he unleashed his soldiers to take out their anger on Alençon. He dropped his shield and, holding his sword by the blade in his left hand, walked over to a brazier which burned nearby. Screams began to ring out through the town in a death knoll. Looking into the flames, he thought of those wretched men who had cursed his mother's name. With a smile, he picked up a torch, and plunged it into the flames until it was fully lit. "I did say burn it all, FitzOsbern."

"You did indeed, William."

"Make sure you find me some live prisoners."

He ran towards the nearest house and hurled the torch, which blazed through the air in a high arc before landing in the thatch. He watched with relish as the fire began to consume it. Throughout the town beyond, buildings were soon set alight.

That morning, Normandy awoke to a fire brighter than any sun.

CHAPTER 29

William felt utterly exhausted. Two days and two nights of hard marching, followed by a dawn assault which ended in fire and blood, had left him drained. All he wanted now was to sleep. He sent men to find lodgings where possible. Some of the houses on the western side had just escaped the flames, though fires still burned in places. William was stood atop the small tower which overlooked the town. The stench of charred wood and burnt flesh filled his nostrils. It was to him like smelling roses. It was the sweet scent of victory over those who had thought to overthrow him for a foreign purse and had sought to sully the memory of his mother.

He turned his back on the town, looking out instead at the plain beyond, where gentle rolling hills should have been home to field upon field of grain and cattle. From the ashes of Alençon would Normandy grow anew. William was sure of that. He would settle loyal men here, though no fort could stand. His present lookout post would be torn down, for he would not risk it falling again into the hands of iniquity.

Squinting in the morning sun, he could just make out a group of riders coming up to the crest of one of the hills to the south. Travellers? He dismissed the notion; no one with any sense would head towards so great a plume of smoke. Were these Geoffrey's scouts, come to see what forces William had? They continued to draw near and did not hesitate to ride right up to the gates. The sentries William had posted further out intercepted them. After a brief discussion, they were allowed through.

A few moments later and William smiled as his guest climbed up the wooden steps to join him.

"God, I see, has granted you victory, my good Duke." Lanfranc smiled heartily, though the bags under his eyes told of weary weeks spent on the road back from Rome.

"He has indeed, though we have paid for it in Norman blood." William looked down at his hands, covered in small cuts. His chainmail had links broken all over it. Down in the ditch, the bodies of some eighty commoners waited to be buried. The crows had not wasted any time in feeding. The bodies of the dozen knights who had fallen had been removed with more solemnity to a church which miraculously remained standing in the centre of the town.

"And what news do you bring me from Rome? Did the Almighty grant you victory there?"

Lanfranc looked down at the smouldering town, his usual grave air returning.

"His Holiness *was* kind enough to grant me an audience. He explained to some extent the ecumenical concerns which led him to prohibit your intended marriage, my lord."

William clenched his hands on the parapet, liking little the way Lanfranc was headed.

"It seems," Lanfranc continued, "that His Holiness wishes to redress the blatant disregard for doctrine which has of late spread like a rot through our great Church. As you know, he sought at Rheims to put an end to the flouting of God's laws, such as the celibacy of priests. In the same manner, he does not feel he can endorse a marriage which is not canonical."

"I see," William said through gritted teeth. "And what did you answer to that?"

"I agree wholeheartedly with His Holiness that it is a practice which ought to be stamped out."

"You said what?" It was all William could do to stop himself from seizing the Italian there and then and throwing him off the ramparts into the flames below.

"I have never made any secret of my beliefs, my lord Duke. The true values of our beloved Church are ever more tainted with the worldly ambitions of men. Unless we bring Christians back to the righteous way soon, I fear we might slip back into the darkness of pagan ways."

"And you thought that the best way of serving your lord, did you?"

"Above all earthly lords, I serve the one true spiritual Lord."

"So it was pointless, was it?"

"Not quite, my lord. I explained to His Holiness that Normandy needs a strong and virtuous prince to rule over it; only that way could faith and order be restored to the Church and the land of Normandy. I gave him my word that you were a true lover of the Church and a faithful servant of His Holiness. I also extolled the many learned virtues of the lady Matilda, insisting that so wise a daughter of Charlemagne could only ever be a force for good."

"And?" William's patience was wearing thin.

"And His Holiness requests that you follow my advice on ecclesiastical matters. Provided that you make some penance for your sins and follow the laws of God, he is prepared to lift the Papal ban on your marriage to the lady Matilda in this... unique circumstance."

William could hardly contain himself. He threw his arms around the cleric and thumped him hard on the back.

"Thank you, Father Lanfranc! Thank you! You have done that which I would have entrusted to no other. I shall not forget it."

"And the penance, my lord Duke," Lanfranc cautioned him, though the faintest hint of a smile was visible at the corners of his lips.

"Yes, of course. Of course we shall make a penance." William looked once more over the town. His eyes caught on the cross which stood up from the Church. "We shall found abbeys, Matilda and I. We shall found such abbeys as to be the envy of Christendom. The work will be instructed as soon as this war is over. I had already intended to build up the town of Caen, that I may strengthen my hold on Lower Normandy. Now, together, we shall build the town with God's word at the heart of it."

Lanfranc seemed satisfied. After a tactful pause to let William appreciate the news, he cleared his throat.

"Yes, Lanfranc?" William could hardly concentrate on anything else, even forgetting his tiredness.

"My lord, you made one other request of me for my visit to Rome."

William's smile faded. He turned sharply to look into the Italian's eyes in an unspoken question.

"Yes, my lord," Lanfranc said. "I have found out who raised the complaint with His Holiness. The Pope himself could never, you understand, break the solemnity of the confessional."

William took the hint in Lanfranc's raised eyebrows.

"I would never dare imagine such a thing. Let us suppose you heard a rumour while on your travels," he said with what was the closest he could come to an earnest expression.

"Let us suppose so. It seems that, upon his banishment, your cousin Guy did not return to Burgundy. He found refuge elsewhere before travelling on to Rome."

"Guy? So that is how he thanks me for sparing his life."

"Indeed, though it appears it was not his idea."

"I can well believe that. My foolish cousin possesses not the intellect for such cunning."

"Quite." Lanfranc paused, unsure of whether to continue.

"Spit it out, then."

"I regret to have to inform you that someone much nearer to you is behind this."

"Montgomery," William muttered. "I still can't believe it."

"It was not Roger Montgomery, my lord. It was your uncle, the Count of Talou and Arques."

"Arques? A traitor? Not possible. He has served me loyally since my childhood."

"It is possible, my lord. Indeed it is true."

"Why should he turn on me now after so many years of protecting me?"

"Because, my lord, you no longer need protecting. Therefore, you no longer need him. So long as you were not of age, he had control of the land. He was prepared to stand by you at the Vale of Dunes for the simple reason that you were following his advice, however reluctantly. He must have thought that he could retain some control. Now you are a Duke in your own right and with your own mind. Though I trust you will continue to seek council from those around you, you are no longer bound to one man alone. That you might now marry a lady of good breeding and sire an heir? That is a thought which repelled him."

William ran his hand through his red hair. How could he have been so blind?

"Of course," Lanfranc said after a moment's hesitation, "this also raises the question of how far his treachery went. That he was behind the delays to the grain supplies is certain. FitzOsbern told me, when I arrived, of the circumstances which led you to attack here. A spy? Your uncle must have sent him to dupe Montgomery. That you won in spite of it is surely a sign that God approves of your plans."

"Anything else?"

"The thought did occur that, as he was so eager to control the Council…"

"Jesus Christ," William muttered, before quickly begging the cleric's pardon. "You think he was responsible for my guardians' deaths? For my great-uncle the Archbishop's?"

Lanfranc shrugged.

"We may never know, my lord."

"I could now think him capable of the darkest of deeds. He was with my father when he died. Osbern was always evasive on the subject, as though he had thought something awry."

"Perhaps it would be best not to speculate. It serves little purpose. You have all you need to arrest him; the word of the Pope, no less."

"Now I can appreciate true loyalty. FitzOsbern has been baying for my uncle's blood for years. This time he may have it."

240

"Indeed, your steward has already served you well. Without his watchful eye, who's to know what Arques might have tried?"

"Loyalty, my good Lanfranc; nothing deserves so much reward when given, nor so much punishment when forgotten."

A scream sounded from within the town. Then came another. Again and again was the calm of midday broken by the chilling sounds. William sensed Lanfranc shudder beside him.

"My lord," he said, "what...?"

"The townsfolk and garrison," William said, with no expression other than a slight smile. "They mocked my late mother and I promised that I would have their hands and feet cut off for that insult. Do you know, I don't think they truly believed that I would actually go through with it? But I would be a savage indeed not to do so. In punishing these few men who are guilty of treason, I send out a message to all who would defy me. If the threat of such treatment dissuades them from raising the sword, then I save not only Normandy but their very souls. Is that not just of me?"

"God must surely forgive this one act of cruelty if it is to ensure future peace."

"Amen," William said. He thought Lanfranc was perhaps less convinced by his own words than William was himself, though.

"I told you Arques couldn't be trusted!" said FitzOsbern.

"He's family," William snapped. "I couldn't very well arrest him just because you had a bad feeling. He always served my father well and he continued to appear loyal throughout my minority."

"He's always coveted your coronet, you know he has. He was just too wily a fox to get caught."

"You can drop the insolent tone right away. I did the only thing I could do without evidence."

William knew his friend was right, but he was damned if he was going to admit it. After all, what could he have done? Arques had not yet been caught committing any crime, though William was sure to uncover more than one in his digging into his uncle's affairs."

"So," FitzOsbern said, "what's to be done now?"

"What else would you have me do with a criminal? He's to be arrested."

"Arrested? Why not just slip a knife between his shoulder blades? He doesn't know we're onto him and it will save the mess of a trial."

"He is a lord of Normandy, the son of a duke and a member of my council. His treason must be exposed publicly and his punishment deemed lawful and fitting."

"A dagger in the dark was good enough for Ranulf. Why have it any different for Arques?"

"Because Ranulf was different. His treachery was personal. His motives were inherently malevolent. He wanted to kill me for his own satisfaction. Arques is a lord who has grown too big for his boots. He is rejecting my authority to enhance his own, of course, and must be publicly punished. But it is purely political."

"I don't know how you can be so calm about this!" FitzOsbern said. "I really don't. Your own uncle turned against you, tried to overthrow you, yet you don't want his death."

"Families will always feud where power is involved. Normandy has seen it before and we will no doubt see it again. If I have him murdered, it will merely cause grief and his supporters will turn on me like dogs. If he is shamed, though, in public with incontestable proof as to his guilt, then they will think twice before supporting him. Rats will always flee a sinking ship. They need to preserve their own interests."

"Fine," FitzOsbern said. "I'll assemble my men at once. I'll have him in chains before the next sun down." He turned and picked up his shield.

"Hold!" William ordered. FitzOsbern stopped in surprise. "You're not going. I've already sent Montgomery to arrest him."

"Montgomery? Why him? You trust him with such a task?"

"Because you're too eager. It's all too personal for you. You have always wanted to see him fall and I need someone who can keep a certain distance on this one."

"So you don't trust me."

"I would trust you with my life. You are a brother to me. I need Arques to come as quietly as possible and he would never hand himself over to you."

William could tell his friend was hardly satisfied with the explanation.

"Rest assured though, FitzOsbern; I will make sure that you have plenty of time to gloat later."

The young steward smiled at the thought.

"As you command, William. But if he tries to slip the knot, I get to drag him back by the scrotum."

"Done," William said, smiling back at his friend.

"So what do we do now?" FitzOsbern asked.

"Now, we take Domfront and take it fast, else Geoffrey will beat us to it." William said. "We can't risk him reinforcing it. If he

243

bases his army there, he'll be able to strike right at the heart of Normandy."

"Excellent. Good idea. Just one question: how are we going to do that? Fire won't work against Domfront's stone walls. And it's built high up on a cliff with only a steep and narrow path leading up to it, we can't get siege engines within range and the place is bristling with spears."

"Don't you trust me?" William asked with a smile.

"Of course I do. I always have."

"So are you afraid then?"

"Never," FitzOsbern said, appalled at the very notion. "But we'll have to think of something, or the men will be cut to pieces. Geoffrey will be able to stroll over and take the rest of the duchy single-handed."

"I'll think of something, don't you worry," William said, with more confidence than he felt.

"Just so long as you're sure."

"We have no choice. The men are dropping like flies from illness and lack of food. Geoffrey is said to be on the move and I won't have an army to fight him with unless I take Domfront soon. I would sooner lose men to arrow and spear than watch them waste away."

FitzOsbern nodded.

"I can't fault you on that, William. In fact, I'm sure every one of the men feels the same way. Even the cowards know that staying in damp trenches or soggy tents will be the death of them."

"Hmm. Anyway, after Geoffrey, there's my uncle to deal with. I can't afford to give him the time to gain support. I must show

244

strength now. This victory has at least raised the men's spirits. They might as well die at Domfront while they are still keen to go."

He looked back at the smoking remains of the tower.

"Tell the men they have one hour to pillage and find what food they want. Then we leave."

CHAPTER 30

Night was closing in around them as they arrived at the clearing by the old hermit's home. William had to send riders to the rear to make sure none of the stragglers took the opportunity to skulk away into the darkness. He would need every man to break through the gate – if they ever got that far. On the path leading up, ten good men might hold back an army long enough to die of old age.

"Any news, De Warenne?" he asked the captain he had left in charge of their besieging force. De Warenne was still young, perhaps in his late twenties, and full of the confidence that youth gives. William knew he was ambitious, but also cunning. He was pleased De Warenne had tried nothing foolish in his absence.

"No news, my lord. The mud is still sloppy. The men are still ill. The enemy is still shut up in the castle."

William grunted.

"We'll wait here for the rest of the army to catch up," he told FitzOsbern. "As soon as everyone has had a chance to arm themselves properly, we'll attack."

"Attack my lord?" De Warenne raised an eyebrow.

"Why, De Warenne; did you have something else planned for this evening?"

FitzOsbern grinned at De Warenne's discomfort.

"No, my lord. Of course not. I wish you had sent word, though; we might have made more preparations."

"I didn't want to risk a leak. Not after Arques."

"Of course, my lord."

"And I did tell you to have a battering ram ready and waiting at all times. You do have it, don't you?"

"Of course, my lord."

"Then go and fetch it."

With that De Warenne hurried off.

"So what are we going to do?" FitzOsbern asked.

"I told you; don't worry. With any luck we'll catch them off guard. They won't know we're here yet. No camp fires!" He barked the last order loud enough for his captains and sergeants to relay it. He didn't want to light up his army for the enemy to see or for his men to get cosy. "I'll be back. Keep an eye on the men."

FitzOsbern knew better than to question him.

William walked over to the lake. Behind the old hovel, out of sight of the soldiers, he let out a heavy sigh and put his head in his hands. How the Hell was he going to take Domfront? Even if he reached the gate, the doors seemed solid enough to take a month's battering without giving in, and all the time arrows, spears and rocks would be pouring down on them. He thought of all those men who had followed him thus far. By the morning, most of them would be dead. He could not let them go home, though. Geoffrey was approaching. He could feel it in his very bones. If they abandoned Domfront, it would be tantamount to letting Geoffrey march in and take whatever he wanted. The families in this area and perhaps the whole of Lower Normandy would be at his mercy; he was not called Geoffrey the Hammer for his kindness. So William would lead his soldiers to their deaths and be in front of them every step of the way. No leader can expect his men to do what he himself is not prepared to do.

William sank to his knees and prayed. It was as good a plan as any, for nothing short of a miracle would bring victory here. As he lifted his head, some movement on the far bank of the lake caught his eye. Across the shimmering water, he could just make out the shape of a man. He blinked and it disappeared. A shiver went down his spine.

"FitzOsbern! De Warenne! To me!"

A moment later, they appeared at his side, panting heavily. FitzOsbern had drawn his sword.

"What is it, my lord?" FitzOsbern addressed him formerly in front of De Warenne.

"Someone's out there." He nodded to the place where he'd seen the dark shape.

"A lone man, was it?" De Warenne guessed. William nodded.

"So you've seen it too, my lord," De Warenne continued. "It's the ghost of the mad hermit. He's been seen more than once these past months."

"Don't be a damned fool," William spat. "We're being watched! Send someone after him before he alerts the castle. Quick, man!"

De Warenne blanched and shouted at the nearest troops.

"God help us from superstitious fools," William said.

"Let's hope he helps us up there as well," FitzOsbern said.

"This will make things that bit trickier."

"Yes, because it was going to be so easy," FitzOsbern said. William grunted.

"Come on, let's get it over with. And pray it was a ghost. That would be a relief compared to an awoken garrison, armed and waiting."

FitzOsbern grinned.

William winced as the ram creaked again. The dead of night seemed to amplify the noise tenfold. They had not waited for the stragglers; they would just have to catch up. William and his vanguard, all good steady troops, crept forward, ever closer to the high walls of Domfront. The narrow path leading up to the fort was torturous as they hurried as fast as they could – which was not fast at all, given that they were weighed down by De Warenne's battering ram, a long and heavy tree trunk with handles and an iron cap to stop the trunk splitting when it hit the gate. The men seemed to realise that this was the best William had come up with, as they reluctantly advanced; but advance, they did. William hissed an order and all those who did not have their hands full with the ram lifted their shields to form a shell above them in anticipation of all the missiles which would soon be falling from the sky. William glanced at FitzOsbern, who had taken his usual position to his right. William was grateful for it; whoever stood to one's right would be the one responsible for watching your unguarded arm and protecting it with his shield. No braver or fiercer warrior could be found than his trusted friend. He saw him watching and winked.

"We'll give them Hell yet, William."

William nodded and turned his attention back to the matter at hand. As he looked up at the parapets, he frowned. Why was there no one there? He had expected the wall to be packed with soldiers, yet in the poor light of the half moon he could not make out a single man. Perhaps they were crouched down and waiting. All the same, it seemed odd. Then came a sound he had not expected. It was the sound of a heavy wooden bar sliding out of place and the creaking of massive hinges. A crack of light appeared from within the castle as the great doors began to swing open.

"Halt!" William shouted. "Look out, they're preparing a sortie!"

Men waited with baited breath for the dreaded sound of hooves as hundreds of knights would soon be sallying out of the castle to trample them down.

"What are the fools doing?" FitzOsbern said. "Why give away their advantage?"

"Maybe they're just as keen as we are to get it over with," De Warenne said from behind. "They've been holed up for almost two years."

"FitzOsbern's right, though; they should just wait."

A dull thud and the occasional curse told William that the men carrying the battering ram had dropped the heavy trunk before everyone was ready.

"Silence!" FitzOsbern barked back at them.

Shields wavered as every pair of eyes seemed fixed on the gate. It was almost fully open now, and behind it? Nothing. Just an empty bailey. Where were all the knights?

"Wait here, De Warenne."

William and FitzOsbern crept forward slowly, with just a half-dozen of their best men. After seconds that passed like hours, they were almost under the gate's archway. A lone figure stepped out. FitzOsbern made to rush at the man, but William pulled him back by his shoulder. The solitary figure had his arms outstretched in peace. The torch light from inside lit up his face.

William stood astounded. How was this possible? The man stepped forwards and bowed.

"Greetings, my lord duke."

William frowned.

"Greetings, Nigel of the Cotentin."

"Domfront is yours for the taking," he said in a matter of fact voice. "Be quick, though; my men have dealt with the sentries, but the army will soon be roused if someone raises the alarm."

William turned and waved De Warenne and the rest forwards.

"De Warenne, hurry. Secure the castle, and have a mind not to kill any of Nigel's men. Report back when it's done."

"Yes, my lord," De Warenne said, as puzzled as William.

William pulled Nigel to one side as his vanguard flooded past them as stealthily as their chainmail and weapons would allow. The task would be an easy one now that the gate was open.

"Tell me, Nigel; what are you doing here of all places?"

"And have you forgotten you were banished?" FitzOsbern raised an eyebrow.

"I do beg my lord duke's forgiveness for this intrusion, but it was done with good intentions."

"Really?" FitzOsbern said. "Well perhaps you could explain how you came to be in these traitors' castle. Was one rebellion not enough for you?"

"I came months ago, my lord duke," Nigel said, ignoring FitzOsbern's barbed words. "I could not bear to think of Normandy in danger. I convinced the Bellêmes I was on their side. It didn't take much convincing."

"I bet it didn't," FitzOsbern said, earning a spiteful look from Nigel.

251

"I gained their trust, biding my time. I had a man posted near your camp at the lake, where he could see you coming. When you arrived this evening, he gave me the signal I had been waiting for. I told the others my men would help keep watch tonight. The few rebels who chose to stand guard with us were soon dispatched."

"The other rebels, you mean," FitzOsbern said.

"I never meant to rebel against my duke, I swear it," Nigel pleaded. "Your uncle Arques…"

"Go on," William said. "Arques is no longer in favour, and no more loyal than you were yourself."

"Arques was always so heavy-handed and took what he pleased. I had hoped we might remove him from your side, but he was too crafty for that. Guy presented the only way out or so I foolishly thought." Nigel knelt down and put his palms together. "I realise I was wrong. I was a traitor to Arques, and yes, I betrayed you, too. But I was never a traitor to Normandy. Never, my lord duke."

William put his hands over Nigel's. "I forgive you, Nigel. Although your sentence is not complete, I do believe your heart is pure. Normandy will have need of men such as you. Do you swear to stay loyal from this moment on?"

"I do, my lord duke."

"Then I hereby pardon you. You are again Count of the Cotentin, with all but a third of those possessions you had in yesteryear. Stand up."

"Thank you, my lord," Nigel said, getting to his feet.

"You are fortunate that our duke is so forgiving," FitzOsbern said, glancing at William. "But as he has forgiven you, I cannot rightly hold the grudge. I embrace you now as a brother."

He leaned in to kiss Nigel on the cheeks, his hand firmly holding his shoulders. As he leaned in, he whispered to the Count. "If you so much as think of betraying Duke William again, I will personally rip out your guts with my bare hands."

He stood back and smiled at Nigel, who even in the poor light of that evening seemed pale.

"Are we all friends again?" William asked.

"We are," said FitzOsbern smiling.

Screaming could be heard from within the walls.

"Ah," said William, "I see our hosts have woken up at last. Shall we go in?"

CHAPTER 31

William was awoken by the urgent calls of a horn blasting short, sharp notes from somewhere beyond the keep. He opened his eyes to find that it was mid-day and he was lying against a stack of grain sacks. He winced as his neck and back did not thank him for the awkward position. He must have dozed off some time ago. He had been working hard on the defences and had not properly slept in a long while. He'd only sat down to catch his breath for a moment.

The horn repeated its cry, which was soon echoed by other horns around the castle and the surrounding defences, right down to the lower forts from which they had besieged Domfront those past two years.

"William, get up!" FitzOsbern was shaking him vigorously by the shoulder.

"What is it?" William frowned and reached for his sword belt. He hastily strapped it on as they strode across the yard to the southern watch tower. They were greeted at the top of the ladder by a worried Nigel who looked as though he had not slept at all.

"My lord Duke, Count Geoffrey of Anjou is here. Our scouts report that he comes with a considerable army. His vanguard is down there already," he said, pointing to the expanse of land beyond the great rock on which the fortress of Domfront stood. William could make out a large group of knights, pennants high in the breeze, no doubt assessing the situation. A great plume of dust further off to the south-east told of an approaching army.

"Send word to our outposts; they are to hold their position but under no circumstance are they to sally out and engage the enemy. I won't have Geoffrey besiege us from our own forts."

"Yes my lord," Nigel nodded.

"And send riders to Montgomery; he should be at Arques castle. He is to spare what men he can to bolster the defences of Falaise. The lady Matilda must be kept safe and Falaise will be Geoffrey's next target."

As Nigel turned to leave, FitzOsbern gave a scoff of surprise.

"What the Hell are they playing at?"

William looked down at the knights who, to his amazement, were making their way up the hill towards the castle, taking care to give the smaller forts a wide birth.

"Are they mad?" Nigel wondered aloud.

William looked at the keep and then back at the knights, chuckling to himself. The others frowned at such a reaction.

"Care to share the joke?" FitzOsbern asked.

"It may have escaped your notice, my lords, but no one has thought to take down the flag."

They looked up at the keep. Surely enough, the Angevin flag still flew boldly where the Bellêmes had raised it two years earlier.

"They think we still haven't taken the castle?"

"Indeed, lord Nigel."

"They're in for a bit of a surprise then," FitzOsbern said with a grin.

"I shall have it taken down at once," Nigel said.

"No, no," William bade him. "Not just yet. Boy, fetch me my bow."

A squire hurried away, before returning shortly afterwards with William's bow. It was the largest the boy had ever seen. Even Nigel raised his eyebrows. Few men could string such a bow, let alone use it with any accuracy. William had inherited his father's solid frame and practised as hard as any of his knights. He drew back the string and patiently waited. Once the knights were within range, he breathed out and loosed the arrow. It flew through the air in a high arc before embedding itself in the leading knight's shield, right in the symbol of Anjou.

William chuckled again as the knight's horse reared. The men beat a hasty retreat.

"Now you may raise our flag," he said to Nigel.

Further down, the main army was coming into view. A lone man rode forwards to meet the fleeing vanguard. His bodyguards in turn hurried after him.

"Geoffrey," William said under his breath. "We meet again."

After much gesticulating and pointing towards the castle, the army stopped. It turned. It left. Count Geoffrey the Hammer of Anjou took a last look at Domfront. William waved down to him. Though they were some distance away from each other, William's fiery hair left Geoffrey in no doubt of whom he was. Geoffrey nodded in reluctant salutation before touching his spurs to his horse's flanks and heading off back into the depths of the forests.

"Why does he go, my lord?" Nigel asked.

"Why should he stay?" William shrugged. "He came expecting to gain two mighty forts on our border whence he might launch an assault of Normandy itself – or at the very least cause us much grief. What did he find? He found that far from

256

having the use of the forts, they are in even more hostile hands than before, he has no support left from the Bellêmes and he would need a sustained campaign – with supply lines stretching right across Maine, no less – in order even to have a chance of gaining access to Normandy. He is quite right to leave."

"It was lucky for us that we took this place just in time then," Nigel said.

"Lucky? Luck is for the superstitious. We make our own luck, with God's help."

William took a heavy swig of wine. They were feasting in the clearing, as the lake was covered in the early morning mist. In the end, the fort had fallen with barely a sword raised, except against those poor souls who had been forced to suffer the consequences of many months of frustrating waiting and starving in the rain. William had called his men off as soon as they had vented their initial fury, though. He laughed aloud again. Relief. Pure and unbridled relief swept over him. Only a few hours earlier he had accepted that he and his men might all be dead before dawn. Yet dawn had come and they were victorious – and with a new ally to strengthen their numbers. As William raised his glass to Nigel, sat opposite, he remembered what a mighty and unflinching stand the Count of the Cotentin had fought at the Vale of Dunes. Such determination would be of use, now that it was put to William's purpose. Even FitzOsbern was now laughing with Nigel as if they had never so much as quarrelled.

"Excuse me, my lords," William said grandly, "I need a piss."

They all laughed at their duke's declaration. William got up and walked over to the hovel. He loosened his breaches and relieved himself, a broad grin on his face. Looking across the lake, he saw a lone man standing guard and chuckled. He waved at the man, who slowly raised a hand in return, before appearing to melt away into the mist. William was still laughing as he got back to the table.

"What is it, my lord?" Nigel asked, with an equally big grin.

"Your man standing guard across the lake; you might have told him to join us. He's done his job well enough, but we really don't need him now."

Nigel frowned. "But my lord, he is here," he said, pointing to a soldier drinking at the end of the table.

"Wait a minute…" William rubbed his head, trying to get his thoughts straight despite the tiredness and the drink. "If he's here… Who did I just see across the lake?"

They looked at each other before rushing to their feet and staring across the lake. There was no sign of anyone there.

"I told you," De Warenne said. "The ghost of a lone hermit."

'Don't start that again," William said, though he hoped no one noticed him touch the small cross which hung at his neck.

CHAPTER 32

LONDON, ENGLAND. JUNE, 1051 A.D.

It had been ten years since Edward had left the Norman court. In that time he had gained thirty years' worth of age on his face, William thought, as he looked intently at the English King. Edward's beard and wavy hair had turned a pale shade of grey. He seemed shorter, somehow, as though the burden of Kingship had physically weighed him down. Deep lines ran across his face, the ploughing of many years' labour.

Of course, William himself had been but an adolescent then and was bound to see a greater difference in one who was over thirty years his senior. Now William was a confident war lord in his twenties, victor of two successful campaigns against rebels and invaders alike. Still, he could tell that kingship had taken its toll on Edward. It was said that he had not been seen to smile since his brother's death. His had not been a happy life. Forced to flee England as a young boy, he had suffered the neglect of his mother Emma of Normandy who had married the invader Cnut on her husband's death. She had let Cnut's sons claim the throne after his death – the eldest, Harold Harefoot, then butchered Alfred with Godwin's help. Edward returned to an England which he no longer recognised. He had enjoyed Normandy, had grown to love its people, its ways and speak its tongue. Kingship was nought but a burden. To then be forced to marry Godwin's daughter was the supreme insult.

Now, though, he had finally rid himself of the hateful Godwin family. The men were banished across the seas and the wife locked in a nunnery. She was lucky, William thought. Others would not have shown such mercy for the sins of the father.

Edward had sent word William was to join him at the earliest opportunity. The Norman duke had stayed as steadfast an ally as his father before him.

"Tell me of Normandy, my good Duke," Edward said looking out across the river Thames. "What of its fields and its churches? What of its people and its music?"

"They thrive, my lord King. The summer has been kind. The harvest promises to be a good one. Our granaries will, with God's help, be full to bursting. Our people can hope to see even the harshest winter through."

Edward smiled.

"Our people, yes. They are our people. My heart never left Normandy's shores, no matter how hardly pressed into service my body and mind have been in this land. I am glad to hear this, Duke William."

"Our Church thrives also. There is a new abbot at Le Bec, an Italian who has brought fresh life to the place. He is a man of great learning and promises to use all his zeal to return our holy places to their former glory and righteousness."

""You speak of Lanfranc?"

William nodded, impressed that the King of England should consider it worth his while to keep informed of minor religious appointments across the sea. "I have heard of him," Edward said. "I gather that he and your uncle Mauger were not exactly the greatest of friends."

"My uncle ruled as a count, not a prince of the cloth, and an unfaithful count at that. Lanfranc warned me of it. Mauger never did care about anything other than his own riches and power. He would bend his knee neither to me nor to the Holy Father." William shrugged. "He paid the price and so did Arques and the other traitors."

"My congratulations for that; I hear it was a fine campaign."

"It was two years of hunger, mud and waiting in ceaseless rain."

"Yet to manage to keep two besieging armies together in such conditions and still have the strength to storm two castles at the end of it was no small feat." He gave William a side-ways glance which reminded him of King Henry's calculating manner. "The boy I knew during my exile has turned into a formidable warlord. Anjou and France must be quaking in their boots."

"Thank you, my good King, but I shall not rest quietly so long as Geoffrey Martel draws breath."

"But without Arques, Mauger and the others, you are now free to rule as you see fit."

"As are you."

"Godwin still has friends at court."

"I wonder that a man like that has any true friends. Surely the English remember how he sided with the Danes. He merely goes with whoever wins."

"But whoever he goes with *does* win. That's just it. Many in this country did not want me as their king. When Godwin accepted me, though, the rest followed suit. Even Leofric of Mercia, Godwin's bitter rival, swore his allegiance to me once Godwin had sworn his – though I suspect Leofric was just relieved not to have to bend his knee to Godwin himself."

"Why did Godwin accept you?"

"He needed my protection – at least for a time. He divided this country. When Cnut's younger son died, the country was not ready for Godwin to rule. He needed to show he was truly English and what better way than reinstating the line of Wessex. Of course, the price was that I should marry his daughter."

"And now?"

"Godwin could still overthrow me. He needs men, though. No doubt he hopes to find them in Flanders."

"My wife swears that her father the Count will not give him any troops."

"Let us hope that no one else will, then."

"Would he have much support if he were to return under arms?"

William watched as a trading barge moved down the Thames, the river which was the lifeblood of London.

"The English bend over to whoever is strongest in their lands. The North will not support him. His arm does not stretch far in Leofric's old home. As for the South, many have cause to resent his heavy-handed manner. He would nonetheless find some support there. His own lands are extensive and their inhabitants know whom they should turn to for rewards."

"So he is indeed a threat, still," William said.

"He is," Edward agreed. "At least I no longer have to listen to his daughter's ceaseless nagging."

"I gather there was little love there."

Edward suddenly turned his back to the river and looked William in the eyes, as though such a word seemed foreign coming from the mouth of a warlord.

"Even princes are entitled to some love in their lives, my good king," William said.

"Well there was certainly none between her and I. Every day I spent in her company was like having Godwin's eyes watching my every move. And she kept expecting children!" Edward sounded offended by the very notion. "Yet I can't stand the sight of her. All I see in her face is that of my brother's killer. Oh, Alfred!"

Edward turned back towards the river and shivered. William felt uncomfortable at such a display of emotion, yet Edward had clearly been holding this back for many long years. He had heard many rumours of Edward's personal life, some less savoury than others, such as a fondness for other men. But seeing the English King shaking thus from grief, all these years later, he saw only a lonely man and cared little for any of the gossip. It all seemed so heartless. He searched clumsily for a way of steering the conversation to happier thoughts.

"Would you take another wife? You could seek an annulment, if your current wife were to take vows?"

Edward shook his head, regaining his composure.

"The Church would not back it. Nor do the Witan care for such things - and it is full of Godwin's men."

"You would let a council of lesser men dictate your future?"

"You must understand, William, that things are not as simple as in Normandy, here. A lord is not free to rule as he sees fit. He must seek the approval of the Witan on all great matters of state. I sometimes feel I cannot take a piss without their say so."

They walked away from the Thames, heading back into the city. Though Winchester had long stood alone as the Royal

263

capital, London was the thriving centre of trade. Great arteries ran out from the Thames' estuary to bring goods from Europe and beyond into the heartland of England. Though the Romans had recognised the importance of the place, the Britons and Saxons had let it crumble for centuries. Now, though, Edward was easing it towards a new age of prosperity.

"Let us think of happier things, though," Edward said. "Now that Godwin and his dogs are gone, I can finally flex my muscles a little in the Witan. Godwin's old possessions are now mine by right. With those, I can buy favours. I can build influence. I can bestow positions."

"Indeed," William said, with interest, "Archbishop Robert was thrilled with his elevation to Canterbury."

"I needed someone I could trust and no one in England seemed worthy of performing God's work."

They came out of a narrow street and William stopped in amazement. In front of them was perhaps the largest building site he had ever seen. Masons swarmed like bees around mounds of stone. Men with arms as thick as tree trunks wielded huge saws to cut the granite to the right sized blocks. More of the massive slabs were being pulled up from the down along heavy wooden runners, the oxen and their drivers struggling to shift the great loads. Young boys ran around purposefully delivering messages, fetching tools and handing out skins of water.

Most impressive of all was what stood in the centre of this orderly chaos. Rising out of the clouds of dust, a titanic abbey was reaching up towards the Heavens. Only the foundations and lower segments were in place, yet it already dwarfed the surrounding buildings with its almighty presence.

"Well?" Edward smiled at William, full of a new pride. "What do you think of my West Minster?"

William marvelled at the sight.

"It is wonderful, King Edward. Wonderful."

"I thought it might please you."

"It is surely one of a kind!"

"Almost one of a kind," Edward said. "It just so happens that you know the architect of this creation." He waved over a cleric who had been deep in conversation with a group of builders.

"Archbishop Robert," William said with true pleasure. "I am happy to find you here."

"Thank you, my lord Duke. You are very kind. I am also glad to see you safe and victorious. I never doubted that God would see you through your ordeals."

"Thank you. I gather that you are behind this wonder."

"Did I not say," Edward interrupted, "that the Archbishop was the only man to relay the foundations of the Church? I had no idea that he would take it so literally."

"The King is too generous," the Archbishop said. "He has been the true driving force behind this creation. As in so many things, his steady hand is guiding England away from its worldly squabbles and back to the light of Christ, no matter how perilous the work."

"Amen," said William, noting the effect the flattery was having on the King.

"The people need a focal point for their praise," Edward said. "Alfred the Great gave them Winchester. I am giving them this West Minster in the new heart of the land."

"They will not forget this gift of yours, my king," the cleric said.

"Tell me, Archbishop," William said, "how is Osbern? My Steward urged me to send his greetings to his brother."

"He is doing exceptionally well. Though he lacks the bravery of a warrior, he is ideally suited to the cloth, armed with much humility and a hunger for reading."

William smiled to himself; how different he was to FitzOsbern, whose greatest hunger was for hunting, women and fighting – and whenever possible all three.

"In leaving Normandy with you, King Edward, he has, I think, been saved from the darkest period of our land."

"But do not think," the Archbishop said with a grin, "to lure him back, good Duke William. He is a servant of God in England, now."

"Thank you, Archbishop. We won't keep you from your important work any longer."

He took the hint, bowed and left them.

"You see, Duke William, what I am doing for the people of this country," Edward said. "I am bringing them back into God's love. I have given them peace. So long as I live, I can keep the rival Earls from warring too much, for they dare not risk losing the chance of inheriting my crown. I can feel the strength leaving my body, William, as much as if I had already lived a thousand lives. I hold on for the safety of my people."

"They have much to thank you for. And I am sure that – "

The King put up a hand to stop him.

"When I am gone, this land will set itself on fire. The Earls will fight over the succession, caring little for what damage they cause. Fractioned nations cannot stay alive. They fall prey to raiders and invaders, ever keen to exploit weakness. I cannot risk the turmoil of one of my Earls sitting on my throne."

He looked William in the eyes.

"You must be king when I am gone, William."

"What?" William

"Do not deny that you had not already thought on it. My crown is one of the most coveted in the west. This land is good and fertile, my warriors are fierce and the sea offers much protection. That is why my Earls keep trying to take it from me."

"The English will never have me for their king."

"Many of them did not want *me* as their king, yet here I stand. England needs a strong master. You already have much experience in dealing with quarrelsome vassals. You have shown your strength and your reputation grows."

"But I know little of the land," William protested, earning himself a sly look from the King.

"Do you think I have not noticed the change in my clerics? How many of them have broad shoulders and scars? You have been watching my court very closely, have you not?"

William looked away.

"I thank you," Edward continued, "for your concern, but let us not pretend that you do not want to be king. You have been eyeing my crown for some time. I do not blame you. Young men need ambition and you have the means of achieving greatness. For my part, I need to know that when I die I will leave my country in safe hands. Let us therefore be happy that our desires are so concurrent."

William saw that Edward was smiling.

"Will you promise to protect this country from itself when I am gone?"

"I will."

"Then you shall be the next king of England."

And just like that, it was done. They agreed not to make William's nomination general knowledge yet. Though William would have liked it to be recognised, Edward could not risk a rebellion from any Earl who wanted the crown for himself. So long as they each thought they had a chance, the English lords would obey their King.

After a night of feasting and being entertained by Edward's jesters, William sailed home to Normandy, to his new wife Matilda and to the peace which at last reigned in his land.

.IV.

THE HAMMER AND THE LILY

Chapter 33

William laughed. It was a laugh full of mirth and bonhomie. Heads turned to take in the sight, for the duke's temper was infamous. He was quite transformed on that evening and he cared little who saw it. He beamed with joy as he looked into the eyes of his beautiful wife-to-be sat beside him. She returned his gaze, full of life, love and lust.

He breathed in deeply. The fresh air of late summer filled his lungs, just as the scent of roast venison teased his nostrils. Tonight was a time for celebration. After three years of warring, the fighting and a long trip across the waters, he was finally able to enjoy peace. Anjou had been seen off. King Henry had accepted a truce on terms honourable enough for both parties to keep their heads high – though perhaps the crown had lost some of its lustre. Corrupt rebels had been banished to ignominy. Peace reigned over Normandy once more.

By way of a reward, he had found Montgomery a young wife. Though Roger was thrilled, it was not a disinterested choice – for William had decided his friend should marry none other than Mabel, daughter and heiress of the lord of Bellême and Alençon. This was the man Montgomery himself had dispatched at Alençon. That particular detail, he suspected, might not need to be revealed to the young lady. At Matilda's suggestion, William had ordered a feast, that they may celebrate their betrothal at the same time as his own to Matilda. Glancing across, William was amused to see the wide grin on Roger's usually stern and unreadable countenance. His new wife seemed rather less

270

enthusiastic. She would learn, he thought. Few marriages were ever born out of love. Amongst the lower order, perhaps such joys were more common, but girls who had land or pedigree had to accept their lot. Happiness thereafter would be down to hard work and resignation. Luckily for William, he had fallen for the very woman whom politics dictated he should marry.

Matilda had seen to the preparations personally. She had made diplomatic invitations, allowed only entertainers of good taste and selected the finest wines of France. At present, William gulped a crisp white wine from the county of Champagne. It was lighter than his usual cask, but Matilda insisted he drink it, having teased him with some truth that his preference was nought but coarse and vulgar swill. It was a small price to pay for having her at his side. He would just have to get used to it – when not on campaign.

"So tell me, my good Count," William turned to Baldwin of Flanders who sat in the place of honour to his right, as befits the father of the bride, "how is the rest of your family?"

"All very well, Duke William; I thank you for the kind thought."

"Your sister…Judith? She is well also?"

Baldwin fidgeted. The red tinge which lit his face was perhaps not all due to the wine.

"She is well, thank you."

"Missing her husband, no doubt."

Matilda put a gentle hand on William's own, the subtlest of warnings. He pretended to ignore it.

"She is indeed. Though I expect she will be joining him soon," the count said.

271

"I must confess to liking Tostig. He struck me as a good man and true lover of the Church... in spite of his family," William added pointedly.

"He is indeed. I would hardly have authorised the union, were he not so."

"Of course. I meant no offence." William smiled as affably as he could.

"None was taken." Baldwin seemed more at ease.

"A TOAST!" William shouted across the field in which they held the feast. "A toast to Lady Judith of Flanders!"

All those in earshot stood and raised their cups before drinking deeply, though more than one puzzled look could be seen. FitzOsbern caught William's eye. He gave him a knowing wink, as the two friends shared the joke.

"She will be joining him, you say?" he asked, sitting back down. "Has he chosen a place to settle then?"

"I rather think he will eventually want to make his way back to his own home."

"England?" William could barely hide his surprise. "Do you think that he will be allowed to return?"

"Who knows what will happen? Godwin can be a very persuasive man."

"Enough to persuade you, you mean?"

Baldwin turned from scarlet to crimson at that.

"Husband," Matilda said, "please."

"It was a simple question. I do hope you will forgive me if it was out of place."

"There is nothing to forgive," Baldwin said, putting on his best courtly smile. He was well versed in these matters. "I told

Godwin that he would have no more assistance from Flanders than the hospitality which his rank afforded him. For anything further, I was clear that he would have to look elsewhere."

William nodded his appreciation of Baldwin's position.

"You do think that he will return to England, though?" he insisted.

"I believe that it was always his intention. As for his success in so doing, your friend King Edward is best placed to answer that question."

William nodded in agreement. He hid his anger at having been kept so much in the dark by his new ally. He had, of course, known that Flanders had offered Tostig Godwinson hospitality. That the Godwins had been freely allowed to find support for a return to England was news to him. Baldwin had not given him the slightest note of warning that Tostig was leaving – nor had Matilda. Had she known of it? No. How could she possibly? All the same, William made a mental note to better organise his intelligence sources in Flanders.

He leaned over to kiss Matilda on the cheek. Her pale skin felt so soft under his touch. What a delicate creature she was, the very paragon of the innocent and virtuous courtly lady. Yet her eyes held something mischievous as if some unknown strength lay hidden away in the depths of her soul.

As he leaned back in his chair, William noticed FitzOsbern talking to one of the guards. There was nothing the least unusual about his steward keeping a close eye on security at court, but there was something about their faces, the urgency of their exchange which awakened William's instincts, even on so festive an occasion.

With a final word from FitzOsbern, the guard faded into the darkness of the night. FitzOsbern saw William's inquisitive look and approached the dais. Rather than bow before the gathered lords, as would be custom, he discretely went round behind William's chair and whispered into his ear.

"You'd best come, William."

William nodded, keeping a courtly smile on his face. There was no point in worrying the gathered guests until he knew what the matter was.

"Forgive me, Count Baldwin. I must see to the sentries."

"You do not have captains to do that for you?"

"Of course; but I like to check on them myself. It keeps them on their toes. The last thing we want with such august company assembled is distracted guards."

The count nodded, though William doubted he actually believed him. As he followed FitzOsbern towards a small tent in an adjacent field, his friend remained utterly silent. After a while it became unbearable.

"Are you going to tell me or do I have to guess?"

FitzOsbern sighed. "You had better hear it from the horse's mouth. You won't like it though, I warn you," he said, lifting the flap of the tent for William to duck inside.

As he went in, he saw that there was a small group of men crowded therein. Sat on a travelling chest, clothes dirty from what had clearly been a rough journey, was Archbishop Robert of Canterbury, the Norman Edward had elevated to the prelacy of the English Church.

"My lord Archbishop!" William said. "You are a long way from your flock."

"No, my lord duke; I am back among them."

"How so?" William looked around at the mournful faces of an erstwhile noble company. The Archbishop put the cuff of his sleeve up to his eye and sighed. William could not help being moved to pity to see a once great man so utterly broken and spent. "What happened?"

"Godwin."

"Godwin," William repeated the cursed name. "We heard just this very evening that he had set sail with the intention of regaining England. I wish I could have given you some warning."

"He certainly made it to England. Word had barely reached us that he had landed when he and his sons were already upon us with a whole army. They landed at Pevensey and were joined by many of their men of Wessex there. We weren't prepared. There was nothing to be done."

"The King?"

"He wanted to raise an army to fight them. It might have worked. We could have fallen back into the north and struck out with an army of Mercians. It could have worked, but Earl Leofric refused."

"Leofric refused to fight for his King? Christ. Is there any Saxon of loyal heart?" William spat. "I thought he and Godwin hated each other."

"They are bitter rivals, it is true, but I think he has grown weary. England has known so many revolts and civil wars in recent years, so many kings overthrown. Leofric did what he thought would bring the best chance of a lasting balance. He may not like Godwin, but at least the Earl keeps peace and stability in his part of the country."

"So what *did* Edward do?"

"What could he do? He accepted Godwin's terms. Godwin and his sons are reinstated to their offices. His daughter has been sent for to warm the King's bed. And I… I am banished, along with most other Normans at court."

"I bet he was thrilled with that," FitzOsbern said.

"The King is furious, but whoever controls the warriors controls the country. In England, there are many small lords who are charged with raising troops. Their allegiance is to a king who they rarely see and who has little influence on their daily lives. When powerful earls such as Godwin and Leofric have a tight hold on their lands, the lesser ealdormen and thegns naturally obey them. They are the ones who can make daily life difficult or good. Why serve a king who is far off?"

"Honour? Oaths? Duty?" FitzOsbern suggested.

"Honour does not protect the crops. Oaths do not put food in your children's mouths. Duty doesn't keep looting Scots, wild Welsh and violent Vikings at bay," the archbishop said.

"You say the lady Edith is to return to the King's bed?" William asked.

"She is," the cleric said. "Little good it will do, though. Edward has no desire for her. Who can blame him, after what happened to his brother? They say, God have mercy on him, that he has no taste for women. To my knowledge, his bed stayed cold even during Edith's dismissal to the nunnery."

"No risk of him producing a little Godwin to inherit his crown, then." FitzOsbern said.

"It won't matter much to Godwin, mind." the archbishop said.

"How so? Does he not want a king for a grandson?" William asked.

"I rather think he wants the crown for himself. He is likely to have it, too. The King is sickly. When he passes, Godwin will use his daughter's marriage to claim kinship to the crown. As head of Edith's family, he is in a strong position. The Witan will hardly object to a man of his standing."

"And what if the Witan has already been instructed to approve another man as king?" William said.

"Another man?" Robert frowned. "What other man? I have heard talk of the old King Edmund Ironside's son, but no one knows where he is – or even if he is still alive. He left the shores of England a long time ago."

"It is not Ironside's son of whom I speak. But if one who had long supported the house of Alfred the Great was recommended by Edward as a suitable successor, even when would-be heroes such as Godwin were turning against the King, how then would the lords of the Witan vote?"

The archbishop looked at William through a mist of tiredness and blinked.

"You don't mean…"

William saw him trying to get his weary brain around the question.

"How would you convince Edward to make so bold a move?" Robert said. "A foreign monarch would not sit well with the people."

"Cnut managed to govern England, though he was Danish. His sons Harefoot and Harthacanute also did in turn. A king may be popular and the worst ruler in Christendom. I do not seek

277

popularity; only justice and God's peace. As to the King's approval, I already have it."

"What?" Robert baulked. "Forgive me, lord duke, I mean no offence. But I had no idea the King was serious in putting your name forward. I heard him muse on it one night, when he was downcast, but..."

"And why should he not? Can a tyrant of Godwin's ilk truly be a rightful king of England?"

"It is true that Godwin's position has outgrown that of a humble Earl. But people follow a strong leader for the promise of stability and gifts."

"Only if he doesn't get in the way of their interests. Leofric's house controls much of England, does it not?"

"Most of what is north of the Thames, certainly. But Godwin's eldest has forged an alliance of some power through his meddling in Wales. And Leofric backed Godwin's return, remember."

"No; he merely didn't risk open war to oppose it. And this is but one event in a lifetime of feuding between them. There's no telling how he would react to an attempt by Godwin to seize the throne."

"Leofric would be content to hold an independent North if Godwin offered it as price for his crown."

"Just as he would tolerate any who would make such an offer."

"All I can say, my lord, is that I know the Witan. Their pride and self-serving will be a great obstacle to your accession to England's throne. It would take quite some arguing from Edward to talk them into even considering it and no one in England is even aware of his intentions yet, so you had best wish him a long life."

"Godwin's wings can yet be clipped. I need you back in England to press my case. Your dismissal was the most unwilling act of a man being leaned on by a bully. If we petition the Holy See, you may yet be reinstated as head of the English Church."

"Thank you, my lord duke, but no. I would rather not."

"I'm sorry?" William asked, flabbergasted. "What on earth do you mean? You are the rightful leader of Edward's church."

"I am a tired old man, my lord. That is what I am." Robert contemplated the dregs of wine, as if the bottom of his cup concealed the mysteries of Heaven and Earth. "For how many long years have I been at Edward's court? I have been constantly embroiled in its games of politics, suffering the workings and tricks of a people who never wanted me there. For all that time, I lost my way, lost sight of God, whom I had sworn I would serve my whole life. I turned away from an incorruptible Lord to serve the corrupted lords of this world. So I must decline your offer, my lord. I will not return to England. This is a battle you must fight without me. Forgive me."

He let his cup fall to the ground and buried his face in his hands. For the first time in his life, William saw him not as the mighty and righteous prince of Christianity he had always known, but as an exhausted old man, whom the exertions of life had utterly worn down. He could tell that any further arguing would be futile.

"Where will you go?" He asked Robert, who looked up through tearful eyes.

"Back to my old priory. There I will return to the true fold of God's service and seek his forgiveness, until the last of my strength finally leaves these all too weary bones."

"Then go with God, Robert. Normandy will always have a place for one such as you."

William backed out of the tent and headed off in the direction of the feast.

"A bad business, eh?" said FitzOsbern. "A pity Godwin wasn't disposed of in Flanders."

"A pity? I rather think he had Baldwin's blessing. This way he is sure to back a winner, no matter who loses."

CHAPTER 34

CAEN, LOWER NORMANDY. 1053 A.D.

"King Henry is not best pleased, my lord."

"What a coincidence," William said; "I am not best pleased with King Henry."

William had brought Lanfranc with him to Caen, where he was overseeing the construction of a new ducal castle. From inside the chapel of Saint Giles, just on the next hill, they could hear the hammering and shouting of the men who had already set about the task of clearing away the few remaining houses and preparing the ground from which the castle would rise.

Nor would the castle be William's only presence there. As part of the deal Lanfranc had struck with the Pope on William's behalf, the Duke of Normandy and his new Duchess Matilda were each to found an abbey, the first for monks, the second for nuns. Thus would they pay the penance for their marriage and allay the Church's concerns. Two hills, one either side of the castle, would become home to William's Abbey of Saint Stephen and Matilda's Abbey of the Holy Trinity. Together with the castle, these three new buildings would tower over the town.

Word had spread across the region. Traders from all over Northern France had come in the hope of selling their wares to William's followers. Some had even settled, knowing that Caen might soon be a great hub of commerce, under the protection of the fort's ramparts and the watchful eye of the duke.

William was glad of their enthusiasm, for it all served to strengthen his message to the barons of Lower Normandy; there would be no repeat of the rebellion of Valognes. Though he had pardoned one of the rebellion's instigators, this new castle was being built in the heart of Nigel's own viscounty of the Cotentin. William thus told all the men of Lower Normandy that no more would he be far away in Rouen. From this castle, he would stamp out any hint of dissent. From these abbeys would God judge the evil deeds of miscreants.

"So what," William said, lighting a candle in his mother's memory, "is King Henry not best pleased about?"

"Your plans, my lord," Lanfranc said. "He greatly respected your uncle Arques, who no doubt kept him informed of your projects. Now he is in the dark and grows anxious."

"What can the King of France possibly have to fear from me?"

"He fears what you might become, my lord. The crown of France no longer shines as it did when it rested on Charlemagne's head. The King's vassal dukes and counts ride roughshod through the land, making war on each other and barely paying lip service to the King's orders. How long until one of you turns his sword on the crown itself?"

"Henry is a fool. He should know better by now than to think Normandy can be cowed into meek submission by threats."

"He should," Lanfranc agreed, "but he is no fool. He is an old hand at this game. Your reign over Normandy remains fragile. Your barons showed once again that they are reluctant to support you in times of crisis. Though Arques helped disrupt supplies, there were not enough to begin with. Nor was the service of arms which all your vassal barons owed very forthcoming. And Arques still holds out."

"So what do you suggest?" William asked, ever so slightly irritated at the prior's lecturing tone.

"You must bring your barons to heel."

"Did I not do so at the Vale of Dunes? Did I not do so at Alençon and within the bloody walls of Domfront?"

"For a time, yes; but there are ways other than the sword. Beat a dog and it will fear you. Feed it and it will follow you. Do both and it will obey you."

William looked into the flame of the candle, pondering the cleric's words.

"Tell me, father Lanfranc; what do you want out of this?"

He turned to stare into the Italian's eyes.

"Me, my lord? I want only that which our Lord God wants: a peaceful and God-fearing Normandy."

"And you believe we can make Normandy peaceful?"

"I believe I can make Normandy God-fearing. The rest I leave to you, my lord."

William laughed.

"Yet you would not accept the archbishopric. Will you not reconsider and change the Church in Normandy from a position of power?"

"Our Lord Jesus had no such position to change men for the better. Why should I take such an office when speech and faith are all that are needed to bring men back to the Light? Besides, your new archbishop was His Holiness' candidate. You would do well to keep Rome pleased. You may one day need to call on its good favour once more."

"Have it your way, then. You know you have a free hand to make what changes to the church you deem for the best. In this, I would trust no one else's judgement."

Lanfranc bowed in acknowledgement.

"I would ask one favour of you, though. Take my brother Odo under your wing. I need men I can trust, but he has much to learn of the ways of the Church. He will need your guidance."

"Does he want my guidance?" Lanfranc asked, spreading his arms.

"He will have it, whether he wants it or not."

The prior grunted.

"And you, my lord duke?"

"If you want peace, prepare for war. My dogs shall know their place."

"Look around you, my lords. What do you see?"

The gathered barons looked around themselves. They stood in a field on a rolling hill, with wheat reaching their knees. It swayed in the gentle breeze. At the top of the hill was a small chapel, with a single cross erected beside it. They had answered William's summons to meet him in Caen. After two rebellions in four years, none wished to seem reluctant to obey. Those who could not attend in person had sent their eldest sons.

"Well, my lords?" William prompted them further.

There was a shuffling of feet. Men suddenly found the clouds fascinating or fiddled with their belts.

"That is what I thought," William said, scowling in contempt. "For those of you who have not already guessed the blindingly obvious, you are currently stood in the Vale of Dunes. If I feel the need to formally introduce you to the place, it is because so few of you have seen it. Your duke was under threat from villainous traitors, yet where were you?"

He wandered among the men. Most would not hold his gaze.

"Some of you answered the call," he said, patting fitzOsbern on the back, receiving a nod of recognition. "Some, but not many. The rest of you kept well away - stayed safe and warm in your halls, making love to your women when you should have been making war with our enemies."

"We would have, come, my lord - " one man started, only to be silenced by a swiftly raised hand.

"Give me no excuses," William said; "I have heard them all before. The fact is that you were too cowardly to stand up for Normandy. You reneged on your duty. I shall not rely on your courage any more. You all owe service to your duke or must pay for men to be hired to take your place. You all know that."

"We will provide such monies as you require, my lord duke," said one, to chimes of agreement throughout.

"You will indeed," William said. "Yet I will not be waiting for war to happen before preparing our defences. From now on, every baron will be required to pay for service of arms, regardless of whether we be at peace or war. These monies will be used for your own protection."

"But my lord, that is not the Norman way."

"It is my way," William said, "and I am Normandy. If you do not like it, you should have thought of that when you let better men than you die on this field, when the sun scorched the ground and the crows called out for blood."

"You cannot do this, my lord, I -"

The protest was cut short by the sight of FitzOsbern stepped forward and pulling his sword part of the way out of its scabbard. The message was clear.

"My lord of Montgomery," William said, turning to Roger, "and my steward FitzOsbern will be visiting each of you in turn to assess what your fair contribution should be. This money is for the protection of Normandy, which is the first duty of any lord. As such, any refusal to cooperate with these men or any of their chosen agents shall be treated as treason. For that offence, we have but one punishment."

William nodded at FitzOsbern, who let his sword fall but into its sheath.

"Now, let us return to Caen. To thank my loyal subjects, you shall join me for a feast."

CHAPTER 35

It was a spring day when the monk arrived at Caen. A soft, warm wind gently stirred the branches of the trees, wafting the scent of blossom from the apple orchards across the field where William was putting his men through their paces. They probably did not need the extra practice, having already trained hard for most of the previous month. William did not care. He was not going to let his men have the time to get soft. Besides, the efficiency of a cavalry charge relies much on keeping a close formation to harness the horses' combined impetus and prevent the enemy from escaping through any gaps in the line. That could only be achieved through constant and rigorous training.

"Do it again!" he shouted at them. "You'll never stand a chance against Anjou if you can't even keep your horses in a straight bloody line. Do it again."

William was being hard on them today; harder than usual, that is. They knew it; yet not one of them begrudged him it. He needed to keep his mind busy.

"De Warenne your group's too slow! Keep up, man!" he fumed.

Normally he would have gone hunting, but this was the season when many of the woodland creatures were rearing their young. It was best to let those young grow into healthy beasts which would later provide more food. The hunting packs would have to wait until later in the summer.

The animals weren't the only ones for whom spring brought the promise of new life. If William was putting his knights through such rigorous exercise, it was precisely because Matilda was

287

lying in expecting their first child – perhaps at this very moment she could be in labour. William, of course, could not be present. It was not the done thing. The Duchess was in her private chambers, locked away from the world, with only her maids in attendance. Nor did William wish to be there with her. He loved his wife deeply. He may have chosen her out of political calculation, but their relationship had soon turned into something deeper than that. He had been so overwhelmed by love and lust, so in awe of her intellectual talents, that she had become an inseparable part of himself. He was a brave warrior, fearing little for his own safety. He could face open battle and the intrigues of his court easily enough. The incessant plotting of his barons no longer made him anxious. He had even gone so far as to defy his beloved Church and the Pope himself in order to be with her.

The present situation, however, was totally out of his control. The thought of his love suffering behind those closed doors filled him with dread. So often, women who shut themselves away with maids in order to give birth, never came out again. William sometimes thought that a woman's chances in childbirth were slimmer than those of a warrior on a battlefield. All he could do was pray. That was not enough for him. All his life, he had sought to control that which happened to him. He could not now stay inactive and patiently wait. He threw himself into constantly training his men and took out his frustration on them. These were his most loyal knights, who had followed him into the bloody fields of the Vale of Dunes and over the walls of Alençon. They trusted him and accepted, now, to be treated like dirt, for they knew he had need of it; anything to keep his wife's trials out of his thoughts, even for a moment or two. Besides, he was their duke. Their lives were his to command – as were their deaths.

And so William made them sweat and they obeyed.

They were just lining up for a fresh charge when William spotted a boy running towards him.

"Ready!" FitzOsbern shouted. "CHARGE!"

They shot off, their warhorses digging up great clumps of earth with their hooves. The boy, blissfully unaware, so focused on reaching William, ran right into their path.

William swore. None of the knights had seen him, for their heads were down. Two hundred horses shook the ground as they thundered onwards. William put his spurs to his horse's flanks. He waved a warning which no one saw, shouted a command which no one heard. The hooves came closer. The boy at last realised the danger he was in and tried to turn back. It was too late. The knights were almost upon him, carried forwards by their sheer momentum, when William reached him. He grabbed him by the collar and lifted him bodily, as though the boy were no more than a small bag of potatoes, pulling the boy onto the pommel of his saddle. The child let out a small yelp, though whether out of surprise or the pain of the pommel digging into him, William could not tell. Nor did he care. He veered his horse round with all the skill of an accomplished rider and kicked the steed forwards just before the knights came level with him.

Eventually, their impetus ran out and they came to a slow canter. William roared at them to halt. As the order passed down the line, William stopped his own mount and threw the boy unceremoniously to the ground. The men gathered around him, wondering how this lad had come to be on their duke's horse. He swore again.

"What do you think you're playing at, running out in front of a cavalry charge? Are you trying to get yourself killed?"

The boy looked up, muttering something, clearly in shock, though whether because he had almost been ridden over or because he was now being shouted at by the Duke of Normandy was hard to tell.

"Well? Speak up, boy!" The lad would have to toughen up soon if he ever wanted to win his spurs. No lord would want a weakling in his conroi. The boy cleared his throat. He could not have been more than twelve or thirteen.

"Your pardon, my lord," he said, scrambling to his feet hastily to kneel before William. "I was told to find you as quickly as possible."

William's heart quickened, pounded like a hammer against his chest. *Please God,* he thought, *not Matilda.*

"You have news of the Duchess?" His mouth felt dry.

"No, my lord." The boy's mouth quivered. "I was just sent to find you."

Damn this waiting.

"Well who sent you, then, for God's sake?" William gripped his reins tightly under his leather glove.

"The Bishop of Bayeux, my lord." The boy gulped, perhaps thinking William meant to hit him as punishment for his behaviour.

William turned to FitzOsbern.

"Odo? When did he arrive?"

FitzOsbern shrugged. "Perhaps he's come to pray for the Duchess?"

William wondered what could have brought his brother out of Caen at this time. Odo was not the sentimental type, so FitzOsbern's explanation seemed unlikely.

"Bigod," William said to one of his men, "you take over the training. I don't want any slacking. FitzOsbern, Montgomery; you two come with me."

The three of them spurred off towards the castle, leaving the boy to make his own way back. Arriving at the keep, William hastily leaped out of his saddle and threw the reins to a stable boy.

"Any news of the Duchess?" he asked the captain of the guards.

"None, my lord duke. She is still lying in."

"Where is the Bishop of Bayeux?"

"He awaits you in the chapel."

Business not pleasure then, William thought. Odo would normally have set himself down in his chamber or the hall with a flagon of beer and something to tuck into – whether food or a wench. William and his companions went across the bailey and into the small chapel.

It took William's eyes a while to adjust to the gloom inside after the brightness of the spring sun. At first the place seemed empty. Compared to the din of the training ground, where metal beat against wood and horses pounded the ground to mud, this small house of God seemed eerily quiet. It was as if the workings of the outside world could not touch it.

As they walked along the central aisle, crossing themselves before the great silver crucifix which stood on the altar, he could at last make out the shadowy outlines of two figures in one corner. They were deep in conversation and scarce seemed to notice the arrivals, though they could hardly have failed to hear the dull echo of the heavy wooden door swinging shut. Their hurried whispers seemed to mimic the breeze which blew outside and whistled in the chapel.

Odo sat facing the aisle, but the other man had his back to William, who could only see his robes and tonsured hair. The diminutive man wore a thick black cloak. A Benedictine monk, then, William thought. He must have come down from the abbey at Fécamp.

"Ah, William!" his brother said, looking up. "I was beginning to think that the boy I sent had got lost."

"Actually, he did; he managed to find himself in the middle of a cavalry charge."

Odo laughed. The sound echoed through the chapel, filling every alcove. It seemed quite unnatural after the serious whispering.

"Well, if you will insist on working them so hard. I heard they don't even need to plough the fields any more, so much do your cavalry dig them up. You might try doing it when they actually need ploughing."

"I don't like men sitting idle," William grunted.

"Better not join the Church, then. That's all we seem to do." Odo winked. Sensing that William was in no mood for levity, he swiftly moved on to the matter at hand. "I believe you already know Brother Osbern."

"Osbern?" William looked at FitzOsbern's brother. The boy had grown into a man, much as he had himself, though he looked nothing like FitzOsbern, save for the eyes. Both had their father the old steward's piercing blue eyes.

"Osbern," FitzOsbern said, embracing his brother. "It's so good to see you. You are well?"

"I am, brother," Osbern said, though he seemed utterly exhausted.

"You've recently arrived from England?" William said.

"Yesterday, my lord," the monk said.

"We rode from Bayeux at first light," Odo explained. It must be an urgent matter indeed for such haste. A worrying thought crossed William's mind.

"Is the King well? Godwin hasn't caused him any harm, has he?" William's concern was genuine. Edward was a good man and a true friend of Normandy.

"The King is well, my lord, in spite of his usual tiredness. Such is the burden of kingship." The monk smiled with thin lips and made the sign of the cross. "We pray that his good health continues."

"He's certainly in better health than Godwin," Odo said. "Wait until you hear this. Tell him, Osbern."

The monk gave Odo an irritated look, as though the bishop had just spoiled a good story. William gave him a quizzical look.

"The Earl Godwin," the monk said "is dead."

William could not hide his surprise.

"Dead? How? When?"

"At Easter. The King's court had gathered at Winchester, as is the custom. During the main feast, the Earl had stood up to praise the King. Despite what had passed between them – their mutual dislike is no secret – Godwin spoke of Edward as a just ruler and a great king. He raised a toast and drank from his cup. It had barely touched his lips before he started to choke. His son Harold tried to save him, thumping him hard on the back." Osbern shrugged. "Nothing could be done. The Earl fell to the ground, his body gave several wild spasms before he lay still, eyes bulging. His life was gone."

William looked at his friends. Their faces all bore the same suspicions he had.

"What are people saying at court?"

The monk shrugged again. "There are always rumours, my lord."

"And what of Harold? How did he take it?"

"He and his father were never close. Yet Godwin was still his father."

"Does he think the death an accident?"

"The death *was* an accident," the monk said pointedly. "Even the greatest lord on Earth cannot refuse to answer when the Lord above us all calls for him."

"Amen," Odo said, though William did not miss the small wink in the darkness of the chapel.

"Thank you, Brother Osbern, for your news," William said. "Welcome to Normandy. The captain of the guard will have someone bring you food and water."

The Benedictine took the hint, his leave and the welcome offer of sustenance. He bowed and made his way out. William carefully waited until the wooden door had swung closed once more.

Montgomery let out a heavy sigh, as if a great weight had just been lifted from him.

"Well," Odo said "what do you make of that?"

"Poison," FitzOsbern said. "It must have been."

"It certainly sounds like it," Montgomery said. "But poisoned by whom; that is the real question."

"I hardly think that matters." William said, putting an end to the speculation before it had even begun. "Godwin had a spectacular talent for making enemies wherever he went. Any one of them might have had cause to kill him."

"Would Edward?" FitzOsbern voiced aloud what they had all been privately wondering.

"Kings do not poison," William said. "Let's have no more talk like that."

Odo looked as though he was about to support FitzOsbern's point but thought better of it.

William actually agreed with them, in his heart of hearts. Edward may well have had Godwin killed. It would even have been the right thing to do. Godwin was a vassal of the King of England, yet he strutted around as though he were the one giving orders. If vassals no longer had to obey their sovereigns and could even countermand their king's orders, the very fabric of society would be torn apart. In England, it had already started to fray. Countries without a strong king have ever fallen prey to foreign aggressors. Though Edward had tried to bring his foremost earl to heel, Godwin had dared go so far as to bring an army into London to make demands on his king. What could Edward have done? The only real shame was that he didn't have the Earl of Wessex killed sooner. Had Godwin been done away with while still in exile, it would have saved everyone a lot of trouble – and preserved Norman influence in England.

"So what happens now?" FitzOsbern said.

"Harold's grip on power will never be as strong as his father's," Odo said. "He's going to have to accept some amount of compromise."

"I heard he did well in the Welsh wars," William said.

"He did," Odo conceded, "but there's a big difference between fending off a rabble of cattle rustlers and being the most powerful man in the land."

"He can still be dangerous," Montgomery said. "We need to act quickly or we'll regret it. If we let him do as he pleases, he could soon enough become a danger to Edward."

"And to anything Edward may have promised Normandy," FitzOsbern added with a knowing glance at William.

"What to do though?" William asked them. "If I go in too heavy-handed, it would merely risk uniting the English thegns against me."

"To Hell with them," FitzOsbern said. "I say we give Edward whatever help he needs."

"Remember that we are in a house of God, FitzOsbern. It doesn't do to blaspheme here." Montgomery said touchily. "Especially when we need Him on our side."

William noted that Odo, the only Bishop among them, had made no reproof.

"Besides," Montgomery continued "we can't exactly send over a ship full of Norman knights. Or have you forgotten what happened last time? Our countrymen went over to help

Edward's brother reclaim his throne from the Danes and they were slaughtered on a hillside near London."

"Montgomery is right," William said. "There is no point doing anything so obvious; it would merely be used against both us and the King. No, this calls for something a bit more subtle."

"Such as?" FitzOsbern asked, far from satisfied.

"For a start, I shall send Hubert of Ryes back to England as my ambassador. There can be no official objection to that. We may even find some of the English more willing to do business with us, now that Godwin is no longer there to stir things up."

"Is that it?" FitzOsbern spat. "Send one man? He'll achieve nothing on his own."

"Do not underestimate Hubert. He is far cleverer than people give him credit for. That's what makes him such a brilliant ambassador; no one expects him to be underhand."

FitzOsbern did have a point though, William thought. Hubert would need some support out there. Norman nobles at this English court would ring alarm bells. William sat down on a nearby pew. There had to be some way around the problem. It had taken long enough to be rid of Godwin; they could not now afford to let Harold take his place.

"You know," William said, "sometimes I wish we could just do as Rollo did here. I wish we could just gather an army and sail right up the Thames estuary and take whatever lands we wanted." He leant back, wistfully thinking of the bygone days of the Viking warlords, when a man's only limitations were the weather, the reach of his sword arm and his own ambition. He laughed.

"I'm afraid those times are passed. Now we must justify our actions with proven legitimacy. Great councils and far away bishops must give their approval before we can act."

"A pity," FitzOsbern said. "A bit of good old-fashioned raiding is just what we could all do with. A damn sight better than all this endless practicing."

William smiled at the resentment in his friend's voice. He'd make them sweat, whether they liked it or not.

"So, what are we to do?" Odo asked.

"There is only one thing we can do; trust in Edward's abilities. He has been in tight spots before with the Godwins. Remember that not all the English wish to see Harold on the throne. The Mercians have ever been fierce rivals. If they put forward a claimant, the dissent might just give us the time to take control of the country."

"By force of arms?" Montgomery asked.

"How else? Diplomacy has its limits. I find spears to be a much better argument for power."

"England is a powerful country."

"So was Charlemagne's France," William said. "Look at it now. Henry can't even control his clergy, let alone his vassal lords."

"It would take quite some army to capture England. A formidable force," Montgomery said. "Far greater than any which you could muster."

"We have allies," William said patiently. "And I intend to make more - also by force, if need be. Besides, England is a big prize. What knight in his own mind would pass up such an opportunity?"

"Not I, for one," FitzOsbern said.

"Anyway, it might not come to that," Odo said. "The English will have to take Edward's choice into account."

"All the same," William said, "we need to plan today for war tomorrow."

"We might as well," FitzOsbern said, "since we have no better idea. I still think we should…"

FitzOsbern's voice trailed away as the urgent footsteps of someone rushing up the flagstones of the aisle were heard. William pushed past his friends to meet the newcomer. It was the captain of the guard.

"My lord," he called, "the Duchess -"

"Oh God!" William said, crossing himself.

He ran past the man and was out the door so fast that he did not hear the rest of what the captain had to say. His heart pounded against his chest. A thousand thoughts did battle in his head. After all he had been through to make Matilda his own, he could not bear the idea of losing her now. As he took the steps leading up to the keep two at a time, he glanced to the east. Among the houses which sprawled around the castle, he could make out a large area which had been cleared of houses. That was the site they had chosen together for Matilda's abbey for women – the Trinity Abbey. Normally the place would have been a hive of activity, with large clouds of dust rising up into the air from men digging the foundations or sawing the large stone blocks into the desired pieces of masonry.

That day there was no work. As a mark of respect for the Duchess, no men were allowed on the site. Only a small group of nuns stood vigil, praying for Matilda and her child to come safely through their ordeal.

William felt as though he had a lump in his throat on which he might choke. They were building these abbeys to ask forgiveness from God for a marriage which the Pope himself had deemed unacceptable. The Pope had eventually relented; but had God? What if the Almighty chose to punish him by preventing the marriage from providing children? What if he punished William with Matilda's death?

He prayed through gasping breath as he reached the door of the keep. In his haste, he slipped, his feet flying out from under him. He was oblivious to the great gash which a piece of stone opened up in his arm as he tried to catch himself. He picked himself up and carried on running.

He thundered into the keep, almost knocking over one of the sentries who hadn't enough time to move out of his way. A lesser man might have faltered when climbing the steep staircase leading to their private chambers, but William was a strapping man in his mid-twenties, made resilient through constant training and sheer force of character. In any case, his only thoughts were for his wife. He reached the top and hammered on the heavy wooden door.

"Open up! Open up for your duke!" he bellowed, voice trembling, catching in his throat.

One of Matilda's ladies opened the door and curtsied. William walked past her into the small chamber.

Matilda was laid on the bed, her small body almost lost amongst the blood-stained sheets. William had never seen so much blood, not even on the battlefield. Her face was whiter than

300

the sheets, a maid gently dabbed at it with a cloth to remove the beads of sweat which glistened there like early morning dew. For all the world she seemed a lifeless corpse, a shadow of herself.

"Christ," he muttered.

Matilda heard and turned towards him. She smiled. She smiled and it was as if colour and life came pouring over her anew.

"Of all the things you could have said," she said in a soft voice "you chose blasphemy as the first word your son should hear."

"My son?" William asked, stunned. The words seemed unreal.

"Your son," Matilda repeated. As he stepped closer, he saw that she held a small bundle in her arms.

"My son," he said the words again, just for the sheer pleasure of hearing them roll off his tongue.

He sat on the edge of the bed and leant over to kiss his wife gently on the cheek. He carefully pulled away an edge of cloth from the bundle. A tiny pink face looked back up at him with small but curious eyes which searched around, trying to make sense of this new world that presented itself to him. An overwhelming feeling of warmth came over William, as all the troubles of the wider world faded away into an utterly insignificant fleck on the horizon.

The boy was unmistakably Matilda's. Of course, any newborn baby seems small, but aside from her same diminutive figure, he also had his mother's small nose and brown eyes.

The boy reached out with a little hand. With the clumsiness of one who has not yet learned to assess distances, he just missed William's hand. William smiled and moved his hand closer. The baby grabbed it, wrapping its whole hand around William's smallest finger.

William had never thought he would be the affectionate type of father. He had had to get by on his own. Even before Duke Robert's untimely death, the two of them had never been close. The Duke had been a great believer in letting his son make mistakes on his own and learn from them; a future duke would rely on none but himself. Osbern the Steward and Archbishop Robert, the Duke's uncle, had both respected that wish and had not sought to replace the fallen duke as a father figure – though William had grown attached to both of them. They had made him get on with learning for himself.

William had never felt any great emotion at seeing children playing. He encouraged his barons to put their sons into training as early as possible and saw little reason to take any interest in them until they started showing some promise. Besides, so many infants did not make it through their first winters that it was best not to become too attached until they had reached the age of eleven or twelve.

Looking down at his newborn son, though, he realised that it would be impossible to keep his distance. As the little boy clasped his finger as tightly as he could, needing to hold on to something solid in the vastness of the world, a tear came to William's eye, in spite of himself. With the arrival of this son – this firstborn son and heir – his own world became a better place. He had saved his dukedom from both internal enemies, secured his northern border through marriage with a daughter of Flanders, and beaten off the threat of Anjou. Now he had given his people what they so greatly needed; a future. He had given them an heir, an irrefutable and legitimate male heir, of royal blood, no less.

As he looked into the eyes of the boy safely cradled in Matilda's arms, he thought how peaceful the babe seemed. One day, William knew, this descendant of Charlemagne would be called upon to continue William's work of safeguarding the lands passed down from one duke to the next since the founding of Normandy by the great Viking Rollo. For now, though, it was up to William to give the boy his best chance in life. He looked up at Matilda. She smiled back at him, glowing with the pride which only a mother can ever know.

"What shall we call him, my love?" she asked.

For William, there could be only one answer.

"Robert," he said, stroking the child's smooth head.

"Robert," Matilda repeated the name of her son.

It was the first duty of a wife to produce an heir. It was the only duty which most lords deemed of any consequence; to continue the man's lineage, so that his lands may be more secure through the knowledge of a successor being lined up. Opportunists might seek to exploit the fragility of a land which had no heir-apparent. Matilda had performed her duty and come out alive herself.

"Tell me," she said after a while, "what is Odo doing in Caen?"

"Odo?" William said, astounded that even at such a time his wife was fully aware of the goings-on of court. Odo had barely arrived, yet a message had already reached her. God help any man who should cross so purposeful a lady.

"Yes, they say he arrived while you were off training the men."

303

"Oh, he came to ask after your health," William said with a dismissive shrug. He could tell the answer did not satisfy her curiosity. "And he wanted to discuss an opportunity."

"What sort of opportunity?" she said, kissing her boy's forehead. William could tell she was anxious; why shouldn't she be? Having just put a baby into the world, it was only natural she should want to keep danger at bay.

"Just some trade," he said, not entirely untruthfully. "We can talk about it later. For now, you need to rest."

He called one of her ladies over to take care of the boy. He kissed him before the child was removed to a small cot at the far end of the room.

He took Matilda's hand in his.

"Thank you, my love," he said. "Get some sleep. You've earned it." He kissed her and left the room.

As the door closed behind him, he breathed a great sigh of relief. At last, the worst was over. Matilda was alive. He had a son… He had a son.

He turned to the captain who had joined him outside the chambers.

"Guard them with your life," he said. "And have a boy fetch my best horse."

The captain looked puzzled.

"I have business with regards to England," he said.

CHAPTER 36

ARQUES, UPPER NORMANDY. OCTOBER, 1053 A.D.

"So the old dog won't budge," William said, as he entered Montgomery's tent.

"No, my lord; I'm afraid not."

"Yet dirty work is afoot," he said, gratefully taking the goblet of watered wine Montgomery had poured for him.

William had been receiving regular despatches from the besieging force at his uncle's castle of Arques. It was certainly a formidable structure. William felt a fool for having let him have it. Arques was the strongest fort that side of Rouen. It had long served to keep the house of Ponthieu in check on Normandy's north-eastern borders. Built on the vital produce of the salt marshes, Ponthieu controlled the main road from Normandy to Flanders, which meant it could cause trouble for any merchants seeking to go between the two.

Arques had, until recently, offered shelter to the merchants and from its high walls riders could sally forth to intervene in any misdeeds the house of Ponthieu might plan. Now Arques was home to William's rebel uncle and the latest despatch had contained the very news he had feared; Arques had done a deal with Ponthieu. If the house of Ponthieu supported him in defiance, he would support Ponthieu once he was back in favour - or on the ducal throne itself. William could not afford to have the two border castles unite against him. He had raised a force of hired swords to supplement his household milites and break the siege.

"What is the latest news?" he asked Montgomery.

"We know that Arques is growing desperately short of supplies," Roger said. "Indeed, I am amazed your uncle has held out for this long."

"This was no spur of the moment desertion; it was years in the planning. No doubt he made arrangements to have provisions smuggled in regularly."

"I have been doing my best to stop them, my lord," Roger said, throwing his arms out in apology. "Arques knows his lands well and the marshes and woods in these parts afford much cover to those who roam abroad at night."

"Roger," William said, raising a hand to stop his friend's apology, "I know as well as any that you do not have enough men to hold an effective screen around the castle. It was never my intention that you should. I simply wanted to see who would support my uncle, so as to know whom I could trust in these parts. Besides, there is no way I could afford to spare the men to besiege Arques so soon after our campaign against the Bellême lands."

"No, my lord. That is true."

"Carry on with your report. What is this of Ponthieu?"

"One of our agents, a tavern landlord in the town, sent word that two milites from Ponthieu had sneaked in to parlay with Arques."

"How do we know that any deal was reached?" William asked. "They might have been rebuffed."

Montgomery shook his head.

"The landlord offered them hospitality before they left."

"Hospitality?"

"A couple of local girls and as much beer as they cared for."

306

"I see," William said, grinning. "So nature took its course and they proved as able to keep a secret as to keep their breeches on."

"There you have it, my lord. FitzOsbern set off a week ago with a small party to patrol the border. Any sign of the relief force and we will hear of it long before they reach the castle gate."

"Has there been any communication from Arques himself?"

"Not for some months, my lord. His last message was one of scorn. He said that he would not treat with one from such a recently ennobled family as myself or with a knave so impudent as the Steward."

William scoffed. How characteristic of his uncle to be so contemptuous of others, even when he was the ignominious one in all this.

"Would you care to take a tour of our positions, my lord?"

"Thank you, Roger. I am sure you have everything under control, but I will nonetheless show myself before the castle, that my uncle should know whom he now faces."

A guard pulled aside the tent flap for them, as they stepped out to inspect the men. William's mercenaries were causing a stir in the camp, as they made space for themselves. These were the lordless men who followed no banner other than that which paid the most. William's new taxation policy was starting at last to replenish the ducal coffers, enabling him to hire the men needed to break Arques. The household milites of the lords who had been besieging the castle for the past year and a half did not take kindly to being disturbed by men they saw as little more than thugs.

It was not long before a fight broke out over places around a campfire.

"You build your own fire," one of the Normans barked at a tall bearded Breton who had pushed him to one side so that he could sit down.

"This one is lit already," the surly Breton said, in his guttural Celtic accent. "And I've been marching all day."

"I don't care if you've been marching all year; this is our fire. You're paid to be here, so you can damn well make your own fire and leave this one to your betters."

The Norman shoved the Breton in the shoulder, earning him a swift punch by way of an answer. Soon the other Normans around the fire had leapt to their feet and were reaching for their weapons, as the Breton's friends rushed over.

"Enough!" William shouted, stepping in between the two groups.

"What's it to you?" asked a boisterous young man, intent on showing his mettle before his comrades.

"This is Duke William, you cur," Montgomery said, striding forwards, his hand resting on his own sword's pommel.

The lad looked from Montgomery to William and flushed crimson at his gaffe. He bowed hurriedly, the others quickly doing the same.

"Forgive me, my lord, I did not recognise you."

"You speak when you are spoken to, boy," Montgomery said.

"Look at me," William said, taking off his nasal-guard helmet. "All of you, look at me and remember this face. You take orders from me. You fight for me. I am in command. It is as simple as that. You men of Normandy should know better. And you who are in my pay should listen closely; I tolerate no disorder in my camp. Any man caught brawling will be flogged raw. Any man caught stealing will be hanged from the nearest tree. Any man who brings whores into my camp without authorisation from one of my officers will have his offending member cut off. Do I make myself clear?"

A silence had fallen around the group. Soldiers from other camp fires had come closer to see what the fuss was about.

"I asked you a question," William said in a steely voice. "Do I make myself clear?"

"Yes, my lord," the men said as one.

"Now," he said, turning to the two men who had started the fight, "what would you prefer? To share a cup of beer with each other or to have your backs flogged until you can't lie down for a month?"

The Norman reluctantly filled a cup and held it out for the Breton, who bowed thanks and drank it.

"Good," William said. "You'll have enough fighting to do soon enough. When you do, all shall share in the spoils."

"Long life to our duke William!" the Norman shouted.

"Long live the duke!" the gathered men echoed.

William carried on through the camp to look out at the castle, from which they were just over an arrow's flight away. His uncle had clearly taken good care of the place. Wooden defences had been added at the top of the stone walls and soaked animal hides and moss protected the wooden parts from the threat of fire. Arques would have heard how William had burned Alençon to the ground.

"It won't be fun trying to take that brute," Montgomery said.

"It won't come to that," William answered. "Arques needs supplies, not just now, but for months to come. If we stop those supplies at their source, he will know that holding out further is pointless. Every day he stands against me, he aggravates his eventual punishment. He is no fool. He wants to end this on favourable terms. He no doubt hopes I will offer him an honourable way of backing down, that way he might even get to keep some of his lands."

"And will you?"

"I am not inclined to give him the satisfaction," William said with a wink. "Not if we have a chance of slapping down Ponthieu at the same time."

He looked back at the castle.

"Do you know, Roger," he said, "I am rather enjoying this. My uncle may be much slower than a boar, but he is much more challenging to hunt."

"My lord," a voice said.

William grunted.

"My lord," the voice insisted, shaking his shoulder. William instinctively reached for his sword, which he always kept by him when he slept. He squinted, as a candle's light pierced through the dark.

"What is it, Roger?" he said, through gritted teeth. "I had just got comfortable."

"Word has come from FitzOsbern. An enemy force is on its way as we speak."

William leapt to his feet.

"How many men?"

"He could not tell. Enough to oblige him to send for reinforcements, though."

William took a deep swig from a jug left by his bed.

"You there," he growled at a guard, pulling aside the flap of his tent. "Help me with my hauberk. Quickly now!"

He pulled on his leather shoes, cursing as a stone had found its way into one of them. He threw out the offending article.

"How far away are they?"

"About three hours' ride."

"A dawn assault on our camp?"

"I'd say that was their plan, yes."

"Good, then we shall beat them at their own game," William said, before turning to the guard he had summoned. "Get a damn move on, man. I'll die of old age before you have that mail on me."

"I'll have the men assemble," Montgomery said, bowing himself out of the tent.

William lifted his arms and leaned forwards so that the guard could pull the heavy mail hauberk over his head.

"Don't be shy, man. Yank it down hard."

Hauberks were always closely fitted and yet cumbersome at the same time. The recent feasting had made William's that bit tighter. By rights, he should have called in an adolescent to help him, but he had no time for decorum. He was eager to lock horns with Ponthieu.

Before long, they were making their way at a brisk pace to join FitzOsbern. Their progress was made all the quicker, if slightly less ordered than William cared for, as Norman and mercenary jostled for position, both troops eager to be the first into the fray.

William rode at the front, closely following FitzOsbern's messenger who acted as their guide to him.

"Who goes there?" came a challenge from a cope of trees just ahead.

"Duke William," the guide answered.

"Come forward, my lord," the sentry called, relieved at hearing a familiar voice.

"Wait here," William said to his men. He spurred his mount through the trees, where he found FitzOsbern. His friend motioned for him to be silent, before pointing down the hill on which they presently found themselves. Through the woods, William could just make out soldiers on the move.

"So Ponthieu has come, has he?"

FitzOsbern frowned.

"Didn't my messenger tell you?"

"Tell me what?"

"The King is here."

William could not hide his surprise.

"Henry? Here? Are you sure?"

"I had to check for myself, when my scouts told me. There he was, bold as brass, his standard caught in the light of the moon."

"The wily devil," William said. "So much for the bonds of fealty. He's got another thing coming, if he thinks to supplant me with my uncle. Have they spotted you?"

FitzOsbern shook his head.

"Typical French. They think so highly of themselves, they've been merrily marching along, speaking loud as they pleased. They must think us miles away."

"Well then, my friend, let's show them what real warriors are made of. French pride will meet the Norman sword."

The relief force was making poor progress. The carts they had brought with them to resupply Arques would have slowed them down at the best of times, but in the late autumn mists, the ground simply turned to sludge under the soldiers' feet, causing the wooden wheels to sink in. Men struggled in the dark to heave them out, only to have them sink in again a few feet further along the path. The campaign season was all but over. No sensible commander would have tried such a march under normal circumstances; but Henry had no choice. He would know as well as William that Arques could not survive another winter without restocking in food and other vital supplies. Perhaps the king thought that a march this late in the year would be unexpected. After all, who would be foolish enough to embark on a perilous journey to war in late October?

Yet he should have properly scouted ahead. Night time cannot hide all secrets. Night time does not last forever. Already, William could see the first rays of light creeping through the branches from the east. He would have liked to take time to choose his moment, making sure the terrain either side was favourable, yet he could not risk being spotted and missing this golden opportunity.

Montgomery joined them on the ridge.

"Alright," William said softly, "this is the plan. Montgomery, you take two Norman conrois to cut off their retreat. I'll have our archers soften them up. If we're lucky, they'll be in complete disarray. Then I'll lead the hired swords and the rest of our men and hit them in the centre."

"Right," Montgomery said, before heading back down their lines to assemble his household milites and order another conroi join them.

"Ready?" William asked FitzOsbern.

The steward grinned with a flash of teeth in the pale half light. His archers had been in pale in the woods even before William had arrived; a standard precaution, though William knew his friend was spoiling for a fight. Alençon had been some time ago and they had known little other than small skirmishes around Arques since then.

"Spear," William said to his squire, who dutifully handed him a throwing spear. "When I say, let them have it," he told FitzOsbern, who nodded to his archers. They notched their arrows and drew back on the strings, each man picking his target.

They waited in silence. It was, for those who have known war, one of those eerie, unnatural silences which forebode imminent danger. Had the French had their wits about them, they might have paid heed and prepared themselves. Had they only listened, they might have lived.

William was listening, and he heard the hoot of an owl further up the road.

"Roger's in position," he said. "Now let's teach these fools a lesson."

314

FitzOsbern lowered his arms and instantly an autumn rain fell upon the French troops. Cries pierced the silence, as men were hit. Horses bolted and soldiers scrambled to grab their weapons from the carts.

Another flight of arrows struck home.

"Normandy!" William shouted. "God helps!"

His riders thundered down the slope, the milites following their lord's flag - the mercenaries following the scent of money.

King Henry turned in his saddle in alarm. The march had been long and tediously slow, but they had finally been nearing their destination when the Norman came out of nowhere.

"Ponthieu!" he fumed.

"My lord King," Enguerrand of Ponthieu said, making haste to join his sovereign.

"Where the Hell did they come from? Why did your scouts not spot them before they were upon us?"

"I do not know, good my king."

"I thought you knew these parts."

"Indeed, my lord, I have known them all my life."

Henry looked at the carnage unfolding behind them, as more and more soldiers erupted from the woods.

"Get over there and deal with them!"

"Yes, my liege," Ponthieu said, replacing his helmet. "Ponthieu! With me!" he ordered his milites. They formed up around him. He gritted his teeth at what he was about to do. The Normans were already slaughtering the centre of his line. It was carnage.

315

"For the King!" he shouted, spurring his steed towards the whirlwind of spears and blades.

William threw himself down the hill, his horse half skidding down the muddy slope. A group of four spearmen were stood by a cart. They realised the danger too late. As his horse leapt off the slope William hurled his javelin at the nearest man. The metal point went straight through the quilted wool and stuffing of his gambeson. As the man fell like an ox, William drew his sword. He ploughed into the remaining three, who had not had the sense to level their spears at him. These were no trained milites, merely levies of the commoners which Henry had brought with him to do the donkey work. The impact from his powerful warhorse threw them to the ground. The most sensible of the three stayed down and hid himself under the cart. Hardly a noble action, but commoners have more use for life than for noble heroics. Another scrambled to his feet and reached into the cart for his shield, only to receive a spear in the back from one of many knights who streamed like a torrent down the hillside to wash away the French.

William pricked his spurs back. His men would deal with the remaining spearman. He had to keep moving. A rider who stays still is little more than a large target. He glanced back and saw that the milites of his conroi were hard on his heels. He wheeled them to the left and pressed on up the French lines, hacking down as he passed French foot soldiers. Most would not stand. They dived under and in between carts to flee into the safety of darkness. From the ridge, the Norman archers picked them off, men falling face first into the mud, arrow shafts protruding from their backs.

"Ponthieu!"

William heard them before he saw them. A conroi of knights, under the banner of Ponthieu, charged at him head on.

"Normandy!" he shouted, standing up in his stirrups that his men would see him.

As he raced level with the first rider from Ponthieu, he twisted sharply in his saddle. The spear which had been thrown at him glanced harmlessly off his shield and he let the knight past only to bring his sword back against his opponent's neck. The man's chainmail stopped the blade from digging in, but the blow sent him off-balance, so that FitzOsbern, close behind, easily pushed him clean out of his stirrups. William heard a yelp as the rest of his conroi rode over him.

He charged at the next man and they thundered into each other. The space between the carts and the ridge was small and it was soon filled with knights. So packed were they, that any thought of charging or withdrawing was quickly forgotten, as the fight turned into a shoving contest. William raised his shield to deflect the occasional blade, though he could do little other than put his weight behind it and push.

Behind the nasal guard and rim of his helmet, he could see little of what was going on. A curse to his right told him that FitzOsbern was covering his sword arm with his own shield. All around, the men of Normandy and of Ponthieu goaded each other with insults, being able to exchange no other blows.

Surely, William thought, the weight of numbers would soon tell. His forces greatly outnumbered Henry and Enguerrand's, yet the enemy wouldn't give any ground.

Suddenly, he felt the earth shake as something heavy thumped to the ground with a crash. It was followed by the sound of horses whinnying in agony and men shrieking in alarm.

He chanced a peak over the rim of his shield and saw what was causing the commotion. A number of his hired swords had dismounted and were presently stood atop the carts, one of which they had overturned, from where they hacked down with axes and stabbed with long spears to wound the nearest of Ponthieu's horses. As the beasts fell to the ground, bringing down their rider with them, the mercenaries leaped down from the carts and drew long knives to slit throats.

William tried to push his steed forward, but it edged back, in spite of its training. He sensed the other horses nearby growing nervous at the sight of the injured warhorses of Ponthieu flailing their hooves in agony, until they were put out of their misery. By then, the hired swords were in amongst Ponthieu's milites, pulling men from their mounts and promptly despatching them, with no thought of taking prisoners. William saw Ponthieu's flag waver and then fall, though he could see neither its bearer nor Ponthieu himself.

King Henry saw the brutal attack by William's men. Curse the duke for having brought in hired thugs. Of course, Henry himself had also paid for soldiers of fortune to follow his banner, but never had he seen such a callous slaughter of nobility.

"Come", he said to his household knights. "There is nothing more we can do here."

"Should we fall back down the road, my lord? We may be able to force a way through."

"What? Do you wish to be cut down along with Ponthieu? No. We press on to Arques."

"But my lord King, we have lost the supplies."

"I can see that, thank you very much. We press on to Arques because we know there cannot be many guards left there when such a force is here. We cannot help the Count of Arques, anymore, but we can at least hope for a safer route home."

He took one last look at the devastation, turned his steed, and disappeared into the trees.

Montgomery arrived on the other side of the carts with his two conrois, having successfully taken a number of prisoners among those who had tried to flee at the rear. William made his way over to join him.

"Jesus Christ," Montgomery said.

William was taken aback; his friend rarely swore. He followed Montgomery's gaze. There, in the mud, lay Enguerrand of Ponthieu. His corpse had been hacked almost beyond recognition. A hired sword was busy stripping it of its rings and chainmail, along with anything else of value he could find. All around, others were engaged in this same business. William could not blame them for looting. After all, these were nought but the spoils of war. Yet there was something ignominious in seeing the Count of Ponthieu defiled by a common soldier.

"You there," William said. "Desist this instant."

The man did not hear him - or pretended not to.

"Are you deaf man, I said -"

He was cut short by Montgomery swinging himself down from his saddle. His face showed only hatred. William had never seen Roger this angry. He was always the calm one, rising above any situation, immovable to outbursts. Now William watched as Montgomery grabbed a rope from his pack. He briskly tied a knot and marched over to the looter, who was too busy in his enterprise to notice. Roger threw the loop around the man's throat. There was a stifled protest, as the looter tried to release himself. FitzOsbern leapt down to join Montgomery, and between the two of them, they dragged the man over to the nearest tree. Roger tossed the other end of the rope over a solid branch and yanked his hand. Puffing as he pulled, he lifted him clear off his feet.

All those around, of Ponthieu and Normandy alike, stopped what they were doing to watch the ghastly spectacle. The man writhed, clutching at the rope round his neck, pitifully trying to free himself. He began to lift himself up, releasing the pressure for a while, when FitzOsbern caught hold of his legs and put all his weight on them. There was a nasty crack like a whip and the man fell limp. Montgomery let the corpse drop to the mud.

He stepped forward, breathing heavily.

"You dogs of war," he said, pointing at the hired swords. "You may not fight for honour, yet we are all subject to the same rules of war. When a man surrenders, you take him prisoner. When a man comes from noble stock, you show him respect, even in death. Fail to do so and this will be the price you pay," he said, looking at the corpse.

320

The Norman knights, and those few remaining survivors from Ponthieu, began beating their swords against their shields, in recognition of Montgomery's words.

He returned to his horse and pulled himself back into the saddle.

"Feel better?" William asked.

"Much," Roger said, spitting on the soil. "But by Heaven, I wish we did not have to deal with these scum."

"So do I, but they have proven more useful than many of my loyal barons these past years," William said. "Right, now that we have dealt with Ponthieu, we had best return to Arques. I am sure that my uncle will be interested to hear of what happened here."

He turned to the milites of Ponthieu.

"Look after your dead and wounded," he said. "Then go home to Ponthieu and tell Enguerrand's brother Guy that I expect him to know his place - unless he wishes to finish the same way as him."

CHAPTER 37

William gripped the arms of his chair. It was crafted out of solid oak, with ornate patterns carved into the wood. Along the right hand side, Rollo the Viking fought an epic battle to forge his new land of Normandy. On the left, Solomon the Wise brought justice to his people. At the head of the chair's back, a single cross symbolised Rollo's conversion to Christianity. William smiled ruefully at the memory of old Archbishop Robert trying hopelessly to teach William's eight-year-old self the story of the king of Israel.

He recalled that the king had been asked to judge which of two women was the real mother of a baby, and which was an imposter trying to steal the child. Solomon had ordered the infant be cut in two and half given to each of the women. When one of them screamed out, pleading that she would sooner give up the child than see it die, Solomon had known her to be the true mother. Clearly, William thought, he had remembered more than he thought. The Archbishop would have been pleased to know that at least some of his tutelage had sunk in.

This day's judgement would require no such wisdom. Guilt was irrefutable. All the same, he felt nervous. He hid his emotions behind steely resolution. Matilda, sat next to him, seemed to sense his unrest and placed a reassuring hand on his. He held it a few heartbeats, before nodding at De Warenne, who stood guarding the door.

"Bring in the prisoner."

De Warenne pulled on the heavy wooden door. It swung open with a dull creak. The room, packed with barons and clergy, fell silent.

FitzOsbern strode in first, armed with the warlike trappings of his office of steward. In his hand, he held the heavy mace which his father had carried - the same with which he had caved in William Montgomery's skull all those years earlier. Behind him, flanked by four guards, came Arques. Though he suffered the ignominy of having his hands bound, his countenance was one of proud defiance.

FitzOsbern and the guards bowed to William. Arques kept his back straight and glowered at him. FitzOsbern noticed the look.

"Kneel before your duke," he barked.

Arques spat in the steward's direction, earning himself a sharp kick behind the knee. There was a collective murmur as FitzOsbern used all his youthful strength to force the older man to his knees.

William's brother Odo, now wearing the pallium of his bishopric of Bayeux, stepped forward. A monk deferentially unrolled a parchment from which the bishop to read.

"William, Count of Talou and of Arques, you stand accused of deserting your post in time of war, of holding your castle of Arques against your lawful duke, of conspiring with an enemy of your lawful duke, and of unholy treason and sedition against your lawful duke, appointed by God to rule over you and all of Normandy. How do you answer these charges?"

"To you, whelp, I answer nothing. The bishopric of Bayeux is an honourable office for a wise and learned man of experience and honour to hold. It is not for a pup like you. I shall not treat with you."

Odo reddened so much at these words that anyone entering the room then might have wondered which of the two men was being tried.

To his left, William sensed Lanfranc shuffle his feet. The Italian had not approved of William appointing his own brother to the see of Bayeux. Nevertheless, he had been worldly enough to understand William's need for men whom he could trust in all circles of his court. Besides, had it not become a custom for the dukes of Normandy to elevate their own family to such positions? Though he wished that practice be abolished, Lanfranc had been mindful to let it linger a little while longer; for now, it served a useful purpose. In bringing down Arques, William's other uncle Mauger might also be displaced, opening the archbishopric of Rouen, the highest of them all, to a more worthy candidate - one of Lanfranc's choosing.

The scholar stepped forward and cleared his throat purposefully. William motioned him to speak.

"My lord of Arques, you forget yourself. Bishop Odo's appointment received His Holiness' blessing. As such, it is the Will of God and beyond contestation. Do you recall the council at which your brother was appointed to the see of Rouen?"

Arques frowned, wary of what would follow.

"I didn't think you would," Lanfranc said, not waiting for an answer. "Nor indeed can anyone recall it, for there was no council. An appointment which required the approval of both this council and the Holy Father was made by yourselves behind closed doors. For your own profit, you took advantage of your duke's young age to seize the archbishopric, yet now you dare question the authority of a bishop whose appointment was sanctioned by the Holy Father himself? For shame, my lord, for shame!"

It was Arques' turn to redden. For all his years controlling this court, he was no match for one of the greatest scholars in Christendom.;

"Count William of Talou and of Arques," Odo repeated, taking courage from Lanfranc's support, "how do you answer these charges?"

Arques turned his scorn on William.

"For your charges, I am innocent. Who could be held guilty of rebelling against such a pathetic excuse for a duke? I faithfully served him as long as I could. But his recklessness will prove his downfall and that of all Normandy. Why, the very victory with which he thought to make his name at the Vale of Dunes was not his doing, but that of greater men. He insulted his overlord, King Henry of France, and thought to win the day with nought but a rabble of youths."

"I did win the field that day," William snapped. "Despite your pleas to bow to the rebels, I stood firm and saved Normandy."

"You were on the field, but it was not your victory, boy. King Henry won the field for you that day and he would not even have been there if I had not sent an emissary to beg his pardon for your impudence. I persuaded him to save Normandy in spite of your foolishness."

"You turned away from your rightful duke," Odo reprimanded Arques.

"He turned away from me. Think how I saved your duchy when you were a boy, William. All you had to do to keep our land safe was to follow my advice."

"Follow your orders, you mean," William snarled, rising from his seat. The assembled lords bowed. "But you are not duke, uncle. I am duke. You have coveted my office for far too long. You thought to make a puppet of me, yet those strings are now broken."

With that, he pulled out his dagger and cut clean through the belt of his uncle's empty scabbard. He tossed it to the back of the hall, where it fell limp on the floor. "There is one master of Normandy. One alone. Me. Any man who thinks to control me, be he Norman baron or French king, will soon find himself sorely mistaken."

"The King of France is your overlord," Arques said, as if his point had been made.

"And as for your loyalty," William continued, ignoring the interruption, "Did you think that your little dealings would go unnoticed?"

"Dealings? I don't know what you are insinuating."

"I am insinuating nothing; I state it openly. The viscount of Montgomery here has been going through our records. It seems that there are no end of discrepancies dating to the time when you were in charge of levying the taxes."

Arques was visibly stunned that William had taken the time to go through the accounts.

"Tell us," William said, "why it is that so much tax was levied yet my coffers are forever empty."

"Defending the duchy costs money."

"It is not expenditure that we question. What we question is why so little money ever got to the ducal treasury in the first place. I'll tell you why; your crooked collectors brought the money to you and you tried to claim that taxes had not been paid in full, keeping the difference in your own purse. You might have got away with it, except you forgot the records kept by the parish churches."

"Your clergy are the crooked ones," Arques protested.

"Some are," Lanfranc said, "at your own encouragement. But not all are as crooked as you, and those who are will be dealt with in due course, rest assured. Duke William has given me leave to weed them out."

"I served Normandy," Arques insisted.

"You served yourself!" William said. "You are not above the law, uncle. Now you will hear our judgement. Count William of Talou and of Arques, we find you guilty of treason against our person and Normandy, as well as guilty of all the other charges laid before you, and of embezzlement. Your castles and titles are forfeit. No longer Count of Talou. No longer Count of Arques. All here know the punishment for treason."

"Death," FitzOsbern said with unhidden relish.

"Death," William confirmed. "Death is all that you deserve and all which you should get."

His uncle looked unmoved, knowing that the judgement had been a foregone conclusion. FitzOsbern made to lead him out.

"However," William said, raising a hand to stop him, "you are our kin. Though you deserve death, we could not face God on Judgement Day knowing we had sent our own uncle to his death, deserved or not. We therefore commute your sentence to

327

banishment - for life. Never again shall you walk the fields of Normandy. Never again shall you taste the fruit of our orchards. Scurry away to live where it please you. We never want you in our presence ever again."

FitzOsbern looked utterly crestfallen at the reprieve, but knew better than to contradict William in front of the assembled lords.

"Steward," William said to him, "escort our uncle to the border."

"Yes, my lord," FitzOsbern said, bowing and leading the deposed count to the door.

"Oh, and steward," William added; "make sure he has a warm cloak. He has many years to live in the cold before old age finally takes him."

CHAPTER 38

"So how are you finding your Bellême lands, Montgomery?"

"The land is good and fertile, my lord. Thank you," Roger said, taking the goblet offered to him by a squire.

"And Mabel, your wife? Is she good and fertile too?" William grinned.

"I have no doubt that she will be with child before long, if I can find time," Roger said coyly.

"Do not leave it too late, my friend. You will have need of an heir."

"How is the lady Matilda?"

"She is well, thank you. And the boy thrives."

"Two sons in three years," Roger said with a smile. "You don't waste your time."

"That is quite a little empire you now have. With the Hiémois and Bellême lands together, you control half of southern Normandy. Men will covet such possessions."

"For now I have my hands full with restoring order to the Bellême lands."

"Yes, I am sure you have. Be sure to see to your border forts. Not just with Anjou, but also King Henry's lands."

"I have been strengthening them, my lord, but it will take more time. The southern defences of the Bellême lands were sorely neglected. You think an attack imminent, my lord?"

"If it were, we would be too late. We must not show Henry any weakness. The castles are the key to Normandy. Look at Domfront; that held us up for some two years. Without Nigel, I do not know how we would ever have taken it. Henry will not attack there if he knows that such castles as Domfront are being held by you. So see to them."

"I will, my lord," Roger said. "I trust you are finding my contributions to your treasury satisfactory."

"I am indeed, Montgomery. I am indeed. If only everyone were as forthcoming as you we would have no need of these new rules."

"We are doing all we can to collect the funds, my lord. FitzOsbern and I have been working tirelessly to ensure everyone pays their due."

"I know you are. I have every faith in your abilities."

Both men looked up at the sound of shouting in the hallway.

"You cannot go in unannounced!"

"Try and stop me!"

The heavy oak door swung open. In strode a rugged man of about William's own age. He wore a mail hauberk and riding shoes. FitzOsbern rushed in after him. Both men were covered in mud and sweating heavily.

"My lord Duke, I am sorry," FitzOsbern said, speaking formally to William, as he always did when in company. "I tried to stop him."

"Stop me," the other man spat in disgust. "After your behaviour, you had best not dare touch me."

"You're lucky I haven't run a sword through you, Ponthieu!"

"My lords," William said calmly, "would you care to explain?" He snapped his fingers and a guard stepped forward to take the uninvited guest's sword, which still hung in its scabbard. The man looked on the point of exploding at the very notion of giving up his weapon.

"You will lay aside your sword, my lord Guy of Ponthieu. I will have no blades in my hall, as well you know."

"What about his sword?" Ponthieu asked petulantly.

"*He* is my steward," William said curtly. "Now either put aside your sword or get back on your horse and be on your way."

Ponthieu reluctantly handed it over to the guard.

"Now then," William said, "would you care to explain?"

"This man will not pay his taxes," FitzOsbern said, pointing at Ponthieu.

"I have no taxes to pay. Not to Normandy, anyway."

"You most certainly do, you upstart," FitzOsbern shouted.

"Upstart? You call me an upstart?"

"I could call you worse."

"Enough," William said, raising a hand to quell FitzOsbern's protest. "My lord of Ponthieu, why will you not pay your dues? These monies are for your protection and that of all Normandy. No one is exempt from contributing. I have already confiscated lands from two barons who refused to pay. I cannot make you an exception."

"My protection?" Ponthieu echoed. "*My* protection? Would that be the same protection you showed my brother when your mercenaries hacked him up and stripped him down to his shirt and breeches?"

"Your brother was a traitor! He supported my uncle's rebellion. Had he been more honourable, he would not even have been there when my men rightfully brought justice on those persons who sought to harm my duchy."

"Persons such as your overlord - and my overlord - the King of France, you mean?"

331

"The King is a separate matter. He is indeed our overlord, yet he forgot himself in interfering in the internal matters of Normandy."

"He judged you and found you wanting, *Duke* William," Guy spat. "The truth is that he put more faith in my brother than in you."

"Then he must have been disappointed that your brother led him straight into a trap."

"How dare you insult my dead brother?"

"It is no insult to state the truth. Your brother led the vanguard and so your brother should have sent out proper scouts to keep a lookout. He did not and he paid the price."

FitzOsbern sniggered.

"Now," William said, "back to the matter in hand. Will you pay for protection? Or would you share your brother's fate?"

"Ponthieu needs no protection. I have my own men to defend *my* lands. Nor is it for you to impose any levy on me whatsoever, Duke William. Ponthieu is not in Normandy. Ponthieu never has been in Normandy. Ponthieu never will be in Normandy. Is that clear enough? I hold my lands directly from the king. If you have a problem with that, I suggest you take the matter up with him."

"Some of your lands lie outside my jurisdiction," William agreed. "But not all. All those lands which lie to the west of the river Somme are Norman lands. If you wish to keep those Norman lands, you had best pay Norman taxes."

"This is outrageous! I will not hear of it!"

"It is the law. Everything from the Somme to the Seslune is Normandy. It is all land paid for with the blood of my forebears -

and land I will defend with my own blood. By every law, defeating the lord of Ponthieu made me Ponthieu overlord."

"What duty I owed you for those lands west of the Somme, I have paid tenfold by keeping your eastern border safe," Ponthieu growled. "Though I owe you little, with so little of my lands being west of the Somme. I have nonetheless held firm."

"You have held firm for your own profit. And how much profit do you reap from the salt marshes there? My people struggle every autumn to scrape together enough salt to stop their meat from rotting after the slaughter. Their cattle do not survive rough winters, and without salt the animals are lost and no food is to be had. Yet you happily withhold salt unless they pay exorbitant prices. I have let you get away with the foul practice for long enough. Now it is time you repaid them by contributing to their protection."

"I will not!"

William gripped the arms of his chair.

"My lord Guy," he said, struggling to measure his tone, "my steward here will be returning to Ponthieu in a fortnight's time to collect your taxes. If you do not pay him then, I will move to confiscate your Norman lands. Is that clear?"

"The King will hear of this," Ponthieu said.

"Be sure to give him my regards when you see him," William said, raising his goblet in a toast.

Ponthieu grabbed his sword back from the guard and stormed out.

"See him safely on his way, FitzOsbern," William said.

His friend bowed and left the hall.

CHAPTER 39

"We should strike the French now!" Robert shouted, to a murmur of approval from a number of the gathered lords. "The King has yet to take any of our castles. If he does, he will be able to strike from a position of greater strength and be all the harder to drive out."

"I agree," Odo said, doing his best at being solemn in his bishop's garb, in spite of eagerness. "Though the Church could never advocate violence, the cause is just. Normandy has been invaded. We must defend ourselves."

"The King remains our overlord. We must act carefully," William said. "He has many men with him."

"Then let us meet him with even more," Robert said. He had grown in confidence since William had formally appointed him Count of Mortain. "We have the means."

"But not the time," Nigel of the Cotentin said. "The King is less than a week's march from us. If we face him in the field today, we have no certainty of victory."

"You would know all about that," FitzOsbern said.

"Indeed I would," Nigel said coolly. "Which is why I urge caution, my lord," he added, turning to William.

"Is it caution to step back and let our enemies help themselves?" Robert asked.

"Though I - unlike you - have faced my lord of the Cotentin on the battlefield myself," FitzOsbern said to William's two half-brothers, "I am inclined to agree with him."

William was pleased to see that FitzOsbern, at least, had learned from their experiences. Then again, his brothers would learn soon enough. They had yet to face the test battle.

"But your lands of Crespon are not threatened, are they, steward FitzOsbern?" said another baron.

The hall filled with a cacophony of shouting as the lords of William's court argued over the best course of action. It only died down when the door creaked open to admit the last arrival, Roger Montgomery. He was fully armoured in his mail hauberk and coif, with mail forearm and shin guards. He was drenched right through with sweat. William raised a hand for silence. Montgomery knelt before the duke's heavy wooden throne.

"Well?" William said, motioning his friend to stand. "You bring news?"

"I do, my lord," Roger said. "As soon as I heard of the invasion, I marshalled my milites and levied the commons of the Hiémois. I had to assure myself that no French troops were on my lands, for fear I had not done my duty. They had crossed further east, by Evreux, following the western bank of the Seine."

"Yes, we know that," Odo said, impatiently.

"Then you no doubt also know that the King has sent a second force across the river Epte and into the Norman Vexin."

Odo fell silent and looked at William, who gritted his teeth.

"You are certain of this?"

"I'm afraid so, my lord. We came across some of the stragglers of their baggage train."

"Who commands them?"

"The King's brother."

William got up and walked over to the window, looking out over the town of Rouen.

The Vexin, he thought. Why would Henry divide his forces?

"Ponthieu," he muttered.

"My lord?" asked Bigod.

"Bloody Ponthieu! That's why he's sent his brother through the Vexin. What else lies in that direction?" William fumed. "That damned Guy of Ponthieu must have promised the King his support. Robert! I would wager any money that he is on his way to join the King's brother."

"There is something else, my lord Duke," Montgomery said in a low voice.

"Go on," William said.

"The scouts I sent after the King's main force tell me his ranks are swelled by a new ally."

"What ally?" William asked, though in his heart he knew the answer.

"Geoffrey, Count of Anjou."

"That settles it," Odo said. "If Anjou has invaded, we must defeat them in battle or they will see fit to take the whole of Normandy."

"If Anjou has joined the King, we have all the more reason for caution," FitzOsbern said.

"Prior Lanfranc," William said, turning to the cleric who stood in a corner by the fire, warming his Italian bones from the Norman winter's chill. "You have been very quiet in all this. Tell me; what are your thoughts?"

"My lord Duke," he said, bowing reverently, "it is not for men of the cloth to advise on military matters."

Odo blanched at the thinly veiled rebuke. As Bishop of Bayeux, Odo was the senior clergyman present, yet the prior's reputation was unmatched in all France.

"Indulge me," William insisted.

"The King of France remains your liege-lord, as you have said yourself. An open attack on him would be... difficult to reconcile with your vassal duties. Were it possible to avoid facing him in battle, your honour would be preserved."

"What loss of honour is there in defending our lands?" Odo said, determined to regain face. Lanfranc cast him an irritated glance and waved his hand as if to swat away a fly.

"Fortify your castles, my lord Duke. That is my advice."

"We thank you, father," William said. "Montgomery?"

"My lord, I agree entirely with the good prior. Our forts are strong and could withstand any assault. Henry will not stray far from the river Somme. He needs it for supplies."

"And if he does?" Robert asked. "If he decides to live off the land?"

"Then we strip the land bare. Herd the cattle far out of reach. What stores can be moved in time, we take behind our walls. The rest, we burn."

"We will still need to do something about Ponthieu," FitzOsbern said. "The two armies must not be allowed to unite."

"Indeed," William said. "I intend to make an example of Guy of Ponthieu, for it seems his brother's death did not teach him a lesson."

He stroked the stubble on his chin as he considered matters.

"Very well. Montgomery, Robert; you two take a force north and deal with Ponthieu. Avoid open battle with the King's brother

337

if at all possible, but above all stop them from crossing the Seine. FitzOsbern; you see to clearing the land of any supplies from which the King might profit. Then join me. I will assemble our army, with what levies and hired swords are available, to head the King off. I shall not meet him in battle if it can be avoided. I merely wish to make a show of strength. With any luck, Henry will see sense and go home to his whores," he said, adding hastily to Lanfranc "forgive me father."

"God will forgive you, my lord. I shall serve you," the Italian answered with the rare glint of a smile.

William had been camped by the Seine for days that went by without any sign of Henry pushing further into Normandy. He must have realised his growing risk of isolation. Ponthieu, they had heard, had as of yet made no attempt to cross the river, on seeing Montgomery's harrying force, contenting himself with pillaging the land and probing for weak spots.

When night fell, it came without a moon. Low clouds covered the land. The only light came from the glow of fires from yet more plundered villages. William marvelled that Henry's men were still finding anything to burn. The area covered by the red tint showed the awesome size of the King's army.

"William," Odo's voice came from the darkness.

"What is it, brother?"

As Odo came into the light, William saw he was anxious.

"King Henry; his whole camp is on the move."

"A dawn attack?"

"Looks like it."

"Damn. FitzOsbern, sound the call to arms."

338

The Steward nodded and hurried off to assemble the army.

"It's a good job we've kept a close eye on them," Odo said.

"No, brother; it's sensible military practice," William said. "Still, I'm glad the men stayed alert. I would have wagered any money on Ponthieu being the one to attack, rather than Henry."

"Perhaps Ponthieu is also attacking on his side. Have you heard from Montgomery?"

"No, I haven't, and you can be sure that Roger would find a way to get word to me if he were under attack. He's perhaps the cleverest man I know." William thought back to all he'd been through with the Montgomery family. That he should now trust Montgomery as much as his father had trusted Montgomery's father was astounding, given the history with old Osbern.

He looked at Odo.

"What are you doing here, Odo? You're a bishop," he said, as if realising it for the first time.

"I came to give your men spiritual guidance, that is all." He smiled at William with a flash of teeth.

"Well just make sure you keep well back. You know men of the cloth are forbidden to draw blood."

"I am indeed aware of that fact and have come equipped for any trouble."

He held up a heavy mace, little more than an oak branch, smoothed out and caped with flanged iron.

"The fighting bishop of Bayeux," William said with raised eyebrows.

"This way I won't draw blood. Doctrine says nothing about bruising or breaking bones, though."

William could not help but chuckle at his brother.

"Just make sure Lanfranc doesn't hear about this, or there'll be Hell to pay."

"Now, now, William; no blasphemy, please," Odo said, wagging his finger in mock disapproval. "Besides, are you going to tell him?"

"Not if you watch my back, I won't," he said. "Come on; let's get started. I won't let Henry get the better of us."

He waved to their squires who had been waiting nearby and now brought up their horses. William swung himself up into the saddle. He patted his steed's neck.

"Come, my friend," he told it; "we have work to do."

He took a spear from the squire and spurred forwards. After much scrambling in the dark to hastily find swords and don chainmail hauberks, William's army was at last drawn up in battle formation. He could tell his men were nervous at facing such a mighty force as the King's, yet those nerves were mixed with a sense of relief at finally being able to do something instead of just wait while Henry's men plundered the land.

FitzOsbern joined them. He had formed the infantry up in the centre, with a large group of cavalry on each flank.

"Ready when you are, William."

"How far away is the King's army?"

FitzOsbern shrugged. "Not seen them yet."

"They can't be far away," Odo said. "Our scouts told us their camp was a hive of activity."

"Alright," William said. "Let's get it over with."

The night was growing old as they headed off to meet the King's army and resolve matters once and for all. It was slow going as they picked their way through the darkness. William

340

was all the more cautious for not wanting to walk his men straight into an ambush. He knew Henry was a wily leader. That was how a king kept his crown.

The hairs on William's neck stood up. Where was the King? They had advanced no small distance and still there was no sign of him. Eventually, they reached the ridge beyond which his scouts had told him Henry's army was encamped. William let out a deep sigh and closed his eyes, readying himself to face whatever was the other side of the rising land. He drew his sword. The steel softly sang out, its blade glowing crimson in the first light of dawn.

William looked at FitzOsbern and Odo. They nodded back to him. And they were off.

William touched his spurs to his horse's flanks and galloped over the rise.

Up the ridge they went, spear in hand, leaving their infantry to bring up the rear. William hated heading into the unknown, but he had not wanted to warn Henry of their arrival by sending scouts ahead. He gritted his teeth and reassured himself with the thought that his men were the best knights in all France. They would see off whatever the King might throw at them. They would put the fear of God into the French.

"Normandy!"

The war cry echoed through the night as they reached the top of the ridge and looked down to their enemy.

Then they stopped. It was very sudden and horses shunted into each other as the men in the rear ranks had no time to realise that their comrades in front had halted. Confusion followed as each tried to find the reason for their stopping the charge so immediately.

William sat still on his horse and threw his spear to the ground in frustration.

"How is this possible?" FitzOsbern wondered aloud.

William gave no answer. He was too angry. He had slipped up and Normandy would now pay the price.

"Tell the men to wait here," he said, before slowly making his way down to the King's camp. He was so angry. Nothing had prepared him for this.

Henry was gone. The camp was deserted. He picked his way through the empty tents. The campfires still smouldered. Everywhere, there were signs of the French having left in a hurry. A wagon lay abandoned. Tents were partly dismantled, their guide ropes tangled up where the occupants had given up struggling with them in the dark. William reached the centre of the camp where the King's tent still stood. What was so urgent that Henry would leave this? William had not advanced until Henry's camp was already seen to be stirring, so it could not be out of fright.

He turned to face the glimmer of dawn in the distance. They had marched for some time, yet the light grew little. Then it struck him. He was looking North, not East. That was not dawn; it was fire. Only one thing could explain it.

"Henry's outmanoeuvred us," he said to FitzOsbern and Odo. "He's linked up with Ponthieu and they now set our land ablaze."

"Ponthieu," FitzOsbern spat. "That traitor."

"What town are they at? Rouen?" Odo suggested.

"No," William said. "Rouen is further West. They can't be far from it though. Mortemer, perhaps."

"What shall we do?"

"The only thing we can do; cross the Seine and join Montgomery as soon as possible. Let's just hope he can hold them for long enough. If they get to Rouen before us, it will cost us a heavy ransom."

He took off his helmet and ran his fingers through his red hair. It was already drenched in sweat and they had a lot more heavy riding to do even before they could join battle."

"William, look!"

He followed FitzOsbern's gaze and saw a small group of riders coming towards them from out of the night. He drew his sword.

"Now that's a fine way to greet your own brother."

"Robert," William said in astonishment. "What on earth are you doing here? You're supposed to be with Montgomery. Is he alright?"

Robert laughed at William's concern.

"Montgomery is fine. He's more than fine. He's as smug as I've ever seen him."

"Smug?"

"He has every right to be. We've just given Ponthieu a thrashing he'll not soon forget. I see news reached Henry quicker than we could get to you, though. It looks like he's scarpered."

"Are you sure of all this?"

"Positive. I've come straight from the battlefield, if you can call it that. Henry was nowhere to be seen. He's probably half-way to Paris, by now."

"How did it happen?" William asked. "I didn't think you had enough men to take on Ponthieu."

"Ponthieu got careless," Robert said. "Montgomery had been organising the evacuation of Mortemer when our scouts told us Ponthieu was almost upon us. The place had never been considered sufficiently populated or strategic to build any serious defences. In times of crisis, people would go to nearby Rouen. We knew we couldn't hold it and so fell back. When Ponthieu's men arrived, they found it well stocked in food, drink and the people's possessions. It was too plump a bird for them to resist. They lost themselves in drinking and riotous looting. Ponthieu had no chance of maintaining discipline."

"I'm not surprised. He's used to letting the income from his salt marshes fill his coffers and never took any real care with law and order in his lands," William said. "So what happened next?"

"Roger had guessed that there would be a chance of this happening, so we stayed near the town and waited until night fall. Then we moved in. The rebels hadn't even put a guard on the outskirts. We rode straight in there unmolested and found Ponthieu's men brawling in the street. We rode them down before they even knew what was happening."

"And the fire?" William looked at the glow in the distance.

"Some of them tried to take shelter in the houses. Montgomery did not want to risk our men's lives by storming them, so instead he burned the houses to the ground."

William looked at FitzOsbern, who raised his eyebrows. Even he could not help but admire Montgomery's ruthless efficiency.

"Where is Ponthieu now?"

"Montgomery has him prisoner, awaiting your justice," Robert said.

"And oh how I will enjoy it," William said with relish.

"William; there is something else you should know."

"Go on," William did not like the tone in Robert's voice.

"Montgomery's father was there."

"What!" FitzOsbern spat, clutching the pommel of his sword in anger. He may have learned to accept Roger, but he had not forgotten the sins of the father or of the elder brother.

"He was with Ponthieu. He must have come in by boat or else we would have stopped him. There's no way he can have crossed the whole of Normandy unspotted."

"How did Roger react to his father's presence?" FitzOsbern asked. The seed of doubt was ever present where a Montgomery was concerned, even then.

"He was furious. His father tried to convince him to side with Ponthieu. The King would allow a Montgomery to become duke if they helped to defeat you. It seems the old man underestimated his son's loyalty, though. He would not let his father back onto his lands, would not give him back his title of Count of the Hiémois and declared himself your loyal servant to the end."

William was touched at Roger's loyalty. He had renounced his own father in order to serve his duke. Not many men would have done the same in his position.

"Where is he now?"

"He's scurried off to join the King."

"You mean Roger let him go?" FitzOsbern looked appalled.

"He can't harm us any more," William said dismissively. "He knows he has no support in Normandy. Even his own son is against him. If he wants to grow old and sad at Henry's court, let him do so. The once great Roger Montgomery the elder is fleeing in the night like a thief. His humiliation is complete. That is punishment enough."

"Congratulations, William," Robert said. "You have seen off the King of France without even bloodying your sword."

"We have sent him running, but I have not yet defeated him. Henry is a sly old dog," William said through gritted teeth. "He'll be back."

Yet as the dawn came, Normandy could at last rest.

CHAPTER 40

William stood still as a statue. He felt the strain of the bow as he pulled the taught string back past his chin. Others would have struggled to draw the bow, yet William kept it steady enough to take aim. The years of hard fighting and copious amounts of eager hunting had made him something of an expert archer.

He breathed in deeply. The stag slowly walked through the clearing. William had been tracking it since just after dawn. He had waited until the ideal opportunity, patiently letting the animal go about its business all morning.

Now was the time to deliver the killing blow. He was about to loose his arrow when something caught his eye; movement amidst the trees to his right. Any number of wild animals could be responsible for disturbing the leaves, yet William trusted his senses. He gently eased the tension on his bow, but kept the arrow nocked firmly in place on the string. He crept slowly, crouching so as to keep a low profile and not alarm the stag. He took up a position partly hidden by a thick oak tree. His eyes stayed fixed on the spot where he had seen movement. The seconds seemed to stretch into minutes.

There it was again, unmistakable this time. Someone was coming through the trees towards him. He pulled back the bow string once more, ready to loose his arrow in a split-second.

"William," shouted an all too familiar voice. "Where the Hell are you?"

He swore as the stag, startled by the shouting, ran off towards the safety of the trees. He quickly turned and shot his arrow, which flew harmlessly past the beast. Then the creature had disappeared. William rounded on his uninvited guest.

"Hasn't anyone ever told you not to creep up on a man when he's out hunting? I could have stuck an arrow in you! Given that you just cost me a whole morning's work, I may just do that."

Robert laughed.

"Seeing how you shoot, I'd say I'm pretty safe."

William glared at his brother.

"Perhaps you fancy a little competition, if you think yourself better."

"Thank you, but not this time. I've actually come to offer you a much better quarry to pursue."

"Quarry? Robert, I hope this isn't another one of your tavern girls, because my wife might have a thing or two to say about that;"

"Matilda is a lovely girl, brother, but as duke you are entitled to have some pleasures."

"I see Odo has not preached enough about moral virtue, Robert. As count of Mortain, you have a duty to show the example."

Robert threw his hand down, dismissing that detail.

"Either way, it is irrelevant. It isn't a tavern girl. I've had an unexpected visitor on my lands and I thought it worth bringing him here."

William raised his eyebrows inquisitively.

"Count Herbert of Maine," Robert explained.

"Herbert? What brings the young count into Normandy?"

"Oh, nothing really; a change of air," Robert said. "That and the fact that Geoffrey of Anjou has invaded Maine and already taken the town of Le Mans."

William's jaw dropped. "What? How did this happen? My spies told me nothing of an army moving into Maine."

"That's because an army wasn't needed. It seems Geoffrey bought the allegiance of the leading men. By the time he reached Le Mans, Herbert had already been sent packing."

"The town's garrison did nothing to stop it?"

"Herbert doesn't have Geoffrey's reputation."

There was much truth in that. Soldiers follow strong leaders. Geoffrey was perhaps the most successful warlord in France. Only William had shown himself capable of besting him.

"So where is the good count now?"

"I have sent him and his Bishop Gervase to Caen under escort. For their protection, of course," Robert added, with a twinkle in the eyes.

"Gervase of Bellême," William asked. "Will I never see the end of that wretched family? They're like rats, turning up all over the place."

"They are indeed and you will have this particular rat locked up as a guest until the situation is resolved."

"I thought the King put the Bishopric of Le Mans under Anjou's control, so what does Gervase care?"

"Herbert is still his count. If he gets back in, then Gervase will lose everything. This way he thinks he can see who wins and then resume his post afterwards."

"A Bellême playing one count off against another. Why does that not surprise me?"

349

William sat in his hall at Caen, with Matilda at his side. The smell of roasting goose floated tantalisingly through the air. The kitchen was busying itself for the coming feast to welcome Count Herbert to the Norman court. Before the pleasures of the evening could commence, though, the initial formalities had to be respected. William nodded to his brother as he entered with the guests. Herbert walked up to William, his head held high in spite of the circumstances. The bishop followed, glancing suspiciously around. He knew that he was not the most welcome person in the land.

"Greetings, Count Herbert! Welcome to Normandy," William said with a smile and outstretched arms. "And welcome, Bishop Gervase. What a pleasure to have one of such a great family back in Normandy."

Behind them, Robert grinned, as the bishop reddened in the face.

"Thank you, Duke William. I must apologise; we left in too much of a hurry for me to bring you a fitting gift."

Enough time to secure half the treasury of Le Mans, William thought.

"Your presence here is gift enough, good count," Matilda said in the silkiest of voices.

William thought he saw Herbert blush. He could not help but admire Matilda's way with men of rank.

"Thank you, Duchess Matilda. You are too kind."

"My brother, here," William said, "tells me that you have an unwanted visitor in Le Mans."

"I'm afraid so," Herbert said, fidgeting. "Geoffrey of Anjou came down upon us. My vassals meekly gave in, rather than stand up to him."

"You must not blame yourself for that," William said, meaning none of it. "In these hard times, no lord is safe from rebellion. I have known my share of it." He glanced at Gervase.

"They shall yet learn to regret it. Anjou is not invincible. I shall return and take back my rightful seat."

"I have no doubt of it," William said. "But come; let us think on it no more for tonight. Tonight is your feast. You are safe and among friends, here. We will have plenty of time to discuss things further on the morrow."

"I will not forget such generosity, Duke William."

William nodded his thanks, stood up and clapped his hands twice. Servants appeared from every corner of the room to set up tables and bring in food.

The feast was exquisite. William was impressed by the quality of the whole thing, given how little time they had had to prepare. Most occasions of the sort would have taken weeks, even months, in the planning, yet this had all been thrown together in a matter of hours. Matilda was not a lady to let surprises get the better of her. William knew she would have been commanding the servants and maids imperially. Geese had been swiftly executed, plucked and stuffed. The boys had been made to build up fires, the guards to polish their armour until it shone. Floors had been swept, privies cleaned, fresh straw lain in the stable for their guests' horses. No detail was too insignificant to receive Matilda's attention.

The food itself was divine. The goose fell off the bone, succulent and tender. Bowls of cereals, mixed with the apples which grew in great orchards throughout the land, complimented it to perfection. The freshly baked bread helped somewhat to soak up the fine wine which Matilda had ordered to be served.

Count Herbert drank as fully as any other there, seeking to forget his troubles for the night. William watched him carefully. Here was a fine gift indeed. Matilda had not been wrong there. The perfect excuse for delivering a blow against Anjou. Yet how to go about it? He certainly wasn't going to rush in there impetuously and risk his own men's lives. It was not his land.

It would have to be thought on. Intelligence would need gathering. With what strength did Geoffrey intend to garrison the castle of Maine? Would Brittany interfere? How would King Henry react? Most important of all; what would he get out of it, if successful?

As William saw the childless Herbert drink heavily, the seed of an idea planted itself in his head. He would start making the necessary enquiries in the morning. For now, though, he kissed Matilda on the cheek and gave her the most fleeting of winks. She smiled and nodded. They slipped away discretely, leaving Robert, Odo and FitzOsbern to entertain their guests.

"So tell me," William asked Herbert as they walked out to the stables, "have you heard from your people in Maine?"

"Not a thing. It's been nearly three weeks since Geoffrey took Le Mans and not a single messenger has reached me."

"I've heard that all those who would not cooperate were immediately locked up."

"You got someone into the city?" Herbert asked in surprise.

"I have people of use, yes. I make it my business to know what goes on outside Normandy."

"You can trust this source?"

"With my life," William said. "Well, with yours, anyway."

Herbert did not share the joke.

"What other information did this report give?"

William thought about it for a while, wondering just how much to tell Herbert. He decided there was little to be gained from holding anything back.

"Your county, I am sorry to say, is over-run. Not just Le Mans; Geoffrey has taken every town, garrisoned every fort with his men. Not one castle made any serious attempt to stop him."

"This cannot be true."

"I'm afraid it is."

"He cannot possibly have taken my whole county in a month."

"I don't believe he *did* do it in a month. This was years in the planning. Even Joshua's own trumpets wouldn't have brought down some of the castles if they had truly wanted to resist."

"What are you suggesting; that I let it happen?" Herbert was red in the face now, a muscle in his temple twitching away like a mad man trying to get out of a cage.

"Your vassal lords were bought, Herbert," William said, dropping the formalities. "They were in Anjou's pay long before he started moving any troops about. You might as well have left scarecrows to do their job."

"How dare you!"

"I am trying to help you, Herbert," William said, grabbing the count by the shoulder. "Look around you. How many of your men

353

are here? You can trust none of them. They do not stand beside you. I do."

Herbert shook William's hand off his shoulder. William left him and went to saddle his horse. He would normally have had a servant do it for him, but he felt Herbert needed some time to think.

After a while, his guest joined him in the stables;

"You are right, William. I should have been more watchful of my men's allegiance. I had never thought it possible that they could turn on me so fully."

"No lord is ever completely safe, however well guarded. I learnt that the hard way at an early age."

"Will you help me win back my county?"

"I will," William said. Herbert looked relieved. "But I will ask this: would you risk letting those traitors back in when you die? They will take over your land once again if you do not leave a strong heir."

William watched closely for some sign of his thoughts. He did not need to wait long.

"You can have it, William."

"Pardon?" He was taken aback by the ease with which Herbert acquiesced to his implied request.

"You can have my county, if I die before you. I shall name you my heir."

"Thank you, Herbert. You honour me with such a vow. Let us hope that you will outlive me by many years, though. You are the younger of us."

William thought it unlikely, given the count's poor constitution and great thirst.

But what other choice did the poor man have?

CHAPTER 41

A VILLAGE NORTH OF LISIEUX, LOWER NORMANDY. SPRING, 1057 A.D.

William watched the long line of women and children, of old men and young lads, of cows, sheep, plough-horses and pigs trudging in a sprawling and ramshackle trail along the muddy track. Behind them, a spreading plume of smoke told their village's fate.

King Henry had returned.

Joined by Geoffrey of Anjou, the King had launched a surprise attack. This time, to Normandy's despair, he had taken care not to divide his forces. The lesson of Mortemer had been learned.

And so one mighty army had crossed into the Hiémois. Seeing this tidal wave of steel, Roger had been quick-witted enough to gather his provisions and levies before hastily closing the gates of his castles in the Montgomery and Bellême lands, now formidable thanks to much work strengthening their defences. He had hoped to stall the King long enough for William to raise an army and drive out the invaders.

Yet Henry's next move stunned them all.

Anyone would have expected Henry to secure the border castles and ensure his supply lines were safe before advancing further. Yet the King brazenly ploughed on, leaving only a token force to keep an eye on Montgomery. He had led the combined armies of Anjou and France deeper and deeper into Normandy's heartlands. Such a move was startlingly out of character for the French king, who had always been so cautious and calculating.

But Henry was growing old, with rumours of ill-health spreading throughout his kingdom and beyond. How many more chances would he have at a decisive victory to recover some of his ancestors' lost power? With the ever belligerent Geoffrey of Anjou at his side, he had clearly chosen to make an almighty push to break the Norman.

Roger had managed to extricate himself with his household knights, leaving his levies and the older men of his guard under the command of his steward to hold the castles. He had joined William in Rouen where, after a heated council of war, the barons of Normandy accepted William's orders. They were to adopt the same burned land strategy which had served them so well three years earlier.

The King's armies would be hard pressed to get supplies so far into Normandy. Yet Henry had come prepared, it seemed. He must have brought provisions to last many weeks, for he showed no sign of slowing down.

The people of Normandy, defiant as ever when faced with foreign aggression, were nonetheless growing weary and angry. Why were their armed men standing by and letting the French and Angevins trample their lands? This was not the way of Rollo's North Men. To see the crops destroyed and houses emptied rather than leave a scrap of food or silver to the French was little consolation.

William's gaze was drawn to a woman in the convoy of fleeing villagers. Her face was old, marked by the many plough-lines her fields had known through the years. Her hair, wrapped in a threadbare veil, was the colour of ash. Loose braids clung to her brow which glistened with sweat. The burden of time weighed down on her shoulder, forcing her to hunch. Yet for all this, it was her eyes which captured William's attention.

They were steely blue, lit with grim determination. Suddenly, William was transported back to that autumn day in 1035 - it felt like a lifetime ago - when he had been told of his father's death. In this old peasant woman's eyes was the look of old Steward Osbern. Poor old Osbern. How William wished he had had him longer. His hand would surely have kept Normandy in check. Had he lived, William might have had a childhood, instead of this continuous struggle to survive.

Sensing his gaze, the woman looked up. She saw the group of noble lords, resplendent in the best mail, helmets and weapons money could buy, sat upon their powerful warhorses - sat, and doing nothing. Her eyes settled on the ringlet of gold around William's helmet. She pursed her lips, stepped up close to him, and raised her arm. It rose slowly, as if requiring a titanic effort. She pointed at William.

"You, boy," she said with the stern voice of a grandmother chastising a village lad, "why are you just sat there? Where is your mettle?"

"Move along, old woman," Robert said, "you know not whom you address."

"I address the Duke here," she said in contempt.

"If you know him to be your duke, why do you feel you may speak to him so? Move along, I say, before I get angry."

The woman spat in Robert's direction.

"You do not fear me," William said.

"I do not," she answered. "I am too old to fear anything, anymore."

"Not even death?"

"Especially not death. I have never been closer to God - and you have never been further from Him, *my lord*."

"How so? I am building abbeys. I have long supported the Church. What more would you have?"

"If God made you duke, then why are you not performing that function?"

"I am, good lady."

She pointed to the plume of smoke.

"You are not. I can remember the days of Richard the Fearless. He would not have stood by like this."

"I do not stand by. I will crush Anjou and France. I will make our lands safe and, many years from now, your aged granddaughter will say that she remembers the day William the Bastard defeated the King of France."

"Be sure that you do," she said.

William walked his horse down to the stream by which he was resting his forces. He ran his fingers through the creature's mane as it thankfully lapped the cool water. His men were itching for a fight. He could feel it. To have the King of France march across their land uninvited was galling enough. For Geoffrey of Anjou to accompany him with an army was downright insulting. Though Montgomery managed to get most people out in time, it was heartbreaking to see the red glow through the night and know that it drew its life from the death of more Norman homes which burned by the hand of Anjou's knights.

Anjou and Normandy had ever been rivals. When the power of one flowed, the other's ebbed. Herbert of Maine knew it all too

359

well, for his lands lay between the two and were oft caught up in the game of power. The people of Maine owed their present allegiance not to their count, but to Geoffrey of Anjou.

King Henry had taken great pleasure in stoking the rivalry, for, though Maine suffered, the Crown profited. Normandy and Anjou were lands powerful enough to challenge the King's authority. Whichever was the greatest threat at any time, Henry supported the other. He would let them waste their armies and finances against each other. By giving them war, he believed he would save his beloved France.

And so, through this unbecoming kingly game, the Hammer of Anjou was beating its way through Normandy with all impunity, knowing that the anvil of Henry's authority would keep William firmly in place. And the land of Normandy burned again. And William could do nothing to put out those fires – until that morning.

The sound of hooves announced the return of FitzOsbern's scouting party.

"William," he shouted, fighting for breath after the hard ride. "I bring you news." He leaped from the saddle, barely giving his horse time to come to a stop. William hurried over to meet him.

"What is it, FitzOsbern? Have you seen the King's army?"

"Seen it? I almost rode into it. Henry is on the march!"

"Which way?"

"West," FitzOsbern said. "He's headed for Caen."

"Caen? How far away from the town is he?"

"Two days at the most. His scouts will be there even sooner. There's no way Montgomery will get the people out in time."

"Christ," William muttered. He would not want to evacuate the town, even if he could. For the past five years, he had been building the place with Matilda. With their twin abbeys and its growing castle, it was to represent all the renewed strength of the dukes of Normandy. To abandon it now would be an admission of defeat. How quickly would his vassals switch their allegiance then?

"Where exactly are they at the moment?"

"When I saw them, half a day's ride away, to the north."

William turned away and walked down to the stream, leaving FitzOsbern to pass the information on to the other lords who had gathered to hear the latest news. He ignored the inevitable mutterings and talk of doom and gloom.

He crouched on the bank and cupped his hands to splash his face with the cool water. He had to act and act fast, or he would lose his coronet without a single fight. As he looked into the glimmering stream, he realised that the answer was staring him in the face.

"Got him," he shouted so suddenly that it made more than one of the lords jump. "Got him, by God!"

"What is it my lord?"

"It's so brilliantly simple. It's so obvious that Henry's completely overlooked it. At least I hope he's overlooked it. We'll know soon enough." William was grinning to himself, relishing the prospect of dealing with his enemies once and for all.

"What is so obvious?" FitzOsbern asked.

"Don't you see it? Henry's made a terrible mistake. Terrible!"

The lords looked at each other, clearly seeking to reassure themselves that they were not imbeciles for not following

William's thinking. William was sure Montgomery would have reached the conclusion by now. He sighed in disappointment, whilst secretly enjoying the moment.

"Henry knows I will not attack him directly. Yet he is only strong enough to threaten our towns so long as he has Anjou at his side. With Henry at Anjou's side, I cannot attack Anjou's forces either."

"Yes, but what is new now?"

"To reach Caen, he must pass through Varaville."

FitzOsbern smiled in realisation.

"Geoffrey's a dead man," he said.

"But William," his half-brother Robert of Mortain said, "I still don't see how you mean to separate Anjou from the King."

"If you were on the march against an enemy's town, what would you expect that enemy to do?"

"Reinforce the town in all haste, of course, buying time to assemble a relief force to break the siege."

"Exactly. That is what Henry and Geoffrey will expect to see and so that is what we shall give them,"

William picked up a stick and laid out his plan in the mud for all his lords to see.

"A battle, at last," FitzOsbern exclaimed, punching Mortain in the shoulder with such enthusiasm that the man tripped and fell back into the stream, to the sound of much laughter around him.

William leaned down and held out a hand to help the soaked baron up.

"Let us hope, Robert, that King Henry is as bad on water as you!"

From his hiding place amidst the trees, high at the top of a hill, William could see everything. Below him, along a well-used track winding between the hills, two armies made their way West. It was a glorious sight. These brave conquerors must have smelt victory. Thus far, they had advanced with very little opposition in their path. They left burning villages in their wake. The only sign that the Norman duke was doing anything at all to defend his land was the pesky raids on their supply wagons; even those had ceased abruptly. The Normans had lost heart. All that was left was to take Caen, Duke William's pride and joy, and Normandy would be forced to formally submit. Then would Normandy's orchards be sliced up and dished out among the victors. Anjou would secure its north-eastern border, with the fertile land and strong forts adding to Angevin prestige. King Henry would never need fear Norman upstarts ever again.

William smiled. *The fools. The poor unsuspecting fools.* Ahead of them lay a strip of silver which ran as far as the sea and beyond that strip a plain. From there it would be an easy ride to Caen.

He watched closely as the King's army, leading the way, started to cross the river. The ford was narrow; so much so that three men could only just walk across it side by side. Horses could make their way easily enough, though more than one was nervous. The supply wagons caused the greatest trouble. Their wheels kept getting struck in the mud, weighed down by their heavy loads. So slow was the progress that the army of Anjou had soon caught up with the King's. Men threw down their packs and rested as they waited for their turn to cross. Squires led their knights' horses to water as officers gesticulated to hurry things along.

William's army had been hidden in the tree-covered hills since before dawn and he sensed their impatience. They saw nothing of the enemy, having been ordered to keep well out of sight. Thus far, William thought, they had been fortunate that Geoffrey's men were tired from marching and too confident of their safety to venture so far as to properly scout their surroundings. Had they done so, the Normans would have found themselves at Anjou's mercy, trapped by sea and by river. It was a gamble William had had to take in order to seize this God-given opportunity. He only hoped Montgomery was playing his part. If not, he would soon find the King's men turning back to help Anjou cut him down.

He looked up. The sun was past its zenith and gradually headed into the afternoon. He smiled to himself. The King was Hell-bent on taking Caen, yet on this occasion, time was on William's side.

He heard a twig snap behind him and instinctively reached for his sword. He whipped it round in time to touch it against the intruder's chest.

"Easy there, William," FitzOsbern said, gently pushing the blade aside.

William grinned and sheathed his sword.

"Just practicing."

"Practice any harder and you'll have to fight Anjou without a steward." FitzOsbern winked.

"Now that would be a pity; I'm counting on you to let people know of my exploits."

"Now how am I supposed to see any of your exploits when I'll be so far ahead of you?"

"We'll see about that," William said. "In fact, we shall see very soon indeed. Look."

He pointed at the ford, where there was a distinctive change in the activity. Men struggled to pull a cart up the bank before giving up and hastily unloading as much of it as possible. Even from their vantage point, the reason was clear enough. The river Dives was rising, and rising fast. Normandy's tides were notorious with waters coming in swiftly from the sea. On this day, Normandy was much angered and filled the Dives at great speed. Though most of the King's men had got across, Geoffrey's army was still on the east bank, with no other crossing for miles. They were close to the sea at this point and it was too much to risk crossing on horseback. They would have to wait for the next low tide. William, on the other hand, had waited long enough.

"Tell the knights to mount and form up. Have Robert bring up the archers. It's time to teach Geoffrey a lesson, once and for all."

FitzOsbern grinned. William could not help but admire his friend's unquenchable appetite for a good fight. They crept back out of sight and quickly went to rejoin their army. William mounted his horse as FitzOsbern gave the orders. Men who had been passing the time eating, sharpening weapons or playing dice dropped everything at a moment's notice and mounted up. Robert assembled the archers and headed up the slope.

365

"Wait until you see us coming up the next hill, then give them all you've got," William called to him. "Don't stop shooting until we're almost upon them."

Robert waved back and soon disappeared amidst the trees on the hills. William turned back to his men and lifted off his helmet.

"Listen up, men! I do not ask you to attack your king. Henry of France is on the other bank of the Dives and no threat to us. Our quarrel is with Anjou. Too many times has the impudent Geoffrey ventured into our fair land of Normandy. Too much damage and too great an insult has he already caused. Well, it ends today! Today the Hammer of Anjou will beat for the last time. It will beat and it will break against the mettle of Normandy. We are the sons of Rollo. We are the warriors from the North. Today, we take back what is ours and trample the lilies of Anjou into the dirt!"

His men cheered. William was sure the sound could not have reached Anjou's men beyond the hills, but it mattered little either way. They would have no hope of drawing up their lines in time.

He led his men up the hill next to Robert's. He paused as he reached the crest. Down on the plain, all was peaceful. Men still sat around waiting. Even the knights and sergeants had given up trying to cross and just waited, still oblivious to the presence of another army just above their heads. He heard a shout from the next hill. Robert had given the order and a great swooshing sound blew down the hill as hundreds of bow strings were released simultaneously, sending arrows in an arc high into the air. Someone down below cried in horror at the darkening sky – too late. The first wave of arrows rained down upon Anjou's men, punching through metal, leather and flesh. The Angevins turned to see whence this storm was coming, while desperately taking cover under shields, wagons or anything at hand which might offer shelter from the arrows. Again and again the arrows came down, leaving no moment of respite for Geoffrey's men to form up for the imminent cavalry charge, save a group of knights who were just out of reach.

William looked at his men. Though nervous, they were clearly relishing the sight of Anjou's deserved suffering. He turned to FitzOsbern.

"Ready?"

"Let's show them how it's done," FitzOsbern said through gritted teeth.

"No prisoners until the area's secure," William said to his men. "We will have ransoms enough from King Henry's men once this is over. Kill the Angevin scum."

He nudged his horse a few paces in front of his line and raised his spear.

"God helps," he shouted.

"God helps!" The cry rang out across the plain.

He pulled his helmet back on, wheeled his horse round and charged down the slope. His men were well-trained. They were battle hardened. They knew the business of war. Despite the steep slope, they kept a good solid line, starting at a soft canter and gradually accelerating, each man timing his pace to avoid any gaps in their line. As they neared the panicked foe, William began to worry that the archers might not stop shooting at all, such was their rate of fire. He was about twenty feet from the closest Angevin when the last arrow struck the ground. Spears

367

then flew overhead, as his knights were eager to get killing before they had even made contact with the enemy.

William picked out his first target; a dismounted knight who bravely stepped forward to meet the Normans. William quickly despatched him with a throw of his spear. He had no time to draw his sword before meeting the next foe, a spearman, and instead, gave his steed a sharp kick in the flank. The trained horse pulled hard left, pressing against FitzOsbern's own mount. The man was knocked down between the two horses and trampled under them.

The charge was a massacre as the Angevin infantry and those knights who had not had time to mount were slaughtered without mercy. From the other side of the river, the French troops, fully prepared for battle, could do little but watch the destruction of Geoffrey's army. Their archers hurried forward to try to help, but the two sides were so tightly locked together in battle that the French archers dared not risk hitting their Angevin allies. They had to content themselves with picking off any Norman careless enough to stray away from the main fray.

William hacked down left and right. Slashing away, taking no time to even check what wounds he was inflicting. All he knew was that these men were on his land, had been harming his people and were now getting everything they deserved. He shouted at his men to keep pressing forwards. He could not risk Geoffrey's men regrouping. His army was no bigger than Anjou's, so to win he would have to keep up the pressure and use all his momentum to drive the invaders out.

He felt someone pull at his leg and looked down to see an Angevin foot soldier snarling up at him, trying to pull him out of the saddle. He kicked him hard in the face and turned his horse about sharply, pushing the man back. His steed needed no further encouragement to crush the Angevin's skull with his hooves.

"William, look out!"

He turned back to face the front just as he heard FitzOsbern's warning. A spear flew past his face and he saw a group of some four-score enemy knights charging towards him in a desperate counter-attack.

"Geoffrey," he said, seeing the Count's banner in the centre of the group.

"There he is, William," FitzOsbern said, coming up to him. "Let's take him."

"Form up! Form up," William shouted. "God helps!"

Ignoring the remainder of Anjou's infantry, his disciplined knights closed up the line and charged head-on at Geoffrey's men. The impact was brutal as horses collided and men clashed against each other.

The first blow William felt was a spear embedding itself in his shield, its point even digging through his chainmail to cut into his arm. He grimaced and hacked down with his sword so hard that the spear snapped in one stroke, leaving only the very tip weighing down the shield. His horse snapped its jaws at others nearby, in a contest of intimidation.

William stabbed out towards his attacker, hoping to land a blow of his own before the Angevin could draw his sword, but it was parried by the knight's neighbour. William was forced to bring his shield forward to cover himself while he dealt with this new threat. The man kept stabbing his spear towards William's

369

head and only his long years of training let William deflect the blow with his sword. The enemy knight kept his distance thanks to the longer weapon and William was wondering how to close the distance when FitzOsbern slammed bodily into the man, knocking him off balance before cutting his throat with a backslash of his sword.

William grabbed the opportunity and threw his shield ahead of him, punching the other knight in the face with its steel rim. He pushed forwards and finished him off with a sharp stab in the throat.

"Normandy," he roared. "God helps Normandy!"

He searched through the thick of the battle, looking for Geoffrey. What he wouldn't give to capture the Angevin Count himself. He pushed past two riders who were locked together in fierce fighting and there was Geoffrey. His rival was fending off three Normans at once, in as brutal a defence as William had ever seen. Geoffrey's sword flickered in the afternoon sun so fast that William's eyes could barely follow it. As he watched, he saw one of the Norman knights fall to the ground.

This was Count Geoffrey, the Hammer of Anjou, doing what he did best. He was already over fifty, yet even now he would not give in. So long as he stood his ground, his loyal knights stayed with him. William had not seen him close up since the Council of Rheims some eight years earlier. Geoffrey had put on weight and grown more grey in his beard. Yet he fought on valiantly.

"Geoffrey," William shouted. "You're finished, Geoffrey! Come and fight me, now. Fight me man to man!"

Geoffrey pulled away from his fight with a final token blow of his sword. He made to head towards William when he realised that the Norman cavalry was moving around behind him. He would soon be surrounded. He looked for a way around the situation, but realised he had an inevitable choice. He saluted William with his sword, turned his horse around and fled the field before the Normans could cut him off completely. His small party, the remnants of a great invading army which had sought to take the whole duchy away from William, was forced to gallop away towards the safety of the boats which they knew waited on the banks of the Seine for news of the attack on Caen.

"Geoffrey, you coward!" William spat in the Count's direction. He knew that Geoffrey had made the only sensible decision, though. Even if he had killed William, he would have been captured. At best, he would have spent years locked up in a Norman gaol while his kinsmen tried to raise a ransom. At worst he would have been cut down by the Normans in retribution for killing their duke.

Robert and FitzOsbern rode up to William, who looked daggers at the Count of Anjou ignominiously fleeing the field. William's men would not catch him. They were too busy taking the easy pickings in the spoils of war.

"So the little shit got away, did he," FitzOsbern said. "Well here's something to give you heart, William; you've annihilated his army, captured and killed his best commanders, saved Normandy..."

"And let's not forget," Robert said, "that just across that small stretch of water, you have trapped King Henry of France, no less."

William smiled grimly.

"I haven't got Geoffrey, though. I'll never rest easy so long as he is alive," he said. He looked up at the sky which was turning crimson as the afternoon grew old. He breathed in deeply Normandy's air, made sweet by the smell of crushed grass. "But as you say: our land is safe. For that, we can thank God."

"I still don't understand," Robert said, as William washed his hands in the river, happily smiling at Henry's stranded army; "how did you know that the King would be leading the march? He could have let Count Geoffrey lead the way. If he had, Caen would be in flames by now and we would be left on this bank with a king whom we couldn't attack."

William wiped his hands on his breeches and stood up. Every muscle in his body ached.

"Henry wanted Caen to submit peacefully. No overlord wants to shed his vassals' blood if he can avoid it. It makes him look bad. If Geoffrey had led the way, the town would never have meekly surrendered. It would have been a blood bath. Just imagine all those frustrated Angevin soldiers let loose on Caen. No man would have lived, no girl stayed unharmed. They would even have looted the churches, given half the chance and what would the Pope have preached then?"

"Surely the King knew we were coming, though. Why did he not deal with us before taking Caen at his leisure?"

"Henry saw our army at Caen," William said with a sly smile.

Mortain raised his eyebrows in an unspoken question.

"I sent word to Montgomery that he was to erect as many tents as possible on the outskirts of Caen and to fly all the pennants he had from the ramparts. When Henry's scouts neared Caen, they would have seen enough camp fires to keep a whole army warm throughout the night. Faced with such a report, what else was Henry to deduce but that we were waiting for him at the town?"

"And he didn't bother sending scouts to keep an eye behind him?"

"He sent one or two small scouting parties; they were dealt with."

"He should have investigated why they did not return," Robert said, his voice full of scorn.

"He should," William agreed, "But when such a golden opportunity was presented to him, he saw what he wanted to see. Unwanted news is seldom listened to by great men when it gets in the way of their brilliant plans."

"You think the King great?"

"He thinks himself great; that is all that matters." William smiled, seeing the distant figure of the King gesticulating wildly at a group of knights who had no doubt been chosen to take the blame. "Though I suspect his sun may not be shining quite so brightly now."

CHAPTER 42

As King Henry of France entered the great hall in Caen, William stepped down from the wooden raised platform on which he sat for formal occasions and bowed in obeisance. The assembled lords all followed suit, though William noted the reluctance of more than one of them.

The King looked weary, yet he walked in gracefully with his head held high. He may be defeated, but he was still king.

William had beaten him in the most humiliating of ways, ambushing and cutting off the King's army without even having to raise his finger against the King. Only the blood of Anjou had stained his sword. He had kept his honour, had kept his dukedom. Now, to the victor: the spoils.

"Duke William," Henry said, holding out his hand for William to kiss the royal ring, "we thank you for your hospitality."

"My lord King is comfortable, I trust."

"We are quite comfortable, for our vassal has shown us his love."

"You know the Duchess Matilda, of course," William said, as she stepped forward and curtseyed.

"How could we not remember a daughter of Charlemagne?" Henry said with a smile. "The good Count Baldwin your father is well? You must miss him, Duchess, being so far away."

"He is well; thank you, my lord King," she said. "And it is not so far. Indeed, Normandy and Flanders seem closer than ever."

William struggled to disguise his smile. Though dwarfed by the august company, only Matilda could show the King of France such cheek in such a courteous fashion. Henry took the barb in good humour. He was well versed in this game.

"My lord King," William said, "please have a seat."

Henry took up the chair from which William had just risen in the middle of the dais. Always one to play at being king, William thought, regardless of any actual power.

"I assume, Duke William," Henry said, "that you have one or two favours to request. Perhaps the ladies would like to leave us while we discuss this." He nodded to Matilda, expecting her to oblige. She stood her ground.

"There is nothing which the Duchess my wife cannot hear. We are as one," William said. He had waited a long time for this moment. He was going to savour it to its fullest.

"As you wish," Henry conceded, his voice resentful to the utmost. "We shall hear your requests."

"My requests, lord King, are only what was rightfully Normandy's all along. Too many times have we been subjected to the ambitions of our neighbours. Jealousy breeds ill will. Therefore, we wish for you to confirm all the Bellême lands as Norman. Count Geoffrey of Anjou must be banned from any further advances into Normandy. His boots have dirtied our soil for long enough."

Henry thought about it for a while. Quite what he thought was pointless, for he had little choice in the matter.

"Agreed," he said at length. "I will have a cleric draw up the deeds. Thus is our pleasure."

"And Maine," William said. "Count Herbert asked us to look after his lands. He named us his successor. You will order

Geoffrey of Anjou to withdraw from that county. It is under the protection of Normandy."

"Very well. It shall be done."

William knew as well as the King that Henry could order what he liked. Geoffrey would never obey that order. Yet it mattered not. All that mattered was that, when the time came, William's legitimate succession there would be beyond contestation.

"We thank you, my lord King."

"*We* grant you these requests," Henry said, in a voice which showed clear irritation at William's use of the royal pronoun. "We grant them for they are fair."

"One more thing," William said. "Those castles which you garrisoned with your troops must be given back to my people. You may be our overlord, but you had no right to take them. Perhaps if you had not given Geoffrey your ear, you would not have made such a foolish mistake."

If the King had seemed somewhat embarrassed before, he was now scarlet with anger. Yet what could he do? If he admonished William, he would find his ransom a great deal more expensive. He was surprised the Norman had not handed him over to one of his enemies. The King of France had many.

"I have already instructed my men to return to Paris," Henry lied, in an effort to save his honour. "So you need not fear on that score."

"Normandy never fears. Normandy survives."

Thus it was concluded.

That was the last time William saw the King of France. Henry died three years later, leaving his eight-year-old son Philip as king. William could not exactly complain. Tragic as any death is, Henry had been no friend to Normandy. Save for the Vale of Dunes, his greatest act in Normandy's favour was to take effect after his death. William had heard it rumoured, but now it was confirmed. As guardian of the infant king – and *de facto* regent – Henry had chosen none other than Baldwin of Flanders, Matilda's father. Thus, whether by chance or by fate, Normandy's southern border was secure.

CHAPTER 43

CAEN, LOWER NORMANDY. NOVEMBER, 1060 A.D.

William stroked Matilda's hair. Already she had given him three sons, Robert, Richard and William, as well as two daughters. William saw little of himself in the eldest. Robert was short, shy and resembled only his mother. Richard, though, showed more promise. William would have to see how Robert grew up, though. As Matilda so often told him: warriors have no patience.

"What did you think of me?" he asked her. "The very first time you saw me, when I rode into your father's yard?"

She turned round to look at him, her flowing hair falling down over her bosom."

"I thought that you looked muddy and exhausted," she teased. "I thought that you were badly shaven, worse dressed and had no sense of decorum."

She laughed at his vexed face.

"And," she added, "I thought you were the most handsome and foolhardy man I had ever seen. Are you happy now?"

"I would be happier with a kiss," he said. She obliged him, then frowned.

"Why the questions?"

"Because I care deeply about what you think of me," he said, more earnestly than he could have admitted to anyone else. Indeed, he would have been ashamed to admit it to any of his lords, even those closest to him. "You don't regret it, do you? Your choice?"

"What choice?" she asked, only half teasing this time. "You were the Duke of Normandy, my father's chosen ally to secure his county. Who was I to stand in the way of such an alliance?"

"But you would have chosen me anyway, had we been in different positions?"

"No, I would not," she said. "You made your position. Without it, you would not be the man I know and love. You made it yourself, and you make me happy, even if your taste in wine remains appalling."

He laughed out loud. There was a bang on the door.

"Enter," he said. FitzOsbern and Montgomery strode in.

"Ah, my good friends. To what do we owe the pleasure?"

One look at their faces told him it was a grave matter.

"William," FitzOsbern said, "Geoffrey of Anjou is dead."

William stood up, lost for words.

"He died in his sleep, so we are told," Montgomery said. "In his monastery, where he knew he would end his days."

"That a man such as him could enter the orders is beyond me," FitzOsbern said.

"He had much to atone for," Matilda said.

"He did indeed, my lady."

William looked into the flames which rose in the hearth. King Henry had died but five months earlier. Now so had the Hammer of Anjou.

"Geoffrey is dead," he repeated, the words echoing strangely in the small room. "All my life I have been wary of the threat from Anjou. He was the best warlord in France. He was my greatest rival. It sounds funny, but an age has ended."

"An age has begun," Matilda said, getting up and standing by him. "You are the uncontested master of northern France. You have won."

William turned around and kissed her cheek.

"Thank you, my dear," he said softly, before turning to his friends. "But we do have one task ahead of us now."

William looked out across the vast expanse of fields in front of him. The land which had once been turned to mud and ashes was alive once more. Here, at Alençon, where he had spent seemingly endless months under the rain in wind-battered tents, now wheat swayed in a gentle breeze. The dark clouds had been banished from Normandy. He breathed in deeply, filling his lungs with the sweet air of midsummer. He was fully armed, with his chainmail hauberk newly scrubbed clean by a squire. His horse waited eagerly to be set loose upon the rolling countryside.

"This place brings back memories," FitzOsbern said, approaching with Roger, Odo and Robert.

"It does indeed," William said, "yet how different things are now."

"How many rebels defeated?" Robert said. "King Henry and Count Geoffrey gone. Infants in their place. No one can stand in your way now, brother."

"There will always be those who try," William said. "We can never rest easy. Yet today is our day. Herbert gave us a gift with his death. Let's go and claim what is ours."

He turned his horse to face his men, all four-thousand of them; knights, men-at-arms, archers and commoners, assembled before the newly rebuilt walls of Alençon. He took off his helmet so they could all know him by his fiery red hair.

"Men of Normandy," he shouted, "bravest and noblest warriors! We have come a long way together. We have come through bloody rebellion. I now forgive those who wronged me all those years ago. We stand united. When our beloved land burned at the hands of fickle France and fearful Anjou, you stood calm. From the ashes our land rose once again, greater even than before. Those foreign powers tried to take what was rightfully yours. With me, you bloodied your swords and bled yourselves. Thus you paid for victory. Your Duke is eternally grateful that you did your duty. Now I call on you to do your duty once more!" He pointed behind him. "Look over there! Across those fields and beyond the river lies Maine. Its count, the sorrowful Herbert, was overthrown in the very same sort of rebellion as Geoffrey of Anjou tried to instigate in our own land. Geoffrey failed here. Now we must confound the very villainy which he left in Maine."

William paused, hoping his words were having the desired effect.

"Before his untimely death, Count Herbert came to me. He asked me to free his lands from the grasping hands of iniquity. Most humbly did I accept to take on that heavy burden of responsibility. Today, with you, we will fulfil that vow and take back Herbert's county with the late King Henry's blessing. Under Normandy's protection, Maine will thrive. Will you help me free our cousins from tyranny? Will you be the brave Normans whom I know ever stand up against Evil? Will you do God's work on this glorious day and be rewarded with the spoils of war?"

An almighty cry rang out across the fields.

"Yes!" A whole army roared as one.

"Then come," William shouted, drawing his sword. "We march on Maine! God helps!"

"God helps!"

The land of Normandy had awoken from its winter slumber, and William no longer needed to run.

William now went forth as the conqueror.

.V.

THE NARROW SEA

CHAPTER 44

THE NARROW SEA. 1064 A.D.

"Hold on tight!"

Yet another wave crashed into the bow. Water splashed over the side of the small boat, covering the rowers who gripped their oars for dear life. They were already drenched from many long hours of struggling through the storm. It seemed as though it might never end. The low and menacing clouds darkened the sky. Below them, the sea was a vast black abyss which threatened to swallow them at any moment. The only specks of light were the white flecks on the surface which showed the crests of the waves swelling around, throwing their craft hither and thither.

It was a game. The oarsmen knew it. They knew it and prayed, for God was playing with their lives. The squall which had caught them out tugged at the mast. The single square sail suddenly tore along an old patch that had been poorly repaired. The men continued to dig in their oars, for what little good it did. It kept them busy. No man wants to sit back and let fate take its course. All strive to have some small control when death draws near. And so they rowed.

In the stern, next to the captain of this small vessel who kept a firm hold of the tiller and seemed alone to be unafraid, sat perhaps the bravest warlord of all England. And he was trembling out of cold and fear.

Harold Godwinson hated ships. He was the great Earl of Wessex, the most powerful lord in the land – many said he was more so than King Edward himself. He had beaten countless Welsh armies into submission, had fought off raids by Irish, Scots and Danes alike. He had even seen off incursions into Wessex by the rival house of mighty Leofric of Mercia

Yet at that moment, he would have given everything he owned to be able to fight against all those enemies at once rather than be sat on that damned boat.

He held on tightly to his sword, though it served him little purpose on that boat lost in the middle of the narrow sea between England and France. It was nothing more than a dead lump of metal to weigh him down should things turn ill, yet it gave him comfort.

The storm had come suddenly. When they had set off from England, the sea had been calm as a mill pond. Yet as England's green hills had faded into the distance and the Norman coast appeared before them, the sky had turned angry and the winds swiftly picked up. The sea had awoken.

"Row, men! Row for your lives!" The captain struggled to make himself heard above the roar of the storm. The rain came down so hard they were forced to squint and could barely see a thing. The captain tried to turn into the waves, hoping to ride it out until it passed. To attempt making for the land would have been suicide.

"Look out," Harold cried. Too late. In turning, they were hit full on the side by a fierce wave. The strength of it brought the mast crashing down. It smashed a hole in the boat, through which water soon started to flood. The captain pulled hard on the tiller, which strained and finally broke.

Harold braced himself for the next wave. As it came, he was thrown bodily from the boat. Ice cold water covered his head. He held his breath as he was dragged down. He frantically pulled off his sword belt. The weapon was his most cherished possession, but he had no choice if he was to live. The knot stuck and he panicked, before remembering his small dagger. He cut the leather and let the heavy weight sink below. He kicked upwards, though he was a poor swimmer. He somehow managed to reach the surface and gasped for air, his mouth full of salty water. A piece of timber floated nearby and he grabbed hold of it.

Searching through the crashing waves, he could see no sign of the boat or any of his companions. He called out. It was of no use. Nothing could be heard through the cacophony of the squall.

He held on tight and prayed, fighting to keep his head above water. The minutes dragged into hours and he steadily grew numb in the freezing sea.

At length, exhausted, the world turned black.

The waves thundered about his head, yet he felt he was no longer being thrown about. Every part of his body ached. He stretched his fingers and found that he was lying face down on sand. The thundering of the waves was in fact the hooves of horses which drew nearer. He opened his eyes a crack. The bright sunshine worsened his headache. Barely three feet away, he could just make out a body lying on the beach. The captain's dead eyes stared back at him from amidst broken timber - all that remained of his boat. No doubt other bodies would wash ashore in time, though some may never return from the depths of the sea.

He closed his eyes, wishing only to sleep, when he heard a man dismount next to him. A strong arm pulled him round so that he lay on his back.

"Is he alive?" asked an authoritative voice.

"Just about, my lord."

"Wake him, if you can."

The order was followed by a hard slap across the face, which Harold really did not need. He grunted. He opened his eyes in time to see another slap headed his way. He grabbed the man's wrist.

"Touch me again and I'll break your neck."

The man looked startled at the Saxon's menacing voice, but kept calm and backed away.

"Who are you, Englishman?" the rider asked in Latin. Harold turned to see he was a man in fine clothes with an expensive war horse. He was clearly the lord of these parts, though Harold knew not where he was.

"I am Harold Godwinson, Earl of Wessex."

The lord's face lost its colour. He turned to mutter something to his small escort of knights who swiftly dismounted and seized Harold. They tied his arms behind his back, showing little care as they did it, before pulling him to his feet. Harold was well-built and it took two of them to keep him up as his aching legs buckled.

Harold looked up at the lord.

"Welcome to Normandy, Earl Harold."

"Who are you?"

The lord turned his horse to head up off the beach. He paused a moment to look back at his captive.

"I am Guy, Lord of Ponthieu."

THE END

ACKNOWLEDGEMENTS

When I strolled into an English bookshop just off Place de la Concorde in Paris on a sunny spring afternoon in 2011, I perused the shelves and picked up a book on William the Conqueror by a certain David Bates. Though I confess, through my own ignorance, the author's name meant little to me at the time, I soon found myself swept away by his account of the fascinating story of a man who lived almost a millennium ago. I had to know more about William the Conqueror, about what made him a man capable of such deeds. This was not some bogey-man who arrived out of the blue in 1066 to kill the last true Saxon king of England, as some popular accounts would have it, but a man of flesh and blood with the same passions and weaknesses, dreams and fears, qualities and character flaws as anyone of us might have.

Since that day in 2011, I have not only had the pleasure of reading many more of David Bates' immense contributions to Anglo-Norman historical study, but also the honour of his answering my many questions on the subject. For that help, and for lighting the fire of curiosity, I am eternally indebted and grateful.

A great many more people have contributed to this book. First of all, I must thank the members of the Battle Conference of Anglo-Norman Studies who were kind enough to welcome a neophyte novelist and history enthusiast into their midst, and had the generosity and patience to share some of their wisdom. In particular, thanks are owed to Daniel Brown & Kate Weikert for their advice and encouragement, and to John Gillingham, who made a throw-away comment which led to a massive improvement in the narrative. Thanks also go to Caen historian Jean-Paul Hauguel for showing me around the presumed site of the battle of Val-ès-Dunes and supplying much-needed insight into the local place names and topography.

Any errors or omissions are my own.

The staff at the British Library were invaluable in helping me to access "the World's knowledge", as they so aptly put it.

Though I have sought to be as faithful to the historical facts of William's fascinating life and times, many inaccuracies will no doubt have crept into the pages of this volume, as well as a heavy dose of poetic licence. For that, I take full responsibility.

Thanks also go to my many proof-readers and alpha-readers, who gave vital feedback throughout the whole process. Thank you to my parents, Anne and Glenn (who also helped greatly with the cover), to my sister Stephanie and my brother Dominic, to Anna, John, Heather, Annie and Andrea. Apologies to anyone whom I may have omitted.

I must thank Thierry Fétiveau for creating the beautiful and powerful title lettering. More of his beautiful work can be found on his website: www.thierryfetiveau.fr

The drive and perseverance needed to bring this story to paperback could not have been maintained were it not for the constant support, understanding and enthusiasm of my partner, Hannah. If Matilda gave William the nobility to rule, then Hannah has given me the fortitude to write – along with a fair dose of Yorkshire common sense.

Last, but by no means least, I would like to thank you, dear Reader, for having had the patience to indulge me in this first foray into writing.

Roll of Honour

The first print run of this book was only possible thanks to the overwhelming generosity of supporters, both old and new, whose donations financed the publication of this "Author's Own" edition. Every donation mattered hugely, and I am eternally thankful to each and every one of those individuals for giving me this chance to bring William's story to life.

Honourable mentions for outstanding generosity go to the following people.

YAËLE BRETAUD
MARION N. M. CHIVOT
GUILLAUME MABILE
ANNA MARTIN
DOMINIC PICKETT
GLENN PICKETT
ANNE PICKETT
STEPHANIE PICKETT
ANDREW ROBINSON
HANNAH ROBINSON
ZENA ROBINSON
VALENTIN SERVEL

Historical note

How to portray a man whose towering feats link him to one of the most infamous years in English history, almost a millennium after his own lifetime? There are inevitably limitations in attempting to faithfully portray such a person with so great a gap in time and with relatively little contemporaneous information on his character. To be true to the man is nigh on impossible.

For this reason, I set out to write this book with a very clear purpose: to try to invite the reader to view events from a different perspective. We have all heard the myths surrounding the Norman Conquest of 1066, but the introduction of William the Conqueror himself tends to be limited to a brief summary of his ancestry and tenuous claim to the throne. What interested me was to take the reader on a journey through William's formative years, to try to understand what his motivations and perceptions might have been. David Bates wrote in his 2016 edition of *William the Conqueror* that "it can feel as if the biographer's task is to make visible the invisible, and to create a context that makes the narrative plausible" (p.7). This is certainly true of historical fiction, when isolated events need pulling into a coherent and believable narrative, with the added requirement of entertainment. Though not all the actions of a human being may be logical, it is necessary to make the leap from one deed to the next in keeping with the individual's character. In doing so, I hope to have presented one possible perception of William the Conqueror.

As ever with historical fiction, a number of choices had to be made with regards to balancing history and narrative. There are

V

many excellent historians in the field of Anglo-Norman studies and I would strongly advise anyone who has enjoyed this story to look into their works (a list of which can be found in the bibliography on my website). The job of the novelist is to find patterns in the chaos of human existence, to invite the reader on a journey which leads him to question his own perceptions and, above all, to entertain. In so doing, I have exercised that wonderful get-out clause which the world has gifted to authors of fiction – artistic license.

However, I hope to have remained comparatively faithful to the events. This book is the culmination of several years of research and writing, during which I had the pleasure to glimpse William's world through contemporaneous and near contemporaneous sources, modern analyses, discussions with leading historians and visits to the actual places where he made history.

I have chosen to make a few minor alterations, such as bringing forwards or pushing back slightly certain events, such as William's mother's death, for the purpose of narrative. Other more major alterations were driven by a desire to preserve the reader's sanity. Had I attempted to include every person who played a role in William's story, it would have made *War and Peace* look like a light weight novella and resulted in the driest, most convoluted novel on the market. Sadly, for this reason, a great many fascinating men and women have been removed altogether or had some of their deeds attributed to those who did make it into the final cut. I sincerely apologise to them for this injustice.

Nonetheless, I shall now endeavour to make a few clarifications on these choices.

To this day, we know William by two epithets: 'the Conqueror' and 'the Bastard'. However, it is important to note that illegitimacy of birth was probably far less important in the Eleventh Century than in later periods and has often been exaggerated (see David Bates' *The Conqueror's Adolescence* in *Anglo-Norman Studies: Proceedings of the Battle Conference 2002*). If William was born out of wedlock, it should not be taken to mean that his parents did not have a long and recognised relationship. Indeed, Harold Godwinson also had a relationship with a woman who was not his wife (see Barlow's *The Godwins*, 2003, pp.77-78). Such an arrangement was known by the term *more danico* (literally "in the Danish custom"). It seems these relationships were comparatively common (see Bates' *William the Conqueror*, 2016, p.16). It was only later that the Church chose to crack down on 'living in sin'. Nonetheless, the conditions of his birth do appear to have played a factor in forming his character, as is attested in William of Poitiers' account of Duke William's treatment of the prisoners at Alençon in c.1051. As far more learned people than me have written extensively and more convincingly on this subject, I shall not speculate any further than to say that William's illegitimacy appears to have been no great obstruction to his becoming duke of Normandy.

William's father did indeed die while on pilgrimage to the Holy Land. We know little about his death. It would seem that he fell ill on the return journey and succumbed to the illness in Nicea. Given the perils of travel in the Eleventh Century, it is entirely possible, indeed probable, that Duke Robert died of natural causes. However, given his epithet "the Devil" and the turbulence within the Norman nobility - including among members of the ducal household - there will always remain a question mark over whether this death was perhaps given a helping hand by a member of his entourage. This is made all the more plausible when one considers the rumoured reason for his pilgrimage: to purge himself of the sin of fratricide which some may have whispered accelerated his succession to his brother's dukedom.

The instability which followed Duke Robert's death is open to debate. The notion that Normandy descended into anarchy has in recent years been called into question by some of the leading academics of the Anglo-Norman field. What is known is that a number of William's guardians were indeed murdered in the power struggles of the most powerful men of Normandy. So many men were murdered that I could not fit them all into this book.

These quarrels appear to have instilled in William a deep-rooted mistrust for the men of his father's generation, rather than for the families themselves. It seems curious, but he appears to have been perfectly happy to bring into his inner-circle the sons of men whom he mistrusted. The most obvious example of this is Roger Montgomery and his son of the same name. As illustrated in this novel, Roger Montgomery was elevated to his position of wealth and power by William's father. Whether this was out of friendship or a need to keep a control of Lower Normandy, I do not know. When William's father died, it seems that irresolvable tension arose between Montgomery and those appointed to hold Normandy until William's coming of age. The matter came to a crux with Montgomery's banishment. His son William clearly felt the blame lay with Osbern the Steward, or perhaps even William the Bastard himself (as it would have been done in his name), for the steward was murdered at the foot of William's bed.

Osbern's vengeance was in fact meted out by his own steward, Barno de Glos (see Bates' *William the Conqueror*, 2016, p.62). However, I felt that Osbern's son, and William's childhood friend, William FitzOsbern deserved to avenge his father himself – and the reader deserved to keep his sanity rather than having to acquaint himself with yet another character for the sole purpose of one event.

Yet in spite of this treachery, another of Montgomery's sons, Roger, was granted his father's lands, possibly as early as 1043 or 1044. Roger II later went on to become one of William's closest advisers and was instrumental in organising the invasion of England in 1066. Given that FitzOsbern was also a member of William's inner circle, the two men - one the brother of a murderer, the other the son of his victim - would have been called upon to work together closely. By any standards, this is quite remarkable. If William had a hand in the rapprochement, it shows either a total disregard for feelings or brilliant diplomacy. (For the rise of the Montgomery family, see Kathleen Thompson's *The Norman Aristocracy before 1066: the Example of the Montgomerys* in *Historical Research*, Vol. 60, Issue 143, October 1987, pp.251-263.)

The rebellion of 1047 is another case where I used some artistic licence to condense the facts, though hopefully without distorting the truth too much. In his verse *Roman de Rou,* which includes an account of the life of William the Conqueror and was commissioned in the Twelfth Century by King Henry II of England, the Norman writer Wace tells us of how William had gone to settle a dispute between the viscounts Nigel of the Contentin and Ranulf of the Bessin. While in the area, he decided to indulge in a hunting trip to Valognes. William's cousin, Guy of Burgundy, seized upon the unrest to try a coup. Guy was a legitimate descendent of William's grandfather, Duke Richard II, whereas William had the taint of bastardy. However, his claim to the dukedom would have been much weaker than that of William's uncles, had they wished to attempt to succeed Duke Robert. Guy's claim was through his mother, William's aunt Alice; had he been successful, it would have been the first time the dukedom would have passed down via the female line. Since its foundation by Rollo, Normandy had followed the French law of male primogeniture, whereby the most senior male descendent inherits the vast majority of the land. If there is no son, the title passes along to the next branch, as was the case when William's father Robert succeeded his older brother Richard III. That Guy of Burgundy chose to press this feeble claim would imply that he felt he had strong support among the Norman barons.

According to Wace, when Guy tried to assassinate William at Valognes, he was accompanied by both Nigel and Ranulf, as well as two other men; Hamon Long-Teeth and Grimoult. I could not resist keeping Hamon in, if only to attribute to him the account of how a rider from the Cotentin threw King Henry from his saddle during the ensuing battle. Wace goes so far as to point out that, when he was writing in the Twelfth Century, the people of the Contentin still sang the chant that "From Contentin came the lance which brought to earth the king of France" (*Roman de Rou*, lines 3979-3990).

Of Grimoult, Wace is frustratingly vague. We know only that he came from a place called Le Plessis and that, of the five men involved in the plot, he was the one by whom William felt the most betrayed. Though I had Ranulf killed off, it was in fact Grimoult who was found strangled in his gaol.

The Battle of Val-ès-Dunes was undoubtedly a turning point, as it appears to show the defining moment when William truly took on the full role of Duke. Though I have chosen to refer to it as the "Vale of Dunes", the etymology remains unclear, with various contradictory suggestions having been put forward in recent years.

Though the battle was a clear victory for the Franco-Norman army, it clearly left its mark on William. The Duke of Normandy would not undertake another pitched battle until he had to risk everything near Hastings in 1066, with the exception of ambushing Geoffrey of Anjou at Varaville in 1057 as he marched on Caen. For the rest of his military campaigns in northern France before the invasion of England, William chose to place the emphasis on castles, besieging them when on the offensive and retreating behind their walls when on the defensive (see

John Gillingham's essay *William the Bastard at War* in Matthew Strickland's *Anglo-Norman Warfare*, 1992).

Some of the more fanciful scenes in the book may appear odd or even at times offensive to modern readers. None is perhaps more so than William's "rough wooing" of Matilda, when he rides into her father's court and beats her. This scene was, in fact, no invention of mine; it is actually present in medieval sources (see Tracy Borman's *Queen of the Conqueror*, 2011, chap.3). It was important to me not to gloss over any negative aspects of William's character. The purpose of this novel is not to defend, but to present him through the most subjective view possible: his own eyes.

The role of women in the early medieval period is a particularly delicate subject to tackle. They are notably absent from the contemporary sources in many cases, in a male-dominated world. Undoubtedly, women had an influence, yet to exaggerate that influence for a 21st Century audience would have been doing women a disservice. Where there have been – and indeed remain to a certain extent to this day – inequalities and prejudice, it would be wrong to rewrite history rather than recognise the challenges women faced at the time. Yet there remains some hope. The Arthurian legends written in the early and high middle ages do give women a role which might be seen as superior to that of men, as they set men on the necessary courses they must take, often reminding them of their duties. Nonetheless, I do not feel I have fully done justice to the women who helped make history. For that, I sincerely apologise.

William of Talou and Arques is one of the most fascinating characters of William's youth. A younger brother of Duke Robert and his predecessor Duke Richard III, Arques was one of the few constants in William's life, right up until 1051. He is a complex person. One could easily imagine him wanting to succeed his brother, just as his brother had succeeded Richard. The only obstacle in his way would have been William. Though William's illegitimacy may not have been a major obstacle, his age certainly would have been. Normandy was only a little over a century old in 1035, having been formally recognised by the French crown in 911. It had been created by a Viking warlord, Rollo (or Hrolf), and as such would have relied on a certain degree of combativeness to survive, particularly at a time when the northern counties of France were taking advantage of the weak Capetian kings of France to make territorial gains. An indication of a young age being an obstacle to succession is that William's father, Duke Robert I, succeeded William's uncle Richard III despite Richard having a living son, Nicholas. It seems that the only obstruction to Nicholas succeeding his father was the fact that he was only an adolescent (see David Crouch's *The Normans*, 2002, p.47). Talou does not seem to have wanted to be made duke - or perhaps felt he would not have sufficient support (after all, Duke Robert had made his lords swear homage to William before he set off to the Holy Land). He contented himself with a leading role at court. His loyalty to William during the rebellion of Val-ès-Dunes in 1047 won him the formidable castle of Arques by way of a reward from

William. Whether or not he defied William during the campaign against the Bellême lands in 1049-1051 is open for debate. William of Poitiers (the Bastard's notoriously sycophantic biographer and chaplain) alleges that Arques deserted his post during the campaign and went on to hold his castle against William, who could not storm it and was forced to besiege it for several years. The matter was only brought to an end when King Henry I of France attempted to send through supplies to Arques, only to have the relieving force ambushed and turned away by William's troops. Poitiers does not give us a reason for this treason, merely dismissing Arques as "perjurious and proud". One possible explanation would be that Arques saw his grip on the Norman court slipping away as William grew in confidence. It is interesting that King Henry chose, according to Poitiers, to side with Arques rather than uphold William's authority, as he had done at Val-ès-Dunes only four years earlier. Could it be that the French king had told Arques in 1051 of his plans to turn against Normandy? It seems unlikely. Another possible explanation is that the rebellion at Domfront, so soon after Val-ès-Dunes, encouraged King Henry to believe William too weak to rule effectively over Normandy. Helping Arques to carry out a coup would thus put a French puppet in command of Normandy. This would only seem plausible if Poitiers is misleading us in the dates. Why else would the king support Arques if William had already put down the rebellion and Arques was holed up in his castle? In short, we just don't know.

If the power of the kings of France was greatly diminished since the days of Charlemagne, one power was clearly on the rise. The papacy sought to intervene more and more in the day to day running of the churches of Europe - and seemed happy to use its position to get its way with the princes and lords of Europe.

A prime example of this was the Council of Rheims. Called in 1049 by Pope Leo IX, its aim was principally to deal with the great religious matters of the time, namely simony (the act of selling ecclesiastical offices) and the little-respected celibacy of priests. However, we see a number of more political issues being drawn into the Council. A number of noble families took the opportunity to seek papal sanction of marriages - and, by extension, political alliances. Two of them concerned the house of Flanders, as Count Baldwin V sought to marry off his daughter Matilda to William the Bastard, cementing an alliance with Normandy, and his sister Judith to Tostig Godwinson, future earl of Northumbria, forging an alliance with the most powerful family in England. King Henry, it would seem, took exception to this Council, which he appears to have seen as Rome meddling in the affairs of his kingdom, and strictly forbade his clergy from attending. For most of them, such an opportunity proved too much to miss. Diplomacy of the time was a slow affair, as one might imagine with such slow communications. A papal council would thus have represented a rare opportunity to meet many of the great lords and carry out some intense rounds of diplomacy, rather like a modern G7 summit (with the notable difference that diplomacy at these medieval councils actually achieved something). Furthermore, with the growing importance of vassalage, as we might call it today, a papal dispensation might, perhaps, be used as a means of by-passing one's over-lord's permission. What earthly lord had a higher authority than God?

King Edward The Confessor is perhaps the person whose mind we would most like to read with regards to the events leading up to 1066. Exactly what were his intentions for the succession to the English crown? It does not help that his biography, the *Vita Ædwardi Regis qui apud Westmonasterium requiescit* (the "Life of King Edward who rests in Westminster'), was commissioned by his queen, Godwin's daughter Edith. Given that he had her sent away to a nunnery, it is hard to imagine anyone whom he would have wanted any less to direct what history would think of him. The result is that in between dutiful (if not entirely credibly honest) praise for Edward, the *Vita*'s main focus is on making the Godwin family look good under difficult evidence to the contrary (see Frank Barlow's *The Godwins*, 2003, p.12).

The other key question, inevitably, is that of why Edward did not produce any heirs, either male or female. There has been much speculation as to the cause, ranging from impotence to homosexuality to his piety in wanting to stay chaste. The notion of abstinence out of religious devotion seems highly unlikely; producing an heir to maintain a stable realm would never have been a more important duty than when Edward acceded to the throne in 1042. By that time, England had known no fewer than six kings in twenty-nine years - Edward being the seventh. We cannot rule out homosexuality or impotence; neither are attributes which the chronicles of the time, whether English or Norman, would have wanted to connect with an English King from whom their patrons sought to inherit. There does remain another option, which I have chosen to portray in this book. It must not be forgotten that the Anglo-Saxon Chronicle, a comparatively neutral source by the standards of the time, apportions the blame for Edward's brother Alfred's death on Godwin's doorstep. Though Edward would have been under pressure to form an alliance with the Godwin family, as they were growing to be arguably the most powerful in England, it does not seem beyond the realms of possibility that he would have had some trouble in feeling any positive emotions towards his wife; this would certainly explain why he had her sent away to a nunnery once he was strong enough to banish Godwin and his sons. It is, however, worth noting that Edward is not credited with any bastards either, which is more surprising. The absence of references to illegitimate offspring could simply be the Conqueror and Harold Godwinson wishing to write out of history any other candidate, especially given that William himself was illegitimate. We can only guess.

An ever present question when assessing the deeds of the Conqueror is that of cruelty. Was William excessively violent or merely a product of his time? Many historians have sought an answer. Certainly there was a lot of violence in his actions. Contemporary and Twelfth Century sources on both sides of the Channel were shocked by his "harrying of the North", a campaign in Yorkshire of systematically destroying homes, provisions and crops, which was as good as a death sentence for those displaced (see Marc Morris' *The Norman Conquest*, 2013, pp.229-231, for commentaries on Orderic Vitalis and John of Worcester's judgements of the Conqueror's 1069 campaign in Yorkshire). His treatment of the defenders at Alençon was no less brutal, as he had their hands and feet cut off (see William of Poitiers). Yet William was also capable of an astonishing amount of mercy. His uncle Arques, cousin Guy, and the viscounts Ranulf of the Bessin and Nigel of the Cotentin had all committed sins which might have deserved execution. All were allowed to live, albeit in exile. It could be argued that William had a different approach towards members of the nobility. It is possible. However, other of his actions, such as his initial dealings with the English in the early years of the Conquest, lead me to believe that it was more complex than that. This book is not intended as a defence or justification of William's actions.

Whoever William the Conqueror really was, he was certainly a man of flesh and blood, with all the contradictions and idiosyncrasies that entails. He was capable of piety and violence, of humour and ruthlessness, of great political ability and logistical feats. For better or worse, he connected France and England, changing both countries and their relationship in ways which still resonate to this day.

Perhaps the sycophantic chaplain William of Poitiers was right to compare William the Conqueror to Julius Cæsar. Though Poitiers intended it as flattery to his master, both figures remain not only renowned but also controversial. As I watched a re-enactment of the Battle of Hastings, emotions ran high in the crowd. It seems that, in 2017, William the Conqueror is just as capable of dividing opinion – and commanding both praise and damnation – over 950 years after the events of 1066.

FURTHER READING

For those wishing to discover the world in which William lived, I can think of no better place to start than by reading works by two inspirational historians. David Bates' *William the Conqueror* is insightful, vivid and meticulously researched. There are two editions: the 2004 version (first written in 1989) is a much quicker read than the 2016 Yale one, though the latter is obviously more up-to-date and is packed with details.

The late great Frank Barlow's *The Godwins* looks at the complex political situation developing in England in the run up to 1066, through the tumultuous story of Godwin, Earl of Wessex, and his querulous sons.

For overviews of the Norman Conquest, Peter Rex, Ann Williams, and, more recently, Marc Morris have all published fine books.

Those seeking more technical descriptions of arms and fighting styles may wish to look up the handy Osprey books *Norman Knight: AD 950-1204* by Christopher Gravett, *Anglo-Saxon Thegn: AD 449-1066* by Mark Harrison and *Saxon, Viking and Norman* by Terence Wise. Majorie Chibnall's *Military Service in Normandy before 1066* (in *Anglo-Norman Studies V: Proceedings of the Battle Conference*, 1982) gives an in-depth description of the structure of Norman military service and the obligations of vassals. R. Allen Brown's *The Status of the Norman Knight* (in Matthew Strickland's *Anglo-Norman Warfare*, 1989) looks at the emergence of knights in the Eleventh Century. For a study on castles of the Eleventh Century, see Robert Liddiard's *Anglo-Norman Castles* (2003), with particular reference to *Timber Castles – A Reassessment* by Robert Higham (pp.105-118).

For those eager to read the primary sources for the period, no venture into Normandy and the Conquest would be complete without reading at least some of the *Anglo-Saxon Chronicle*, William of Poitier's *Life of William the Conqueror*, Wace's *Roman de Rou,* Bishop Guy of Amiens' *Carmen de Hastingae Proelio* (a vivid account of the Battle of Hastings), and Orderic Vitalis' *Gesta Normannorum Ducum* (the "Deeds of the Dukes of Normandy").

A more comprehensive bibliography is available on my website: www.JosephTPickettAuthor.com

About The Author

Born in Leicestershire, Joseph moved to Nantes, France, at the age of six. A lover of history and literature, he was keen to explore the origins of the complex relationship between England and France through William the Conqueror's story.

Joseph now lives in London, where he can often be found of an evening doing research in the British Library or writing in his favourite wine bars.

His medieval influences include Chrétien de Troyes' prose *Perceval* and the verse *Sir Gawain and the Green Knight*. Though highly romanticised, they offer a glimpse into medieval life, along with wonderful imagery – particularly regarding the role of nature. There was also a strong medieval tradition of 'chansons de geste' (literally 'songs of deeds'), which were vernacular histories, such as Wace's *Roman de Rou* (an account of the deeds of the Norman dukes since the duchy's foundation by Rollo).

Modern influences include Elizabeth Chadwick and Bernard Cornwell, F. Scott Fitzgerald, Jane Austen, Simon Armitage, E.A. Poe, and the inimitable Oscar Wilde.

Joseph is currently seeking representation.

Follow Joseph's writing journey here:

 @NormanScribe

 Joseph T. Pickett – Author

www.JosephTPickettAuthor.com